T0274093

Books by Sara Ella

The Unblemished Trilogy
Unblemished
Unraveling
Unbreakable

Coral

The Curious Realities series
The Wonderland Trials
The Looking-Glass Illusion

THE CURIOUS REALITIES BOOK 2

THE LOOKING-GLASS ILLUSION

SARA ELLA

ENCLAVE

Escape

For Madi, who loves games.

And for Janelle,
who taught me how to play this one.

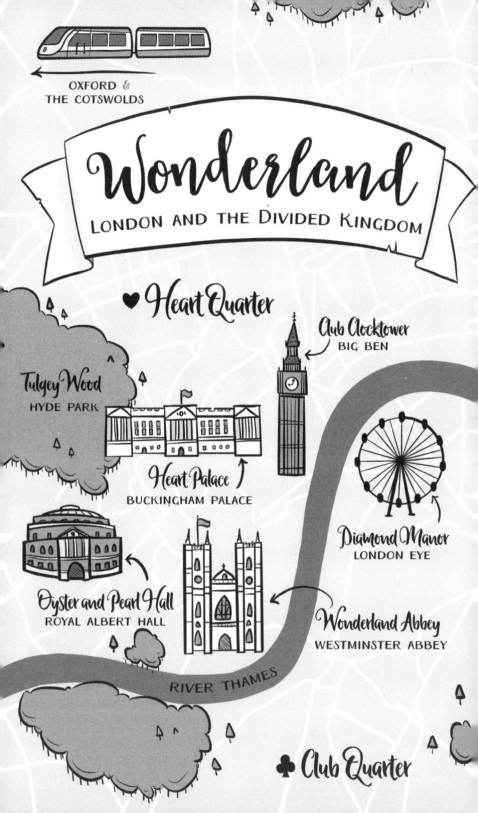

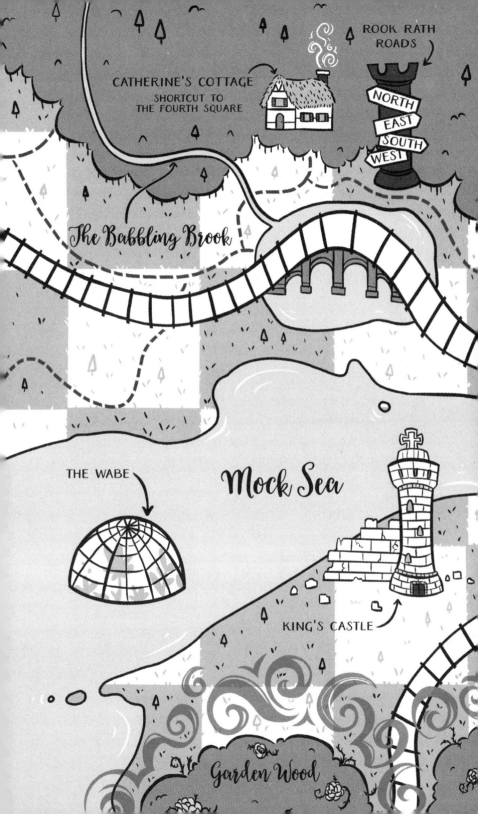

THE EIGHTH SQUARE

Final move. I knew it would be the most difficult, but how would I have expected it to end like this?

This last and most devastating loss.

"Why the long face?" Her Majesty says.

I've tried to remain strong. To keep my tears captive. Now, though, they seem fitting. A necessary release to encompass the moment.

"Poor, pathetic Alice," she jeers. "All alone."

I have nothing—no one—left.

No. I shake my head. *No.*

I'm tempted to sneak a glance behind me, at the squares and obstacles and memories I've left in the dust of what was. But it's no use going back to yesterday. I was a different person then.

Shedding my fear and anger, I clothe myself with resolve instead.

However this ends, I will not cower before lies.

So I rise from where I kneel.

And seek the truth that waits ahead.

THE PAWN

*"I wouldn't mind being a Pawn,
if only I might join—
though of course I should like
to be a Queen best."*

— Lewis Carroll,
Through the Looking-Glass and What Alice Found There

CHESS

Deep breath. She's all right.

We're all right.

As long as we stay together, everything will be all right.

"Ace!" I call her name, but she doesn't respond. "Alice!" I shout through cupped hands.

She's not too far off. Fifty metres directly to my right, give or take a few. Yet she doesn't turn her head in my direction. This doesn't surprise me in the slightest. The Fourth Trial always starts out the same. Attempting to divide us, to pit us against one another until it's every mate for himself.

It's just like her to confound me. I've never been one to ponder on logic or reason unless it concerned my own concerns. The nonsensical has forever intrigued me.

And then there's Ace, who makes perfect sense. Too serious for her own good and the most amusing creature I've had the pleasure of encountering in my seventeen years. I should have known she'd do me in. Now I can't imagine a Wonderland without her.

And that's precisely the predicament in which I find myself. If she discovers what I've done, she'll never forgive me. In fact, I'm quite certain she'd wish for a Wonderland without *me* in it.

If she knew, she'd make sure of it.

I attempt to walk towards her, but it's a futile move. When I try to take a step right, it's as if an invisible wall blocks my path. I've always believed nothing is impossible. But this . . . I release a hefty breath, pushing unkempt hair out of my eyes. So far, this Trial seems to challenge every belief I've ever held, and we've been here mere minutes. If nothing's impossible, why in Wonderland can't I reach her?

I glance over my shoulder, towards the looking glass that stood at the end of my path through the Tulgey Wood in the Club Trial. As I feared, my mirrored image no longer remains. Only a curtain of darkness stares back at me, leaving me to question . . .

What if we're not in Wonderland anymore?

"Ace!"

Her reaction to my panicked voice this time is that of someone waking from a dream. Startled, she turns her head and locks those crystal-blue eyes on mine. The grave expression shading her gaze says everything and nothing.

It's in this moment I notice the vast green meadow upon which we stand. The grass is divided into emerald and sage squares. Several metres off, the squares scatter into forked paths that disappear into a haze of grey, and beyond that, a wooded area much like the one we've only just left behind in the Third Trial.

"What is this place?" I call at the same time Ace shouts, "Are we still in the Tulgey Wood?"

Neither of us answers the other, giving us each the precise answer we need.

This is not, in fact, Wonderland. And if it's Wonderland in fiction? Well, it's not on any map—real or imagined—I've ever seen.

Or have I? A shake of my head does nothing to wake my mixed and lost memories of last year's Heart Trial. The pieces I recall are scarce. There was Kit and—

"I've come back," I whisper. "I'll find you."

Ace tips her chin in the direction of the thick crop of trees, unaware of my empty promise to a brother who can't hear me. The trees stretch onwards with no end in sight. An illusion, imagined by Queen Scarlet's mind? Perhaps. We've faced illusions before. The Spade Trial simulation, after all, tested us to our breaking points. Kit's face in the Hall of Mirrors appears again in my thoughts, a reminder of whom I came for.

And whom I will not leave behind.

A deep rumble, followed by a piercing screech, rises from deep within the forest's leafy bowels.

I tense. The Jabberwock. Just as I'd predicted. The beast is always part of the Heart Trial. If the rumours are true, it takes on a different form depending on what its victims most fear.

Ace moves forwards two squares.

She's so close yet much too far from where I stand. It's no use. We're literal pawns in the queen's last game. The others may be looking to find the Ivory King and the real Wonderland. But, the truth is, I only joined the Knight Society for the sole purpose of finding my brother. If I find out this king—whoever he is—played a part in taking Kit from me?

He'll despise his own crown.

I stare at the life-sized game board ahead and flex my hands at my sides. Chess. Of course it would be my namesake. The one game Kit always wanted to play. I refused upon principle. This is the game that drove our father completely and utterly mad. It was his obsession. An obsession that, for all intents and purposes, eventually led to his demise.

I tug at the collar of my jumpsuit, not quite ready to proceed, but knowing I must if we're ever going to reach the end. To find Kit. To go home.

In the game of chess, a pawn can only move forwards one square until the opportune moment. Two squares if it's the first move.

Until . . .

Another step forwards.

Until that pawn is ready for the kill.

ALICE

It's cruel. Wicked, really. We're supposed to finish the Trials as a team and yet here we are, working together . . . apart.

Curse my incessant curiosity. We should have stayed in the Tulgey Wood.

It was a strange sensation, stepping through the looking glass, silver mist obscuring my vision. It was like being surrounded by water but maintaining the ability to breathe. Once through, everything felt different.

I wait for my teammates to emerge from the mist in our wake, to take their places upon their respective squares. Their paths could not have been much longer than ours. But no one appears. For now, it's just me and Chess against the game.

"Vicious." The word slithers between my teeth like the snake of a queen it describes. I glance towards a sky that is neither light nor dark. Neither clouded nor clear. Is this some illusion like what we experienced during the Spade Trial? Similar to the trickery we encountered at Oyster and Pearl Hall, all of this feels too extravagant to be real. The chessboard meadow. The silver mist behind. Even the sky seems fabricated with its unnatural blue playing in tandem with the jewel-toned greens beneath our feet. Lightning cracks. Thunder booms.

Scarlet *is* watching. Waiting. Anticipating our every move. This is the Heart Trial, after all. How could I have expected anything less? The Wonder Vision bangle on my wrist lights up then seems to glitch and power off at the thought. The WV is just another way for Her Majesty to track and control our every move. She is equal parts villainous schemer and heartless monarch, using the Trials for her own pointed purpose.

Are you proud of me, Charlotte? I want to ask. *All of these fancy phrases and abundant adjectives and nowhere to aim them.* Syntax may be my sister's secret weapon, but it's not mine. The rules pertaining to words won't help us here. Only the rules of the game.

And we must be smart enough to beat it.

The chessboard meadow clued me in at first, but it also seems too obvious. Still, we must explore every possibility, including chess—

My throat constricts.

Chess.

I allow myself to look in his direction. Can he speculate my thoughts as I try to guess his? We're on the same team, yet I can't help but question if we're here for the same reasons. Trust is a fickle, feeble thing. Why can't it make up its mind, for pity's sake?

"Again?" Chess calls.

I nod and swallow. Though we've already tested this move, I try once more. I lift a foot, attempting to step over the line and enter the square to my left. One. Just one. Please work. Please . . .

But the task is as simple as walking through a brick wall. So it's true, then. We *are* the queen's Pawns. I train my attention on the green pastures before us, spanning farther and wider and with more squares than a traditional chessboard contains. It would appear we'll be spending this Trial traipsing across the namesake of the boy I've . . . what? Fallen for? That seems far too cliché and not quite fitting.

Because I didn't fall. I leapt. I leapt into his arms, and I haven't been the same since.

But how do I define what I feel or what we are? We are not clean lines of ink on parchment. We are forwards and backwards. Friends and strangers.

Ace and Chess.

"One more time, Ace," he says.

I scrunch my brows. Is this game his namesake? I don't truly know much about Chess or his past—aside from his desperation to find his younger brother Kit. How can one look towards a future when what's come before are mere scribbles on a solitary page?

The realisation induces the sensation of sinking, and suddenly I feel three inches shorter. I shoo away the memory of drinking Dwindler's Draught, straightening where I stand. This is nonsense. Worrying about my relationship with Chess rather than analysing the task that lies before us? Fear swirls like a dark cloud around me.

"What do you reckon?" Chess shouts past a playful smirk. "We reach the edge of the wood, and the Trial is over?"

If only it were that simple. But, despite the clear truth that this entire expanse of dark- and light-green squares appears to be a chessboard, I sense this Trial is much more complex than either of us can fathom. Bigger than Wonderland itself. The very fact we've stepped off the obvious path and made it through the Tulgey Wood shows this is just the beginning.

Our most recent clue haunts me: *All ways are her ways.* Perhaps our little shortcut was precisely what Queen Scarlet had in mind all along. In an effort to avoid her plans, did we inevitably discover them?

"There's only one way to find out!"

Chess nods then tilts his head back the way we came.

A glance over my shoulder reveals only thick fog, reminding us our other teammates have yet to make their way out of their respective Tulgey Wood mazes. Did they take a wrong turn somewhere? Wander off the path?

"Madi, where are you?" I say more to myself than anything.

"Where, indeed?"

Startled at the familiar voice, I whip my head right, flinging my plaited, straw-coloured hair into my eyes. Charlotte stands beside me in the very next square. She's young, with rich brown ringlets bouncing against her shoulders. Little more than a metre high and resembling the Queen of Hearts more than ever. She circles me, revealing at once she is not another Pawn.

I blink. "How is this possible?"

Despite her youthful complexion, she maintains the serious demeanour I'm so familiar with. "I'd tell you nothing is impossible," she says, "but you already know that, Catherine."

Catherine? *Why are you calling me by my mother's name?* I want to ask. Instead, I say, "Any other sisterly advice?" She might be shorter than I am at the moment, but in her presence, I always feel like a child.

"Only this." She circles me again.

I glance at Chess, who seems preoccupied with his attempts to make it out of his square without moving forwards. Can he see my sister or is she a figment of my imagination?

"He can't help you now," Charlotte trills. "Not until you've reached the Eighth Square."

I gesture towards the Eighth Square ahead. "That shouldn't be too difficult."

"Oh, Catherine." She shakes her head. "You are forever focusing on insignificant details. You never look at the picture as a whole."

There she goes, calling me by my mother's name again. Despite the error, her criticism still stings. I swallow my pride and exhale. "I'm listening. Your advice, oh wise one?"

"Start at the beginning. And when you get to the end . . . stop."

"As if I couldn't have figured that out on my own," I mutter, facing forwards as Charlotte circles me a third time. I glare at the trees, which still seem miles off. Charlotte races past my sideview, then heads straight for the wood.

Just as she disappears from view, the same monstrous sounds rise from the leaves and bark and branches, shaking my bones and unsettling that place deep inside where a new seedling of fear sprouts. I cover my ears and duck down, expecting whatever it is to emerge and attack. But, just as quickly as the noise commenced, it dies, and an eerie calm washes over the field.

What now?

"I think we have to keep going," Chess calls.

"He's right." Madi! The sound of her voice brings a swell of relief. But, just like Chess, who is stuck in his own path of squares, Madi Hatter is too far. Her mane of lavender locks coils around her face, highlighting the fierceness I'm sure ignites her violet gaze.

How can one square between us feel like an entire country?

Player by player, Team Heart appears as if stepping from a dream into the nightmare of our Final Trial. Not one of them is close enough to touch. Try as we might, it seems we are meant to cross this chessboard alone.

Willow Reed with her wide-set eyes and dark crown braid.

Sophia Marigold, sweet smile in place despite the sour circumstances.

Jack B. Nimble, as quick and clever as his name.

And Knave Heart. Scarlet's nephew. A brooding boy I've yet to figure out and have come to trust all the same.

Each player stands tall on their own square. I'm at the centre of the line, with teammates flanking me like a miniature army on either side. There will be no clues this time. No clever hints or riddles we must solve. The only way through this Trial is forwards.

Separate but together.

"What now?" Madi shades her eyes though the sun has yet to grace us with its presence. "How do we find this guy?"

She's referring to the Ivory King—the supposed creator of the real Wonderland. While I know nothing about him, I do have something that might aid us in our quest.

I take *The Adventurer's Almanac* out of my knapsack and

thumb through its pages. The games are listed according to the year they were invented or introduced to society, starting with the most modern and working back to the ones from centuries past.

And here it is. Near the end of the almanac.

CHESS
Date of Origin: Circa AD 600
Place of Origin: India

The chapter is a lengthy one, and rightly so. The game is complex, to say the least. Whoever authored the almanac was a true anorak on the topic. And—it would seem—the author was more obsessed with chess than any other game they recorded.

"Are we just going to keep standing here, waiting for that *thing* in the trees to come out and give us a proper greeting?"

The question comes from Willow, who stands with her arms crossed two squares to Madi's right. As if being summoned, the *thing* we all know to be the Jabberwock screeches from someplace we can't see. The others cover their ears. I ignore Willow's question, wave the book to make my point, and keep reading.

"Oh, excuse me. I didn't know this was library hour."

Was it only weeks ago I would have interpreted Willow's annoyance as contempt? Now I know wit and cynicism come with her territory.

"That's exactly what it is." I give an exaggerated grin. "Now hush! This is the best part."

She huffs but complies.

I take in a quick review of the rules to a game I haven't played in years. Not for lack of interest, but because it always took *for-ev-er*. Card games have the potential to last long enough, but never as drawn out as a game of chess. No sleight of hand or card counting or quick tricks. Nothing is left to chance. A single wrong move can cost you the entire game. And, unlike in Black Hearts, it's not your queen who must be saved.

In chess, the goal is always to save the king.

A flip of the page reveals nothing of consequence. My hope falters. I'd expected to find some rather good advice. The dos and don'ts. Best moves. Popular openings. Instead, I'm met with a children's story. I shouldn't be surprised, really. The entire book is littered with rhymes and riddles. Why should this be any different? I clear my throat and begin to read out loud, projecting my voice so every player can hear.

CHESS—A GAME FOR QUEENS
OR LEGEND OF A CONQUERED KING?

There once was a king who ruled without kindness or compassion. He never wanted for anything. Everyone in the palace feared him, for this king knew the power he held over those lower than he.

One day, a wise man visited the king in his chambers. "Fancy a new game, Your Majesty?" the man inquired.

The king loved games, for he knew no one was clever enough—or foolish enough—to best him. He conceded to the match, and the wise man revealed a curious board, filled with red and white squares. Next, he set up the pieces.

"What are these?" The king picked up a pawn and turned it over in his hand.

"Each piece represents a member of your kingdom, sire. The pawn, the knight, the bishop, the rook, the queen, and, of course, the king." The wise man tapped the final piece, knowing exactly what the king would propose next.

"I shall play the king," he declared. "For no mere pawn can outwit a king."

The wise man shook his head. "That's not how it transpires, I'm afraid. You must play every piece. For without them, your king shall fall before he's begun."

The king bristled. "Surely you don't mean for me to play a lowly pawn?"

"Suit yourself," the wise man said. "Let us begin."

Of course, the king, ever stubborn in his ways, refused to play by the rules. If he moved a pawn, it was in the wrong direction and only to free up the king's path. The game ended before it started. First fell the pawns, followed by the bishop, the knight, and the rook. When the wise man took his opponent's queen, the king simply turned up his nose. "Who needs her? The king is most important."

"Ah," the wise man said. "But without your loyal servants to protect you and a faithful queen by your side, your king will now fall." And with that he took the king's most treasured piece.

While it would make for a good ending to say the king learned his lesson that day, he continued to see himself as the only important piece on his own board. Not long after, his kingdom was seized by a neighbouring nation. One much stronger, with pieces placed strategically from pawn to queen. The king did not learn, but you, dear reader, can.

Never underestimate the least or the small. For they have the power to take down queens and, yes, even checkmate a king.

When I close the almanac and replace it in my rucksack, no one speaks for a long moment. My first conversation with Blanche de Lapin—Royal Advisor to Queen Scarlet—returns to me.

"I hope eet vill be ov use to you een finding your vay."

"Chess?" I say finally. "It's your call. What do you suggest?"

He stands firm. "No way, Ace. You were promoted to Team Queen, remember?"

I want to shake him, but lucky for Chess that's impossible right now. I'm no queen. Not really. But we can't stay here.

"Forwards." I decide and nod at the trees. "We're all Pawns."

I take the first step, and the others follow suit. Unlike in a traditional game of chess, we can all move at once. What other rules will be different? I don't even know if our goal is to capture the king or protect him.

Does the Ivory King know we are here? And what of Queen Scarlet? Is this all part of her plot?

I sigh. To find out, we'll have to play.

A few more metres and our paths will cross over into the wood. Just as in the end of the Club Trial, we will each be on our own. Will it be this way for the remainder of the Heart Trial? And if we can't find Kit or the other missing players . . . What if we fail and we're trapped here forever?

I set my jaw. Move one final square forwards, allowing the silver mist to consume me. In another moment, a canopy of trees shades me. The *what if*s can't keep us from pressing on. As a Pawn, one rule appears to remain the same here.

Even if I wanted to, I can't turn back.

ALICE

For all this dreadful walking, one might have mentioned when supper starts. How long has it been since we left the Club Trial? Hours? Days?

Mere minutes?

Perhaps we're still in the Tulgey Wood, and this is all a grand illusion.

No, that can't be it. This new wood is different. Silent and void of life. Curved trees with thick roots and slender trunks resemble black pawns, their charred branches curving upwards and inwards. The scarce leaves on these trees tremble without a breeze. When they move, not a rustle resounds.

My feet ache. With every bend rounded, I feel as if I've made no progress at all. Each turn is identical to the next, and I half wonder if I'm roaming in a corkscrew direction that simply begins where it ends. Are the others on the same, repeated path? My heart skips a beat. Have any of them come face-to-face with the Jabberwock?

"The Jabberwock takes on many forms, depending on what you most fear."

Chess's words from the evening we met with the other members of the Knight Society haunt me. I've surmised my greatest fear: being alone. Maybe this is how that fear is manifested.

I stop in my tracks and squint into the thick procession of trees. "Is this the best you have for me, beast?" I spin in a full circle. Then another. "You're going to have to do better."

One good turn deserves another, so I twirl a third time.

And stop and blink. I clean my glasses with the hem of my Team Heart jumpsuit sleeve for good measure.

How can *this* be here?

I haven't been to the Foundling House in London since Charlotte and I left ten years ago—not until I happened upon it just before entering Wonderland at the onset of the Trials—and I certainly never expected it to show up in this reality. Am I lost?

I hear laughter, and the familiar sound of distinct joy draws me in. Charlotte. I jog past the waterless fountain and the pitiful garden and up the path to the heavy front door. A quick jiggle of the handle reveals it's locked.

"Odd." I crouch and peer at the brass knob that looks rather like an old man's bulbous nose. "You're never locked."

At my accusation, the keyhole widens. No . . . it—he—yawns.

In another life, I might yelp and leap back. But this sort of oddity no longer surprises me. I daresay it's familiar in a bizarre and comforting way, bearing a striking resemblance to the knob on the door from my old nightmares. The embellishments over the knob arch like eyebrows, while two beady eyes blink beneath them. The knob wiggles of its own accord. Then the brass face speaks. "Haven't you got a key, miss?"

"I do, actually." I tug on the chain of my locket watch, pulling it free from its hiding place beneath my jumpsuit. The tiny key Chess gave me back at The Rabbit Hole in the Normal Reality—the key Charlotte gave him—hangs from the chain like a charm. "It's too small, I'm afraid. Though it was rather useful for opening a secret compartment in a clock once."

"I don't know much about clocks," the face says, peering at my necklace. "But I do know a thing or two about locks." He sniffs. "And your key, my dear, is meant to open the door."

Nothing surprises me anymore, so I attempt to insert the key charm into the hole—mouth—beneath the handle.

The talking knob spits it out at once. "I've made myself clear, and here you are not listening. Do you make a habit of ignoring what's right in front of your nose?"

"It depends on the occasion." I shake my head. Since when did I go about spouting echoes of Chess's witticisms? "If you please, sir, I'd like to understand what you mean."

"I do not *please*, and I am not *pleased*. And my name is not *sir*." He sniffs a second time, and his brass lips quiver. Then he releases a sizable sob.

Oh, dear. If Chess were here, he might offer the knob man a handkerchief. All I have to offer is a listening ear. "What *is* your name?"

My question appears to make him dreadfully emotional as he emits three more sobs before speaking again. "No one has ever asked that of me, miss. The truth is, knobs don't have names, or at least I don't. I have one purpose and one purpose only. As an official shortcut between squares, I'm to make sure no one gets by me without the proper key. If I let the wrong person through, it could endanger the king, you know."

At the mention of the king, my ears tingle. I kneel and lean in. "The Ivory King? Is that who you're meant to protect?"

"Contrariwise. The Ivory King is *what* I'm meant to protect."

"I beg your pardon? Is the Ivory King not a person?"

"Must you ask such *person*-al questions?"

"I do apologise for upsetting you," I say kindly. "It's just that I came here looking for the Ivory King and the real Wonderland, and if you can direct me to them, I'd be much obliged."

"There you go again," the knob says and sniffs. "Ignoring

what's right in front of your nose. I've said it before, and I'll say it again—I can only allow someone with the proper key to pass." He winks.

Sigh. Talking about kings is getting me nowhere. Instead I say, "And I have the proper key?"

"It seems a shame to play a trick on an old knob such as myself. Now, pardon my impatience, but if you don't mind—or even if you do—I'd appreciate it if you would hurry up about continuing to the next square. Or go the long way. It's really up to you."

"Which square am I in now?"

"The Second, obviously. Pawn Wood."

Got it. That would have to make the chessboard field square one. "And if I take the shortcut through the house? Which square will I be in then?"

He exhales his annoyance. "You will have completed the second and begun the third."

I'm inclined to ask more questions. Why is he speaking as if the squares are levels in a game? Are there more shortcuts? Will there be eight squares in all, as young Charlotte mentioned? Does each shortcut require a different key?

Chess comes to mind again. *"Always asking and never doing, Alice."*

I rise and take a step back. The door is a simple structure of solid oak and brass. The elaborate hinges seem to curl around the wood like talons. When I crouch to set my face level with the knob and keyhole again, the enchantment appears to have fallen asleep. His soft snores inspire my own yawn. I'm tempted to get cosy right here and take a catnap. I'm sure Dinah would approve—wherever she is.

Hmm. I suppose I could enter the house some other way. Breaking in would be a small feat, especially considering this house is most likely an illusion to begin with. It's what a common thief would do. And a common thief is who I once was.

Gazing upwards, I examine the windows. Film and grime coat the quartered panes. The chipped paint on the sills begs to be scraped. And there it is—my ticket in. A frame missing its glass. It's not even that high.

The moment the thought occurs, a ladder appears beside the stoop. I blink hard to be sure of what I'm seeing. This didn't appear out of my will or imagination, which only confirms someone is watching. A glance at the sleeping knob reminds me he'll be of no help. If the door won't open, and I can't go around, seeing as I'm still a Pawn, this seems the only thing left to do.

With a check that my rucksack flap is secured, I begin my ascent. The loose rungs twist beneath my grasp, and I nearly fall backwards with my first step. I reposition myself and take a steadying breath. "Since this is the only way," I tell the ladder, "I'd appreciate it if you would cooperate." I half expect it to answer like the brass knob. It doesn't.

Another step. The rung snaps and my foot slips.

"But this is the only way."

All ways are her ways.

Our Club Trial clue rushes my thoughts, washing me with sudden clarity. I shake my head. What am I doing? This is all wrong and precisely what a cheater would do. What *Queen Scarlet* would do. It's sneaky, dishonest, and rotten.

I jump down and steady myself on the stoop once more, dusting myself off and straightening my locket watch. When was the last time I needed the melody inside to wake me? It's strange, but ever since I left the Normal Reality, I haven't needed help waking at all. I wonder . . .

A glance at the knob with no name reveals he's still sleeping quite soundly. I open my locket watch and turn the tiny key-shaped knob on the side, setting it for one minute ahead. I study the clock with its watercolour image of flowers and a riverbank as the seconds tick by. When the second hand reaches the twelve, "All in the Golden Afternoon" begins to play. At the same moment, the knob man blinks his sleepy eyes and, if such a thing were possible, he smiles.

"Now that, my dear, is the proper key." At the release of his words, the face vanishes, and the knob appears as ordinary as any other. A little click resounds, and the door swings inwards.

"How very peculiar." I tuck the locket watch away and enter the Foundling House. Everything inside sleeps in abandonment and disrepair. The dead fireplace and mantle in the sitting room, a dusty looking glass above. A game of chess, its pieces lying on their sides or on the ground like wounded soldiers. Except . . . I tilt my head. Things seem out of place. As if someone rearranged the entire house and flipped everything to the opposite side of where it belongs.

With a shiver, I continue forwards and take the rickety stairs two at a time. The boards bow and creak. When I reach the top, the splintered cap at the crest of the banister topples at my touch.

Down, down, down. The cap rolls step after step until it rests at the stair base with a *thud*.

I inhale. Surely I'm alone. If someone else were present, they would have heard—

Creak, clatter, bump.

Not alone then. I gather my wits. "Hello?"

Two whispering voices, one slightly deeper than the other, reach me from down the shadowed hall.

Creeping forwards, I'm careful to avoid the noisy floorboards I remember well. Framed photographs line these walls, but none utter memories of family or togetherness or a cheerful childhood. The Foundling House was never meant to be permanent, and neither were we.

"Temporary," Charlotte once said. *"That's all we really are."*

As a child, I never understood what she meant. Now . . . now I question if she knew more about our un-permanence than she let on. As Normals. As Wonders.

As sisters.

The pitter-patter of a child's feet invites me closer to the room Charlotte and I once shared. But when I peek inside, I find the space barren, aside from a framed looking glass resting on a tilted easel. Unlike the mirror in the entryway of the house, this one seems oddly familiar.

When I draw near, I discover why.

Rather than my reflection, I see Charlotte's. She's older in this one, sixteen or seventeen maybe. Just as I did in the Tulgey Wood, I step through the glass.

It turns to silver liquid around me. The sensation of drowning isn't as startling this time, and it soon passes. I gasp and open my eyes. The same silvery mist from before envelops me. I wave my hands to clear it away and find I am no longer alone.

Two girls in their teens sit together on a four-poster bed. Intricate carvings wrap the cherrywood posts. The entire space has transformed. No longer the modest Foundling House room, this is a suite, three times in size at least. A settee is angled towards a set of French doors that lead to a balcony on my right, and a claw-footed tub beneath a shelf filled with expensive-looking lotions and soaps waits to my left.

"Catherine, there you are," one of the girls says, popping her head up and beaming. She's blonde like me, though her hair is closer to white than the golden tone of my straw-coloured locks.

I glance over my shoulder to glimpse who she's addressing.

"Catherine," the white-blonde girl says again, "come and sit with us."

Her steel-blue eyes gaze my way and I realise . . .

This girl is talking to me.

First young Charlotte on the chessboard field and now this? Why do I continue to be mistaken for my mother?

I'm inclined to leave the way I came, but when I turn and place splayed fingers on the looking glass, it's solid. My reflection has changed as well. Here, inside the glass, I'm the adolescent version of my mother.

As usual, my curiosity gets the better of me. I accept her invitation, cross the thick antique rug, and sit on the edge of the bed.

"We promised one another, didn't we?" The girl reaches for

my hand, eyes glistening. There's a sad sort of joy there. A look full of both faith and fear.

I take her hand and nod, hoping she'll explain further. My response sticks in my throat and I clear it. "Yes," I say.

"Promises can't last forever," the girl beside her says. It's the first she's spoken since I entered the room. How did I miss it? Dark brown hair with eyes to match. Pointed expression softened only by her long lashes.

I tilt my head, considering her. "What do you mean, Charlotte?"

She glances away, towards the balcony doors. "After Mother's announcement today, one of us will be—"

"Please don't talk that way," the girl holding my hand begs. "Nothing has to change. Not really."

Charlotte turns her head towards the girl and scowls. "You say that now, Cordelia, but you'll see. When one of us is named the next queen—"

"—the others will do everything they can to support her," Cordelia finishes. "We're sisters. A crown can't change that."

Charlotte releases a short laugh. She stares at her hands, studying them. "A crown changes everything."

I almost think I catch her lower lip tremble when she says it. But, just as quickly, she smooths her expression.

"Maybe you're right, Cordelia." Her forced grin looks as if it belongs in an advertisement for the Wonder Gene-suppressing cordial. "Maybe nothing has to change."

I don't know what to say, and I certainly can't figure why Charlotte would be sitting with my mother and the Queen of England in the first place. Did this moment actually occur? Is Charlotte related to royalty? She looks just like Queen Scarlet. Perhaps . . .

I shake the notion away. Too many possibilities that don't make sense pummel me at once. Rain begins to *pitter, patter, pitter* cold and grey beyond the French doors. We sit together quietly for a spell, Cordelia gripping both our hands and Charlotte refusing to make eye contact with either of us.

"I have an idea!" Cordelia bounces off the bed suddenly. "Let's play a game. Just as we used to."

Charlotte rolls her eyes, sighing. "We're not children anymore, Celia."

It's an odd thing to see the young queen-of-England-to-be puff out her lower lip in a pout and put her hands on her hips in the way I so often do. I've seen this woman as an enemy to both Normals and Wonders my entire life. Here, though . . . she seems like I imagine a sister should.

Kind. Warm. Playful.

Her focus fixes on me. "You'll play with me, won't you, Cat?"

I nod, humouring her. Whatever will gain me more information. As trivial as this scene appears, something deep inside tells me it's important somehow, vital even. "I will," I say, scooting off the bed.

"Now you *have* to play, Charlee," Cordelia says, clapping her hands.

At the mention of Charlotte's nickname, my thoughts suddenly turn to Raving and Madi and their lost brother, Stark, jogging my memory, reminding me why I'm here. Whatever I'm witnessing, whether it happened or not, isn't real.

With a groan, the girl who practically raised me rises from her perch on the bed. When she nears us, Cordelia taps her on the shoulder and squeals, "You're it!" Then she bolts from the room.

Charlotte shrugs and gives me a look that seems to say, *Why not? She'll get what she wants anyway,* picks up the skirt of her dress, and chases after Cordelia.

I follow them out of the suite and into the hall. Cordelia's giggles echo throughout what could only be Buckingham Palace. It's nearly identical to the Heart Palace version where our team stayed during the first three Trials. Certain Wonder details are missing. Fantastical things like lifts that grow flowers and vines that stretch into a never-ending sky. My first day in Wonderland with Madi seems like a lifetime ago.

Maybe it was.

I find my way down a winding staircase and onto a plush,

red-carpeted floor. Charlotte and Cordelia are nowhere in sight. I tread carefully, peeking my head around corners, trying not to let the portraits of rulers past lining the walls intimidate me. Is there an exit? Another liquid looking glass where I reenter the Foundling House and the Fourth Trial?

The place is a maze, as I'd expect any palace would be, but this is beyond that. As if the illusion I've found myself in wants me to stay lost until I find whatever it is I'm supposed to stumble upon.

Clang! Crash! "Oh, feathers and treacle and tea!"

I follow the sounds and innocent curse around a corner and down a short flight of steps until I'm standing inside a warm kitchen. The scents of rising dough and fresh pastries mingle with a cloud of settling flour in the air. I glance around, but there doesn't appear to be anyone—

A little girl pops her head up, hardly visible over the butcher block island at the kitchen's centre. "Mummy," she says, "I'm sorry. I was trying to bake a cake for Aunty Charlotte, and the mixing bowl was too high, and I climbed onto the countertop and fell . . ."

She goes on and on, talking with her hands, wiping flour off her cheeks with her floured palms, only making things worse. She looks as if she bathed in the stuff.

I stand there, stunned.

This little girl of five or six is me. Yet it appears I'm seeing her through my mother's—Catherine's—eyes. I glance at my hands. They've aged several years, revealing lines and creases that weren't there moments ago. Did I skip to a different time and place?

A memory rushes back. Vibrant and vivid and completely unexpected.

The Heart Palace kitchen stands almost exactly how I recall. Except, like the Foundling House, everything is flipped. Backwards. On the opposite side of where it is in Wonderland. I skirt the island and stoop to help my younger self, lifting the metal mixing bowl and placing the fallen whisk inside.

"Why were you making a cake?" I ask, recalling the moment but failing to fully remember the reason behind it.

"Because, silly," young Alice explains, scooping spilled flour into the toppled bag. "It's Aunty Charlotte's unbirthday. Madi says you only get one birthday a year, but you get hundreds of unbirthdays. Aunty has been so sad, and I wanted to surprise her with an unbirthday cake."

I fight the urge to laugh at my own naive innocence.

"You think I'm a silly girl, don't you?" Her lower lip quivers, and she turns her face away, no doubt trying not to cry.

Yes, this is most definitely me.

Drawing her gently into a hug, I pat her hair, just as my mother did the day this actually happened. Tears burn and prick my own eyes now, but I refuse to let them fall. I can't see her face or hear the tone of her voice, but in this strange moment I feel her holding me.

Young Alice pulls back and grins. Trails of dried tears amidst the flour coating her skin make her look more caricature than concrete. "What's wrong, Mummy?" Reaching up, she lays her hand on my cheek.

"Oh, nothing at all, my darling." I sigh, hoping this is the right thing to say. I don't know if it's close to what my mother said to me back then, but I do know it's what I would have needed to hear.

So often, I longed for my sister Charlotte to comfort me in this way. But even when we were close, on those good days filled with pleasant memories, she remained at arm's length.

I pull my young self close again, as she buries her head in the space between my neck and shoulder. We stay that way a long time, until she's grown so quiet I'm certain she's fallen asleep in my arms. When I open my eyes, however, I'm alone. Gone are the walls and the kitchen and the girl. The Foundling House and its lawn and fountain have vanished. I'm sitting on the empty floor of the wood, left with only a whisper of what occurred moments ago.

Silver mist settles in the air like tossed flour.

That very same flour dusting my cheek where a little girl touched me.

CHESS

Here in the dark wood, my father finds me.

But he is not welcome.

"You're a sad excuse for a son," he jeers in my mind. *"Can't even learn strategy for a simple game of chess. I should never have named you after it. The game is a masterpiece, and you're . . ."* He laughs dryly to himself. *"You'll never be good enough for the Trials."* My father turns to my brother then.

I was eight, but Kit? He was four. Helpless. Weak.

I've considered this moment since Kit disappeared a year prior. How I placed myself between him and my father that day a decade ago. How I took blow after verbal blow, wishing Thomas Shire would get on with it and hit me already. At least then I'd have something to show for it. A bloodied bruise that would eventually heal. A heroic scar or two. Instead all I acquired were invisible gashes left wide open.

I tried my entire life to protect Kit from those wounds only to—

No. I cannot let guilt or the shadow of my father's memory get the better of me. Not when finding my brother requires every bit of focus I can gather.

Our father is gone. I'm all Kit has now.

The crisscross branches of the thick wood leave scarce room for light along the earthen path. Or what I think is the path. I can only see a metre or two ahead or behind. With nothing but the jumpsuit on my back, I'll need to find shelter and food before nightfall. There are no timeouts, pauses, or lifelines in the Fourth Trial. That much I recall.

What I don't recall is this. *Any* of this. The darkness, solitude, quiet . . . It's enough to drive a person mad. And in that madness, another memory surfaces. A year or so after our father disappeared, and we were left as our grandmother's wards.

"You ruin *everything*!" Kit's accusation rings so clearly in my thoughts it resounds through the trees. Leaves shudder and branches curl, mirroring my internal recoil. At his voice, a picture of the scene unfolds in my mind, then projects as a 3D hologram into the empty space before me.

Is this a trick of the Trial? A Wonder Vision projection? It's how Trial simulations are made to seem so real, after all. I glance at the WV bangle on my wrist. Three pulsing red heart lights stare back. My Fates. Kit's WV has been offline since he lost his final Fate and went missing last year—or so our team was told.

I watch the vision of him before me now. It isn't real. An illusion. A memory. Yet I sense the desire to reach out and touch him. I've pictured this moment and how I might react after not seeing him for this long. How he would react to me.

The urge to touch him fades the longer I stand here, replaced with another, unexpected desire. It's so strong it feels more need than want. Of all the actions I thought I might take at hearing his voice again, a sudden instinct to run was not on my list of possibilities.

My twelve-year-old brother reveals the scale model of Big Ben he constructed with his mind. He'd spent a good two years perfecting his design before finally bringing it to life. It was an impeccable replica, right down to the toll of the bell. I should have kept my big mouth shut.

But that's never been my strong suit.

"You have the most coveted DNA in the world, little brother." My sixteen-year-old self saunters up to him, clapping him on the shoulder. *"Half the Normals out there want to be you, and the other half want to snuff out your brilliance entirely. And here you are, replicating something of theirs, something ordinary, when you could imagine something new. Something brilliant."*

"You're just jealous." He stands tall. *"Wait until I show the minister. He'll have to let me enter the Trials next year. I'll be old enough, and Team Spade's Puzzle Master is about to age out. I'm the best one for the job."*

I couldn't argue with him, but I also didn't want to admit he was right. Kit was always good at figuring out the way things worked. At solving problems. He was born for the Wonderland Trials. Everyone knew it. But he was too young, too naive. By sixteen, after three years of training and competing, the Trials had already changed me, challenged me in ways I couldn't have anticipated. I wanted Kit to hold on to his childhood as long as possible.

The Minister of Spades, however, did not share the sentiment.

The replay memory of me and my brother falters, exchanged for a new one. Now an image of the minister appears before me. This one's more recent, the day of Kit's thirteenth birthday, six months before last season's Trials.

"He'll make a fine Spade player," the minister notes. And then, *"Why the long face, Shire? You ought to be proud."*

"He's too young. The Trials are no place for Kit."

I cringe at my own hypocrisy now. Maybe if I'd trained him better—rather than trying to shelter him—Kit would have been more prepared.

"No younger than you were when I recruited you for the Trials," the minister says, lifting his tattooed hand, a black spade-shaped stone on his ring finger.

"That's different," younger me counters, the argument falling flat as a discarded Joker.

And that was it. I couldn't give the minister a good enough reason. Kit was made the new Puzzle Master of Team Spade. He would have given Jack a run for his money.

The hologram disappears, and the wood ceases its taunting—for now. I shake off the memory and stride deeper into the unknown. Twigs snap. A bird *caws* a sound somewhere between an owl's hoot and an eagle's screech. Branches unfurl and bow, almost as if the trees are alive, welcoming me. Or luring me. Even the dirt path itself fades from brown to red like a carpet rolled out for a king. It's all just a ruse, of course. The title of Team Heart King means nothing here. I'm a Pawn, like my comrades. And if I *am* Team King? Then anything from here on out is designed to bait, trap, and capture me.

I control a shudder. Something about this notion suddenly seems familiar, but I can't quite put my finger on it.

I follow the reddening path, which curves and curls and crosses over itself like the branches overhead. Just when I think I might find my escape into daylight, the way swerves or veers, taking me in a new direction all together.

And then a roar of laughter pierces the silence clean through. I wiggle a finger in my ear. The sound was close, like amped music through a soundbud.

Another turn around yet another bend. I shade my eyes from the abrupt light and look down for a moment or two to adjust my vision. Is this what it's like for Ace with her fractured eyesight? It's awful. I'll have to admit as much if I see her again.

When I see her again.

"Ah, there he is!" a voice crackles as if through a speaker. "I think we made contact, Quincy, ole boy."

When my eyes adjust to the newfound light, three figures come into focus. The one who spoke is a balding, portly gentleman with dark, egg-shaped buttons on his green waistcoat—Mocktur Telle,

Lord of Clubs, though he goes by "Minister" when the occasion suits him. He's as contrary as they come.

The second is a tall and slender woman, who appears almost ghostly. Black and silver jewels drip from her neck and ears and wrists. She is none other than Madame Sevine, Duchess of Diamonds.

The third and final figure stands at ease beside the others, hands concealed in his white trouser pockets, black waistcoat fitted and flawless. He is as familiar as my own reflection, with his slicked dark hair and passive stare.

"Minister of Spades," I say. "Isn't it against the rules for you to interfere with a Trial once it's begun?" I keep my distance, not quite convinced this is, in fact, the man I've always considered a mentor and confidant.

"Unfortunately," the minister begins, "no Spade player has set foot in this Trial. So, technically, I am not interfering as my own team has yet to arrive." A hint of bitterness varnishes his tone.

"You insisted on the transfer," I remind him. "It was your idea I join Team Heart." Shame cloaks me. I've told my team lie after lie. They believe I tricked the minister into transferring me. If they only knew the truth.

The minister's entire form wavers, glitching in and out of view.

This is a hologram then. Another illusion created by the WV. My eyes narrow. Is this part of the Trial? Some obstacle I need to overcome?

"That may be true," the minister concedes. "And yet, I do not recall you keeping your end of our bargain." I don't need him to elaborate, but he continues just the same. "You assured me that by getting close to that Wildflower girl, by gaining her trust—"

"Her name," I interrupt, "is Alice." As I speak, my guilt intensifies. Getting close to Ace may have been a strategy at first, a means to finding Kit. But it became so much more than that. *We* became more than that.

"Irregardless," the minister replies, mocking me with a word we both know is nonsense. "You have yet to deliver on our deal.

That girl is the reason my daughter Charlotte left Wonderland to begin with. She is also the last known link we have to Catherine R. Pillar and the riddle she left behind, which—"

Sevine stops the rant with a piercing glare.

Good. The minister has said too much. I know they wanted Ace to enter the Fourth Trial. Not a problem, of course, since she could have led Team Heart this far without my help. What I do not know is why.

A riddle, eh? As Ace would say, how very curious indeed.

"Perhaps," I pose, "I'd like to make a new deal." One that protects Ace *and* my brother. I shake copper and pink hair from my eyes but keep my gaze fixed on the trio before me. I'm keenly aware of my surroundings. If I need to escape, could I walk right through them? Or should I let this one play out and see what facts, findings, and dare I say, fiddlesticks I can gather?

"You jest!" Mocktur laughs so hard he starts to cough. Though he's not physically present, the echo certainly is. When he finds his voice again, he adds, "That is not an option, lad."

Fine. Let's change the subject. "Tell me," I inquire. "Say Alice can solve her mother's riddle? Suppose she can even convince Charlotte to return to Spade Quarter. What then? Queen Scarlet remains on the throne, and we all know she has no intention of relinquishing her power. It's why the Fourth Trial has been unbeatable since she was crowned champion of the Trials all those years ago."

In response to my history lesson, the three quarter heads exchange glances.

Ah. Seems these three haven't divulged their true intentions. I lean against the nearest tree trunk and cross my arms. My mind is made then. We'll let this one play out.

"It's true," Madame Sevine concedes slowly. "We have desired to balance Wonderland's rule for many years now."

Her innocent tone doesn't fool me. In fact, it only serves to put me more on edge.

"It's time the four Houses share power," she continues. "No

queens. No kings. Each quarter free to govern itself, while working together for the common good of all." She keeps both hands folded neatly in front of her, but her rigid posture suggests she's far more menacing than she appears.

The way she explains their idea for a new Wonderland doesn't sound so bad. But I'm no imbecile. The schemes brewing in the minds of these three are as clear as the sinister smirks on their greedy faces. "And the Trials?" I ask. "What will become of Scarlet's Trials once you *balance* Wonderland's power? Will they conclude with the close of her reign?"

The corner of Madame Sevine's mouth twitches. "The Trials serve their purpose, young Shire. A purpose we were all promised would come to fruition." She shoots a side glance at the minister before returning her gaze to me. "Since the foundation of Wonderland, the Heart Quarter—and its queen—have held the upper hand." She fans her face, the jewels at her wrists clacking and clinking. "Until someone new passes the Fourth Trial, Scarlet holds her title, position, and control."

Interesting. "Why not simply overthrow her?" I shift away from the knobby bark poking my spine, casting a nod towards them. "Three against one. Surely such a feat would be child's play."

"Things don't work that way!" Lord Mocktur huffs. He withdraws a handkerchief from his trouser pocket and dabs it across his forehead. "There are rules, procedures, and of course, the Wonders to consider. They look to Lady Scarlet, trust her. We can't storm Heart Palace and expect their devout loyalty." Even the folds of his neck and chin have turned red by the time he's finished.

It is not lost on me that he refers to Scarlet by her Normal Reality title—*Lady*. The Wonders may recognise her as Queen of Hearts, but these three see her as nothing more than a caterpillar to be squashed. Their true motive is more than apparent. They may say they want to be free to govern themselves, but they each believe one better than the other. They want to use the Trials as a way of proving which quarter is strongest. Which one is fit to rule. But that still doesn't explain why they believe Ace entering the Heart Trial is the key to solving Catherine's riddle.

I take in the Minister of Spades' expression. It's one of hunger for a crown that's always been just out of grasp.

He must sense I see right through him because he says, "Let's not forget why we risked our necks to send this communication in the first place, my friends." He says the word *friends* as if he's sucking on a lemon tart. He eyes me. "Have *you* forgotten, Shire?"

I'm an idiot. This isn't an illusion or a Trial test—it's a transmission. Why did I think he'd let me forget the task he set before me? I scan my WV. Is there a way to block them? How did they hack me in the first place?

"I've done what you asked," I say. Of course they would expect more. "Alice made it to the Fourth Trial. Charlotte has returned to Wonderland." What else could they possibly want? "Now, if you'll excuse me, I'd best be on my way." I push off from the tree, fully intent on marching past this lot. Except, when I try, they stay ahead of me, visible but out of reach.

Blast. I roll my wrist. How do I get this thing to turn off?

"Your way?" Mocktur scoffs, wagging his beefy finger. "I'd watch your words, young man. Really. Some people have no more sense than a baby."

I exhale and stare upwards through the branches. I don't have time for this. "Get on with it then." I look at each of them in turn, casually clasping my hands behind my back, twisting the bangle on my wrist. "What else do you want?"

"We have reason to believe Catherine left behind a series of clues," Madame Sevine says. "Clues which will lead us to solving her riddle and the secret to finishing the Heart Trial."

My heart pounds with each new question. Do they know of the Ivory King? What reason would they have to seek him? Will these supposed clues lead to the real Wonderland? "You're out of luck." I aim my words at the Minister of Spades. "Our team was separated at the onset of the Trial. Alice isn't with me."

"Well, I suppose you'd better find her, sooner rather than later, if you don't mind." Mocktur checks his pocket watch. "The clock is ticking."

"And if I don't find her?" My own challenge surprises me. I want to reunite with Ace and the rest of Team Heart, but not at the expense of whatever these three have planned.

"Then . . ." A new and fourth voice joins the mix. I know her before she appears.

Dinah FeLin.

Grandmother.

She's dressed as proper as always. Lace collar to her neck, adorned with an onyx broach she never takes off. "Then you and Kit and Alice shall face the consequences upon your return, Grandson." Dinah brandishes a small corked bottle filled with purple liquid.

Wonder Gene Cordial. The very thing Wonders avoid at all costs.

I narrow my eyes and step backwards. "You wouldn't."

"Do not underestimate me," Dinah says, tucking the bottle into the folds of her black dress. "Alice is the daughter of Catherine R. Pillar and the last one to see her mother alive. She became Wonder, not by birth but through belief. And somewhere in those muddled memories of hers lies the answer to the puzzle we must solve. For the sake of Wonderland and all who call it home."

"That makes your sweetheart extremely valuable," the minister says pointedly. "Lose what we value, and you'll lose what you hold dear as well."

"She's not my—"

The minister holds up his tattooed hand, the same one that bears his own WV bangle, a black-spade stone at the centre. Unlike Trial players, quarter heads only use the WV for connection to their House players, and not to keep track of Fates.

"Do not lie to me, Chess," the minister says. "I've known you too long. I've never seen you look at anyone the way you look at that girl. Not even my daughter Charlotte." His lips curl, lifting his mustache.

There's no concealing my embarrassment on that one. But I was just a lad when I admired the girl who pretended to be Ace's sister. The minister is playing dirty.

Maybe Ace was right about him all along. Her gut told her he was bad news. Her gut told her a lot I advised her to ignore.

I've made a right mess of things.

A throat clears. All eyes fall to Sevine. Her smile is sickly sweet. "It's your choice, Shire. See this through to the end, and bring us the answers we seek, or risk their lives."

"And what of Heart Quarter?" I ask, already knowing the answer as I glare at my grandmother.

"That is not your concern." Dinah waves a hand, as if batting my question away like one would a pesky moth. "It will all be worked out once this Trial is over. Once the riddle is solved, we can finally unleash the full potential of Wonder Gene power."

My fists clench. This could only mean one thing—Dinah must believe the Ivory King has something other Wonders don't. And she'll do anything to possess it. I should have trusted Ace. She saw right through Dinah when I was convinced my grandmother's motives were pure.

"And if I do this?" I ask. "If I . . ." I swallow, then start again. "If I find Alice and help her solve this riddle, you'll leave us alone? We can go our separate ways?"

"Of course," Dinah says blithely. "Solve the riddle, slay the Jabberwock. Slay the Jabberwock, find the king."

Sweat slicks my palms. "We understand one another then?" My bangle refuses to unclasp, and my hand is too large to slide it off. It's more a shackle than anything.

Dinah nods. "I believe we do."

"We'll be watching," Mocktur says at the same moment one of his waistcoat buttons pops clean off. "Any funny business and you'll rue the day you crossed us."

As I nod, my bangle finally opens, unlinking its connection to my mind and ending the transmission.

A glance at the now-offline Wonder Vision bangle sends my pulse into a panic. I'm terrified but also exhilarated at the newfound freedom. The three lit hearts that represented my remaining Fates no longer stare back at me. I know the band plays a role in the illusions we see in each Trial. The dragon-flamingoes fabricated by the Diamonds. The quicksand floor in the ballroom imagined by the Clubs. It's part of the game. And every game has a master—or a mistress, in our case. Scarlet knows everything about us through this technology, from when we hit our REM sleep cycle to how many calories we've burned in a day. It's unnerving.

Now, it appears, the quarter heads have found their way in too.

I have half a mind to toss the dead device into the wood. Instead, I loop it through my jumpsuit's utility belt. It may come in handy later.

Strolling directly through the spot where my grandmother appeared moments before, I shade my eyes as daylight pours through the widening spaces between branches. I continue on until I meet a fork in the red road. Paths like those in the Tulgey Wood veer off to either side of a tree with a corkscrew trunk. I don't hesitate or ponder which path I ought to take. I head left and follow a sound that perks my ears.

Walking is overrated.

A train's whistle calls.

ALICE

Charlotte.

It doesn't make any sense. And yet I saw her with my own eyes—through my *mother's* eyes, which only makes the encounter more curious. It seems illogical, incomprehensible, improbable, and utterly impossible.

Nothing is impossible.

I've heard these three little words more times than I can count. And yet the questions remain.

Lady Scarlet and Cordelia, Queen of England, were fraternal twins, or that's what history has told us. One born Wonder, the other Normal. But there was no sign of Scarlet anywhere inside that looking glass. Instead I encountered what seemed to be triplets, including my mother. How can that be, when Cordelia and Catherine are decades older than Charlotte?

Unless . . . could it be she's older than twenty-six? Perhaps, but twenty years older? I shake my head, staring at the scuff marks on my trainers. There must be some reasonable explanation.

I rise from the forest floor. The flour that coated my jumpsuit moments ago has dissipated, and the clouds of silver and white no longer fill the air. Something about that silver mist means something. I saw it on the chessboard field and again inside the Foundling House. Memories? Dreams? Illusions?

All three?

Dusting myself off, I make my way forwards, but my focus isn't on the path before me. Instead, I scan my WV, searching for Queen Scarlet's Alias.

When @QueenOfHearts comes up, I stare at her photo. Poised. Proper. Refined. Everything Charlotte is and then some. But the longer I study her face, the more differences I find. At first glance, Scarlet and the woman who raised me look nearly identical, apart from their obvious gap in age. It would be easy to get one confused for the other, maybe even assume they're related.

When I pull up Charlotte's profile, however, it's clear how truly different they are. Both have brown eyes, but Charlotte's are warmer and wide-set. Pink accents her high cheekbones, while Scarlet's appear more sunken, almost hollow. Their noses are different as well. The queen's comes to a point, while Charlotte's is more rounded and button-like. If I didn't know any better, I'd say Charlotte's nose is more like mine.

I narrow my eyes. No, not more. *Just*. Like. Mine.

Hope swells. If the vision I saw holds any truth to the past, that would make Charlotte and my mother Catherine sisters. Which means we'd both have royalty in our blood. Charlotte would be my aunt, just as little Alice said. And Queen Scarlet?

She'd be an imposter.

It's too good to be true. Too wonderful to hope for and also incredibly dangerous. For me and for Charlotte.

I close out both profiles in my view and trudge on, encountering nothing and no one, aside from the whispering wind's song as it stirs up fallen foliage at my ankles. Invisible creatures scamper and scurry among the bushes and shrubs, too quick to catch a glimpse of but leaving me unsettled all the same.

The moment I first laid eyes on Queen Scarlet returns to me as

I round the next curve in the wooded path. She looked so much like the girl I believed to be my sister it took my breath away. Could the queen be the very reason Charlotte avoided Wonderland for so long?

All ways are her ways.

Her ways, indeed. If Scarlet isn't the rightful Queen of Wonderland—or even royalty at all—does anyone else know? Do the other quarter heads realise the woman who leads them isn't who she claims to be?

And what of the Ivory King? What part does he play in all of this?

My pace picks up with each pound of my pulse, and I look around. Perhaps this is all a maze, the labyrinth from the Tulgey Wood extended. I'll most likely end up exactly where I was or somewhere all the more confusing. Still, I can't just stand still. I need to move, to do something that feels like progress or, at the very least, an attempt to find what I came for.

Who I came for. The reason the Knight Society sent me.

"The Ivory King is the designer of the true Wonderland." Charlotte's words echo in my mind, clear as the day refusing to show itself through the branches above.

I answer the memory with words of my own. "True Wonderland?" I ask the pawn-shaped trees. "And what is truth? Everyone in Wonderland seems to see their own version."

The trees don't answer. Of course they don't. They're just trees, after all.

A brook's babble reaches my ears, and I follow the sound, stepping off the path and picking my way through protruding branches and over unearthed roots. When I see the sound's source, I almost cry. Falling to my knees at the edge of the water's bank, I scoop myself a drink.

My lips remain dry.

I make another attempt, and again the water disappears on my skin, leaving behind specks of shimmery silver dust. I stare at my reflection below, watching where it ripples. The brook looks so real. But as I have a third and final go at quenching my thirst, the water, cool to my touch, still vanishes when I try to take a sip.

Now I really do want to cry. Anger trumps sadness, and I rise, brushing soil from my knees and shins. "Is this some sort of jest?" I search for a sky I can't see, for a someone who isn't listening. Or maybe they are. Perhaps this Trial is being livestreamed, and every Wonder in Wonderland is mocking the Wildflower girl who might entertain with her tears.

Not today. As difficult as it may be, I will not let anyone see me cry.

Leaving the false brook behind, I make my way back to the path. It takes longer than I expect. Too long, in fact. Is this the way I came?

I turn in a full circle. Once, twice. This bush with the blackberries wasn't here before, was it? And that poplar tree. It's common, closer to something one might see in the English countryside than in Wonderland. If I didn't know any better I'd say I entered a different wood all together. One in the Normal Reality. This is getting me nowhere.

Retracing what I'm sure were my steps, I attempt to find the brook again. But where trickling water flowed moments before, the ground is now a dry and shallow crevice, littered with stones and twigs. With hands on my hips, I glare at the empty riverbed. "What in all of Wonderland is going on here?"

"What sort of question is that to ask?" a familiar female voice calls.

I whirl.

The voice titters. A few moments later, a young girl in a white lace frock drops down in front of me. "It's a perfect day for tree climbing, wouldn't you agree?"

I stare at her, incredulous. She's younger than when I last saw her. Maybe ten or eleven at most. "Cordelia?"

"Is that any way to address your future queen, Catherine?" She *tsks* and shakes her head. "And how many times do I have to tell you? I hate that awful name. I'd much rather be called Celia, like what Governess Dinah calls me."

Dinah? Chess's grandmother was a governess to the young would-be queen?

I don't know how much of what I'm seeing is history versus illusion, but I'm taking mental notes. If this is accurate, it may be useful later on.

When I don't answer or comment, Cordelia—ahem, *Celia*—flips her hair playfully. "I'm only joking, Cat," she says. "Not about the name of course. I *would* rather you call me Celia. But regarding our kingdom's future queen? I think we both know Charlotte is going to give us some good old-fashioned competition." She turns and links her arm through mine. "Come. The others are probably looking for us."

We walk in sync for a while. Dirt lines the hem of her frock, and her white-blonde hair is mussed. Her appearance looks nothing like the Queen of England now, but I suppose we were all children once. We all loved to run and play and climbs trees. Except . . .

I—Alice, not Catherine, to be clear—wasn't allowed to participate in such frivolous nonsense. Charlotte's stern scoldings and disapproving stares made quite certain of that.

When at last we reach the path, Celia picks up her walk to a brisk stroll. I try to keep up, my arm still linked through hers, but my muscles and bones are heavy, pleading with me to rest. "Would you please slow down?" I unlink my arm and pause to catch my breath. "Where are we going anyway?"

"The cottage of course." She skips ahead, along a pebble-strewn path that looks vastly different from the one I stumbled upon to begin with. "I was merely trying to make up for lost time."

Straightening, I shake my head. "You can't lose something that doesn't belong to you."

"It is far better to be late to where you are going than to be early by always staying where you have been." Warmth fills me. There was a time Chess's words inside my head irked me. Now I just wish he were here to say them to my face.

Celia doubles back, skipping around me before stopping a few feet away. "Well, I suppose that's true. Shall we race, then? If time isn't our own, we might as well make a run for it."

There's a challenge in her gaze I can't turn down. What would my mother do? She was a scientist, after all. In all probability she was a sensible, smart, no-nonsense type of woman.

But the person before me isn't a woman, she's a girl. Which makes me one too. I inhale deeply and adjust my stance. "On your mark . . ."

Celia beams and joins me, lunge at the ready. "Get set . . ."

I return her smile before shoving my glasses up the bridge of my nose and focusing on the path ahead. "Go!" we yell in unison.

A startled starling takes flight from his perch on a low branch. We race past him, my rucksack slapping my spine. Celia squeals, and I'm laughing so hard it only serves to steal my breath too soon. My side aches, and I want to win and surrender at the same time.

"Faster, Cat!" Her voice echoes. "We don't want to be late!"

Late for what? I make another mental note, tallying each detail until it's otherwise proved unimportant.

"Come on! We really mustn't dawdle." Though she's merely a few paces ahead, Celia sounds far away. Like a muffled voice through a pocketscreen's receiver.

The road curves and I lose sight of her. When I round the bend in her wake, a wall of pouring rain divides the path in two. I stop just shy of sprinting into the downpour. The overcorrection does me no favours, causing me to stumble.

I sit, grasping my now-skinned knee. Rain gushes a mere metre from where I sit, abandoned in the dust like a forgotten forget-me-not.

"Celia?" No answer. My voice sounds small, helpless. "Cordelia, are you there?"

Where could she have gone? Certainly she didn't run straight into the rain? Unless . . .

I stretch a timid hand towards the silvery wall of water. What takes place next is both startling and striking.

Rather than rushing like a waterfall over my skin, the rain avoids my hand altogether, curving out and away like a stream skirting a boulder. I draw my arm back and examine my palm and fingers. I'm completely dry.

What now? Whatever lies beyond the wall is unpredictable. I could turn back, attempt to find another way through the wood. I'm alone, defenceless. I've no tea to change my height or form. Nothing but a rucksack with an old book and a few measly trinkets I don't need.

What would my mother do?

The only things I know about Catherine R. Pillar are what I've been told. History has tried to erase her and the work she did, and Wonders and the Gene right along with it.

What if that's the point?

A conversation I've tried to forget surfaces. I don't relish recalling the day Chess left me to fend for myself in London's Hyde Park. But I let myself relive those painful minutes all the same, hoping they'll spark something new. Something I didn't notice before.

"If Pillar had been a Wonder," I'd said, *"nothing could have stopped her."*

"Or, consider this," Chess had replied. *"Nothing did."*

At the same moment I replay his words, a fresh thought solidifies. Lightning flashes, illuminating the curtain of rain.

Nothing stopped my mother.

And nothing is going to stop me.

I stand, wincing at the pain in my knee and the blood staining the fabric of my jumpsuit, and step forwards. The rain retreats to either side of me like drawn drapes. Once I've stepped through, those drapes close with a crash, followed by a boom of thunder.

In a few short seconds I'm drenched. My hair sticks to my face, and my clothes cling to every centimetre of my skin. But the air is warm, and the space around me smells like earth and grass and new beginnings.

Another flash of lightning reveals what awaits ahead.

I bolt for the quaint cottage with a thatched roof and shuttered windows. Puddles splash beneath my steps, spraying dirty rainwater over my ankles and calves. When I reach the stoop, the awning above does little to shelter me from the storm. I wring out my hair and tap the knocker twice. Entering the Foundling House was one thing—the building in London was my home for years. But this could be someone's residence. Best to be polite.

Not a soul comes to answer.

Stepping back to get a better look, I examine the door. How peculiar. It's an exact replica of the one I encountered at the Foundling House back in Pawn Wood. Solid oak and brass. Hinges curling around the wood like talons. A glance at the brass knob, at least, tells me this door has no intention of speaking. It doesn't need to. I know my way in this time.

I withdraw my locket watch on its chain. As the tiny tune plays, my shoulders relax.

The door opens, and I'm certain I've found a new shortcut.

I slip inside as another roar of thunder resounds, causing the walls and windows of the little cottage to shudder in submission. The door closes of its own free will behind me, but the house isn't dark by any means. Cool light streams through the windows, and an oil lamp burns dimly in one corner. I take in the details one after another. Tipped beakers and empty test tubes strewn across a dusty countertop. Dark computer screens and unplugged extension cords. An abandoned stuffed yellow rabbit I can only assume was once white, lying in the centre of a braided rug.

"Hello?" One step forwards. Two. I expect the floorboards to protest, but they remain silent. It's almost as if they, too, fear the unknown. "Celia?"

Not a word.

Attempting to even my stilted breaths, I approach the rug and scoop up the lovey. It's limp in my palm, its neck ragged and in dire need of new stuffing. Two black beady eyes stare back at me.

"Have we met before?" I ask the rabbit, tilting my head to one side. "I feel like—"

The sound of stringed instruments reaches my ears. I look around, but every device left behind by whoever lived here remains dark and silent. The oil lamp suggests there might be more antiques present. I stuff the rabbit into my rucksack and begin my inspection of the house.

There isn't much to see. A short hallway leading to a lone room with two single beds, another oil lamp between them, this one unlit. The beds are made, quilted duvets with matching shams smoothed and tucked. The embroidered curtains match as well, parted to let in the evening light. I back away and find a modest kitchen, which holds a small wood stove crammed in beside a round table and two chairs. But still, not a source of music to be found. Not from a record player, gramophone, or any other ancient form of melody delivery.

After determining the kitchen holds no food, either, I meander back into the main room, choosing to sit on the rug over reclining in the destitute rocking chair by the window. I pull out the rabbit again and turn him over in my hands.

"What do I do now?" I sigh, almost disappointed the lovey doesn't respond after my encounter with the doorknob. "I'm no closer to finishing this Trial or defeating the Jabberwock or finding the Ivory King than when I began." I squeeze the rabbit and hold him close, blinking towards the ceiling to keep any tears at bay.

A glimmer of something catches my eye. There, bouncing off the vaulted rafter, is a distorted reflection of light. I glance at the window. The rain has stopped, and the cool blues of the storm have been exchanged for warmer hues. Sunbeams illuminate the dust in the air and cast shadows across the floor from the furniture and forgotten science experiments.

And then I see it, half concealed by a stool in one corner—a heart-shaped hand mirror with a silver frame, sunlight bouncing off the glass.

Still holding tight to the rabbit, I crawl and retrieve the mirror. When I'm settled on the rug once more, I examine it properly. The silver is tarnished, proving it's real and not some false replica. It's heavy too. Despite the frame's neglected state, the glass remains intact. I drop the rabbit into my lap and cradle the mirror with both hands, peering at my reflection.

"Aren't I a ghastly sight?" I give a little laugh. "Some Team Heart Queen I turned out to be."

At my words, my WV blinks on, layering my vision in a transparent screen that includes our Team Heart score, the remaining Fates for each player, and a map icon. The technology designed by my mother has been acting up since we arrived. It powers on randomly and turns off without warning. Oh, my heart. The invention my mother once intended as an enhancement for the Wonderland experience has only served to—

I shake my head. To what, exactly? We know the WV tracks players and collects data on how we perform. It's how the simulations seemed so real in the Spade and Diamond Trials. I take in my own Fate count, reminded I have only two to get through this entire Trial. What happens if I lose what I have left? Will I end up lost in the Heart Trial, too?

My mouth falls open. Why didn't I think of it before? If the WV tracks players, could it be used to find those who went missing in this Trial? It's worth a shot.

Sliding the mirror into my rucksack for safekeeping, I use my mind to put the WV to work. I pull up Kit Shire's profile first. There's little I can access since he's not been added as a Card to my pack. It shows his name, age, and that he played for Team Spade, along with some of his stats from last year, but no photo. Unlike his brother Chess—Team King—it looks like Kit was the Spade's Puzzle Master. I smile at that, missing my brilliant friend Jack whom I was only just getting to know.

I'll have to look up my teammates next. For now, I select the map icon in Kit's profile, next to where it says "Location," but a little message pops up in my view that makes me want to pull out my hair.

*Location set to private. Please add @KitCat to
your pack to access personal information.*

Really? I don't even bother to look up Stark Hatter. Since he's not one of my Cards, no doubt I'll be greeted with the same message. "Fine," I say to the screen. "Have it your way."

I pull up Chess, my heart pulsing with hope that's only squashed when the screen gets stuck on a rotating clock. His location won't load. Of course it won't. I attempt the others half-heartedly. Madi then Jack then Sophia and Willow and Knave. This has never happened before. Since when does the WV freeze? This isn't decades-old tech, for treacle's sake!

Frustration winning, I yank the bangle from my wrist and chuck it across the room. It bounces off the nearest wall and lands with a *tink*. My shoulders heave. This is a nightmare, cruel and inescapable. Clearly this cottage was only meant to distract me and has nothing to do with moving forwards in the Trial. I have half a mind to leave my bangle here. Fear and doubt creep in, solidifying I don't measure up to the task before me. The chances of making it to the end of all this, when no one has done so since Scarlet herself, is like drawing four aces in a row from a shuffled deck.

It's impossible.

"I just want to go home." The admission is one that surprises me. All I ever desired was to be Wonder. Now part of me longs for my old life with Charlotte, the one before I knew she lied to me.

But then I wouldn't have Madi or Chess or the others. I wouldn't be on a path to possible answers about my mother. I wouldn't be closer to the truth. I pack the rabbit into my rucksack beside the mirror, shouldering the straps as I rise. As I move to retrieve my WV bangle, I resolve to change my posture. Not only for myself, but for every Wonder who's been lied to about what's real.

"I want the truth," I say. Then I snag my bangle and clasp it onto my wrist. I take a closer look.

This can't be right. I compare what I'm seeing to the transparent screen that comes to life in my vision. I remove my glasses, clean the lenses with my jumpsuit, and return them to their perch. The same images stare back at me through my now crystal-clear view. Where there were just two Fates left to my name moments ago, three now blink back. Did I complete some unknown task? If this is a life-sized game of chess, did I progress to the next square? I must be doing something right.

My heart skips. Instead of leaving, I drop my rucksack to the floor, settle into the rocking chair across the room, and turn the bangle over again and again between my fingers. Releasing a yawn, I close my eyes with a small smile. For the first time since being separated from my team, I sense an emotion opposite of fear beginning to emerge.

I sense courage. And where there is courage, there is always hope.

CHESS

The art of train-catching is one I've yet to master. I've never minded being late. It's the early ones you have to watch out for. Tardiness is fashionable, even intentional, if done on purpose.

I look over my shoulder, picking up my pace as the train's whistle grows louder. The minister and other quarter heads, along with Dinah, have gone, though their words still echo on an endless loop in my mind. With the WV off my wrist, can they still track me?

"Solve the riddle, slay the Jabberwock. Slay the Jabberwock, find the king."

My grandmother's words remain the most prominent on repeat. What stock does she hold in all this? The group's motivations to overthrow Scarlet seem weak at best. It's almost as if Dinah and the heads have formed their own team, inserting themselves in the Trials for a reason I can't comprehend. If I learned anything from my misguided and mistrusting father—a master at the game of chess—it's this:

"Everyone has a strategy, m'boy," he often said. *"Only a simpleton reveals his intentions all at once."*

I am not naive. There's more to their strategy here. Just like there's more to mine. I've no aspiration of letting harm come to Ace or Kit or anyone else. I'll find them. And when I do, we can formulate a plan together.

If Ace can forgive me for the mess I've made.

And if my brother can forgive me for leaving him behind.

Pressing on, I sprint for the chug and clatter of the unseen train. The trees thin and soon clear, giving way to grassy flatlands with rolling hills beyond in contrasting greens. Every inch is divided into chessboard squares, just as when we arrived. Tracks appear from nothing, only materialising when the train does. The charging locomotive—an old steam engine—becomes visible around a bend to the south. At least, I think it's south. Could be west. Even east. I search for a station ahead, someplace where the train is bound to stop and I can board. But no such pause exists.

If it doesn't intend to slow down, then I'm just going to have to match its speed.

Sprinting, I leap between two arching trees and run alongside the rapidly forming tracks. The unnatural current caused by the train as it approaches forces me to duck my head and hunch as I pick up speed. The faster I run, the more the train accelerates. Even with all the imagination my Wonder Gene can muster, I'm no match. I'll never make it at this rate. Not on two human legs.

But perhaps on four. Good thing I always keep a few drops of Beast's Blend tea on hand. Just in case.

I pause to catch my breath and slip a small vial from my jumpsuit's utility belt. Then I unscrew the cap, revealing a dropper. Two drops ought to do the trick. I stick out my tongue and let the liquid fall, the taste of bergamot, cinnamon, and cloves spicy and strong. I haven't transformed into animal form since the Spade Trial. It'll be nice to—

And there I go.

The upside of turning into a cat is that I'm far more agile and fearless. And, of course, the peculiar phenomenon remains that, somehow, my clothes disappear and reappear the moment I turn human again. Where they go in the meantime, I'll never know. And I don't rightly care. I'm a cat, after all, not a tailor.

Now, to catch that train.

I dash, dart, fly through the air. Each leap and bound frees me, but my improved speed falls short still.

Oh, blast it all. Run faster, you git.

The nearest car's steps remain a metre away. My paws pound hard and fast on the earth. If Ace could only see me now, she'd miss the train simply by doubling over in giggles. She'd find my struggle hilarious.

I miss her for it.

A hand covered in white, curly hairs reaches out from the car.

Don't mind if I do. An unpleasant yowl escapes my throat as I pursue one final leap with claws outstretched.

The owner of the hand—a man with static white hair, round spectacles, and an unusually long goatee reminiscent of a goat—grabs me by the skin of my neck. Despite the aging colour of his locks, his face exudes youth, and he can't be much older than I am. "Almost missed it," he says. When he chortles it sounds like a bleat.

"Thanks," I say, but it comes out as a meow.

He seems to understand, sets me down on all fours, and removes a pocket watch from his waistcoat. "What say you? Another minute or two until you're in proper form?"

All I can do is purr and hope the bob of my furry head and twitch of my whiskers looks like the nod it's meant to be.

He pivots on the heel of his shiny white dress shoe.

I follow him into the car and down a narrow aisle. Sleeping passengers joggle and snore in their seats. They wear funny hats and ascots and gloves in an array of colours. Who are they? Are they real or figments added to this grand illusion? I've removed my WV connection, so any Trial simulations shouldn't seem as real from here on out. In theory, I ought to be able to decipher between what's fictitious and what isn't.

"Where are we off to?" I say, at last human again and glad to be rid of the hairball that was forming in my throat.

"Follow me, lad," the goat man says without glancing backwards. "You'll see." He leads me into a separate car where private compartments greet us with closed doors and drawn shades.

"It's this one here." He opens the third compartment down and bows, waiting for me to step inside. "After you, lad."

I incline my head and accept the invitation. Let's hope following this stranger isn't the most foolish thing I've done yet. Risks have never frightened me. They can lead to delightful surprises.

Most of the time.

A young man about my age already occupies one of the two plush bench seats. His shoulders hunch, and his forehead presses against the window glass. Oversized headphones cover his ears while his right foot *tap, tap, taps* the floor. A silver bangle with no remaining Fates circles his wrist.

I'd know him anywhere. His purple hair, usually two shades darker than his sister's, has faded to a monochromatic grey, but it's him. A strange ache that is one part disappointed and two parts hopeful turns up uninvited. He's not the Wonder I wanted to find first, but he's still a step closer.

"Have a seat, my boy," our host says. "You've had quite the journey, I presume, and we have a ways to journey still."

"Thank you," I say to the man as I sit beside my oldest rival. He doesn't seem to notice either of us. I clear my throat. "Stark?"

Madi's brother does not respond.

"Stark Hatter?" I tap him on the shoulder this time, attempting to ignore the fact that we have an audience.

He doesn't stir.

I know we played on opposing teams in the games last year, but the least he could do is acknowledge my presence after being gone all this time. "Stark."

"Pardon?" He hangs his headphones around his neck and straightens, his voice monotone at best. "Do I know you?"

I shake my head and blink. This *is* Madi's missing brother. I'm sure of it. I sense the goat man watching us, amused by our exchange. I ignore him and press on.

"Stark, what's happened?" I say. "What have you been doing the past year? Everyone's worried sick. Raving. Madi. I must say, even I've been concerned, despite the fact Team Diamond took the lead last year. I don't hold it against you though, mate." I nudge him with my elbow, hoping this will lighten his mood.

"Raving? Madi?" His brows knit. "Am I meant to recognise these names?"

I look to the goat man as if he has the answers.

One leg crossed over the other, the man clasps laced fingers over his knee. "Don't mind the boy," he says. "He can't help his own memory. The longer you live inside your own mind, the more space you have. And the more space you have, well . . ." He taps his forehead once. "Leave him be, and let's get a spot of something to eat for our journey while I explain the rules. Fancy a smoked brisket?"

I've never been one to turn down a hearty meal. It's not as if I can go anywhere. Stark has placed his headphones over his ears once more, and the train must be moving a hundred miles an hour by now. "Why not?" I say. Maybe, at the very least, I'll get some answers.

"Excellent," the man says. "Buckley's the name, and I'm pleased to make your acquaintance."

"Chess Shire," I say. "Have you been here long, Buckley?"

"Can't say if I have or I haven't. Time flows differently in the King's Trial. One minute an hour has passed, and the next you've barely travelled a second."

The latter part of his explanation is baffling, but it's the first thing he says that has me leaning forwards. "The King's Trial? Come again?"

"I can't, I'm afraid. I already came and left twice now."

I purse my lips. This must be how Ace felt when I spoke to her in infuriating riddles and contradictions. I'll have to apologise for that. And yet, the thought of riddles has me wondering . . .

Is this part of the riddle Ace is meant to solve?

We chug along through the countryside. Soon—or is it soon?—an attendant arrives at our compartment with a meal cart, a silver dome covering three plates. She reveals a tray hidden in the wall beneath the window and serves us. Buckley ties a serviette around his neck and digs in. Stark ignores his supper and turns up the volume on the radio-like device in his hand.

I give him a side-eye and eat. The food is hot and filling, making me forget for just a moment where I am and why I'm here. The reprieve is welcome as Buckley and I dine in silence. Once he finishes his serving, he exchanges it for Stark's. I almost protest, but Madi's brother doesn't seem to notice or care. In fact, he appears to have fallen asleep.

After our meal, the attendant returns and removes our empty dishes. I intertwine my fingers behind my head while Buckley stretches across the bench seat he has to himself.

Stark hasn't eaten or uttered a single word.

"Out with it then," I press. "You mentioned rules and the King's Trial."

"I certainly did at that." Buckley kicks off his shoes and closes his eyes.

"Well?" This bloke is starting to irritate me. Doesn't he see the urgency here? "Care to explain?"

"Don't be in such a rush. I told you, time passes differently here. We're on a loop, you see." He twirls a finger in the air. "We go 'round and 'round in circles until we come back to where we began."

"And where is that, exactly? Where we began?"

"Honestly, it's exhausting explaining everything when you novices arrive." Buckley releases an overdramatic yawn that tells me he's hoping I'll let him sleep. When I don't insist upon it, he sighs and leans in. In a voice hardly above a whisper, he says, "You began at the First Square."

"The chessboard field?"

"Precisely. From there you entered the Second Square—"

"The wood."

"Pawn Wood."

"Same difference."

"Nothing different is ever the same if you have a mind for reason," he says with a wink. "Now, where was I?"

"The Third Square."

"Incorrect. You caught the train at the second and will now likely miss the third entirely. You'll keep returning to the first unless you change position or the Gateway closes. Understand?"

"Change position? Gateway?"

He rolls his eyes. "Don't you know anything? The Gateway opens once per year. There's one right way into Wonderland and many detours along that way. This happens to be one of those detours. The question is, will you change your position and get back on the proper path?"

I'm starting to think I don't, in fact, know anything, but I won't tell him as much. Organising my thoughts, I opt to inquire after the first thing he said. "How does one change position, exactly?"

"Isn't it obvious?" Buckley flicks his white-haired temple. "To change position, you must first change your mind."

"Change my mind about what?"

Stark stirs beside me. He snores softly, and his headphones have fallen around his neck again. The volume is just loud enough I can hear the faint speaking of a girl's voice.

I lean close to Stark's shoulder to get a better listen.

"*. . . and this, ladies and gentlemen, is why the Fourth and final Trial—the Heart Trial—remains shrouded in mystery. Most players never make it there to begin with. Some never return. Those who do escape the clutches of the Jabberwock have little to no memory of it at all. When they try to relay the tale, it's as if their memories of the Fourth Trial have simply . . . vanished.*"

I straighten. Madi Hatter's podcast voice prattles on inaudibly. The Diamonds took the lead in the Trials last year. The queen declared them the victors, despite the fact their Team King—Stark Hatter—was missing when they returned. They couldn't defeat the Jabberwock either, of course. No one has since Queen Scarlet, supposedly. The Diamonds just lasted longer, that's all.

My team—the Spades—barely made it out of the Trial alive. We—I push my hands against my thighs and shake my head. I don't remember. Not what the Jabberwock looked like or how the battle ended. Knave claims I stole his glory, but I can't recall how that happened either. I only remember Kit's face before we escaped . . . I start. Could this all have something to do with the Gateway Buckley mentioned? Did it close after we made it out alive? Is that why Kit and Stark couldn't get back?

I have to know. I return my attention to Buckley, who is now mimicking Stark's snoring. "Who are you?"

He twitches and peeks at me through the slit of his eyelid. "No one of consequence." He smiles to himself. "Then again, according to my coding I am a checkpoint. Now that you're here, you can't very well go back. Not that you'll make it past me, of course." Eyes closed, he nods towards Stark. "He never did."

I'm in over my head here. Still, I ask, "What of the Gateway, then? When does it close?"

Buckley sighs and sits up, clearly disappointed he won't get to snooze. He's quite the character, I'll give him that. If I weren't so intent on finding answers, we might have a good laugh together.

"The Gateway opens once per year for seven days. Seven days to give anyone who enters the chance to seek what's always been there to begin with."

"And the checkpoints? Is there more than just you?"

"What an absurd question! Of course there's more than me. There are several, in fact. There are ways around us, but—"

"—once I cross a checkpoint," I say over him, "I can't turn back."

"Correct."

I eye him as I attempt to take in this information. That explains why Stark is stuck here. Did a checkpoint trap Kit as well? Is this

THE LOOKING-GLASS ILLUSION   55

why the quarter heads send players into the Trial? Because they don't want to risk getting trapped here themselves?

"All right. So I can't turn back. How do I move forwards then?"

Buckley thrusts a pointed finger in the air. "I've said it before and I'll say it again, you can't change positions unless you change your mind. And you can't very well change your mind unless you first change your heart."

"How do I do that?"

He chuckles. "Oh, I can't tell you. It's not written into my code."

My eyes narrow. There he goes again, mentioning a code. I wish Kit or Jack were here. They could solve this puzzle in a heartbeat.

Footsteps pad past our compartment. I ignore them. "What *can* you tell me?"

"It's not a question of *what*, but *when*," Buckley announces. "*When* I can tell you is the thing, my boy."

I mull over this information for a moment, then I search the compartment for a timekeeper of some sort. A clock. A watch. Anything that might denote the *when* this man is referring to.

"I know what you seek, lad, but you won't find it. Not with that attitude. You're too focused on what you're able to touch or feel or see. Tell me," Buckley says, "do you enjoy being a Pawn?"

His question seems off topic. "I haven't been one long enough to know. Do you enjoy it?"

"Oh, I'm not part of the game in *that* way," he says breezily. "I already told you. I'm written into the code. A checkpoint you'll likely never pass before the Gateway closes. And if you're on this train when that happens, then"—he shakes his head—"you'll be stuck here like him." He sends a resigned look in Stark's direction. "It gets rather boring, really. If I were to judge by your appearance, you seem like the bright sort. When I saw you running for the train I thought, 'Now there's a bloke who has a chance.' I hate being disappointed." He checks his pocket watch again then clicks his tongue.

I study him more intently than before. He's checked his watch twice. Mentioned *when* he can tell me something as opposed to *what.* If I've learned anything about the Trials over the years, it's that clues are everywhere. I eye him closer, taking in all the minute details Ace would notice if she were present. Buckley's gaze is all mischief and movement, his eyes an odd thing to behold. I sharpen my focus. His pupils are minuscule—too shrunken to be human. And the lines in his green irises appear to be moving.

Not moving, ticking. I count the seconds as they go by. *Tick, tock, tick, tock.* I find the second hand. The minute hand. The hand that marks the hour. His eyes are not eyes at all, in fact, but two analog clocks. The next time the second hand reaches the spot where the twelve would sit, it moves around counterclockwise. Then, when another minute has passed, the hand turns clockwise again.

It's as if he's restarting time. He said this train is on a loop. But how do I get it to change direction? To move on to a new location rather than continue in a circle?

Buckley strokes his goatee in a thoughtful manner. "You're the first in a while to see it," he remarks. "The boy there made a few feeble attempts. But he couldn't achieve the task before he forgot himself. So there he remains. Helpless. On an endless loop. Never advancing to the next square."

The sound of a cart rattling in the hall approaches, breaking my concentration. The same attendant who served us opens the door. On her cart, three domed plates that smell suspiciously like the brisket we just ate wait.

"Fancy a smoked brisket?" Buckley asks, just as he did previously. I blink. I'm about to decline. Wasn't I going to ask him something?

"Might as well eat," the man before me says. What was his name? "You might be here a while."

I nod, unsure of the last time I had a decent meal. The attendant serves us, though I've lost my appetite. I look to the young man beside me, hoping for something familiar.

But he's asleep. Not that he'd be of much help anyway.

It's not as if we know one another.

I've never seen him before in my life.

ALICE

"The other quarter heads and I will not agree to this, Your Majesty. It goes against everything Wonderland stands for." The Minister of Spades blocks what appears to be a study doorway. Greenish veins pop from his forehead, and his nostrils flare.

At least, that's how I picture his upper half from my hiding place in the cupboard under the bookcase, a thatched door distorting my view. My knees are pulled in to my chest, and my head is bent at an awkward angle. All I truly see of him are the cuffs of his trousers and a pair of black alligator-skin shoes, pointed so sharp at the toe I'm afraid they might snap if I get too close.

Someone else steps into my line of sight. She wears a flowing black mid-calf skirt and a red angel-sleeved blouse. Though shorter than the minister, she carries all the air and authority of a queen.

But the voice that speaks next does not belong to Scarlet.

"Wonderland is a haven, Minister," Charlotte says. "It has been since the day we left Normalcy behind. Since my sister Cordelia gave us no alternative." Sadness coats her words, but they carry an undertone of regret as well. "More than that, Wonderland is a reminder of something greater than ourselves, beyond our special DNA. It's a gift. And I will not squander it."

"Precisely." The minister bolsters his tone. "It is a gift, one that Normals wouldn't know the first thing to do with. We left Normalcy behind, and for good reason. To even consider allowing Normals into our society is the very definition of backwards."

"But they aren't Normals anymore, are they, not if they choose to change?" Though her words carry passion, Charlotte's posture remains poised. "Don't you see? This is our only way forwards. If my sister's child can become Wonder, anything is possible. Catherine believes Alice may even be the key to unifying the realities if—"

"Nonsense," the minister barks. "Unify the realities? I daresay, the Duchess of Diamonds was correct in her assessment. You *have* gone mad."

"Careful, Quincy. I am still your queen. And I have support, even if that support is not from the likes of you."

Doing my best to remain quiet, I shift, but this doesn't resolve the cramp in my leg or the crick in my neck from this tiny cupboard.

Charlotte turns towards the window, just enough so the soft light filtering through the gauzy drapes showcases her profile. I can see her fully now. She's older, forty at least, with modest creases around her eyes and an angle to her delicate jaw that marks maturity. If I didn't know her voice by heart, I'd say this was Scarlet speaking.

But Charlotte is only twenty-six. This can't be real.

"You may be royal by your English blood," the Minister of Spades says. "But things change. The other quarter heads support *my* view on the matter, as does your former governess Dinah."

"This isn't about you," Charlotte says. "It's about all Wonders. Both those born with the gene . . ." She pauses, stealing a side glance that makes me hold my breath. Does she know I'm here, eavesdropping? ". . . and those who, through pure faith, found their way in." Charlotte winks before turning to face the minister once more. "Not faith in you nor me nor any other human Wonder in existence. But belief in the idea of something more concrete than flesh and blood and genes and tests."

"We shall see about that." The minister huffs. I can barely make out his tattooed hand as he straightens his waistcoat. "You may have eccentrics like Lavender Hatter and Blanche de Lapin on your side, but not everyone shares your sentiments and sympathies for the Normals. That girl—"

"Do not insult my niece in front of me. Alice is anything but Normal, and you would do well to remember it."

"She doesn't belong here, Charlotte." The way he addresses her so informally this time—not as a queen or a daughter but as a commoner—gives me chills. "Those of us born with the gene have a right by birth."

"And she has a right by belief," Charlotte says. "Can't you see past your pride and consider that perhaps Wonderland isn't just for those born into it? Anyone might have a chance to share in this amazing gift if we would only allow them the opportunity."

I picture the minister's stare hardening. He shoves both hands into his trouser pockets and backs out of the doorframe. "Wonderland is for Wonders. Anyone less doesn't belong." He slips out of view and into the shadows of the corridor beyond.

The odd dream forces my eyelids open. I knew I'd seen the minister's tattoo somewhere in my past. I was five, hiding in a cupboard and hoping he wouldn't find me. While I didn't understand much at that age, I knew well enough to fear the man.

He didn't like me. He wanted me gone. That part was real.

The rest I don't understand. Are the memories I keep stumbling upon filling in the blanks of my lost childhood? One in which Charlotte was somehow queen and twenty years older, sister to Queen Cordelia and my mother Catherine? It's impossible, wishful thinking. Then again, if my memories *are* returning, and Charlotte *is* royal, that leaves one question unanswered . . .

Who is Lady Scarlet?

I roll over onto my side. That's my first mistake. Because I'm sitting up, not lying down. The wooden rocking chair beneath me is hard as a stale crumpet, and my bones ache in places I didn't know had bones. Did I fall asleep? How much time have I wasted?

Flash, boom, flash, rumble, screech.

The storm has returned. And it's close. But this time, it's brought something far more fearsome with it.

A wild caterwaul that can only mean one thing.

The Jabberwock has found me.

I inhale a sharp breath. All the extra Fates in Wonderland couldn't have prepared me for this. I knew I'd have to confront the beast eventually. I just didn't know it would be so soon.

I bolt from the chair, leaving it rocking with such force it hits the wall. Then I grab my rucksack from the floor and catapult myself towards the bedroom at the heel of the house. The storm bellows again, followed by a howl of wind that rattles the windows. The wardrobe in the back room's corner is too small for me to hide inside, and more than anything, I wish I had a vial of Flourisher's Fate with me. Oh, why didn't I think to come into this Trial more prepared?

"Take your things with you this time, as a return to the palace is unlikely."

I should have better heeded Charlotte's words. I give myself very good advice, but very seldom is it given in time to actually matter.

Something lands on the roof of the cottage.

I scramble under one of the single beds and press flat against the floorboards, willing myself to shrink. To disappear altogether.

Scratch, scrape, scratch!

The awful sound clawing at the window moves me to cover both ears. A talon? A tree branch? I wish I'd left this silly cottage when I had the chance.

"The Jabberwock takes on many forms, depending on what you most fear."

Chess's words do little to soothe. My thoughts drift back to my former nightmares, to the beast that skulked just beyond the walls of the checked hall. I never saw it, but it was always there, waiting. As trapped as I felt inside my own head, it felt better than facing whatever lurked on the outside.

"If you want to get out, you must first go in."

"Don't you think I know that by now?" I protest, elbows digging into the floor. "I'm here, aren't I? I stepped off the obvious path, and where has it gotten me?"

If I had a pillow, I'd bury my face in it and scream.

Rafters groan and creak as the wind and rain continue their abuse. The thunder and lightning seem farther away, teasing that this nightmare will end eventually. Turning over onto my back, I dig through my rucksack and withdraw *The Adventurer's Almanac.* It takes no time at all to find the poem I seek. I skim the first stanza and focus on the second. Charlotte would be proud to know I've retained my poetry vocabulary.

"You're not completely hopeless, after all," I imagine her saying.

I twist the book in the limited space over my face to read the words in the dim light.

> *"Beware the Jabberwock, my son!*
> *The jaws that bite, the claws that catch!*
> *Beware the Jubjub bird, and shun*
> The *frumious Bandersnatch!"*

Nonsense, the lot of it, just as it was before. The rest of the poem goes on to speak of a sword of some sort, a blade that can slay the beast to everyone's joy. The question isn't whether or not the Jabberwock is real—it's as real as the pounding heart about to break from my chest.

The true conundrum is what this ridiculous poem has to do with it?

Whoever wrote these words was off their trolley, or else a deeper meaning lies beneath it all. There are no underlined letters in this one as in "The Crocodile" poem. No hidden message from

Charlotte to help me understand that hearts are wild. Compared to "Jabberwocky," even the raven's writing desk riddle seems simple.

I blink. That's because it is.

Of course. I turn the book upside down, then right side up. No matter which way I situate the tome, the poem remains a torrent of made-up words. It doesn't matter if I read them backwards, forwards, or with my eyes closed. The words don't mean anything. Because they're not real.

I'm so elated at this new discovery, I attempt to sit up, only to hit my forehead on the bed's underbelly of planks in the process. Whatever the Jabberwock is, it's no different than Scarlet's Wonderland, a façade created to mask what we're truly meant to see.

One, two, three deep breaths. I clutch the almanac against my chest. Two grunts and a groan later, I'm standing inside the bedroom, the book tucked under one arm and my rucksack slung over the other.

A curved black talon taps the windowpane.

I want to close my eyes and hide and give way to my nausea. Instead I take out my locket watch and play the tiny melody I've trusted to wake me from my nightmares. Though I'm fully conscious, the tune gives me the courage to speak the words I hope will work.

I clear my throat. "I don't believe in you."

A screech and a caw reply.

This time I fill my lungs and cry, "I do not believe in you!"

In an instant the world outside the window transforms. The storm and howling wind and pelting rain dissipate, retreat, vanish. Once again sunshine filters in, casting a friendly glow over my face. I am not naive. This isn't the last I'll see of the Jabberwock.

But perhaps this is the beginning of the end.

With a silent *thank you* to the book's author, I stow it away. I'm about to leave the world of the cottage behind, certain I've overcome the task young Cordelia led me here to complete. I've thwarted the Jabberwock—for now, at least. Then I hear the music again, this time accompanied by a woman's laughter. I pause. Glasses clink, and I can almost see couples dancing 'round and 'round a grand ballroom.

On instinct, I withdraw the silver hand mirror. Every encounter I've had with a reflection thus far has led me into the past as seen through my mother's eyes. Taking me back to move me forwards.

Leaving the Tulgey Wood behind only to see a young Charlotte skipping off towards a new, more sinister wood.

Finding the replica of the Foundling House and what awaited inside. Three teen sisters and a little Alice with flour on her hands. Two separate memories from separate times, but clearly connected.

Hearing the brook that took me off the path. Meeting young Cordelia, who raced me along a new one.

And now this cottage with its makeshift lab and whispers that a child was once here.

It's all connected, it has to be. What if these are biscuit crumbs left behind to help me find the real Wonderland and the Ivory King?

Tracing my fingers along the mirror's heart-shaped frame, I gaze into my reflection. The hidden music crescendos and my senses heighten. I can taste pastries and treacle and the most delectable tarts with raspberry preserves I've ever had the pleasure of sampling. I press a hand to the glass. Only, it isn't glass at all, but the same silver liquid I've encountered before. My hand goes straight through yet remains completely dry.

Just like at the brook's bank. And the wall of rain.

I swallow and push my hand deeper. It's warm on the other side of the mirror. Wherever the other side so happens to be.

A woman's sharp voice fills my ears.

"Enough secrets, Dinah," the woman says. "Queen Charlotte and that scientist sister of hers are out of control. They must be stopped before Wonderland as we know it ceases to exist."

At the word "exist," I'm pulled through the liquified glass. The brief sensation of drowning squeezes my lungs. I gasp for air, and in a moment, I'm standing on two feet, breathing again, surrounded by candlelight and garlands embellished with dried orange slices and red roses. The music in the background is clearer now, an old Christmas tune about a king and a feast, crisp snow and a brightly shining moon.

And oh, the smells! Beyond the delectable treats I sensed before, now I'm greeted with the scents of pine and cinnamon. Of cocoa and peppermint.

Of Chess.

The thought of him stings. We've not even been apart a day and already it feels like a never-ending game of solitaire.

I turn slowly to survey the room around me. It looks to be a parlour of some sort, with a sitting area situated beside a roaring fire on one side, and a grand piano with several cosy-looking chairs nearby on the other. Paintings deck the already-decked walls, mostly depicting watercolour landscapes. One painting features a stunning portrait of three sisters, two blondes with blue eyes on either side of a brown-eyed brunette I'd know anywhere.

Three royal sisters. Three fraternal triplets.

Cordelia, Queen of England.

Catherine, my mother and the scientist who discovered the Wonder Gene.

And Charlotte. My sister who is really my aunt? But how could she be so much younger than the other two? Even the best beauty products in all of Britain couldn't remove almost thirty years of aging. In the Normal Reality, we celebrate Queen's or King's Day every year. Cordelia is approaching fifty. My mother—if she were here—would be the same age. But Charlotte is only twenty-six.

Something doesn't add up. I'm going to need Jack's help to solve this puzzle. I tuck the ideas and questions away for now, focusing instead on my own altered reflection.

On the wall behind me hangs an enlarged version of the hand mirror I held only moments ago. I'm my mother again, and in this scene—memory—I'm wearing the most lovely sapphire-blue gown. The vibrant colour brings out my—her—eyes, which are framed by black, rectangular glasses. The dress is gathered up at the back, just above my hips, and the fluttery sleeves make me look almost angelic.

I lower my hands to my sides and turn this way and that, relishing the swish of the material as I move. How can I help but stare at her? And why do I miss someone I don't even remember?

Footsteps approach the French doors across the room. The coloured-glass panes distort two figures on the other side.

"In here," Dinah's distinct voice says.

Panic wells and a rush of dread consumes me. Whether these feelings are my own or my mother's—or both—I cannot tell. But the instinct to hide takes over. Picking up the skirts of my gown, I shuffle as quietly as I can across the room. My first thought is to look for a pot of tea to drink to help conceal me, but then how would I know which blend it is? Instead, I slip out another set of doors and onto a balcony, leaving one door cracked just enough so I can listen from behind a potted shrub. It's freezing, and I clench my teeth to keep them from chattering.

Dinah and her companion enter the warmth of the parlour then. Though this memory must be a decade old, Chess's grandmother seems frozen in time. Same black dress and orange-streaked hair. The only thing that appears to be missing is her onyx broach.

Beside her, Madame Sevine—Duchess of Diamonds—saunters across the floor.

"What would you propose we do?" Sevine laughs, stumbling a little. The champagne flute in her hand is empty. "You must have an idea or two, hmm?"

Dinah, ever the gracious hostess apparently, crosses to a sideboard where various refreshments await. She retrieves a fresh champagne bottle from an ice bucket and refills Sevine's glass.

The Duchess raises it to her lips and sips, her smile increasing by the bubble.

Dinah seems to sense their conversation isn't for outside ears. She links an arm through Sevine's and leads her to a pair of wingback chairs by the hearth. They sit and lean close. "I've already spoken with both the Minister of Spades and the Lord of Clubs . . ." Dinah's hushed tone makes it difficult to determine everything she's saying. ". . . Mocktur, the old fool, thinks we ought to toss Charlotte into the Pool of Tears and be done with it."

Sevine giggles, spilling some of her bubbly onto the expensive-looking rug. "Sounds simple enough," she says, not attempting to match Dinah's low volume. "We could make it seem like an accident."

"And then what?" Dinah counters. "The people look to Charlotte. They trust her. Rely on her. It wouldn't bode well for us to do away with such power. It is far better to have loyal subjects than fearful ones. Even if we did get rid of Charlotte, Catherine's research is far too valuable. She can prove useful."

The duchess eyes her, skepticism apparent. "Go on." She nods with another salute of her half-empty glass.

Dinah glances over her shoulder.

I'm so anxious I could burst. Or plummet off this balcony like the icicle I'm slowly becoming.

"Charlotte must be replaced," Dinah says at last.

I shiver. Aside from the chill clutching my heart, the end of my nose is numb and I can no longer feel my toes. How much longer is this memory going to last?

"Replaced?" Sevine asks, her voice going up an octave. "By whom?"

At her question, I lose my balance and the potted shrub I've been hiding behind moves and scrapes stone. Leaves and branches rustle.

Dinah snaps her head in my direction, her heartless, cat-like eyes searching.

I crouch low. Did she see me? Surely my mother was far more elegant in this situation. I can't picture her hiding behind a bush, eavesdropping. She was a brilliant scientist, after all.

And I'm just a silly girl playing dress-up.

Seemingly satisfied they're still alone, Dinah focuses once more on the tipsy duchess. "We replace her with another Charlotte, only slightly altered. A double. A mirrored image. An illusion. Queen *Scarlet* will do nicely, I think."

Sevine throws her head back. The diamonds around her neck *click* and *clack* with every move she makes. "Where are we going to find this Scarlet?"

Dinah smiles with all her teeth and I don't think I've ever seen anything so unsettling. She withdraws a vial then.

I peer through a gap in the shrub's branches. The vial appears to contain some sort of honey-coloured tea. My insides twist into knots.

Sevine's eyes go wide, and she drops her flute. It shatters on the floor as she jumps up. "What is that?"

"This is a special tea blend that I've been perfecting, thanks to the help of Lavender Hatter. She has no idea her concoction will ultimately lead to her beloved queen's demise, of course. With this tea, we will place a better Queen of Hearts on the throne. An upgraded version. One we can control."

"Brilliant," Sevine says.

Evil! I want to scream. I cover my mouth with both hands.

"Do you think Catherine will suspect the switch?"

"Catherine is so preoccupied with her little science experiments," Dinah derides, "she won't even notice. The further Wonders are removed from the real version of Wonderland, the more power we hold. They can no longer decipher truth from lies. First, we change the queen."

"And after that?" Sevine asks.

"It's quite simple really." Dinah's feline grin reflects off the looking glass as she adds, "All that's left is to alter history itself."

ALICE

The feeling of being yanked from a dream through a vortex of death at one hundred kilometres per second doesn't begin to describe the sensation that follows my venture out of the looking-glass memory.

Or was it a nightmare?

The jury's out on that one.

"Is she breathing? Please tell me she's breathing?"

I'd recognize that abrupt tone anywhere. If I wasn't trying to catch my breath, I'd sigh my relief. Willow.

Clothes rustle. Someone's hair tickles my face. My fingers curl around something slender—the hand mirror?

"She's going to be all right. Here, hold this."

The soft voice contrasting Willow's . . . Sophia?

My heart swells. It can't be. They're here, and I'm here, and we're together. I didn't have to go and look for them. Contrariwise, they found me.

The sound of a cork popping from a bottle, followed by pouring liquid, greets my ears. Something cold and hard touches my lips.

I part them, and a lukewarm, peppermint tea finds its way onto my tongue.

Focus Fix. Tears burn against my closed eyelids. How is it possible to miss Madi more than I already do?

"How much longer?" Willow says. Gentle fingers stroke the matted fringe away from my forehead. "This place is unnerving."

"A minute or two," Sophia says.

Invisible weights press against my eyelids. I'm fully awake, but I can't open my eyes.

My thoughts run rampant. Charlotte, Scarlet, Dinah, Sevine. Who *is* Scarlet? How does Lavender Hatter's tea work? Does it give Dinah the ability to control the imposter queen's mind? I suspected Dinah couldn't be trusted, but I didn't expect the confirmation to sting quite like this. It cuts to my core and makes me question Chess once again. He would have been too young at the time, but . . .

Eyes still closed, I twist and turn my head, as if the physical manifestation of my refusal to believe Chess a villain will make it not so. Even now, Chess's words beg me to believe in him.

"You know me," he'd said just after our first kiss.

I nod where I lie. "I know you," I whisper.

"She's waking."

"Here," Sophia says, and I feel two hands slip beneath my shoulders. "Let's help her sit. Maybe that will nudge her into consciousness."

I groan as they assist me into a sitting position. Still, my eyelids won't budge. If Dinah is controlling Scarlet, we're in more trouble than I realised. I've only encountered the Queen of Hearts once up close—in the Heart Palace garden. She was intimidating, to be sure, though Knave didn't seem to fear her one bit.

But Dinah is beyond mere intimidation. She's crafty and cunning, as catlike as her Beast's Blend form suggests. To put her as the mastermind behind all of this means something far worse.

We only need to figure out what, exactly, that worse meaning is.

"Come on, Alice." Sophia's gentle coaxing is what finally urges me to open my eyes and face the light.

A cough. A deep inhale. My lashes flutter, and both of my teammates instantly wrap their arms around me.

The attempt to stand takes everything I have. Without my friends, I might have been here on the cottage floor for days.

They release me at the same time. "We're so glad you're—" Willow starts as Sophia gushes, "I can't believe—"

We all laugh in unison. I take them both in.

Sophia beams, but not even her brilliant smile can hide the sunken purple half-moons beneath her brown eyes. Even her vibrant brown skin looks paler somehow.

Willow's normally tidy crown braid is a frazzled mess of wisps, and a few leaves stick out here and there. She's always been pale, a stunning contrast to her dark hair. Today, though, the effect falls short, and she looks more sickly than I've ever seen her.

I don't look too fine myself, of course. My Team Heart jumpsuit is torn and dirty, as if I've been running through a patch of muddy bramble bushes. The looking glass—or window to the past, it seems—has shattered, leaving only remnants of its former mirrored glory to return pieces of my tattered reflection.

"What happened?" I lean against the wall for support, perusing the state of the cottage. Beyond the windows, daylight reigns. Was I here all night? The memory couldn't have lasted longer than half an hour. Then again, memories are like dreams.

And I know better than anyone that time can be funny in dreams.

"We were separate but both in the wood," Sophia tells me, "trying to find a path that actually led somewhere when we heard the sound of breaking glass and then an awful scream." She glances at Willow.

"It's how we found one another," Willow says with a nod. "I'd been wandering for what seemed like ages. When I heard the scream"—she winces at the sound I don't recall making—"I ran. The path opened into a clearing, and there was Soph." Her voice cracks.

Willow's never been one to get overly emotional. Fatigue and the all-consuming loneliness of the wood must have done her in.

"Then we found you." Sophia looks at me with a teary half-smile.

"We're just glad you're okay," Willow says. "What happened?"

I explain about the looking glasses and reflections and give them the condensed version of my encounters, skipping the details that involve Dinah for now. "Is that how it's been for you?" I ask them.

Their shared looks of confusion seem to question my sanity.

Sophia speaks first. "Silver mist and liquid glass? Rainfall that parts like drapes?" One look at her shoes, then back up at me. "Are you sure you weren't dreaming?"

I furrow my brow. "You don't believe me?"

"It's not that we don't believe you." Willow seems to weigh her words. "This is all some sort of simulation, right? Anything could happen in a Trial. We just haven't run into anything quite so . . ."

"Colourful," Sophia finishes.

Willow nods.

My heart is a sunken cobblestone at the bottom of the Thames. But disappointment soon morphs into defence. Chess would believe me. Madi wouldn't assume I'd been dreaming or that I'd fallen prey to a simulation or an illusion of the Trials. What I saw were my mother's real memories. I'm certain. So I snatch up my rucksack, step between them, and make a beeline for the door, stowing the broken mirror I'm still clutching with my other possessions.

I need air.

Once I'm outside, away from the dusty cottage and the memories and nightmares, the temperature feels brisker than it did yesterday, prickling my skin through my torn jumpsuit. I rub my arms as hopelessness envelops me.

What now?

Where now?

As light trickles through the trees, ushering in the morning, I move farther from the cottage. Fallen leaves crunch beneath my steps, reminding me this strange weather may very well be an illusion too. Back in the Normal Reality, spring bids farewell as summer's heat hovers humid and heavy. In Wonderland, anything goes. I can imagine whatever temperature I wish. Here, it's autumn, maybe almost winter. In the last looking-glass memory, it was Christmastime. Could that be connected to the sudden change in seasons? Or is this another simulation ordered by Scarlet?

By Dinah.

I stop and curl my fingers tightly around the straps of my rucksack. When cautious footsteps approach, I'm tempted to turn and tell them everything. Maybe they'll believe me then. But if Dinah really is controlling the imposter queen and designer of this Trial, she could be listening. I can't let her know what else I've seen. I may have already said too much.

"We need to keep moving," I say as Willow and Sophia flank me on either side. "I've already wasted too much time here. And there's no telling when the Jabberwock will return," I add to see how they'll respond.

"Alice." Willow does nothing to hide the curiosity in her tone. "Did you actually see it?"

Relief washes over me. I open my mouth to begin my description, but something strikes me. "*Actually,*" I admit, "come to think of it, no. I only saw what looked like a talon scraping the window." Which very well could have been a tree branch. "But I heard noises. Horrible, bloodcurdling noises."

Sophia speaks up. "I heard it too. It sounded like . . ." She covers her face with both hands.

"Death." Willow completes the sentence as she takes a step ahead and turns to face us both. "The blasted beast, whatever it was, sounded like it was dying. And like it wanted anyone nearby to die along with it."

Lowering trembling hands, Sophia peeks back down the road to where the cottage awaits. Safe. Cosy. Familiar. "Maybe we should stay here. Camp out until the others find us. We're not equipped to fight. That vial of Focus Fix was the only one Madi gave me."

My eyes widen. "Madi?"

"She gave me one too." Willow withdraws a vial from a pouch at her hip.

"More Focus Fix?" I ask.

Willow uncorks her vial. "Take a whiff."

I do so, and I'm immediately greeted by the scents of lemongrass and ginger. "Flourisher's Fate," I note.

"Madi must have known we'd each need something." Willow draws the vial back and twists the cork in. "For some reason she entrusted me to carry the antidote tea."

I frown. "She didn't give me anything."

"Are you sure about that?" Sophia's lilt is optimistic.

My nod stops halfway. *Am* I sure? Without replying I dig through my rucksack. My hand closes around my old deck of cards. Then the almanac and the tattered fabric of the stuffed rabbit I found. I used to have my silver locket watch in here too, but now I keep it around my neck. I don't feel anything else in here . . . except . . . is that . . . ?

My pulse skips and trips over itself. I pull the incognito vial free.

"So you do have one." Willow leans in. "Which is it?"

I hold it up to the light, which glints off the glass, illuminating the caramel-coloured liquid within. So many teas look the same, it's hard to tell which one this might be. I uncork my vial and pass it once under my nose. I hope to smell lavender and black currant. Dwindler's Draught is the blend I'm most familiar with. Shrinking has proven useful.

But a vision of Willow, no larger than my palm, flashes across my mind.

Well, as long as it doesn't almost kill you, of course.

But this is not that.

"Any guesses?" I ask.

Sophia reaches for the vial. After investigating, she shakes her head. "The scent is floral, but I can't place it." She offers it to Willow.

But Willow only shrugs and returns Madi's gift to me. "Yours is as good as mine."

I inhale the scent again, trying to place it. "Is that . . . ?" Another sniff. "Citrus," I declare. "And chocolate."

Sophia eyes the vial skeptically. "Why wouldn't she label it?"

"Maybe she didn't have time," Willow suggests.

"Whatever her reason," I say firmly, "I trust Madi. She wouldn't have given me this unless she thought it would help. The blend she gave Sophia certainly did."

"But we know what Focus Fix does," Sophia protests. A light breeze tousles her dark locks, and she shudders. "An unknown blend can be dangerous, even deadly. You'd better not use it until we can ask Madi what it is."

I don't argue but I also don't agree. Though I may not have a clue regarding this mystery blend's purpose, Madi knows. And if she entrusted me to have the courage to use it at the proper time, I'll stow it away until then.

We walk in silence for a spell, the only sounds the crunch of our trainers on what has turned into quite the gravel-littered path. At first I thought we were merely backtracking, but I don't recognize this part of the wood. Then again, much of my time here has been spent experiencing the past. For all I know we could be walking towards the chessboard field, no closer to finding the others or finishing the Trial. But, if we're still Pawns, we must be moving forwards. Right?

Frustration brews. Where is the Ivory King? Why doesn't he help us and simply show us the way?

I pose a question. "Have either of you ever made it this far in the Trials?" I can't believe I've never asked this. I don't know much about their stories, aside from the fact they're practically sisters due to Sophia's fractured past.

Sophia kicks a pebble and shakes her head. "This is only

my second year. Team Heart didn't make it to the Fourth Trial last season."

"Same," Willow says. "We were fresh meat together. Our trainer put us through the wringer. Much different from Charlotte's hands-off approach."

My knee-jerk reaction is to come to Charlotte's defence, but Willow isn't wrong. Aside from the time we spent on training obstacles in the Heart Palace courtyard, we've hardly seen my sister.

My aunt. Charlotte is my *aunt*. I don't know that I'll ever get used to thinking of her this way. But I'm not ready to divulge this information yet.

"Who trained you last year?" I ask.

"Blanche," they say in unison. When my eyes widen at their response, Sophia adds, "Don't let Miss Fancy-Pants fool you. She's a pistol."

I reflect on the first time I met the Frenchwoman. I didn't know what to think, what with her helping me cheat during Clash of the Cards and all. But could it be she was trying to show me something that might aid our team in reaching our goal? Blanche *is* part of the Knight Society after all, and Charlotte trusts her. What was it the Minister of Spades said in my memory dream?

"You may have eccentrics like Lavender Hatter and Blanche de Lapin on your side . . ."

When we stop to rest, I'll need to make a list of allies, enemies, and those who remain uncertainties. I hope, for our sakes, Blanche is an ally. As close as she is to Scarlet, having her as an enemy would not bode well.

We walk until we hear the glorious notes of running water. Though I've been fooled before, I'm cautiously hopeful. In Wonderland, we can imagine many things. New clothes. A different hairstyle. We can even alter the colour of the sky. We can make bland food taste like tarts and treacle. Add a little flavour here and a dash of spice there with a flick of our Wonder minds. But, like anything imagined, it fades. Actual sustenance is different. If we were to conjure food out of thin air it would be just that. Even an anomaly of science can't change truth. We need to eat something real.

It feels like an hour has passed since we left the cottage, but there's no true way to gauge the time. My locket watch says six o'clock, yet the sun hangs straight overhead. The WV is no help as the time in the corner of my view appears to have frozen. And yet, my added Fate remains.

Thankfully, the stream we find just ahead appears to be one hundred percent real. I'm more parched than I realised, and I scoop several handfuls into my mouth before my thirst is quenched. The temperature in the air has warmed considerably, bordering on too humid. It's as if we're passing through all four seasons in a single day.

"We can rest here for a while," I suggest. "Get our energy back up."

"You rest," Willow counters. "Soph and I will forage and see if we can find something edible." She curtsies and adds, "Your Majesty." Then she winks before turning on her heel and heading downstream.

Despite being famished and lost, at least Willow has retained her snark. Her silent reminder I'm no longer the Team Ace, but its Queen, is not lost on me.

Except, I don't feel like a queen. My shoulders slump. "Charlotte, where are you when I need you?"

Don't be afraid. I am always with you.

I watch from a distance as my teammates examine the shrubbery and scour the ground. We're quite the trio. An Ace who's not quite fit to be Queen, a Four, and a Two-turned-Ace. Willow has always been more of an Ace than I am anyway. Even now she takes the lead, allowing me a moment of solace to collect my thoughts.

"Hey," Willow calls. "I think we found some truffles!"
I wave and give a thumbs up. I've never been a fan of mushroom texture, but anything is better than starving. I can always imagine it tastes like shortbread or scones. Sigh. I might as well make myself useful too. I have a list to write. I sit on the edge of the bank and take off my trainers and socks, then I dip my aching feet into the running water. Slippery green moss coats the stones beneath the surface. It tickles and I smile. The moment reminds me of a day long ago. When everything was normal and I was just a girl holding my big sister's hand so I wouldn't slip into a stream.

"Careful now, Alice," she'd said that day in the countryside. *"I don't want to lose you."*

I'd giggled. *"You could never lose me, Charlotte. Even when I try to get lost, you always find me."*

Little did I know how true my naive statement was. Charlotte found me in the Cotswolds. She found me in Wonderland. I may not be able to communicate with her now as the WV seems to have a mind of its own in this Trial. But I can't doubt she'll find me here too.

"Come and find me, Charlotte," I say, hoping somehow she can hear.

I take out the almanac. Charlotte's note from before the Club Trial remains tucked away inside. I unfold it and read it even though I have her words memorised. Except . . . something is . . . different . . .

I read the lines again and again. Holding the brief letter up to the light, I peer closer. Oh, my . . . how could I have missed this?

Not all of Charlotte's words are created equal. While they appear upon a quick glance to be written in black ink, a closer inspection reveals some words have been penned in very dark blue.

Frantic to decode what I hope is a clue, I dig through my rucksack. Come on, where's a normal pen when I need it? Imagining one won't help. The ink will only disappear later.

At the thought, the same notepad icon I've used before appears in my WV. This feature, at least, seems to be functional. My original list of FACTS and other theories is still there. I cross off the one I'm certain now is dead wrong.

~~Charlotte is somehow Scarlet's daughter, or at the very least, related to her.~~

I swipe to a blank note with my mind and begin my new list next, trying to recall everything I've learned thus far.

THINGS I'VE LEARNED THROUGH THE LOOKING GLASS:

ALLIES:
- *Charlotte, a.k.a. Wonderland's rightful queen?*
- *Blanche de Lapin, a.k.a. @WhiteRabbit*
- *Lavender Hatter—Someone related to Madi, Raving, and Stark?*

I pause there and add a note next to the question in all caps.

ASK MADI

Next I make a heading for ENEMIES and add Dinah. Then under UNCERTAIN there's the Minister of Spades and the other quarter heads.

Finally I add a section entitled CLUES before turning my attention back to Charlotte's note.

> *See you on the other side of the finish line. No timeouts this round. Take your things with you this time, as a return to **the palace is** unlikely. Don't be **afraid**. I am always with you.*

It takes meticulous attention to detail—my cursed astigmatism does me no favours—but when I'm done, the four words she penned in blue stare back at me in my WV note.

The palace is afraid.

The palace is afraid? Afraid of what? Of whom? The Jabberwock seems most likely, but also far too obvious—

"We have dinner!"

I look up to find Willow beaming and holding two handfuls of washed truffles. They're even less appetizing up close.

Sophia waltzes up beside her with handfuls of her own findings. Some sort of pink fruit with purple leaves and stems. "Frabjous berries!" she declares. "Let's feast!"

ALICE

Willow was right.

Truffles are not like normal mushrooms. They're so much better.

With a little help from her Wonder Gene, Willow transformed the unappetizing fungus into a decadent cream sauce. Sophia created a delightful jam that was so perfect I might just eat jam again tomorrow. And the day after that. I'd eat it yesterday, too, if that were an option. To top it off, Sophia found an almond tree, and that was all Willow needed to imagine a batch of almond-flour scones into being.

As we finish, I lick my lips, savouring the perfect blend of sweet and tart. Jam, jam, jam.

Full and happy, we keep close to the stream as we head downhill for whatever in the wherever it may lead. If this is one giant game of chess, how long until we cross into the next square? If that's how it works. Will we be Pawns for the duration of the Trial? Are there Knights and Rooks and Bishops waiting off in the distance, and if so, are they friends or foes?

All too soon the water slows its trickle, stopping at a boulder dam. We all take a final drink and follow a natural path between two rows of flowering bushes uphill. With newfound energy, I'm the first to reach the hill's crest. Pink, purple, and yellow blossoms tint the world around me, speckling the path ahead as if it were an aisle in a wedding chapel.

My smile falters.

Before, the choice to follow the stream was simple, our path forwards clear, or at the very least sensical. Now we stand at a crossroads. We could venture north, south, east, or west, according to the four arrow signs posted at the intersection's middle. I circle the pole that holds the signs. Every path appears the same. Unassuming. Blanketed with flower petals, sunlight dotting the way between meagre shadows.

It's too quiet. Too . . . friendly.

"Which way do you suppose we ought to go?" Sophia stares up at the signs, searching for hidden clues no doubt.

I'm tempted to treat this crossroads like the one in the Tulgey Wood and avoid it altogether. There, we stepped off the obvious path and found our own ways.

My brows scrunch. Were they our own ways, though? Or were they tests prepared by Queen Scarlet herself? We still ended up here, in the Heart Trial, and it appears we're no closer to finding the real Wonderland or its creator. We've yet to uncover what happened to the missing players. And the Knight Society has been of no assistance whatever.

"We're lost." I plop onto the ground, petals fleeing this way and that. "Maybe we ought to wait here for someone to find us."

"That's your brilliant plan?" Willow stands above me, hands planted on her curvy hips. "Do nothing?"

I shrug, not wanting to deal with her constant need to challenge and push me past my limits. Bitterness creeps in, slow and fickle. Why couldn't Madi or Chess have found me? I stuff the unbidden thought down where I won't be able to access it. What is wrong with me? I ought to be grateful I'm not alone anymore, not wishing for a different set of teammates.

"We could only move forwards before, right?" Sophia muses, nearing the northern path. "But there are four ways we could go. Does that mean the game's changed?"

A torch flicks on in my mind. Maybe she's onto something. I pull out the almanac and thumb through the pages until I've found my dogeared place in the chess section. I trace one finger along the list of various pieces and the rules determining their directions. Pawns can only move forwards unless taking another piece off the board, then they can move on the diagonal, like a Bishop. Knights move in the shape of an L . . . Aha! Here it is.

"We're Rooks. Look at the shape of the signpost." I hop to my feet and study the arrows. Above them, the post's crown is shaped like a rounded turret. Below them, the post's end bevels and curves outwards, like the base of a chess piece. "Or Castles, depending on your preference. We can move in any of these four directions"—I gesture towards each path—"in the shape of a cross." Maybe things are looking up. If the game alters here, it's a sign of progress, of newfound direction.

"But which one do we take?" Sophia peers over my shoulder. "Do you think it makes a difference?"

Right. We still have to answer that trivial question.

"Of course it makes a difference," Willow snaps. I've never heard her speak to her best friend this way. It's different than her usual underlying hints of humour and sarcasm. This seems off.

"Willow, are you all right?" I close the almanac and reach out to her.

She jerks away. Turns her back on us and folds her arms. "Just pick a path already, won't you?"

Shoving the book into my rucksack I let out an exaggerated huff. "Excuse me for trying to include you on important decisions." Maybe my bitterness isn't so hidden after all.

"You're the Team Queen, aren't you?" Why does her question sound more like an accusation? "You don't need us."

I eye her back. When she doesn't turn around, I give Sophia a look.

She seems to catch my meaning because she approaches her best friend with three cautious steps. When she's directly beside her, Sophia says, "Willow?"

Willow bristles but offers no response.

"Willow?" Sophia tries again, glancing at me before continuing. "Arguing won't solve anything." Now Sophia reaches out to her friend, but Willow deflects her gesture.

"Don't touch me!" As soon as she says the words, she whirls. The action is followed by Willow's sudden deafening scream. All colour drains from her face.

The sight causes immediate déjà vu. Where have I seen this before?

"Alice, move!"

It takes a hair of a second too long for me to register Sophia's sudden warning. Before I can react, she charges, knocking me to the ground and out of the way, then she starts shouting orders and commands. The words tumble out of her so quickly they don't make sense. Is she speaking to us?

"Keep your temper!" Sophia bellows.

Willow limps away, towards the northern path. Her hobble draws my gaze and I notice the chunk of torn flesh and fabric at her calf.

My stomach somersaults and a feeling like vertigo makes me dizzy despite the fact I'm not standing.

Sophia continues her strange tirade. "You're nothing but a pile of petals!" she snaps. "Just a bunch of bad-tempered little tyrants!"

"What in the cards, Soph?" My question comes out more like a desperate screech.

Sweat beads at her temple. She's panting, staring daggers at the flower petals on the ground.

But, wait. Some of those petals are *moving*. Not from a light breeze or human disturbance but they're walking, with little legs on tiny colourful, camouflaged bodies.

"Mome raths!" Sophia finally shouts between the words she's hurling at them. "Run!"

I'm frozen. Terrified. No one knows what a mome rath actually is, right? But it appears it's some sort of savage flower with a mind of its own. A flower that bites, no less.

"Alice, move!" Sophia insists again. "Help Willow! I won't be able to hold them off much longer."

It's only then that I see her Flower Mastery in full swing. She's arguing with the mome raths, attempting to convince them to stop their attack. They pile up, one on top of the other, towering higher and higher above Sophia. One giant monster made of snapping, vicious petals.

If I wasn't seeing the horror for myself, I might laugh at such a description. But these little monsters are no laughing matter.

"We mean no harm," Sophia cajoles, arms and hands out in front of her, positioned in defence. Her voice wavers. "Please, we only want to find our way."

The mome raths don't appear to speak in any language I understand. But they rustle and sway, moving ever closer to Sophia.

"Please," she tries again, "let us pass."

Her desperate plea is what finally gives me the will to rise. With fear plastered on her face and alarm infusing her words, Sophia's still standing firm, still fighting.

So what am I afraid of?

Before I can talk myself out of it, I'm up, sprinting past Sophia and the four-way rook sign and catching up to Willow. She's not in good shape. Blood drips down the exposed skin on her calf and agony contorts her face.

I stop directly in her path. "Get on my back."

"Are you insane? You're smaller than I am."

"Small but mighty," I say, hoping my confidence will more than make up for my lack in stature. I swing my rucksack around to my front side, like a kangaroo pouch. "Now get *on*."

She's reluctant but concedes. Once I've got a firm grip on her legs, I say, "Hold tight."

Whether it's the adrenaline or the fear or a mix of both, I

speed walk as fast as my legs will carry me. I'm almost running, and I'm surprised by how much ground I'm able to cover with Willow on my back. My thighs and arms and chest burn, but it's the good kind. The kind that says even if I can't help take down the mome raths, I can still do my part.

"I'm sorry," I blurt.

Willow, whose head has been resting on my shoulder, shifts. "What? Why?" Her voice is weak and far away. She sounds sleepy.

"I was missing Madi and Chess. I shouldn't have snapped at you back there. You were right. I *am* supposed to be leading, but sometimes I feel utterly and completely inadequate. But I'm so grateful—"

Wiggling out of my hold, she slides off my back.

My cheeks warm. There I go again. Saying too much and showing my awkward side.

She limps past me, thumbs looped through her utility belt. "Just stop." She hangs her head and pauses. "I'm the one who's sorry." Her voice breaks. "I don't know what came over me. The anger manifested out of nowhere, and then there was this piercing, stinging pain. It felt like—"

"It's okay," I tell her. "You were bitten by a mome rath. We saw what it did to Mouse in the Club Trial. It's not your fault."

She doesn't nod in agreement. Instead she attempts to peek over her shoulder. "Where's Soph?"

"Taming the little beasts. It was amazing to watch, once I wasn't so terrified," I say. "I've never seen petals act that way."

"At least now we know what they do." She winces against the pain. "The fact that they can camouflage themselves doesn't help, though."

She limps forwards, and I match her stride, hoisting her arm over my shoulder.

I don't know how many minutes we amble along the road that way, but the farther we move the less progress we seem to make. Willow's breaths grow more shallow, and I check myself to keep her pace.

"Should I move slower?"

Willow shakes her head. "No, I can manage."

But she can't. We're moving at snail's speed, and I wish for a bus or train or some other mode of transportation to get us moving.

"We need to stop." I lead her to the path's shoulder and help her sit on a log. Petals no longer line the trail, and our only company seems to be a bird's lacklustre melody from somewhere above. Sophia should catch up shortly. I only hope we chose the right way.

I toss my rucksack to the ground and kneel beside my teammate to examine her wound.

She hisses at my touch. Willow has never been one to shy away from the tough stuff, but one look at her closed eyes tells me a blood wound is not her injury of choice.

It's not mine, either, but here we are. We received minimal first-aid training back at Great Expectations Preparatory Academy in Oxford. How to apply a small bandage or clean a paper cut won't help me here. I doubt anything in the almanac would offer much assistance. "I wish we had a doctor," I say aloud.

At the admission, I almost expect my WV to save the day. To lend me some advice that will solve the puzzle of Willow's bleeding leg. Once again it remains silent. A quick glance at my WV bangle shows I still have three Fate hearts, at least. My eyes widen when I take in Willow's status.

It's like the Diamond Trial on repeat. Her Fates are fading. I have to act. Fast. I attempt what I've done before and transfer my bonus Fate to Willow.

A message I've never seen pops up in my WV view, the letters written in bright red.

Access denied.

My lips press together. I try again.

And, again, I'm denied access. Of course, my WV would fail me when I need it most.

"I think you have to put pressure on it," Willow says,

gulping in air between her words. She's far too pale as she sags where she sits.

Pressure. "Got it." I have no clue what I'm doing, but I have to do *something*. I tear at the already torn fabric covering her right leg.

She grasps the log beneath her, keeping her eyes shut tight. My hands shake.

"How bad is it?" she asks.

Worse than I thought. "You're fine," I tell her. "You're going to be just fine." The wound has spread up her calf like some sort of poison. The scent of something like burnt rubber wrinkles my nose. Are mome raths venomous? No amount of pressure or bandaging is going to help this.

Willow's final remaining heart blinks from the bangle on her wrist.

I jerk my head right, back down the path. Where is Sophia? Would she know some sort of natural remedy? Some kind of pollen that could work as a cure? I should search for her, make sure she's okay, but I can't leave Willow.

"Alice . . ." Panic seeps into her voice. "Just tie it off. We'll clean it and get a proper bandage later."

I shake my head, but she can't see through her closed eyes. Telling her it's more than just a blood wound won't do us any good. Even if it were blood alone, this isn't the Normal Reality. Willow was bitten by something opposite of Normal, so how could anything Normal be the solution?

"Ivory King," I say so quiet I doubt Willow can hear over her ragged breathing, "if you're real, I could use some help right now."

Nothing happens and my heart twists. Did I think it would? Did I really believe some magical solution would manifest out of nowhere?

Taking the extra torn fabric from Willow's jumpsuit, I tie a makeshift tourniquet around the wound's opening. She slides off the log and slumps to one side.

I shake her, smacking her cheek lightly. "Willow!"

No response.

I check her pulse. Her breaths are shallow, but they exist, thank goodness!

Another glance down the road. Still no Sophia. "Help," I say to no one. "Someone? Anyone? Please? Help me!"

On the last word, my rucksack tips over, spilling its contents onto the ground. Sunlight glints off the glass of Madi's mystery vial. I grab it. My hand trembles as I work the cork free. I hold my breath as I gently part Willow's lips and pour every last drop of the tea into her mouth.

One, two, three far-too-long seconds pass.

Willow coughs and sputters, blinking wildly. I exhale at the same moment my gaze falls to her leg. The wound is disappearing, fading into her skin as if it were never present at all.

"What happened?" she asks.

I'm beaming. I knew Madi wouldn't let me down. "Madi happened." I stand and dust off my legs. "Now wait here and rest. I'm going to find Sophia."

I'm elated as I head to the crossroads. But nothing awaits me there aside from the four-way sign. No Sophia or petals or mome raths. I enter the intersection and check each path. Maybe she didn't see which way we went. I try the southern path, then the eastern, and finally the western. "Sophia!" I call.

My voice greets me in an echo. But our team's Flower Master is nowhere to be heard.

At the crossroads once more, I turn this way and that. "Sophia, this isn't funny!"

Nothing.

Panic wells. She must have found Willow. She must have. I spent too much time looking for her along the other paths. She realised she went the wrong way, and we just missed each other. She's been with Willow all this time, and they're laughing and wondering where in Wonderland I am. Of course they are.

But when I reach the log, that irrational panic I was sure would subside has become reality.

Willow is gone.

SQUARE FOUR

THE

KNIGHT

"I don't want to be anybody's prisoner.
I want to be a Queen."

— Lewis Carroll,
Through the Looking-Glass and What Alice Found There

CHESS

I know this place.

These walls.

These faces.

Yet nothing and no one has a name. *I* don't have a name.

Why don't I have a name?

We chug along on the whatever-it-is, the countryside scrolling past in an array of colours I can't define. There's green, yes. That one I recall at least. But the others? They elude me. Perhaps they've forgotten who they are too.

"Pardon," I say to the bloke across from me. "Where are we headed?"

He peers through round spectacles, a half-moon grin tugging at the whiskers on his chin, but disappointment etched across his face. "Nowhere of consequence, unfortunately." The man sighs, waving his hand. "You seemed so different from the others, you know? I suppose that's what I get for hoping this Trial might finally come to an end. That *she* might finally come to an end. Wishful thinking." With that he withdraws a broadsheet from inside his waistcoat, unfolds it with a snap, and proceeds to read.

It seems I remember how news is delivered, but what was that other thing he mentioned? Trial? I sit back and slouch. Why does the word send off a flare of recognition in my mind? I may be lost at the moment, my mind as blank as an empty scoreboard—scoreboard . . . there's another word I'm sure means something important—but this man clearly has no intention of helping me remember what I've forgotten.

Who I've forgotten. Mainly, and first of all, myself.

I shift and turn to the lad beside me. Since I arrived—whenever that was—he's drifted in and out of consciousness, not much for conversation. He seems perfectly settled with not knowing where . . . What's the word for this mode of transportation? Why can't I recall a word as simple as—?

The gentleman clears his throat and changes position, crossing one leg over the other. The movement draws my attention. His paper crinkles, and I can barely spy his bushy white eyebrows over the top edge. My gaze lowers, and I scan the front page. One section inside a bold box stands out.

RIDDLE OF THE DAY

I can fly or I can crawl,
but I shall never stop or stall.
I have hands but no feet;
you may race against me,
but I assure you I can't be beat.
What am I?

I ponder the odd riddle. It's far too simple. "Time," I say, more to myself than to my nameless companions.

The whiskered gentleman folds one corner of his paper down and eyes me with a singular quirked brow. "Pardon?"

I gesture towards the broadsheet. "The riddle on the front. The answer is *time*."

He studies me for a long moment. I get the feeling he's trying to make me uncomfortable, but I remain still, holding his gaze.

"So it is," he finally concedes.

At that, the train—that's right . . . how could I have forgotten?— halts to a screeching stop, launching me from my seat. My head bangs against something hard. I'm on all fours with a nasty ache throbbing at my temples. The position feels familiar. Beast-like. As if I've been here on the ground in this same situation before—

Just as I'm about to remember what I'm sure is key to clearing my confusion, the man tucks his paper under one arm and helps me to my feet.

"Would you look at that." His gaze ventures from me to the sleeping lad to the compartment doors and back to me. His eyes sparkle with delight. "The train has stopped." He claps me hard on the back.

"Great," I say as I stand and straighten my lapels. Except, I have no lapels. I'm not wearing a jacket or coat at all, in fact. My fitted attire is not my taste—red and black and a bit too shiny. It's the sort of thing one would wear if . . . if . . .

If they were playing a game.

No, not a game. A Trial.

My memory jogs to catch up, and I take a deep breath to sprint along with it.

Buckley. The minister and Dinah and the other quarter heads.

The boy with no words and a blank expression on his face is Madi's brother. Stark Hatter. He went missing last year during the Fourth Trial. How long has he gone on like this, unaware of himself or the time passing around him? He doesn't appear to have aged a day, albeit looking a bit haggard and worse for the wear. How many times remembering did it take him to forget completely? Is there any part of him that still knows me? Still knows Madi? She'll be devastated if she sees him like this, all empty stares and hopeless expressions.

And if she's devastated, Ace will be too. I cannot let that happen.

I won't. If Madi found Kit first, I'd want her to do everything she could to help him.

"Sorry about this, mate." I grab Stark by both shoulders and shake him. Hard. I don't have time to be classy, and I'm not going to wait until I've lost my mind again.

"Stark." I stare straight into those glazed-over eyes. "Stark Hatter, Team Diamond King. Wake up. Now."

"Stark?" He shakes his head as if coming out of a trance. Despite his blinks of confusion, I see it. A recognition. A spark.

"You'd better hurry, lads," Buckley warns. "You boys don't have much time before the train resumes."

I turn my head to face him, keeping a hand on Stark's shoulder. I remember the clocks in his eyes. "How do we get past this checkpoint?"

"You have to get off the train." Buckley slides the doors open, peeks his head out into the corridor, then he steps to one side, leaving our path clear.

"Go on," he urges. "You've solved the riddle. All you need to do now is find the answer."

"I would think if I've solved the riddle, I'd have found the answer."

"That, my dear boy, remains to be seen."

Could this man be any more frustrating? I lug Stark to a stand, draping one of his arms over my shoulders.

He reaches for his abandoned headphones and device on the bench.

"Leave them," I say.

Panic glistens at his hairline. His eyes search the empty air, and I know he's looking for a vestige of his sister. He's clinging to his last lifeline, his only connection to anything beyond this train, this Trial—her voice in his headphones.

"You don't need them," I assure him. "I'm taking you to the real thing."

At least, I hope I am.

Stark nods.

Relief swells and I straighten. The only obstacle that remains is getting off this train before it runs away again.

Clapping me once more on the shoulder, Buckley beams. "Tell the next checkpoint I say hello."

"I will." And I have a feeling I'll know what or who that is when I see it. I extend my hand, and he shakes it once.

He says nothing more, but his gaze emits the opposite of what it did before. Where disappointment once lived, bursting pride now resides.

I don't know this man. My gut says he's not even real, a mere figment of the Trial. Yet, in a single look he's touched me, given me something beyond words that my father never could.

"Thank you," I tell him.

"It'll be that way." Buckley points in the direction we came.

Without a glance backwards, I'm pulling Stark along the train's corridor. We race past a slew of private compartments, and I sneak glances inside each one on the slim chance Kit might be here as well.

But they're all empty.

When we reach the end of the car, my pulse thrums as I attempt to push the doors open. Locked from the other side. I bang on the glass window, hoping someone in the next car might hear. But no one comes to our aid.

"You can't go that way." I jump as Stark speaks from behind me, his voice groggy.

I jiggle the knob as hard as I can. "How do you know?"

"Because I've already tried it."

I cease my clearly futile attempt to break through the door, and turn to face him, cocking my head as I do.

"When I first came," he says, "every time I'd find myself again, every time I'd *remember*, I'd try to break free." Hanging his head, he shakes it slowly. "We're never getting out. We're prisoners."

He shoots a sideways glance out the window. The longing in his eyes cuts me to my core.

"We are not prisoners," I announce. I try the door handle again. Blasted lock. "We stopped the train, didn't we?"

"For now."

Since when did Stark become so cynical? So hopeless? He used to be the best and brightest, even better than me, though I'd never admit it out loud. "There's always an answer," I tell him. "Facing the Jabberwock is about conquering our fears, right?" Crouching, I peer through the keyhole. "Tell me, what are you afraid of, Hatter?"

Part of me expects the silent treatment, so I'm surprised when he answers, "I'm afraid of being forgotten."

Now he's getting somewhere. "Problem solved, mate." I shake his shoulder once. "You are one hundred percent unforgettable." At least now that I've remembered, obviously.

"What about you?" he asks in return.

"Me?"

"What are you afraid of?"

I swallow. He gave me an honest answer, and he deserves an honest response. Why can't I bring myself to give him one, then? I pinch the fabric of my jumpsuit near my neck. "I'm afraid of being stuck in this irksome attire for all eternity." It really is starting to chafe.

Stark's eyes narrow. I expect him to call me out, but instead he says, "The other Trials were designed to test our skills on every level, including our wit."

Crossing my arms over my chest, I wait for him to elaborate.

"But this Trial isn't like the others."

"Go on."

He paces the corridor. "The other Trials focused on clues and puzzles. Escaping. Winning." When he walks my way again, he stops. "How long have I been here?"

I stare at my shoes.

"How long?"

I wince at his raised voice. I look up at him and say, "A year."

His jaw works, and he turns his head to gaze out the window

again. The rolling green chessboard hills stretch on for miles. Back home, we can see the layer of the Normal Reality beneath the fantastical, but here, even Wonderland seems hidden. And unlike other Trial simulations, so much of this feels real. Planned and purposeful. Designed.

"A year." Stark leans his head on the window, mumbling the words over and over.

Suddenly he draws himself up, determination on his face. "We have to finish what we started. Not for Team Diamond or Team Spade, but for Wonderland. For all of us." And with that declaration he turns on his heel and strolls away.

It takes me a moment to register the transition from confused and aloof Stark to Team Diamond King. We may not be teammates now, but we have a common goal. Which is precisely why I follow him.

At first I think we're going to rejoin Buckley in the private compartment, but Stark strides past it without a glance. He's speeding up, and I double my pace to match his. How long is this train car?

Midday sunlight, bright and hot, streams through the locomotive's windows, casting long shadows across the floor. Wasn't it about this time when I arrived on the train in the first place? Onto its endless track. When did I lose track of the time?

Endless track. Track. Time.

Could it be so simple?

When we reach the dining car, I scoot past him in the narrow aisle, then I face him as I walk backwards.

"Time flies but never stops," I say, out of breath.

Stark lifts an eyebrow. "Took you long enough."

"Ha! Says the bloke who's been here a year." I regret the words as soon as they're out of my blathering mouth.

But no offense contorts Stark's expression. He merely chuckles. "Touché."

When we find the very place where I boarded the train to begin with, Stark reaches past me to open the door. It's only then I notice just how high we are, on a bridge overlooking an enormous glittering lake. And it's a long way down.

"After you." Stark gestures.

"Are you mental?" I grip the rails on either side of the exit and lean out, releasing a low whistle. "It's hundreds of metres. If the fall didn't kill you, you'd be knocked unconscious by the sheer speed at which you hit the water, and then you would drown."

"Thank you for the physics lesson, Shire." Stark rolls up the sleeves of his Team Diamond jumpsuit and zips the front up to his neck. "Which is why we'll have to fly."

I stare at him. "Did I miss something?"

"No," he says. "I did. For an entire year I missed it." He combs his fingers through his hair. Since waking, the grey and faded shade has returned to a deep purple once again. It's the same length it was a year ago, though, another confirmation he's remained frozen, never moving forwards or backwards. "Time doesn't stop, and yet you stopped the train when you solved Buckley's riddle. You attained the impossible. More than that, you pushed past the boundaries, achieving what we've never been capable of in Wonderland. But the real solution isn't in the answer itself. The real answer is in the question."

My eyes widen. "Since time did something it's never done, then the possibilities are endless."

Stark cracks what I'll bet is his first smile in a while. "Time flies," he says.

And then he shoves me off the train.

ALICE

The northern path is darker than it was before. Colder too.

"Willow!" My throat is dry and my voice cracks. "Sophia!" One, two, three, four more lonely steps. "You're both hilarious." Nothing. "You've pulled my leg. Ha, ha. Very funny."

I half expect them to pop out of the bushes at any moment. We'll have a good laugh. When we catch up with the others, Madi will help me come up with a brilliant payback prank, and this will all be but a memory.

But there is no laughter. No "fooled ya" smiles. My teammates have vanished, leaving me once again on my own.

I press on past the fear and uncertainty that suffocates, closing in like the walls in my nightmares. It took me the first three Trials to figure out my deep-seated fear of being alone. But it's more than that, I think. I've never actually minded independence. I craved and enjoyed it. Being alone, in and of itself, is not so frightening. It can even be fun.

No, it's not aloneness I fear.

It's abandonment.

I shiver at the realisation. The season seems to have changed again, ushering in a winter evening so frigid and cruel, I'll have to find shelter again soon. For the first time since entering this Trial, I'm searching for a looking glass or reflection that will take me away and help me escape the reality of what's to come.

I may never find my teammates. Maybe they're already gone, and I'll be trapped here like Kit and Stark and the other missing Wonders.

"Willow," I call again. This time when I speak, it feels like I'm choking on the surrounding darkness. As if it's more than just nightfall but a living, breathing thing. A poison more potent than any I've encountered.

"Willow!" I try again. "Sophia! Where are you?"

"They aren't here," a smooth voice says.

I whirl and immediately regret it. I can hardly see anything at all, and now I have no clue which direction I'm facing. "Who said that? Where are you?"

Whoever it is gives a low chuckle. A boy. Why is his laugh so familiar? "Don't worry," he says, and a hand touches mine. It's warm despite the chill around us. "Your eyes will adjust soon. Give it a moment."

My first instinct should be to rip my hand away. This strange boy could be an enemy. For all I know, he might be a manifestation of the Jabberwock. But his touch feels oddly familiar. He squeezes my hand and I welcome the unexpected comfort it provides.

I don't return the gesture, but I don't pull away either. After a few blinks, the darkness settles, turning from black to a deep, hazy blue. I blink again and shapes start to take form. Boulders. Trees in the distance to my right or my left and a shoreline ahead.

And a boy who looks strikingly like . . .

"Chess?" My heart constricts and my eyes burn. He found me. We found each other. I chose the right path. Everything is going to be fine.

The boy chuckles again and shakes his head. "Typical." He tilts his head back, copper hair shaggy but lacking the pink streaks I've come to adore. His eyes are striking, but closer to sea glass than turquoise. "What does a guy have to do to get away from his older brother's shadow?" He meets my eyes and winks, then releases my hand. He hooks his thumbs in his trouser pockets and walks towards the nearby sea lapping against sand.

All words fail me, except one. "Kit." My heart swells in a different way now, and emotions clash. Elation. Curiosity. Caution. Hope. Chess will be over the moon to learn I've found his brother. Or did Kit find me? Either way we're together. And I'm not letting him out of my sight.

I bound down the shore, relishing the change in the salted air. Kit pauses at the shoreline. I watch as his shoulders rise and fall with a deep, controlled breath. An ocean breeze tousles his hair and whips at his clothing. Is he waiting for a boat? There's nowhere left to go aside from the water unless we turn back.

Before I reach him, he backs up a metre or two. At first I think he's going to turn around and come to meet me, but then he dashes towards the water at a full sprint. When he's up to his waist in the ocean, he waits, arms outstretched and buoyed by the waves.

When I reach the line where sea-foam meets sand, littered with washed-up pebbles and shells, I stop. "Wait," I call. "Please, don't go. I've only just found you." Could he be an illusion? Did I enter another memory of my mother's? But that doesn't make sense, does it? If she disappeared when I was a child, she couldn't know Kit. He looks to be thirteen or fourteen, the same age he was when he vanished during the Trials a year ago.

"Ah," he says, "and wouldn't it be a pity to lose what you've only just discovered?"

Those are Chess's words. Is this simply a coincidence? Siblings sound alike, don't they? Not that I would know. Charlotte and I are as opposite as night and day. As white and red. But we also aren't sisters.

Cordelia and Charlotte and Catherine are, though. And they're plenty opposite too.

"Kit," I manage around the stopped-up emotions in my throat. "Is it really you?"

He turns to face me. His arms still spread over the mild waves. He sways with the water, letting it move around him. "What is *really*? Do you mean, am I *real*?"

When he words the question that way, I hear how ridiculous it sounds. I can only nod.

"Depends on what your definition of real is. If you mean, am I a living, breathing human, then the short answer is yes. For all intents and purposes, I'm real."

I exhale.

But then he speaks again. "If you mean am I here, standing before you in all my charming glory?"

He is without a doubt Chess's brother.

"Then the answer is more complicated," he adds. "One I can't truly expound upon unless you come with me." At that he immerses himself fully into the water.

I stand, uncertain, and count the seconds away. Ten. Twenty. Thirty.

He's not coming up for air.

Why isn't he coming up for air?

I don't think, I dive. It's freezing, and I regret the decision immediately even if my good conscience scolds me for doing so. But the sensation of ice prickling every centimetre of skin is almost immediately replaced by something warm and soothing and much thicker than the seawater ought to be. It invites me in, and I cease my swim and frantic search and let the feeling envelop me for just a moment.

Then I open my eyes.

I'm sinking down, down, down through a vertical pit-like cave. Fear drowns out every other response. Darkness grips me, and I frantically thrash this way and that, struggling to swim up and out and away to safety. Even back to the familiar wood, where nothing made sense but at least I wasn't dying.

"Don't fight it. Let it see who you are." Kit's voice sounds so much like Chess that I can't help but listen. I will my panicked muscles to relax.

The sensation of melting into a deep state of sleep washes over me, while at the same time, I remain fully conscious. Just as in the wood, my eyes adapt and the veil of darkness lifts, revealing knickknacks and trinkets and other items I recognise. They float around me, trapped within giant bubbles. Bouncing off the walls. I reach out to touch them, but each item remains beyond my grasp.

The clock from Charlotte's coffee table. The one with the compartment where I found her birth certificate. The lost Wonder poster with her face at the centre. Various playing cards float inside bubbles around me too. The Ace of Hearts stands out, the riddle that led me into Wonderland written on one side.

Why is a raven like a writing desk?

A montage of memories plays through my mind at those words. Chess twirling me in a circle. Guiding me by hand through the streets of London. Giving me my first kiss, ensuring I would never feel the same about another boy again.

I sink deeper and more objects come into view—like a collage of my first days in Wonderland. A red-and-white mushroom that looks like a mini replica of the *Champ* bus. Wonderland's coat of arms, studded with gems and stones. Blooming roses like in the Heart Palace courtyard.

Tumbling deeper, I close my eyes and test my breathing. Though my lungs ought to be screaming for air, I'm more alive than I've felt in ages. Deep breath in. Exhale out. Whatever surrounds me, it can't be actual water. Part of the Trial simulation, then?

When I open my eyes again, I will my body to relax. The locket watch around my neck floats free from its prison beneath my clothes. The knockoff silver shines and sparkles anew, just as it did when I was a child. I gasp at the lost memory and cling to it as if it will vanish before I can piece it together with the missing parts of my past.

I sink farther, deeper. Everything I see is like a time capsule. An exam with low marks from my first year in Oxford. A lopsided lamp with a cracked base from the Foundling House. My mother's lab coat that I used to play dress-up in. Warmth pricks my eyes at the sudden memory I wasn't aware I possessed, and I stretch forwards, reaching, trying to snatch the lab coat free. At my touch, the bubble encasing it bursts, and the lab coat disappears, dissipating my hope right along with it.

My mother isn't here.

When I reach the bottom, I don't fall or collapse in a clumsy heap as one might expect. On the contrary, I land on my feet with ease. I gaze up through the tunnel, but it's dark once more. The bubbles have gone and my memories along with them. I heave a sigh and focus on the only source of light ahead, which lies at the end of a long corridor, fashioned of cold metal walls. I tread with caution. Either Kit awaits somewhere nearby, or he was an illusion created to draw me into some sort of trap. The possibility has me stalling.

But then I hear laughter, the kind that makes me think of friends taking tea out on the terrace, a golden sunset as their backdrop, the carefree air their constant companion.

I pick up my pace.

When I round the bend, I enter the last place I expect to find. I don't know what I envisioned, but it certainly wasn't a vast atrium that is both laboratory and conservatory, encased beneath a glass dome several stories high. Above the glass, fish and birds coexist, whether in the air or underwater, I can't tell. The hum of computers and other devices fills the space with the warm buzz of life and learning. Several stone-paved paths branch off into different areas of the atrium, snaking between and around blossoming fruit trees and vegetable gardens with every variety of food imaginable.

My stomach rumbles and my mouth waters. What in all of Wonderland have I gotten myself into?

"Welcome to the Wabe!" Kit approaches, both hands shoved inside the pockets of a crisp white lab coat, his broad smile a replica of his brother's and just as charming.

I take in the sights once more. My reaction is the same as when I first entered. The terms *awe* and *wonder* come to mind, and I don't try to hide my astonishment. My gaze falls to Kit, who is still smiling. "Do you mean the wave? As in waves of the ocean?"

"Nooo," he says, drawing out the word but keeping his tone pleasant. "I mean the Wabe, short for Way Between."

"The way between what?"

"Between Wonderlands, of course."

My heart alights. "Then you must know how to find the real Wonderland and the Ivory King. Have you seen my teammates? I lost two of them in the wood where you found me. Surely—"

Kit nears and places firm hands on my shoulders, encouraging me to slow down and take a breath. "One thing at a time," he says. "First, let's get you settled in. Maybe a meal? A change of clothes?"

I nod and push my glasses up the bridge of my nose. "That sounds nice."

Kit releases me, then he veers right, up one of the stone-paved paths. I follow as he talks, hardly able to keep myself from plucking a luscious orange fruit from a shrub-like tree.

"That's the Tumtum tree," Kit explains, snapping the fruit free from its branch and handing it to me. "The first we've been able to reproduce, thanks to your mother's research."

I hear the lilt in his voice. He knows he's piqued my attention, which means, somehow, he knows *me*. I turn the foreign fruit, no wider than a pack of cards, over in my hand. It has the colouring of a navel orange, but the texture is more plum-like. I hold it up to my nose and inhale. The scent is reminiscent of the jam Sophia made. Sweet and tart and perfectly scrumptious. I can't help myself. I take a bite.

Flavours I don't anticipate dance on my tongue. Tart and sweet, yes, but also salty and savoury. It's like dinner and dessert rolled into one. I swallow and take two more bites. By bite four the fruit is gone, and I'm licking my fingers to enjoy every last drop.

"Satisfied?" Kit asks.

More than satisfied. "I feel as if I've had three full meals today, with multiple courses too."

"That's the beauty of the Tumtum. It was designed to put an end to hunger as we know it. And the flavours are a bit different for everyone. It's quite fascinating."

"My mother designed it?"

"Not quite," Kit says, "but her research aided us in preserving it for now."

He continues along the path and I hurry to keep up with his long strides. "You'll find all sorts of strange things here. Amazing things. Wonderful things. All preserved to keep our world alive."

I think on his words for a moment, turning them over in my mind just as I turned the Tumtum fruit over in my hand. "You called this place the Wabe—the Way Between." I don't add that I realise I've seen the word before, in the "Jabberwocky" poem. For so long I believed it was nonsense, yet I suppose even nonsense means something to someone.

"Indeed," Kit says. "The Way Between is what one might call a hidden level within this Trial. Ever played an old video game?"

"I've heard of them." The way things used to be in the Normal Reality, before the Divide, was a common topic in illegal online chat groups. Video games were mentioned here and there. While the idea sounded appealing—getting lost in a virtual world for hours on end—I never had a chance to play.

"It's completely off the map, you see," he continues. "Scarlet and anyone else with access to that copycat invention can no longer track your whereabouts." He gestures to the bangle on my wrist. "In essence, you no longer exist in their world."

I twist the bangle around as I attempt to pick out the hidden meanings behind his words. "That wasn't you on the beach, was it?"

"He insisted you were smart," Kit says and pauses at the edge of a small bridge that curves over a fishpond. He leans both elbows on the bridge's railing. "And you're correct. It was a projection. A hack, essentially. We accessed your WV and used it to our advantage to bring you here."

"But," I say, rubbing one hand over the other, "I felt your touch."

"WV technology can make you feel many things."

A month ago, I might have gawked at his explanation. Now the idea of projections and virtual illusions and simulated sensations is as familiar as using my Wonder Gene to change the colour of the sky. But one thing he said stands out amidst the rest. "Who insisted I was smart?"

"I've gotten ahead of things here." He turns and extends a hand. "I haven't properly introduced myself. I'm—"

"Kit," I finish for him, shaking his hand. "Your brother has been looking for you."

Something dark crosses his expression. But just as quickly, it vanishes, replaced with his pleasant demeanour once more. "My reputation precedes me. As does yours, Alice."

The well of hope within me bubbles, ready to spring. If he knows me, someone I know must be here. Oh, please let it be Chess. Or Madi.

"Come." Resuming his walk, Kit crosses the bridge. "We have so much more to brief you on. I'm sure you must be overwhelmed."

He's not wrong. But I also don't know how I could possibly rest in a place like this. There is too much to discover. And I have too many questions.

We pass more greenery and botanicals that make this indoor facility feel like an outdoor Eden. Vines climb and curve around archways and tiered gardens scale the white stone walls. Different areas appear to be dedicated to different things. One section is filled to the brim with stacks of old books, while another area seems to be set aside for chemistry experiments. Still another space is arranged like a lounge, complete with a crackling hearth and classical music playing in the background.

I keep an eye on Kit as he leads the way, following but remaining at a distance. His status as Chess's brother doesn't mean he's safe. He's been gone a year, and anything could have happened—changed him—between then and now. At last we wind up a curved ramp that ends at a modest balcony overlooking the entire place. I take it all in, noticing more areas I hadn't seen as we ventured along the path. There's a corner for computers and another made up entirely of screens with various images moving across them. We aren't alone by any means. Others wearing lab coats work away at various stations, noses buried in books or fingers tapping away at computer keys. I don't recognise a soul.

Until a door behind the overlook opens and the last person I expect to see joins us.

"Alice."

I forget all decorum and practically attack him with a huge hug. "Knave!"

His stiff form and lack of response at first makes me falter. We're not exactly close. But then he relaxes and wraps his arms around me with a quick squeeze. "It's good to see you too," he says.

I pull away and relish every familiar inch of him. After losing Willow and Sophia in the wood, I needed this. I needed his black-licorice eyes, ringed with purple. His brooding expression that's really not so bad once it grows on you.

"I hope this answers your question." Kit inclines his head towards my teammate. "Knave here has talked nonstop about how brilliant you are."

I search Knave's eyes. He's always been distant—dare I say rude? I was sure he didn't like me one bit, but the way he doesn't break eye contact says Kit's words ring true.

He thinks I'm brilliant? He never said as much. Why didn't I take the time to get to really know him? I make a silent promise to myself to be a better Team Queen.

Kit clears his throat and elbows Knave. "I was just about to explain how things work down here in the Wabe. You'll require a full tour, of course, and no doubt you'll want to meet with the E.G.G. task force we've put together."

My ears perk. "E.G.G?"

"Extraordinary Gamers Guild," Knave says.

Gamers? That sounds like my kind of guild.

Knave must have noticed my interest, because he gives a half-smile. "I figured you'd get excited with your Mastery and all."

"You found your Mastery. Now use it, oh Master of Games."

Chess's words fill me with the confidence I need.

"Game Master," I say aloud for the first time.

"Game Master," Knave echoes. "You'll fit right in, A."

A? Since when did he give me a nickname?

"Excellent," Kit declares. "The E.G.G. will be glad to have you."

I lean back against the balcony railing, processing everything I've learned. After a moment, I pose the most pressing question. "You said no one can track us here." I hold up the wrist bearing my WV bangle. "How is that possible? The Heart Trial is Scarlet's creation."

"That's what she wants us to believe." Knave's eyes squint at the domed glass ceiling, then at me. "Let's sit down. Have some tea. I've only been here a day longer than you. I'm still trying to make sense of it all too."

I want all the answers, all the explanations. But he's right. I do need to sit and breathe for a spell. But first, "Could I get something to eat?"

"Certainly," Kit says, flashing his brother's smile once again.

Knave and I follow him back down the ramp and into the lab-slash-botanical garden. We veer right along a new stone path that leads to a private alcove beneath a wooden trellis. Moss and ivy hang amidst strings of lights that crisscross overhead. There's a stone fire pit filled with glass beads that stands at the centre of several armchairs set up in a circle. Flames quietly lick the air, warming the space to the perfect temperature. A sideboard against the wall boasts refreshments. The tantalising scents of fresh tea and biscuits draw me in.

I choose the armchair closest to me. It isn't until I let my body melt into the cushions that I realise how tired I am. My eyelids droop and a yawn breaks free.

"Take as long as you need," Kit says. "The other girl nearly collapsed when I brought her in."

"Other girl?"

Knave clears his throat. "Willow."

Adrenaline forces me to my feet. "Where is she?"

"Sleeping in the hospital wing." Knave doesn't elaborate.

I eye him. It's been difficult to have faith in him from the beginning, and his behaviour during past Trials hasn't helped much in the way of making him trustworthy or likable. But whatever else I do or don't believe about him, I don't believe he would hurt anyone.

So I nod and slowly sink back into the chair. Kit moves to the sideboard and soon offers me a small saucer with a biscuit on top. Next he hands me a mug of steaming tea. It smells of lavender and chamomile, like Madi's Tranquil-i-Tea, but there's something else too. Honeysuckle? Vanilla? I raise an eyebrow.

"Don't worry, it won't hurt you," Kit says. "I'm no Tea Master, but my mother taught me how to make a good old-fashioned cup of Seren-i-Tea. Any Wonder who's had the pleasure of crossing paths with the famous Lavender Hatter knows the recipe. It's mild enough that even if you get the proportions wrong, it won't affect you too much." He winks.

"Lavender Hatter?" I ask immediately. And yawn again.

"Madi's mother," the boys say in tandem.

Of course. I had wondered about the name.

"She and my mum were close before—" Kit stops and doesn't finish his sentence.

A memory dawns—the day I first entered Wonderland. There had been a familiarity between Chess and Madi that pricked and prodded in ways that made me question their connection. I sit forwards and set my tea on the edge of the fire pit, suddenly not so sleepy.

Knave is watching me. "We all have a story. Now that you're here, Kit might be able to fill you in on some of your own."

That's right, Kit had mentioned my mother's research. "What can you tell me about Catherine R. Pillar?"

"Funny." Kit glances sideways at Knave. "I was hoping to ask you that very question."

I look at them for a moment. It's clear when Kit went missing from Team Spade last year, Knave suffered the loss too. Though I have a feeling nothing will be forthcoming until we start the tour.

I rise like the Team Queen I'm supposed to be, ignoring my Seren-i-Tea but grabbing my biscuit to eat on the way to wherever we're going. "Enough rest," I tell them, anticipation filling me with renewed energy. "I want to know everything."

CHESS

Everything they tell you about your whole life flashing before your eyes at the threat of sudden death is true, give or take a few minor details.

For one, there are certain parts of my life I'd prefer to leave out. My father's constant disapproval—right up until the day he went insane and ceased to exist as we knew him—for example. I don't need to relive that. The moment it pops into my mind it's gone, plummeting into the abyss that's no doubt at the bottom of this lake.

But Ace? That's where I'd like to camp out. Doesn't matter that I've never actually been camping. My father never had time for such frivolous activities, and training for the Trials didn't require roughing it in that way. Pushing our minds to their limits, sure. Building fires and singing songs around those fires, not so much.

But back to the memories I'd like to remember before this whole drowning thing renders me unconscious.

The first thing that occurs to me is I never did get a second kiss. If I live through this—if *we* live through this—that kiss'll be my number-one priority. As long as Ace is game, of course.

For now, two things happen in succession, pulling me up and out and away from my reverie. One, I feel as if my arm will be ripped from its socket, and two, I gulp in sweet, precious air. Did air always taste this good?

I'm getting carried away. Back to the part where I almost died . . .

It's rather unpleasant being shoved off a train only to fall face-first into an immense—and positively frigid—body of water. It's not the same as jumping into a pond or a pool. When you're descending at such great speed, the sheer force of wind velocity makes it hard enough to breathe as it is. Add the whole water-filling-your-lungs predicament, and you've got number one on the list of lousiest ways to die. Never before has my belief in my own impossible abilities been so thoroughly tested. When the shock of what was happening wore off, I was able to collect my thoughts and put them into action.

If this whole thing is a simulation, what's to stop me from flying? That single question made it possible. I instantly ceased falling, took control of gravity, and soared through the air as if I had wings. For the most invigorating thirty seconds or so, I could fly. I was flying.

And then I looked down. Doubt became my anchor, pulling me and any hope I had to make it out of this alive right along with it.

To be fair, it's rather a difficult feat to maintain belief in the impossible when plunging to certain doom.

And that's the story of how I died. The end.

"Come *on*, Shire! Don't quit on me now."

"Ace?" Something burns. Everything burns. My eyes. My throat. Even breathing sets my chest ablaze.

Breathing. I can breathe.

I cough and sputter, rolling over onto one side only to cough and sputter some more.

Someone pats me hard on the back. "There you go," a familiar voice says. "That's it. Welcome back, man."

An American accent that doesn't belong to Madi. It can only be . . . "Stark." I rasp. Ouch. Talking burns too. "You tried to kill me."

"That part's on you. Why'd you look down?"

He tries to help me sit, but I bat him away with one hand.

"I looked down," I croak but sound somewhat more normal than before, "because there was nowhere else to look." My eyes find their focus. Stark is dripping wet but appears much less worse for the wear than I feel. I don't have to ask for details to know what took place.

Stark didn't fall. He didn't look down. He flew and landed on his own two feet right here on this grassy shore. When he noticed I didn't follow in his footsteps, he dove into the water after me, once again proving he certainly earned that Team Diamond win—even if he wasn't around to enjoy it.

"No wonder the Spades ended up in second last year," I say.

"Did they?" Stark says but doesn't sound surprised. With a yank, he forces me to my feet.

"You're a git," I tell him, though the insult is half-hearted.

"And *you're* welcome." He arches his back and stretches this way and that, showing off just how unscathed he came out of the ordeal.

I roll and rub the back of my neck. When I look up, I notice the train has either vanished from the bridge or moved on.

"What do you suppose the next checkpoint is?"

"Pardon?"

"The next checkpoint," Stark repeats. "Buckley told us to say hello for him."

Right. I might be tempted to clasp my WV bangle onto my wrist again . . . if its GPS system worked the same here. For now the device remains hooked onto my utility belt. I've no intention of using it again unless necessary.

"There's one way to find out." I begin the trudge uphill, towards what I hope is a road or a path or a clear direction of some sort.

Stark races past me. "You always were a sore loser," he calls before he sprints up and over the hill's crest.

Lost to me once more.

"*Solve the riddle, slay the Jabberwock. Slay the Jabberwock, find the king.*"

Much like the train on a never-ending loop, these are the words that race around my mind. I look ahead at Stark, who I finally managed to catch up with. We both played a part in solving Buckley's riddle. Too bad it's not going to get me any closer to completing Dinah's task.

There must be more to the quarter heads and their motives. I just can't figure out what.

"How long do you suppose we can keep this up?"

Stark's question jars me from my thoughts. I take a gander at our surroundings. We've been walking along this country road with wide-open spaces on either side of us for some time. From the train we could see the altering shades of green that made up the chessboard square pattern. From here it just looks like overgrown grass. Normal grass. For all we know, we could be in the Normal Reality at this point. There's no way to tell since we can't see the contrast in layers of what's Normal against all that's Wonder.

"Are you going to answer?" Stark says over his shoulder. "Or are you planning to keep acting as if we're playing for opposing teams?"

"Sorry, mate." In a few strides I'm shoulder to shoulder with him. "I've got a lot on my mind."

"Care to share with the class?" He spreads his arms wide. "We're all ears around here."

I open my mouth but stop short. My expression relaxes into an uneasy smile. A jest. He's making a jest. Since when did I become the serious one?

"I see. You're going to ignore me. Interesting strategy, Shire."

"I'm not ignoring you. I'm thinking."

"Sounds painful," Stark says.

"It is."

He laughs. "It's been so long, I'd almost forgotten what it was like."

"What *what* was like?" I watch him in my peripheral vision. Though he's been lost—a prisoner in his own mind—for a year, nothing about his demeanour suggests he's anything but perfectly sane.

"When we were kids," he says, "my mom and your mom would have tea, and we'd all play together. Raving would boss us around, and you and I would—"

"—pretend to be knights," I join in. "Fighting the dragon to try and save Princess Madi."

"She hated having to be the princess." Stark muses. "Do you remember what she used to say?"

How could I forget? Doing my best impression of Madi from ten years ago, I whine, "Why can't I be the dragon? Let Raving be the boring old princess."

But Stark isn't playing any longer. He stares off into the distance. "It wasn't her fault," he says.

I blink, unsure what he's getting at. "What wasn't whose fault?"

"My mom. I know she was the one driving that day, but it was an accident." He turns to me. "Shire, you can't—"

"I'm not discussing this," I say, cutting him off. I pivot on my heel and continue my trek along the road. Wherever this leads, it's better than here.

"You're going to have to talk about it eventually!"

I don't stick around to hear what else he might say. Let him catch up if he wants. I certainly didn't come here to dig up old memories.

Looking back is not my style.

We travel a long stint in silence. Stark doesn't mention anything about our mums again. The brisket from the train has long since worn off, and the familiar pangs of hunger and thirst join us on our quest. Still, we don't stop until we reach an L-shaped fork in the road, where we can either keep straight or take a hard right down a steep hill.

"I say we go straight." Stark says the first words either of us have spoken since our tension began over an hour ago.

I mumble under my breath.

"What?" He faces me.

"You would say that," I say louder, regretting this new controversy I've started.

"Excuse me?"

I shake my head. "It's nothing."

"No, go on," he insists. "If you have something to say, Shire, say it to my face."

"Fine, Hatter, I will." I look him straight in the eye, enunciating every next word. "Going straight is the easy choice. The road is flat and familiar." I gesture down the hill, towards the unknown. "If we go down, that likely means we'll have to go up at some point or another. Which means work. But you never did know the meaning of real work. You're a Diamond, after all."

"What are you implying?" Stepping closer, he's all hot air with his puffed-out chest and unblinking glare. But taller doesn't always mean wiser.

"Diamonds have it made. Everyone knows." I hold up a hand. "Don't worry, though. As soon as we make it out of here, you can go back to your cushy life in your glittering manor back in fake Wonderland." I instantly rue what I can't take back.

Stark's eyes go wide and then narrow. "Fake? Wonderland? Explain."

Great, now I've gone and done it. "Your sister can fill you in." I don't have time for this. He's slowed me down as it is. I might've found Ace and Kit by now if not for him. I move to head down the hill when Stark grabs my arm and yanks me back.

"You know," he says through gritted teeth, "I was going to help you finish this Trial. I was even considering giving you credit if we made it to the end. Now you're on your own. Good luck."

I free myself from his grasp. "Lay off, mate."

"No." He flexes his fingers at his sides, backing away, towards the straight road. "You've made it perfectly clear I am not your mate." Walking along the even path, he leaves me at the fork to make my own choice.

I'm about to let him go his own way. I have bigger things to worry about than babysitting his sorry behind. But at the sound of galloping hooves, I jerk my head around. There, in the distance, is that . . . ?

A midnight-black horse comes racing into view. The rider—or ninja?—on top leans forwards, determination squaring his broad shoulders. I stand and stare, expecting him to halt. Could this be the next checkpoint? Will there be another riddle to solve?

But he doesn't stop. He charges.

Stark shouts something, but I don't register his words.

A searing pain shoots through the back of my skull. My limbs tingle, and my ears turn to ice.

Numbness consumes me. Then the world shifts to shadows.

I'm yanked into consciousness courtesy of someone dousing my face with freezing water. I gasp and blink, moving to sit so I can catch my breath.

"That's blasted cold!"

"How else did you expect me to wake you? Sorry, Shire, but if it's true love's kiss you're after, you'll have to wait for Alice."

I never thought I'd be so relieved to hear Madi Hatter's voice. Rubbing at my eyes, I try to get some clarity of vision. Shapes and colours start to take dimension. Madi stands over me, lavender hair pulled back tight off her face. A scowl masks her usually amused expression.

"What did I do now?"

She helps me to my feet, then gives me a light shove to the shoulder. "That's for not having Alice with you."

I lift my hands in true surrender, hesitating, waiting to see what she'll do next.

Then she throws her arms around me like she used to when she was younger. When both of our mums were still alive and she was like a little sister to me.

"And that," Madi says, hands on her hips in her typical stance, "was for finding my brother." I almost think I detect a hint of a sob in her words. But her expression remains perfectly radiant, not a tear in sight.

As she steps back, I take in our surroundings. Every smelly inch. New details come into focus. The grime under Madi's fingernails. The scent of something foul—like animal droppings. A single turn about the confined space reveals my worst fear. Okay, perhaps not my worst fear, but this definitely isn't looking good.

"Is this a jail cell?"

Madi's mouth twitches. "Is it that obvious?"

I study the three stone walls and spiked iron bars reaching from floor to ceiling and ceiling to floor.

"I've already tried escaping," Madi says. "Any and all Wonder Gene-ness seems to be cut off in here. The bars won't disappear, and you can't walk through them."

My hand grazes one of the bars. It's solid, but that's never been a problem before. Not when I've walked through walls. "Have you tried transforming them into something else?"

"Like what?"

"Like, I don't know, pasta?" I'm a little amused at my own ridiculous suggestion. "Something we could break or easily slip through."

"Pasta? That's what you're going with?" It's Stark who speaks. He's been awfully quiet.

I search for him, which isn't hard to do in here. There's nowhere for him to go. Except, where is he?

Madi juts her head towards one wall. "He's in the next cell over."

"With me!"

I startle at the new voice. "Jack?"

"Nice to see—er, hear—you, mate."

"Good to hear you too. Glad you're safe," I say earnestly.

Someone laughs, though I can't tell if it's Jack or Stark.

"Welcome to the Fourth Square," Madi announces. "Where no one is safe and everyone's a prisoner. But now that you two slackers have arrived, maybe we can solve old Knightley's riddle."

"Knightley? Wasn't he a character in a Normal-banned book?"

"Don't mind Madi," Jack says. "She's taken to giving our captor a nickname to make him seem more human."

Captor. Human. Riddle. "Checkpoint!" I clutch my head. "This is the next checkpoint!"

Madi eyes me. "Next? I think you mean first."

We stare at each other and then it occurs to me—maybe we haven't shared the same experiences. Could it be they've travelled a different course? One that doesn't involve time-loop trains and free falling? Buckley mentioned it was possible to go around checkpoints.

"Take a seat," I say. "We have a lot of ground to cover."

ALICE

"Right this way. We have a lot of ground to cover, and we're short on time."

Kit plays the role of tour guide as we exit the atrium via the overlook and wind higher into the walls of the Wabe. It's sort of like a human-sized ant colony. Long corridors switchback into other long corridors. Walls made of clear glass allow us to view the botanical laboratory and all its moving parts, from the computer station to the alcove where I spent a mere five minutes relaxing. From what I can tell, the lab and its indoor gardens make up the central hub, and the corridors lead to various recessed rooms.

There's a room for reading and another for rest. Still another for research and one for brainstorming.

"It's like a giant training facility," I say, more to myself than to the boys.

"And every team in Scarlet's Wonderland wishes they had access to it," Knave says.

When we reach our destination door, Kit knocks once, and it slides open at his command. "Welcome to the Archives." He steps aside as we enter what looks like a massive library. Charlotte would trip over herself just to stand here. "This is the place you can find records of any and every Wonder thing that's ever happened, dating back decades before Pillar's research ever began. There are blank spaces, of course, but we've pieced together a solid timeline for the most part."

Rows and rows of bookcases of every size, colour, and shape crowd the room that doesn't appear to have an end in sight. There are shelves made of ladders and ones that hang from the rafters high overhead. Circular shelves create windows between some of the bookcases, and benches are crammed into every available corner and nook.

"This is incredible." Even I can appreciate its magnificence. It's almost as if every book, tome, and story banned from the Normal Reality found its way here. Out of habit, I glance up, expecting a mere thought to reveal Charlotte's WV profile. I need to see her face. My heart sinks a little when nothing happens, Wonder Vision failing to function once again. I swallow as I venture deeper into the Archives to keep from turning into a puddle on the floor. Knave and Kit do not need to see my waterworks.

My fingers flutter along the spines on the shelves. I pay close attention to the way each section is divided. It's an interesting mix of past and present. Leatherbound tomes that seem so fragile they might fall apart at my touch are lined up next to books loaded onto individual tablets. I remove one of the tablets, and the screen lights up immediately.

I read the title out loud. *"The Collected Works of Gyre and Gimble.* Who are Gyre and Gimble?"

"I remember these." Knave's voice close to my ear startles me. He's so quiet, I didn't realise he'd followed me up the aisle. "When I was younger, I'd stay with my aunt and sneak into the Heart Palace library to read for hours. She'd always scold me when she found me in there."

Aunt? That's right. Knave is Scarlet's nephew. What did Blanche call him? Knave Civilius Heart.

A conversation comes back to me. An argument between Knave and Chess in the Hall of Mirrors during the Spade Trial . . .

"*I had to take on my aunt's name and hide out in Heart Palace to save myself from humiliation,*" Knave had said. "*Do you even comprehend the damage your fear caused?*"

What if Knave is the enemy? He and Chess were at odds. Then again, Knave didn't seem too chummy with his aunt the one time I saw them speak.

"*No one ever actually wins the Trials, do they, my darling aunt?*"

Just when I think I have it all figured out—whom to trust versus whom to question—I feel like I'm starting from square one again.

I slide the tablet into its slot on the shelf and move on down the row. I'm about to ask Kit where I should begin to learn more about my mother, but I don't have to. When I reach the aisle's end, her face is all I see. I gasp and bring a hand to my mouth as I pass beneath an ivy-adorned archway and enter a large nook dedicated entirely to her. A gold plate engraved with her name greets me from the nearest bookcase.

IN MEMORY OF CATHERINE R. PILLAR
Renowned Genome Researcher, Beloved Mother and Sister

Photos of her line the curved nook walls. One of her shaking hands with the Minister of Spades and another of her dressed in full lab garb, white coat and protective goggles included. I peer closer, studying every centimetre, including the way her hair strayed from behind her ears. I catch myself inadvertently tucking a wandering lock of my own hair back in its place and one corner of my mouth turns up.

Loads of books and tablets line these shelves as well. A fish tank makes up most of the ceiling, reflecting off the white walls and giving the illusion of being underwater. Then again, I suppose we are underwater, aren't we?

I don't know where Kit and Knave meandered off to, but I'm grateful for the moment of solace. I feel as if I'm on sacred ground.

Just when I'm thinking I don't know where to begin, Charlotte's words, and not my mother's, come to mind.

"*Start at the beginning. And when you get to the end, stop.*"

I pause for a moment, then reach for the first book on the top shelf. When I pull it free, I see it's not a book but a portfolio held together by a large elastic band. I take it and choose an egg-shaped chair that hangs from one of the rafters like a swing. I sit back and let the chair sway as I tug the band off.

Pages of varied sizes fall out, and a few flutter to the floor. They smell of scribbled ink and candlelit nights. I gather them into a neat stack and flip through each one, trying to make sense of the words. Torn graph pages with mathematical equations. Shorthand notes I can't decipher. I'm about to give up and move on to something more coherent when I notice what looks to be a journal entry from a few years before I was born. I nestle deeper into the egg swing and soak in every messy word.

We had a breakthrough today. Cordelia is coming around to the idea of proposing a new ministerial department—the Ministry of Wonder Relations. Charlotte is on board, of course, but she holds out little hope Cordelia will follow through. My own hope is that, with the perfection of Wonder Vision, our sister, Her Majesty the Queen of England, will finally catch a glimpse into the world we call Wonderland. Maybe then she'll believe.

I close my eyes, picturing the three sisters giggling and running down the stairs of Buckingham Palace.

"Come across anything significant?"

I look up to find Knave and Kit nearby, watching me. Expecting? Hoping?

Tucking the entry away, I wrap the elastic around the portfolio and rise. "What can you tell me about Wonder Vision?" As I hold up my bangled wrist for emphasis, I notice all three of my once-red hearts are no longer lit. My very real heart stops at the sight. I flick the bangle with two fingers, but nothing happens. I check my view. No icons, no notifications hover before my eyes. No Trial stats or card requests or—

"I tried to tell you." Kit's voice breaks through my thoughts. "It doesn't work down here." He holds up his arm to reveal that the Spade bangle on his wrist is unlit too.

Knave follows suit, indicating his Fates have disappeared as well.

"While Scarlet would like everyone to believe this Trial is her own creation," Kit says, "the truth is she has very little control—if any at all—over what happens here. If she did, off-grid pockets like the Wabe wouldn't exist. It's places like this that give us a chance of actually finding what we've lost. As if Wonderland itself wants us to seek it out."

"Wonderland." I breathe the word, which somehow feels just as sacred on my lips as the preserved memories that surround me.

"Wonderland," the boys echo together.

I shelve the portfolio and reach for a tablet this time, but Kit places a hand on my wrist and stops me. "Wait," he says. "I think there's something you'll want to see first." He moves to the largest framed photo on the wall—one of my mother smiling widely, glasses askew on her nose. Kit touches the frame, and the image wavers, revealing it's not a photograph at all but a digital film screen.

Adjusting my own glasses, I still and stare intently as she begins to speak.

"Perhaps our greatest discovery of all," she says to the camera, "is that the Wonder Gene is not limited in the way we understood genetics in previous decades." She removes her glasses, wiping them on the corner of her lab coat. "It's not the same as, say, being born with blue eyes because your parents have them or the ability to roll your tongue due to the fact someone else who shares your DNA can—though it's worth noting both concepts have fallen under fire in recent years." With that she gives a gleam of a smile before putting her glasses back on. Then she rolls her tongue and crosses her eyes.

I can't help but laugh while Knave and Kit chuckle behind me. Whoever's holding the camera seems amused too because the image shakes and blurs for a moment before refocusing.

My mother winks, whether at the camera or the person beyond, I can't tell. "The Wonder Gene," she continues, "defies all logic and reason as we know them. I guess there are some things even science can't explain." There's a thoughtful pause. An instant where she turns her head, looking off into the distance at something before returning her attention to her audience.

"I might even go so far as to say the Wonder Gene is not a gene at all. Genes make up who we are to a certain degree. In essence, they are the characteristics we are born with—we don't choose them. We might dye our hair or wear coloured contacts to alter our eyes. Physical features can be enhanced or covered up or modified. Other genes manifest through disease or disability, again not something we choose to carry or pass on to the next generation."

I'm nodding along, memorising her tone of voice. The way she fidgets with the right temple of her glasses.

"When I first discovered the Wonder Gene, I categorised it as such because our research and tests supported the idea. You were either born with the gene or you were not."

Goose pimples raise the hairs on my arms and neck.

"But that theory has been tested—defied, really." She beckons someone to join her.

I know it's Charlotte before she faces the camera. Her brown hair shines beneath the lights, and her crimson blouse sits on her elegant shoulders just so. When she does fully turn, I gasp and wrestle with my emotions.

Charlotte holds a little girl of two or three years, an almost-new rabbit lovey with soft white fur clutched in her tiny grasp.

I reach out and touch the screen with my fingertips. My hair is a shade lighter here, more white-blonde than yellow. Charlotte tries to hand me to my mother, but I cling to her, frowning and burying my face into her shoulder.

Charlotte rubs my back while my mother gives my hair a single stroke, a strange look I can't define in her eyes. Then she's all business again, straightening her lab coat and addressing her unseen audience.

"It all comes down to believing in the impossible, and this is our proof." She holds out both hands in a way that makes it look like I'm a prop on display.

Charlotte whispers something in my ear, no doubt trying to coax me to smile for the recording.

But I'm as stubborn as ever, keeping my face hidden.

My mother shoots a stern look towards us both, but she doesn't press the issue. "Have you ever wondered why a child raised by someone who is not their blood relation takes on certain traits or characteristics? Stepchildren and even foster or adopted children, when with a caregiver for an extended period of time, begin to act and even look like that person. Why?"

I pause the recording and consider her question. Charlotte raised me. Though now I know we actually are related by blood— not as sisters but as aunt and niece—I think the presented idea still applies. I'm more like Charlotte than I've ever wanted to admit. And I miss her. It's then I realise that since Charlotte stepped into the frame, my wholehearted attention has been on her. Not on the mother I lost.

Charlotte is not my sister. She's not really my aunt. In the most real and true sense of the word, Charlotte is more my mother than my real mother was.

My trembling hand touches the screen, and the recording

resumes. "Belief in and of itself," Catherine continues, "can alter the very fabric of our DNA. By simply believing in another reality, that reality becomes concrete, tangible, true. And, just as anyone can become Wonder, so anyone can *unbecome* Wonder. We all choose what to believe. Our beliefs shape who we are. They change us. And that's what having the Wonder Gene is all about."

The screen goes dark and I'm still trembling. No one has to say it aloud for me to know what I've just witnessed. This is it. This is Catherine R. Pillar's Theory of Impossibility.

I don't know how long we stand there in silence. Knave places a firm and friendly hand on my shoulder. "All right, A?"

I sniff, but I don't cry. "All right," I manage. As much as seeing the recording shook me, a showcase of all I've lost, it also reminded me what I still have left to lose. What I refuse to lose. I face the boys. "All right," I say more firmly. "What's next?"

The study room at the back of the Archives is far too cold. I fold my arms over my chest and hunch down in my chair to keep from shivering. Our professors at Great Expectations used this method a lot. They figured frigid temperatures in the classroom made it easier to stay awake and focus. The exact opposite is true for me. All chilled air makes me want to do is bundle up and hibernate.

". . . it's given us an entirely new perspective on Wonder Vision," Kit is saying. "Fascinating, isn't it?"

I force a wide-eyed blink, though I didn't catch most of whatever he just said.

He must notice because he repeats himself, pacing back and forth in front of a digital map depicting Wonderland. It's a replica of the map I discovered inside the clock at Charlotte's flat, but with Wonder locations replacing London's.

A blush blooms on my cheeks. I nod so he knows not to relay the same information a third time. Wonder Vision. We're talking about Wonder Vision. Got it. Also, how in all of London is this kid only fourteen? He's clearly a genius, and the longer he speaks the less like his brother he seems.

Not that Chess isn't brilliant, of course. He's just a different sort of brilliant.

My sort of brilliant.

Chess, I miss you.

Kit clears his throat noticeably, drawing my attention out of the clouds. Could this room be any more uninspiring with its white walls and lack of colour? Besides, Kit's been talking for the past hour. While everything he's saying is fascinating, I'm also downright drained. If I thought Scarlet's Wonderland was difficult to comprehend, this is an entirely new level.

I change positions in my rather uncomfortable metal chair for the hundredth time to keep from falling asleep.

"Take a look at this, for instance." Kit taps something into a digital keypad on the screen and the map shifts to a 3D model. Two outlines of London in separate colours stacked one on top of the other. London in gold and Wonderland as we know it in blue. "Wonder Vision was originally designed to suspend a person's disbelief just long enough to provide a glimpse into another reality. It was meant to be a temporary enhancement, not a replacement."

He taps the screen again and another layer is added in bright red, but this one is unique and nothing like London at all. It shows mountains and valleys and rivers branching off in every which way imaginable, the iconic serpent shape of the Thames nowhere in sight, instead replaced with slithering train tracks.

"This Trial falls somewhere in the middle of the second reality and the third." Kit points to the space between the blue Wonderland layer and the unfamiliar red one above it. "We've been led to think the Heart Trial belongs to Scarlet, when really it was formed out of necessity. We have reason to believe this Trial is Wonderland's way of protecting itself from those who don't truly believe it exists."

I nod, curious, following along as best I can. He keeps referring to an invisible "we." His explanation reminds me of Dinah's divided diagram on the paper serviette. The memory makes me uneasy, and I squirm. If Dinah can't be trusted, should I be questioning Kit's loyalty too?

"Scarlet took things too far." Knave rises from the chair beside me and approaches the map. "She used Wonder Vision to create a new reality, one that acted as a barrier between Normalcy and the real Wonderland."

"But," I say, unable to abandon the voice of logic and reason that lives permanently in the back of my mind, "how does that work if only players wear the bangles?"

"The bangles are new," Knave explains. "Something they've been testing on the players."

"Why?"

Kit taps the screen and the image changes once more, wiping away the maps and revealing something else. Something I don't expect to see.

Pushing my glasses up the bridge of my nose, I peer at the recording. It's me in an empty, white-walled room, not much different from this one. I'm looking this way and that, my expression transitioning from awe to wonder to surprise. I reach out, grasping at air.

I can sense Kit watching me, waiting to see if I'll catch on.

While I may not be privy to all the ins and outs—the secrets and lies—of what's happening on a grander scale around here, I know a memory when I see one.

"This is when I entered the Wabe." At my words the replay comes to life. It's still me, but the scene around me alters, revealing the vertical tunnel and objects encased in individual bubbles. "It felt like I was falling, and bits and pieces of my memories were falling with me."

"But?"

"It was an illusion."

"Were this another Trial," Kit says, "I'd give you extra points for that one." His countenance remains neutral, but the pride in his tone is undeniable. "Using Pillar's research the way it was intended, our team here at the Wabe replicated Wonder Vision technology to dive into your subconscious. Hopes. Fears. Ideas. Dreams. Everything that drives you–that makes you who you are– transformed from an internal existence to an external reality."

Feeling suddenly exposed, my gaze descends to my bangle then rises again. "The WV started tracking me when I left London and entered Scarlet's Wonderland. Has it been tapping into my thoughts and memories, as well?"

"Not down here," Kit assures me. "But, yes. Scarlet has used it to manipulate and control the players."

"I didn't want to believe it at first either." Knave's voice has a similar effect on the screen. It goes dark and lights up moments later, revealing Knave in a similar state. Falling. Surrounded by objects that must mean something to him. Headphones. A book. A pet's collar.

"So you're telling me . . ." My brain hurts. "What *are* you telling me?"

"We're telling you that Wonders are so far removed from the real Wonderland, Scarlet no longer needs Wonder Vision to keep them trapped in her own diluted version of our world."

I sit up. "But Madi said the WV was designed specifically for the Trials. How could every Wonder be fooled if only players wear the bangles?"

"We've all been deceived," Knave says softly.

Kit's fingers move swiftly over the keypad on the screen, and it blinks off. "The bangles are the next step up."

That's right. What did Madi call them? Wonder Vision 8.0.

"This must all be extremely overwhelming and fairly exhausting," Knave says.

I want to soak in as much information as I can in the least amount of time possible. And we won't accomplish anything if I'm not awake. "A little," I admit. "But I need to know one thing before I can think about resting."

"What's that?" Kit asks.

"The other missing Wonders–the players. Where are they? What's happened to them?" *What happened to* you? I want to add.

But I don't. He doesn't look lost at all. If I didn't know any better, I'd guess he wants to be here.

"I can't speak for anyone else." Kit pulls over a chair and takes a seat. "I only know if the Wabe's director hadn't found me, I might never have kept my wits. An encounter with the Jabberwock is not something to be trifled with. Once you see it, your greatest fear comes to life. You can't unsee it." His eyes change as he speaks, glazing over, staring into nothing.

We wait for Kit to say more, but when he doesn't, Knave continues for him. "We do know that this Trial has a mind of its own. Scarlet doesn't control it any more than we can control Wonder Vision."

"Do you think the Ivory King created the Trial?"

Knave hesitates, glancing from me to Kit and back again. He hasn't been here much longer than I have. This must be a lot for him to process too.

Kit comes out of whatever trance he was in and answers, "Ivory King or not, we believe the true version of Wonderland was hidden at some point to be kept safe from Scarlet and those loyal to her, so she couldn't destroy it entirely."

"Hidden." I repeat the word. "All right. That's nothing we didn't already assume." Otherwise, we wouldn't be searching in the first place. "So how do we find it?"

Their eyes fix on me, and suspicion builds. Have they planned this moment from the second we entered the Archives?

"Why are you looking at me like that?"

"Zey are looking at you like zat," a familiar female voice from behind me says, "because you, dear Alice, are zee only vun who can solve Pillar's riddle and open zee door to Vonderland. You are zee key."

I whirl. And gape. Because those pink-rimmed brown eyes framed by transparent lashes belong to none other than Scarlet's royal advisor.

Blanche de Lapin.

CHESS

There is more than one way to navigate the Heart Trial. Or so it would seem. We've all had different experiences that led us here. Varied paths that pulled us apart and—eventually—drew us back together.

That's the part I'm counting on.

"Tell me more about the Fourth Square."

I sit with knees bent against the cell wall with Madi on my right and the bars to my left. Whoever this Knightley person is, he still hasn't shown his face, leaving us to our own devices. We spent a good stint swapping stories, comparing experiences. It appears Stark and I are the only ones who encountered a train.

Jack entered the wood initially, only to find himself navigating a maze of hedges and thorns. Madi's story is one for the books, though, and included a series of underground tunnels that eventually landed her right on Knightley's doorstep.

"The Fourth Square," Madi explains loudly so the others can hear, "is halfway to the eighth."

I elbow her. "Oh, really, halfway to the eighth, you say? That's loads helpful, thanks."

She ignores me.

"First of all, you're welcome."

"For what?"

"For my uncanny ability to coax information out of anyone." Her gaze shifts to the darkness beyond the bars. "I was the first of us four to arrive. Before Knightley threw me in this cell, I did a little snooping. Any guesses as to where we are?"

"I know!" Jack pipes in.

"Quiet. Let him guess."

I look towards the ceiling to make it appear as if I'm thinking hard. After a minute or so I shrug. "I give up. Tell me."

Madi rises, dusting herself off and turning to face me as if preparing to give a grand speech. "This miniature prison is one of several levels in a castle keep."

"We're in a castle?"

"No. A castle *keep*. I've no idea what happened to the rest of it–if there was a rest of it to begin with. This keep stands on a hill overlooking the entire Trial. These cells are on the topmost level." Madi lifts a horizontal palm above her head then brings it down a notch. "The middle level contains Knightley's chambers."

"And the bottom?" Stark's voice asks.

"An undercroft," Madi says knowingly.

I'm trying to work out what this could possibly mean. "Why would a cellar matter?"

"It matters because the undercroft is set up like barracks, with at least a dozen beds, two water closets, and a storehouse of supplies!"

"You think Knightley is planning to hold us here for a while?"

"I also," Madi continues over my words, "found something of interest in Knightley's chambers." Her eyes light up.

Now she has my full attention.

But before Madi gets another word in, Jack blurts, "It's a strategy map. For the game of chess!"

Madi sulks and glares at the wall. "I'm telling the story, Jack!"

"But you're taking too long."

Madi huffs. "As I was saying, before I was so rudely interrupted"—she ups her volume, no doubt for Jack's sake—"I discovered an entire wall, covered with notes and scribbles and analyses, all dedicated to dissecting and understanding the game of chess. Which means whoever Knightley is, he's trying to beat the Trial too."

My pulse rate begins to rise. "You think Knightley could be one of the missing players?"

"I do." Her voice mounts in excitement.

Could he . . . could he possibly be Kit? "When's the last time you saw him?"

It's Jack who answers. "That's the thing, mate. We haven't actually seen him, not his face anyway. He's only been up here to bring new prisoners . . ." He pauses. I wish I could see his face. "Or to take one."

My eyes widen as Madi toes the floor.

"And you failed to tell me this, why?" I demand, jumping to my feet.

"We didn't want you to worry."

I don't have to look in a mirror to know all colour drains from my face. "Who was here with you?"

Madi and Jack reply in unison. "Sophia."

Odd how chunks of memories keep returning the longer I'm inside this Trial, as if each one is a fragment broken off and left behind until I've retrieved it. A week ago, I couldn't have told a soul anything about the Fourth Trial aside from the need to defeat the Jabberwock, and even then, I couldn't explain what the beast actually is. Yet, with each passing moment in this place, I recall a bit more.

Kit, shouting for help.

Knave, demanding I turn back.

My other Spade teammates, never casting a second glance in my brother's direction.

My head is bent, and my hands dangle over my knees as I sit. Once again, I am both failure and fraud. I left Kit, and now I'm betraying Ace and the others. But if I can find Kit and Ace first, before Grandmother and the quarter heads intervene, maybe we stand a chance at winning this thing for good.

"I think I've got an idea." Stark's words drift from the opposite cell, pulling me into the present. His voice is thick with exhaustion, and I wonder if he ever experienced any true sleep on that train.

"Let's hear it," Madi says, leaning against the shared wall, ear pressed to stone.

"We create a diversion and make a ruckus," Stark says. "Get Knightley's attention. He'll have to come up to find out what's going on."

But Jack brings reason in this scenario. "I think we're better off waiting until he feeds us next. Then we use the element of surprise. If he has to check into a commotion, he'll arrive on guard."

That makes sense.

"It might work if we knew when mealtime was." Madi glances at the barred window, which lets in a great deal less light than it did when I arrived. It could be late afternoon or even dusk at this point. "Meals are sporadic. When I first got here, Knightley fed me twice within a few hours. Today, though, we haven't seen food at all."

The others continue bouncing ideas back and forth, none of them holding much substance. I wish they would stop rambling for a moment so I can think, but the sound of a creaking door silences everything.

Firm but cautious footsteps approach.

Slowly, I stand, placing my body like a shield in front of Madi. On a normal day, she'd protest. Today, though, she must be just as nervous as I am because she doesn't budge.

Someone breathes beyond the bars, cloaked in darkness.

Knightley's lack of courage to reveal his identity tells me all I need to know.

"Show your face," I demand.

Nothing. No movement at all.

"Coward," I mutter under my breath.

That does it. There's a shuffle, and then a black-clad human form emerges from the shadows. He's smaller than I would have imagined, masked like some rogue ninja. Still, he doesn't utter a word.

"Where's Sophia?" I press. "Have you harmed her?"

Knightley doesn't move or respond.

"Answer me!"

Madi puts her hand on the crook of my arm.

But her silent warning doesn't cause me to back down. If this is Kit and he's playing some sort of revenge game, it isn't funny, not if Sophia's safety is on the line.

"She told me you'd be the most stubborn," the stranger finally says in a low voice. But not low enough. Knightley is a . . . girl?

Why does this terrify me even more?

I scan her frame with new eyes. She's clearly attempted to hide it with the black clothing from her mask right down to her mid-calf boots, but I see it now. The soft curve at her waist and the feminine dip between her shoulders and neck.

None of this, however, moves me to speak with chivalry or decorum. "I don't care what she told you." I'm seething. Partly because she's not Kit and partly due to the fact she won't answer my question. So I ask again, punctuating each word. "Where is Sophia?"

Knightley emits a close-lipped laugh. Then she seemingly disappears. But a loud cranking sound soon follows, and the spiked bars retreat into the floor and ceiling. "Follow me," Knightley says. "And try to be quite quick about it."

We don't immediately obey, either out of shock that we've been set free or the fact our captor so easily turned her back on four people who likely want to attack her and make their escape.

Jack is the first to emerge. He pokes his head around the wall and grins. "What are you slowcoaches waiting for?" He follows Knightley into the unknown.

The midlevel chambers of the tower are exactly as Madi described them. Every inch of the curved, black stone walls is plastered with layers upon layers of images, layouts, and paragraphs overflowing with notes. A modest fire crackles inside a wood stove, and rugs with intricate designs in red and black thread decorate the floor. A hammock hangs off to the left in front of an ajar door I assume—and hope—leads to a washroom. Unlike the cells where we were kept, this level smells like freshly ground coffee and roasted nuts.

But the best sight of all is Sophia, sitting cross-legged on a floral rug beneath an arching window much like the ones inside Wonderland Abbey. A telescope is positioned near the window, angled towards the sky. Sophia's right arm is exposed, wrapped in . . . red feathers?

Madi's the first to kneel beside our teammate. "You're injured." Madi glares towards the door.

I hadn't even noticed Knightley standing behind the door where we entered from the stairwell. Though I can't see her eyes, I feel her intense stare.

"I was injured before Erin found me," Sophia clarifies. "She used borogove feathers to heal my wound."

Erin? We all turn at once. I don't know what a borogove is. I suppose it doesn't matter. Sophia is here. She's alive. While I selfishly wish it were Ace sitting before me, I'm grateful we have one less teammate to worry about.

"I liked Knightley better," Jack declares, always speaking before he thinks. "It's more mysterious. Erin is just so—"

"Normal?" the woman in black says, fingering the hilt of the weapon at her waist. There's an Irish cadence to her accent that makes me wonder if she chose to stay in England after the Divide or if she ended up stranded there.

Jack gulps and nods awkwardly.

"I *was* Normal." Knightley, who is now Erin, unsheathes a dagger and flips it in the air. Whether she does this out of habit or to remind us all not to cross her, I can't guess. "For the first eighteen years of my life, I lived in London, unaware another world lay just beyond it. When I entered the Wonderland Trials as a Wildflower ten years ago, I had no idea what I was getting myself into."

Ten years? She must've arrived around the same time Charlotte fled with Ace.

She converses quite easily now. "I'm not particularly skilled at games or puzzles as my mastery is related to medicine. I played the Two position for the Clubs and mostly waited on the sidelines in case one of my teammates became injured." At that, Erin sheathes and checks the weapon. Then she joins Sophia on the floor, peeking beneath the feathers plastered to Sophia's skin with some sort of goo. Seemingly satisfied, she rises. "When we made it to the Fourth Trial, I was elated. I truly believed we might win." She lifts a hand and pulls her mask free. Auburn locks fall to her waist and a constellation of freckles shoots across her nose and cheeks. "I've been trapped here since then. This keep is my prison."

I'm grateful for her explanation but blasted angry at this information. "So you felt compelled to make it our prison as well?" I can't help but raise my voice. Does she have any idea how much time we've wasted?

"I had to be sure you meant no harm," she fires back. "Please understand. I've encountered the worst sorts of people in my ten years here."

My ire dims. Ten years. At least she's being honest to strangers when I haven't been upfront with my own teammates—especially with Ace.

We're all speechless for a spell. Erin moves to the wood stove and ladles coffee from a cast-iron kettle into a tin mug. She kneels beside Sophia again and hands her the hot drink.

Madi intervenes just as Sophia brings the mug to her lips. Drawing the mug towards her nose, Madi inhales with closed eyes. We all watch, waiting for her assessment.

Madi eventually nods and opens her eyes. "Interesting combination," she says to Erin. "I'm a Tea Master, but I wouldn't have thought to pair coffee with lemon."

"I'm glad you approve." Erin offers a genuine smile. "I've only ever used tea and coffee for medicinal purposes. I'd be fascinated to learn other uses and interminglings."

"Absolutely," Madi declares. I can tell she means it.

The tangible tension in the room lifts measurably. Shoulders relax and jaws unclench. One by one, we lower ourselves to the rugs, forming a misshapen circle of sorts. Erin serves coffee to each of us. Though it's not sweetened, the taste is surprisingly refreshing and hits the spot. Next she offers us each a wooden bowl of mixed roasted nuts. Cashews and almonds and walnuts with a hint of salt.

A later gander at the window reveals evening has fallen, and I check off another day in my head. Two days down. Buckley said the Gateway would remain open for seven.

Five days to go and then what? We get booted back to square one? Are we doomed to leave this Trial only to have our memories of it wiped completely clean? It's hard to imagine but it's happened before. It's happened to me.

I stare into my now-empty bowl. I still see Kit in my nightmares. The hurt on his face when I didn't turn back. What type of person leaves his kid brother behind? Ever since our mum died and our father—I don't actually know what happened to him, and I don't rightly care—it's been me, Kit, and Grandmother. Now even she clearly can't be trusted. And the Minister of Spades? He took us under his wing and gave us a place to belong. Now I mean nothing more to him than an end goal.

Kit's the only family I have left, and I abandoned him when he needed me most. He would have fought his way through fire to get to me. I should have done as much. But, frustratingly, I can't recall what happened that fateful day. I only remember Kit's hoarse hollers.

"Chess! Wait! Come back!"

I put my forehead on my knees.

Maybe the Jabberwock isn't the beast.

Maybe I am.

ALICE

Whatever they may tell you, there is a key to winning every game.

Some revolve around the key of strategy, while others rely purely on the key of chance. But no matter what you play or how you play it, there's always experience to consider. How well do you know the game? Are you mere acquaintances? Or have you gone a few rounds? Do you know all the ins and outs and highs and lows? Are you familiar with every possibility and probability? What are you willing to risk in order to gain your expected outcome?

These are the questions that go through any well-versed card player's mind before peeking at the hand they've been dealt. There are so many ways it could go, after all. You might hold a poor hand. Or you might hide a grin to keep the others at your table from suspecting you've already won. However you begin a game, the only thing that truly counts is how you end it. Every decision, every choice you make, directly affects the outcome. Do you draw or discard? Play fair or cheat?

I have one such choice to make now as I lock eyes with the woman who wears more hats than Madi Hatter herself.

"What are you doing here?" I want to ask how she got into the Trial since she isn't a player, but instead I skip to a different question. "Did Charlotte come with you?"

Blanche purses her pink lips. "I am ere on Knight Society bizness. Charlotte," Blanche announces, "haz gone missing."

"Missing?" Again? "How is that possible?"

"Nothing is impossible," Kit counters.

I shoot him a glare for using what's become an overused and cliché phrase these days. Does he have to act so much like Chess right now?

He immediately takes a keen interest in the blank wall to his left.

"As for vut I am doing ere, I should sink eet vould be obvious."

I study her. Part of a good card player's skillset is being observant, aware of facial expressions and tics and tells. I now notice Blanche sports a white lab coat. It's plain compared to her usual lace and frills.

The next thing I pick up on is that the bangle circling her wrist—which previously bore the word "Advisor" and a ruby-red heart rather than four Fate lights—is missing.

"Where's your WV bangle?"

"Now zat," Blanche remarks, "eez zee obvious question." She crosses to me and places a hand on each of my shoulders. "You really do look joost like her, you know."

I don't have to ask who she means. And it's a compliment. My mother was stunning, smart, and sophisticated. But I feel a sizable stone lodge itself in my ribcage at the comparison. Is it because the more I learn about Catherine, the more I realise what's expected of me?

I might as well jump in headfirst. Games have never scared me before. So why should they now?

Because the fate of Wonderland depends on winning this one.

I try to shake away my internal voice of no-nonsense, straight-to-the-point logic as I say, "Tell me about this riddle."

Blanche nods approvingly. "Catherine left behind clues,"

she explains. "Together zee clues form a riddle. Vun only you can solve."

I eye her with one brow raised.

"You ave a right to be skeptical," she says. "Een fact, you should be. Everything you ave been raised to believe eez, ov course, a lie."

I stand frozen. When I first learned Charlotte hadn't been truthful most of my life, I needed to sit down. Now I remain standing, despite the fact that Knave pulls a chair over for me.

Since when did he become such a gentleman?

"Thank you, but I don't need to sit," I say to him and level my gaze at Blanche. "I need you to explain."

"Certainly," Blanche says. "But I think new introductions are in order."

I startle. Her sudden change in accent trips me up and makes me do a double take. Rather than of French origin, her British English is quite crisp and clear.

She offers a hand. "Professor Rabekah White—Blanche was my cover during my time in the palace. I worked with your mother for years."

I shake her hand numbly. Things have gone inside out. She's like a completely different person.

"And also," she gestures towards Knave, "your cousin. Knave Heart."

My mouth drops open. "Cousin?"

Knave nods, offering a half smile. "If it's any consolation, I've only recently learned the news myself."

Is this why he's been so kind since I arrived?

Maybe I do need that chair after all.

Rabekah launches into a detailed explanation about how my mother is the fraternal triplet of the Queen of Hearts and Queen Cordelia. I focus on her lips and the practiced way they move, as if she's rehearsed this. Her avoidance of the Queen of Heart's name does not elude me.

Does Blanche—Rabekah—know Scarlet is a fraud?

"So you see," she concludes, "it's really quite simple once you put all the pieces together."

"But, if the Queen of Hearts is your aunt," I say to Knave, "does that mean Cordelia, Queen of England, is your *mother*?" How have I failed to make this connection before?

He shrugs. Because being a crown prince is no big deal, obviously. "Actually, it was a huge scandal. The Queen of England, the very definition of all that is anti-Wonder, ends up with a Wonder son? She couldn't bring herself to Register me, but she also couldn't let a soul know what I truly was."

It doesn't take being the daughter of a genius scientist to fill in the blanks. "She sent you to Wonderland. To keep you safe."

"She asked my aunt to look after me." Knave pauses and then adds, "My *real* aunt." The way he says it so pointedly can only mean one thing.

He knows.

My knees weaken. I collapse into the chair Knave provided. All at once this room with its scarce seating, blank walls, and single transparent screen feels claustrophobic. Removing my glasses, I pinch the bridge of my nose. My voice is almost a whisper. "You've been inside the looking glass."

Blanche—Rabekah . . . am I ever going to get used to the change?—lowers herself beside me. Though she's wearing a white pencil skirt to her knees, somehow she still manages grace and poise. "That's just the thing, Alice." She pats my hand gently. "No one can enter the looking glasses but you."

When we entered this Trial, I thought I had no blood relatives who remained. Now I have an aunt and a cousin.

Things really have become curiouser and curiouser.

Knave walks beside me in silence. We navigate the corridors overlooking the Wabe's central hub with all its strange plants and interesting alcoves. I'm grateful Knave seems to be aware of where he's going. I don't have the energy to get lost. My feet drag, and I'm regretting not resting before visiting the Archives after all.

Knave clears his throat, stuffing his hands in his lab coat pockets. "I'm sure you must have questions."

Do I ever. "Yes, I do."

"I'm an open book. Ask away."

Except, I'm not sure what to ask, or how to organise my thoughts into something coherent. It is nice not to have Kit or Blanche—*Rabekah*—listening in. But where to begin? We round a bend into another corridor. This one is lined with doors on either side, each with a different gold-plated number. Sconces shaped like raindrops hang above every entryway, casting a pool of warm light at each threshold.

It's reminiscent of a hotel I visited back in London. Though we could never afford to stay, Charlotte let me join her once on a job hunt. I was very young, and it was just before Charlotte was offered the position in Oxford. She stood, inquiring at the front desk, and I took the liberty to explore when she wasn't looking. I had felt like the scolding I received when she found me, fear blazing in her eyes, was worth it. The hotel was a palace, and for thirty minutes, I was its queen.

I realise we've stopped before one of the numbered doors—the three—which are apparently not arranged in any particular order.

Knave stands aside. "This one is already coded to your thermal signature." When I give him a quizzical look, he explains, "We downloaded your WV data when you entered the Wabe before it went offline."

Ah. Now the tunnel journey makes more sense. It wasn't simply a trip down memory lane after all.

Unlocking a door with no knob is something I'm getting used to, so I don't need further instruction. I place my palm against the smooth surface, and it slides left, retracting into the doorframe. Once inside I find quaint, almost old-fashioned accommodations. A single bed with a quilted pastel coverlet, a nightstand, a lamp. There's an antique desk and matching chair against the wall to my left, an oval looking glass hanging above it. I pause before my reflection.

As if sensing my thoughts, Knave speaks up from where he waits just inside the room. "It's not one of Catherine's. It won't turn to liquid at your touch."

I never do get to asking my questions. I have too many. Instead of responding, I move deeper into my new space, tossing my rucksack onto the bed. I find a wardrobe with a few sets of clean clothes, a water closet, and a cabinet with snacks and glass bottles of water. It's like a little girl's room, and for a moment, I'm reminded of the cottage back in the wood. Do Knave and Kit know about that from my WV data too? Do they know everything?

I make my way out onto the balcony. The air underneath the glass dome is humid, which is most likely due to the ocean saltwater and the fact that the central hub is basically a greenhouse. After a few minutes, my cousin joins me.

Cousin.

Elbows bent, Knave leans against the balcony railing beside me, hangs his head back, and gazes towards the dome.

"I should have known when something changed," he says suddenly. "I was just a kid, but I should have sensed something wasn't right. Scarlet was always rather cross with me. When I went to live with her after the Trials last year, she avoided me entirely. I only took on the name of Heart because I had to." He turns and drapes his hands over the rail.

"I have one memory of Charlotte from before she disappeared. I was five or six. I was playing in the courtyard garden, and I fell into a rose bush. I was a blubbering mess, wailing like you wouldn't believe. Though she was the Queen of Hearts and could have had anyone in her household tend to me, she chose to take care of me herself. She cleaned each wound. Bandaged every cut and scrape."

I bite the inside of my cheek to keep from crying. My voice is thick with emotion. "Sounds like Charlotte." I try to laugh but it's half-hearted, failing to cover the ache I feel. "Always had to do things her own way."

I turn to face him. "I still don't understand any of this. How they replaced Charlotte and how Dinah was able to find someone who looks just like her. But Charlotte hasn't aged like Cordelia and . . ." My voice trails. *How my mother would have aged*, is what I ought to say. Instead I press on, letting one question after another pour out like a spilled cup of tea. "And what about the Wonders? The Trials? This is supposed to mark the twenty-fifth year. Is that a lie too? How has Dinah been able to fool an entire population of people into believing in a fake Wonderland, an imposter queen, another timeline, and a different history?"

If I expected a profound response, I don't get one. "I don't have all the answers," is Knave's only reply.

Of course you don't. I'm grateful I only think the dark thought rather than say it. None of this is his fault.

"What I do know," he adds, "is that, given enough fear, people will do or believe most anything. They'll behave in ways they never would have and believe a lie because it's easier, more convenient, than the truth. I'm guilty of it too. They replaced Charlotte with Scarlet, and I went along with it."

"You were just a child."

"Even so"—he shakes his head—"I should have recognised my own family. But Scarlet looked so much like her. Their names sound similar. It's obvious now they're nothing alike, and I'm kicking myself for being so stupid and allowing whoever is behind all of this to convince me of a false reality."

I study him. His eyes are brown, like Charlotte's. His hair is brown too. He may be Cordelia's son, but Knave resembles our aunt in more ways than one. Always serious, never wavering.

"Anyway, I'll let you get some rest." He goes inside and I follow. When he reaches the corridor, he turns. "But if you can't sleep, you might want to check the nightstand drawer. There's something inside you may find of interest."

With that he's gone. I close the door and exhale. Then, in a few steps, I collapse, fully clothed, onto the single bed. I don't bother to kick off my trainers or take off my glasses or climb beneath the covers. Whatever's inside that drawer can wait. For now, sleep is the only thing I find of interest. So I close my eyes and let it find me.

Another turn on my mattress and it's confirmed.

A few measly hours of sleep are all I'm going to get.

It's dark beyond the French doors that lead to the balcony. I sit up and switch on the lamp. I still can't get over how normal some things are, even in a new reality.

Maybe Wonders and Normals aren't so different. My mother said as much, didn't she?

"Just as anyone can become Wonder, so anyone can unbecome *Wonder. We all have a choice what to believe."*

Rubbing the sleep from my eyes, I head for the water closet. Soon I'm sinking into a warm bath. Every muscle cries out in gratitude. It is then and only then—with the door closed and the opening to finally be myself—that I allow myself to cry.

And cry.

And cry.

Perhaps it's all the pent-up emotion I've bottled and stored. It could be that I'm simply exhausted or famished or all of the above. My body and mind have been pushed beyond every limitation. I'm drained and done and discouraged. So I weep until I have nothing left. Until my fingertips wrinkle and my skin is splotchy and red.

I slowly rise from the now-lukewarm water, wrap myself in a towel, and wander to the wardrobe beside my bed. The clothes within are simple, reminding me of how little Charlotte and I had for so many years, but we always made the best of it. I layer a white camisole beneath a sky-blue button-down blouse, then select a simple pair of fitted black trousers. The blouse is loose, and I'm practically swimming in it. I roll up the long sleeves to my elbows and knot the shirt tails at my hips. The trousers are too long as well, so I roll them up at the ankles. A quick glance at the looking glass over the desk only shows the top half of my chosen ensemble. It's not Madi Hatter-worthy but it will have to do.

Opting to leave the WV bangle off and stay barefoot until I have somewhere important to be, I peruse the snack stash next. My throat is parched, and the tepid bottled water soothes as it goes down. Needing a bit of savoury, salty, and sweet, I choose a beef stick, bag of potato crisps, and a package of shortbread. Not the healthiest bites, but plenty filling.

When I can't put it off any longer, I reach for the nightstand drawer. I've been avoiding it for reasons I don't understand. Maybe it's my reluctance to find further shocking revelations.

I pull the drawer open, place my hand inside, and my fingers close around the spine of a book. I draw it out and lift the hard cover only to discover it's not a cover but a lid. Where I expect to find pages, a secret safe resides.

A safe that requires a key.

My breath catches. I don't believe in coincidences, and this is anything but. This is intentional on purpose and entirely planned. Withdrawing my locket watch from beneath my blouse, I hold up the tiny key attached to the silver chain. The same key that unlocked Charlotte's clock.

It slides into the keyhole without hindrance. One quarter turn and the lock clicks open. I lift the book safe's interior lid and stare at what's inside. My pulse *thrum, thrum, thrums* in my ears.

A pair of corded soundbuds.

An archaic-looking device with five buttons. Play. Pause. Stop. Fast-forward. Reverse.

And a yellowed note.

I raise the note up to the light and notice familiar handwriting—the same handwriting I've seen in the margins of *The Adventurer's Almanac*, on a map of Scarlet's Wonderland, and across an envelope bearing my name.

"This audio diary chronicles the final days of Catherine R.

Pillar's life and my reign as Wonderland's queen," I read aloud, then pause and swallow.

The handwriting is Charlotte's.

ALICE

Charlotte knew.

She knew this entire time what happened to my mother, and she never breathed a word.

I'm cross all over again. So cross, in fact, I can no longer see her words through the blur of my furious tears.

I have half a mind to take my frustrations out on Knave—if I could find him. The Wabe is a maze. Without my WV as a guide, I'm lost until someone returns for me.

"Chess," I tell the ceiling, "where are you when I need you?"

Before I face whatever the audio diary holds, I reach for my rucksack and pull out the almanac. I've known from the first time I laid eyes on it that some of the handwriting was Charlotte's. But there are other notes penned in a different hand I've never been able to place. My mother's?

Only one way to find out. I plug the soundbuds into the device and stick one in each ear, relishing the familiar feeling of comfort they bring. In this moment I realise just how much I've missed Madi's podcast. I take a deep breath and press play.

Charlotte's voice greets me through the tiny speakers.

"Fourth of May 2085, Heart Palace."

This is from the year Charlotte fled with me to Normal London. "It has become exceedingly clear the quarter heads fully intend to do whatever it takes to overthrow me. My royal advisor and former governess, Dinah FeLin, has convinced them my vision for Wonderland is all wrong. And so I've turned to the only soul in this reality or the next on whom I can rely. Catherine.

"Wonderland is fading for even the most dedicated believers. They've abandoned truth for comfort and given themselves over to temporary pleasures in lieu of what's truly lasting. Intent on protecting itself, our beloved reality retreats into hiding bit by bit, in hopes that one day we might seek it again."

The audio goes silent, leaving only soft static to fill in the blank space. Charlotte speaks of Wonderland as if it's a person and not a place. This matters, but I can't begin to comprehend why. And so I wait with bated breath for the next recording to begin.

"Sixth of May 2085, Heart Palace. Dinah has stolen the blueprints for Wonder Vision. We can't begin to understand what she might want with them, as the invention was only ever intended to offer a glimpse of Wonderland to those who desired to believe in the impossible. Our best guess is that she intends to use Wonder Vision to keep Wonders distracted, submerged so deeply within a lie that they never come out the other side. We will not allow Alice or Knave to grow up under her rule."

My heart is racing. She wanted to get Knave out too? Of course she did. Fresh tears prick my eyes. Something must have gone horribly wrong in order for her to leave him behind.

I pause the recordings and move to the desk. I don't have to search long to find a pen in the top drawer. I uncap it and return to the bed, flipping to the inside back cover of the almanac. In the past I would have used the WV's digital notepad, but it's no good to me down here. I'll have to take notes the old-fashioned way.

For the next hour or so, I listen intently, scrutinising Charlotte's words and tone. Each new recording ups my anxiety. She sounds rushed, distraught, and worst of all, afraid. Charlotte speaks of Dinah's intentions and of being nearly poisoned.

My heart stills. Is that what Dinah's secret tea was? Poison for Charlotte? I make a note and continue listening.

Next she lays out my mother's detailed plans and how Lavender Hatter helped her concoct a brew using the leaves of a particular plant that could only be found in the real Wonderland. Lavender preserved a few of these plants before Wonderland was lost. Should Charlotte drink a single drop every day, the tea would work together with the Gene to keep her appearance youthful.

". . . Infinity Infusion," Charlotte is saying. "Dangerous should it fall into the wrong hands, but ultimately my only option if I hope to remain hidden. They'd never think to look for us at a Foundling House. They'll be searching for a woman in her mid-thirties, while I'll appear no older than sixteen. Of course, Dinah has a few tricks up her sleeve, but we won't be biding our time to find out what they are. My heart breaks as the Gateway to Wonderland is now nearly closed. I only hope this isn't the last time I'll lay eyes on our beloved reality."

Dawn in its fullest form has broken through the panes of the balcony door. I ought to find Knave or the hospital wing where Willow's being kept. My lack of sleep is catching up to me, but I can't stop listening.

I wish I had stopped listening.

"Second of June 2085, Tulgey Wood. It's far worse than we feared. If we ever want to find Wonderland again, we'll have to brave its Trials. Catherine suspects that, in an effort to shield itself from those who seek to destroy it—or worse, wield its power—Wonderland has set up a series of Trials that must be passed before anyone can set foot in the reality again. I've warned her it's far too dangerous, but Cat insists on trying to make it through on her own. We don't know what awaits beyond the Gateway, but I'm afraid it's like nothing we've faced before. I must go after her and press her to see reason, but I can't leave Alice and Knave behind. I'll have to take them with me . . ."

The longer I tune in, the more pieces fall into place. Charlotte wasn't competing for Team Heart the year she took me. She *was* Team Heart, attempting to stop my mother from getting lost in this place, this Trial. Or, really, *these* Trials, as each square I've encountered has been a Trial of its own. When she didn't succeed, Charlotte did the only thing she could. She fled to the Normal Reality to protect me.

The Trials aren't twenty-five years old. They didn't even exist before Dinah put Scarlet on the throne and carried out the grandest lie ever told.

I know what happened to me, but what about Knave?

I gather my things, shove them into my rucksack, and swing it over my shoulder.

Maze or no maze, there's no time like the present to find out.

The Wabe is already buzzing to life as I weave my way through the vein-like corridors. I keep close to the outer passages that overlook the central, domed hub. Narrow paths and stairways climb and curve and switchback. When I happen upon a digital map embedded in a wall, I sigh.

Finally, something that makes sense for a change.

The map shows I'm not far from the hospital wing. Two lefts and a right later, I'm staring at a circular opening in the wall as tall as it is wide. When I step through, a bell-like voice from a hidden speaker says, "Welcome to the hospital wing."

A woman sits at a tall desk directly to my right. I freeze. She looks strikingly similar to Nurse Humpty—a.k.a. The Ref from the Diamond Trial timeout—with her pale skin and oval glasses. I remind myself *that* nurse was only a simulation. One of many illusions created and enhanced by our WV during the Trials. *This* nurse appears to be perfectly real.

She looks up from whatever was holding her attention when I walked in and smiles. Now I see she doesn't really look like

Humpty at all. Her glasses are more round than oval, and her skin is closer to pinkish cream than alabaster white. A once-over of her clothing says she's not a nurse either. A casually dressed secretary perhaps?

I clear my throat to ask after Willow, but the woman beats me to it.

"Alice?" she asks.

I nod, surprised.

"I'm Lorina. I oversee the hospital wing." She rises and comes around the desk to meet me, her like-new trainers squeaking on the floor. "Miss Reed has been awake and demand—" She clears her throat and starts again. "She's been asking for you. If you would follow me."

Anticipation at seeing Willow grows as I follow Lorina down yet another corridor that leads to several more circular openings—intentional holes in the walls that give this part of the Wabe a modern feel.

"You will find her room down at the end there." Lorina gestures ahead. "I'll be at the front desk if you need me."

I thank her with a smile, and we go our separate ways. My nerves take over when I reach the opening that leads to Willow, not knowing if she'll be cross with me for leaving her or blame me for Sophia's disappearance. Either way I have to face her, so I muster my courage and enter.

The hospital rooms I'm familiar with are sterile and plain, emitting a strange smell that's a mix of antiseptic and death. This is nothing like that. A bubble-shaped window carves out the wall on one side, and easels and art supplies line the wall on the other. Canvases sit on the easels. Some are blank while others bear paintings of daffodils and daisies and every flower one might imagine.

"They thought it'd be therapeutic," Willow says and I jump.

I search the space for her. There's a brightly coloured shag rug that takes up half the room. An indoor plant bursts to life with orange blossoms beside a tall floor lamp with a copper base. I'm a little jealous of Willow's accommodations compared to mine, then I immediately chastise myself for it. She's here because she's hurt, not because she's on holiday.

"Willow?" I still don't see her. Has she disappeared from this reality as Chess did from mine?

"Over here," is all she says.

Motion in one corner catches my eye. I'd thought it was just decoration, but now I see that giant cocoon-like basket is a chair. Willow swivels to face me, nestled on a cushion inside the large opening on the opposite side.

"Good morning," she says, but she isn't smiling. In fact, she looks livid.

I want to reach out and hug her, but instead my gaze finds the spot where her leg was bitten. Her footless tights cover it, but she must sense I want to see what's underneath, so she rolls up the fabric to her knee. "All better," she declares.

My eyes widen. I almost don't believe what I'm witnessing, though I watched the transformation take place myself. Her skin is smooth. There's no sign of a bite or healing wound at all.

"Then why—?"

"Why am I still in the hospital wing?" She laughs mirthlessly. "Some wounds are more than skin deep, or so they tell me." Her chin juts towards the various easels and canvases. "They think I need a creative outlet to process my emotions after being bitten and losing Soph. Apparently, mome rath bites are more than skin deep too."

A weighty dread takes over my thoughts. Did the mome rath venom do something to her mind . . . or her personality?

"And Madi's tea?"

"Whatever it was, it worked, though you'll have to ask her what was in it. *If* you ever see her again."

The jab in her comment isn't lost on me. She lost her best friend. Maybe she feels it would be fair for me to lose mine too.

"You shouldn't have helped me." She looks away. "You should

have stayed with Sophia. Kit would have found me regardless. He's the reason I survived."

She has every right to feel this way, but something inside me breaks open at her words. "I did what I thought was best. What *Sophia* told me to do. She's the Flower Master, not me."

"Clearly."

"What would you have had me do? You needed help."

"No," she snaps. "I would have been fine." It's on the word *fine* that her voice cracks, and my heart softens.

She's not lashing out because she blames me. She's acting like this because she feels guilty.

"Willow." I kneel on the rug that feels like cashmere. I force calm and understanding into my tone. "It wasn't your fault."

"Isn't it though?" Her voice breaks again. "First the Diamond Trial and now this?" She rolls down her tights, as if the mere sight of her healed skin shames her. "I'm supposed to be the strong one. When Sophia needed me, twice I've just—"

I take both of her hands in mine. "You've just been human," I say softly. "Everyone needs someone sometimes."

Willow sniffs, and I think it might be the closest I've ever seen her come to crying. "Those sound like the lyrics to some oversentimental song."

A smile lifts the corners of my mouth. "Who knows? Anything is possible."

She returns my smile with a small one of her own, but it doesn't reach her eyes. "It's my job to keep her safe." She hangs her head. "I failed her."

I release her hands and sit back. "We'll find her," I promise.

Willow doesn't show any sign she agrees, but she also doesn't argue.

For the first time, I feel as if I might not be so bad at this Team Queen thing after all.

"Chin up," I tell her. Then I utter the words I never thought would come out of my mouth. They belong to Charlotte and always made me feel small. Now I take ownership, using them to encourage rather than condescend. Perhaps that's how Charlotte meant them all along. "Crying won't help, you know."

Willow's smile lights the room.

By the time I leave the hospital wing, it's well into the afternoon. As I watched Willow paint her feelings, Lorina had lunch brought for us—meats and cheeses and sliced fruits. Satisfied Willow will be fine given some time, I'm on my way to find Knave.

I want to trust my cousin. But I still question whose side he's really on. He pulled a knife on us in the Hall of Mirrors. He's been arrogant, angry, and all-out aggressive. It's no secret he has a temper, yet wouldn't anyone after what he's been through? Including whatever happened between Chess and Kit in last year's Heart Trial.

What *did* happen? Something deep inside tells me it's somehow related to my mother's disappearance and this Gateway the audio diary mentioned.

And what of Knave's relationship with Charlotte now? He's clearly jaded towards her. Did he recognise Scarlet as an imposter when Charlotte came in as our trainer? Why wouldn't he say anything then?

I refer to the map I passed earlier and head straight for the Wabe's atrium lab. I'm getting used to relying on my own instincts, rather than on my WV for guidance. It's a good feeling, reminding me I don't need Wonder Vision to confirm what I already know.

I am Wonder. It's time I start acting like one.

It takes several wrong turns, but eventually the sound of rushing water and the whir of computers reach my ears. The arched entry to the atrium welcomes me to the split paths that weave between botanicals and various stations and alcoves forming their own labyrinth. I'm about to act on impulse and veer left. But then the sound of quiet laughter draws me straight ahead and around the curve of a brick wall acting as a planter for several sapling trees.

And there he is. Leaning back in a desk chair, watching something play out in full colour on a large screen.

He doesn't appear to notice me at first. The screen's light splashes his face in an odd sort of blue-orange glow. I watch him, searching for similarities that prove we are family. He's serious and intense, and his smile is a rare sight, just like Charlotte's. But what about me? Are we alike at all?

I'm halfway hoping he'll suddenly reach for a pair of glasses I haven't seen before. At least then we'd have the poor eyesight in common. He doesn't, of course, so I keep watching, trying to pinpoint any trait we share.

But there's nothing aside from the fact that whether I *feel* related to him or not—Knave is my cousin. And, more than that, he's my teammate. I have every right to doubt him, but he also has every right not to trust me. I lived, safe and sound and cared for, in the Normal Reality with Charlotte for ten years.

He must want answers too.

I draw a rolling chair up beside him and shift my attention to the screen. He glances at me out of the corner of his eye but makes no move to speak. The animated short that's playing invites an old memory, one I'd forgotten I possessed.

"I remember these," I say. "They used to let us watch them on Saturday mornings at the Foundling House."

Knave nods, rocking a bit in his chair. "I can't tell you how many times I used to wish to be Normal. Normal kid. Normal family. Normal life. When no one was looking, I'd flip one of these on and pretend, just for an hour, that I wasn't Wonder. That my mother wasn't the Queen of England, ashamed to call me son. That I was anywhere else but Wonderland."

My heart aches at this unexpected admission. Knave's alias, @ *SirKnaveTheBrave,* makes sense now. He is brave. And we have more in common than I saw on the surface.

"I always thought my parents didn't want me." I retrieve the diary safe from my rucksack and lay it on my lap, smoothing my fingers over the lid. "When I learned Charlotte wasn't really my sister, it broke me. Then I find out she's my aunt and Wonderland's rightful queen? The more I get to know her past, the better I understand what she was trying to do." I look at Knave, and the words gush out. "I'm so sorry I didn't see you or try to understand you." I place a tentative hand on his arm. "But I'm here now. If you need me."

He exhales, then points a remote at the screen and it goes dark. "Come on," he says, surprising me by grabbing my hand. It's playful. Friendly. The way I imagine having a cousin at a young age would have been. "I want to show you something."

CHESS

Sleep is perhaps the most necessary enemy I've encountered. If I could opt to stay awake permanently, I might. It would eliminate a torrent of troubles. For one, I wouldn't be trapped in the same vicious nightmare, doomed to relive the same shameful memory night in and night out.

When I wake, it's morning, or so I presume. Except, it's too warm, and orange light batters my eyelids. I turn over and groan.

"Morning, sunshine. Or should I say, afternoon?"

I stretch across the bed. Except, this isn't a bed. It's a rug. That would explain the pinch in my neck and the sharp pain in my lower back. I open my eyes to find Madi standing over me, a grin that looks far too satisfied plastered across her face.

"You drool in your sleep," she says.

Her observance warrants a second groan as I sit up and stretch my neck.

"How long was I asleep?"

Madi moves to the wood stove, pours a cup of tea, and hands

it to me. "It's a few hours old, but it'll do the trick." When I don't partake, she chides, "Chess Shire, you know me better than that."

I eye the tea. Now that Madi and Stark have been reunited, I wouldn't put it past them to play some sort of practical joke.

She rolls her eyes. "It's *Focus Fix*, you git."

I sniff the strong scent of peppermint and down the lukewarm liquid in several long gulps. Then my face twists and I gag.

Madi smirks. "Too bitter?"

All I can do is nod in between coughs.

"Sorry. We're fresh out of treacle."

Once the wretched taste has worn off, I stand and survey the room. Erin's quarters. "Did we all sleep in here?" I scratch my itchy scalp. I'm in dire need of a wash—despite my less than desirable dip in the lake—and it's starting to manifest in ways I'd prefer not to make public.

"The rest of us slept down in the undercroft." Madi hikes a thumb towards the stairwell. "Knightley was right about this keep being her prison. She can only leave on horseback, and even then, she can only go as far backwards as the fork in the road where she found you and Stark."

"How far can she move forwards?"

"Knightley will explain everything in detail once you've had a chance to clean up."

I look at her, amused. "Does Erin care that you keep calling her Knightley?"

Madi shrugs. Not because she's insensitive, but because, unless Erin says otherwise, Madi is going to assume the lost player has been waiting her whole life for someone to care enough to give her a nickname.

I cross to the window and look outside. Chessboard fields span the landscape around the keep as far as the eye can see. "So this *is* a checkpoint." I say it more to myself than to Madi. "Did Erin mention if there's a riddle to solve?"

"Fewer questions and more washing." Madi grabs me by the sleeve and shoves me towards the water closet. "There are fresh towels and clean clothes. The trousers were a little small on Stark, but they should fit you just fine."

The Hatter boys have always given me a hard time for being shorter than they are. There's something so ordinary about Madi's playful jab that hits me in just the wrong spot. I tense and turn away, welcoming the solace of the small space that features a simple wash basin, standing shower, and loo. As ancient as this keep appears, at least it has this much.

"I'll meet you downstairs when you're finished." Madi closes the door behind her.

I exhale. Standing under the spray of tepid water with weak pressure may not be ideal, but it's exactly what I need.

Dressed in the dullest colours I think I've ever donned—a grey shirt, tan trousers, and brown boots—with hair uncombed but stubble, at least, shaved, I exit Erin's chambers and hurry down the spiralling stairwell. My WV bangle hangs from my belt loop, a constant reminder at my hip that, eventually, I'll have to face the poor decisions I've made.

But not quite yet.

Madi wasn't kidding when she said the undercroft is set up like barracks. Metal bunks line the walls of the circular room. The stone floor is barren, and the crisscrossing archways above give the illusion the space is larger than it actually is.

Or perhaps it feels large because I'm the only one down here. "Hello?" I say it loud enough that my voice ricochets off the rafters.

Someone makes a shushing noise. Madi and Sophia playing tricks? I poke my head inside one water closet and then the other. Nothing, and no one jumps out to scare me.

Odd.

A door slams somewhere in the distance. It's then I realise the sounds are wafting through the cracked round window. It's placed too high in the stone for me to peer through, so I push open a monstrous wooden door and step out into the sunlight. The scent of nearby hay assaults my nose and makes me sneeze. After a few blinks, my watery eyes adjust, and a small barn across the way comes into focus. I jog over to find my teammates inside.

But what I stumble upon is not a barn at all. Or not fully one, anyway. These are stables and—

"Welcome," Madi says in a hushed tone, "to the game room."

My mouth hangs open and I close it abruptly. "This is . . ."

"Incredible," Jack whispers nearby.

"Remarkable," Madi adds.

But Stark doesn't follow suit. "A mad house," he mutters.

If I thought Erin's chambers revealed a bit of her crazed side, that was nothing compared to what lies before me now. The first stall to my left is dedicated to her midnight black steed. The mare whinnies and neighs, and her giant nostrils flare, making her appear more wild than tame. Her coat has a silk sheen to it that suggests Erin brushes her more than once a day. Fresh golden hay carpets the stall floor.

I resist the urge to sneeze again and move on.

In every subsequent stall, a different chess game is set up on a small table or bale of hay or barrel or crate. Stools sit on either side of each game and more strategy notes and diagrams adorn the walls and posts and stall doors. It's like looking at a foreign language for all the arrows and graphs and data Erin has drawn— or crossed off.

In the final stall at the end to my right, Erin and Sophia sit, a game in progress between them. Some of the pieces are carved from wood, and others from stone. Sophia plays red and Erin plays white. In fact, all the sets are white versus red rather than the traditional white against black. My mind darts to whom we're fighting against, and what we came for.

To find the real Wonderland and its creator. To end Scarlet's rule. Whatever Dinah and the quarter heads want with the Ivory King, I still haven't guessed. Honestly, as long as Ace and Kit are safe, I don't rightly care.

Madi sidles up beside me and puts a finger to her lips. At first I tense, wondering if somehow she's reading my mind and attempting to silence my guilt-ridden thoughts. I used to play a similar game with Ace. She thought I was inside her head—her dreams—when her subconscious was simply hovering between her reality and mine.

". . . *perhaps my reality is just different from yours,*" she told me once during our first argument.

She had no idea how true her statement was then.

I nod at Madi, knowing all too well the ins and outs of chess etiquette and sportsmanship. I once made the mistake of asking my father a question during a game he was playing against himself. That game ended with him flipping the board over in a rage, sending the black onyx queen piece directly into my right eye.

The bruise it left behind eventually healed, but a dark spot in the corner of my iris remained, a constant reminder of the man who despised my existence. I never forgave the game after that. Instead I studied it from the shadows. Watching and waiting for the day my father would invite me to play. I dreamed of that day— the day I would finally beat him. Maybe then he'd consider me worthy of being his son.

No such fantasy became my reality.

Game day arrived when I was twelve. He sat to begin a new solo match. One round could take him days to complete. He'd stare at the board until he looked ill, with sunken eyes and sullen cheeks. Sometimes he wouldn't eat for days. He filled in the gaps with his favourite scotch whisky.

But on this particular day, he was sober.

He looked me straight in the eyes, smiled beneath his handlebar mustache, and said, "Fancy a game, son?"

It's like he knew what I'd been planning, and in eight moves, he intended to take it away. And he did, along with any semblance of pride I'd gained in the time I'd spent perfecting my strategy. Still, I must have done something right that day. When I turned thirteen, I received an invitation from Team Spade. I didn't question what position I'd be playing or why. I only cared about getting as far away from my father as possible. On one condition, of course. That the Minister of Spades allow me to bring Kit along too. He made an exception so long as Kit behaved. "You have extraordinary cunning and conniving wit," the minister told me. "I have an eye for these things. I'd bet this year's Trials you're a Game Master. You see a game from every possible angle. You find loopholes and problems and figure out how to overcome those problems. Mark my words, Chess Shire, one day you'll rule the Spades as king."

I couldn't tell if he was talking about Team King or something else at the time, but either way my hopes were high, my doubts low, and everything else in between was, well, possible. I haven't seen my father since. Rumours spread that he'd eventually gone off his rocker and ended up ranting and raving in the Normal Reality, where authorities detained and Registered him. It wasn't hard to picture. The spiral started when my mum passed.

I never inquired after him. He deserved whatever fate found him there.

"Checkmate." Erin draws me out of my own spiral and successfully ends her game with Sophia.

I applaud quietly, but I'm the only one. Erin's mouth is turned down, and when I look over my shoulder to take in the others' expressions, they're all rather solemn too.

"Why such long faces?"

"Nothing happened," Madi says.

I furrow a brow as Erin exits the stall, shoves past our lot, and moves to the next game, choosing to play white this time instead of red.

I glance at Madi. "Care to explain?"

"Knightley has been playing these games of chess—which were already set up when she arrived—on her own since she reached this checkpoint." She pauses, as if waiting for Erin to jump in.

When she doesn't, Madi continues. "A handful of players have come and gone over the years, but none of them stayed or bothered to help her. They pillaged supplies and abandoned Knightley and the checkpoint. Goodness knows what happened to them. Probably taken out by the Jabberwock." Madi shudders, then motions to Erin who seems to be in some sort of stupor. "No matter how many times she plays, though, nothing changes. Not since her horse appeared. They can't travel beyond certain boundaries, though they've tried."

I incline my head towards the previous game. "We're here now, so something's changed. She just beat Sophia."

At the mention of her name, Sophia pipes up. "It's not about winning."

"What do you mean?"

"Knightley isn't sure," Jack says. "When she first arrived, she was bright enough to figure out the games needed to be played, at least. She's been playing them solo all this time."

I cringe at the word "solo," thinking of my father.

"The first game gave me my horse," Erin says to the board. "I figured if I played and finished each game, I'd eventually have everything I needed to move on to the next square, to win the Trial. I've tried beginning every game with white, then with red. I've attempted hundreds of openings and variants. I've taken the king with every piece from pawn to queen. I've looked at this game forwards and backwards and inside out. I have played every day, sometimes for hours a day, for ten years." Her trembling fingers hover over a white pawn. "The keep never fails. I am never hungry or thirsty or cold. But these games have made me wish the supplies didn't replenish each season."

I don't know what to say, and no one else does either. This, at least, explains her fascination—obsession?—with chess. If I were stuck here all alone with nothing else to do to pass the time, I might grow a little obsessed too.

And that's precisely why I've avoided this game for so long. Because it was my father's obsession, and I watched it destroy him. The game plus his drinking turned him into a man my mother didn't recognise. If it hadn't been for him, maybe my mum and the Hatters' mother wouldn't have been in a car together that day.

Funny how the Wonder Gene can grant you the most Wonderful things imaginable, making you feel invincible at times. But, Wonder or Normal, the Gene can't stop a car from speeding through a red light at an intersection.

It doesn't prevent a windshield from shattering.

It won't change a thing if you're not wearing a seatbelt.

And it sure as Spades can't bring anyone back from the dead.

I should sit across from Knightley and play a round, help her solve this checkpoint's riddle.

Instead I turn on my heel and walk in the opposite direction.

ALICE

There's nothing quite like running through the corridors of a secret . . . what would I call the Wabe? A bunker? It's part lab, part library, part greenhouse. It has everything, really. We could survive down here as long as we wanted.

Something inside aches at the thought of comfort and a place to call home. I'm tired of searching for truth only to end up sorely disappointed.

I'm also tired of being lied to.

The rush of adrenaline I feel at sprinting after my cousin through the halls, solid white walls to our right and glass overlooking the atrium to our left, is curiously freeing. We pass a few strangers here and there, teenagers and adults alike. Some give us the side eye while others laugh as we run by. Are they lost players? People who worked with my mother? Both? I consider swinging past the hospital wing so we can invite Willow to join us, but I decide against it. She needs her rest, and I'm not sure she'd be up for a race just yet. Not until we find Sophia.

"This way," Knave calls over his shoulder.

In the past, a run like this would have done me in. The Trials are good for something, it seems. They've certainly made me stronger.

In more ways than one.

When we reach the tip top of a spiralling iron staircase that seems as if it will never end, I pause to catch my breath. "This had better be worth it," I pant at Knave.

"Oh, it's worth it."

He's not even winded. After seeing him tackle killer hedgehogs in the Diamond Trial, there's no wondering why he was chosen to play the Ten position. He's certainly the most physically capable of Team Heart. "I never asked you," I huff. "What's your Mastery?" I had assumed he was a Beast Master, if such a thing exists, but that was a guess. He never let on what skill he specialised in.

Knave glances down at me as he untwists the wheel of a hatch above us. When he lifts the door, it groans. He climbs out, then gives me a hand up.

Once I'm standing on a small wooden platform, I take in the view.

We're surrounded by ocean. Waves crash, and the spray of seawater moistens my face and hair. The salty air plays tricks on my tongue, and I spy the shore where I first met Kit as well as the wood beyond where I encountered the Jabberwock. The same place where Willow and Sophia found me, and I lost them.

"It seems so real, doesn't it?" Knave remarks.

His question isn't what I expect. My eyes are still on the shoreline as I ask, "Isn't it?"

In the corner of my vision, I catch him shake his head. "The ocean is an illusion, concealing us from view. It's almost as if we're in yet another reality here. From what Kit and Rabekah tell me, we know little about the Wabe's origins. We don't have a clue as to whether your mother found it or if she designed it. Her fingerprints are all over this place, though."

I think about the book safe in my rucksack. The recording she left. And the looking-glass clues, as well.

"To answer your question, my Mastery is Agility." He sighs. "Everyone expects me to be fast and strong. I was chosen to play the Ten, after all. But I'm clever too. I'm more than just a speedy pair of legs."

With every word he utters, I relate to him more and more. I know what it's like to only be taken at face value. To be looked at like a weed rather than a dandelion with a thousand wishes, hopes, and dreams waiting to be granted.

We don't speak for a long time, the illusory ocean's rock and sway acting as white noise. I sought Knave out for a reason, but he doesn't seem to have any desire to dig up buried memories. When he's ready, I'll be here. For now, there's another question pressing on my heart.

"Can you tell me more about the looking glasses? Why am I the only one who can enter them?"

Scratching his head, Knave flips around and leans his bent arms on the platform's railing, just has he did on the balcony last night. We're gazing in opposite directions now. A pair of misfits with different skills, different ideas, different ways of viewing things, but also very much on the same page.

"I've only been here a day longer than you have, but," he says, "the professor and Kit gave me the short version if you want to hear it."

I almost say I *am* the short version, but I save my dry humour for Chess and stay silent.

"Basically, Professor White and her team have gathered that your mother left behind clues coded specifically to your DNA."

I think of the door opening at my thermal signature.

"While they can't unlock the clues like you can, they have been able to pinpoint their locations."

My ears perk at this. Finally, we're getting somewhere.

"There are eight in all, one for each square in this Trial."

Eight. I count backwards in my head. As far as I know, I've entered five of these memories.

First, when I entered this Trial through the looking glass in the Tulgey Wood. I saw Charlotte as a little girl on the chessboard field when no one else could.

Second and possibly third were at the Foundling House replica in Pawn Wood. The two separate memories within one looking glass. Three sisters, all in line for the throne, and little me crying over spilled flour.

Fourth was at the babbling brook, where a young Cordelia raced me to the cottage.

Fifth was inside the heart-shaped hand mirror, when my mother overheard Dinah's wicked plotting.

Five down. Three to go.

Now to organise these clues in a way that leads us to the real Wonderland. Why would my mother leave behind a riddle hidden within memories and not simply be straightforward about things? It's infuriating. Unless . . .

Unless she knew Dinah would be searching for these clues. The woman is clever, there's no denying that. But this doesn't explain what she would gain from finding the real Wonderland or the Ivory King. If she wants everyone to keep on believing her lies, why unveil the truth?

I turn around to face the same direction as Knave. Unlike the familiar shoreline and wood, the place where Knave fixes his gaze is dark and unwelcoming. It's hard to tell what lies beyond the darkness. It's like a cloud of black ink, hovering over the artificial water.

"It only grows more difficult from here," Knave says. "The professor thinks we might really have a shot, though."

"What's different this time?" I tense, sensing I may very well know the answer.

Knave confirms my worst fears. "You."

"Are you saying I'm the chosen one?" I laugh because the idea is absurd.

"No." Knave fixes his serious gaze on me. "I don't think it works like that. I think we all have the opportunity to be chosen.

It's just a matter of accepting the invitation. You did once, apparently. The professor says you *became* Wonder."

It's strange to hear him say this aloud when I've kept that little tidbit to myself since learning the truth from Charlotte.

"What you've done is impossible, yet you didn't even have to try. You just . . . did it. You believed. How much more are you capable of?"

Others are relying on me, those connected by blood and friends who became my family through all of this. I think long and hard on Knave's words as I stare at the inky blackness waiting across the water. Does the Jabberwock lurk there, ready to rear its claws again when we least suspect it?

Except, we do suspect it.

"What do you think?" Knave is regarding me. In the past, I might have thought his stare menacing. Now I see beyond my first impressions and search his heart.

And mine.

"I'm in," I say. Because, together, we can prepare for whatever awaits.

"I had no doubts." Knave pulls me towards the hatch. "Which is why it's time you met the members of the E.G.G."

"The bridge will last for exactly ten minutes."

I still can't get used to Rabekah's real name or her English accent. She will always and forever be Blanche—all French and frills—to me.

We're seated in an oval-shaped conference room at an oval table. The ceiling matches the theme with an oval skylight. Kit and Willow are present along with several new faces. Though we ran through brief introductions when we first sat down, I've already forgotten most everyone's names. There are a few Wonder adults the professor recruited to join the Knight Society's mission. An elderly gentleman with a white ponytail. A middle-aged woman with a frizzy hairline and keen brown eyes. And, to my surprise, Raving Hatter is present as well. Either his silver hair is longer than when I last saw him, or the absence of his top hat makes it seem that way. He looks older somehow too, as if Charlotte's disappearance has aged him. The remainder of the group is made up of players who have gone missing over the years—Game Masters, like me. But not every stray player is here. Some have yet to be found, including Stark Hatter.

According to Kit, everyone in attendance has chosen to make their home in the Wabe, opting to remain even when the Gateway reopens—which I've learned happens once per year for seven days.

"Better here than living a lie," Kit said during introductions. "Even if we never finish the Trial, at least we'll have tried."

I couldn't agree more.

"Kit, Knave, and Willow will accompany you, Alice," the professor says now. "But the rest of us will need to remain behind. The bridge isn't stable enough to hold more than four."

Raving shoves away from the table, rising in protest. "It can hold five. I insist you send me." He flings one arm towards the skylight. "My siblings could be somewhere out there."

"They could also find their way here," Rabekah counters.

Raving lowers himself into his chair. I can see the internal debate flicker across his face. Stay here and hope Madi and Stark or even Charlotte turn up. Or go looking for them and risk getting lost in the process.

"Now then," Rabekah says, "let's talk strategy."

The next hour is spent bouncing ideas back and forth. I'm in my element with these gamers. They speak my language and I smile inside.

"The entry point of the Sixth Square is here," one boy with freckles that match his hair says. He uses a pen with a red light on one end to point at a digital map at the table's centre. The map is half finished, with only some of the locations labelled.

Point of Entry.

Pawn Wood.

Mock Sea.

Strange train tracks weave around the map. The chessboard pattern spans every inch of terrain. But the rest? The dark spot Knave and I viewed from the rails and beyond? Only question marks and blanks label these places.

"What do you know about the Sixth Square?" I lean forwards, hoping for an answer.

I don't get one. "No one's returned from that part of the Trial," Kit states. "Which most likely means no one has ever made it past that section either."

The news is disheartening, but not knowing what to expect has never stopped us before.

Once we reach a general consensus that we really have no strategy—that we're taking a huge risk and all we can do is hope going in prepared is enough—Rabekah calls the meeting to a close.

"That's it?" Despite everything they've done to aid in her recovery, Willow is still not quite herself. She's never been one to wear fear on her sleeve, but her voice of caution is perhaps the most reasonable protest thus far. "You could be sending us straight into the Jabberwock's lair."

"Your worries are warranted"—the professor nods—"but do not think for a moment I'd send you in without protection." She focuses on me. "You have the almanac?"

I snag my rucksack from its place on the floor. "Check."

"And the audio journal?"

"Double check."

"Very well," Rabekah says. "You'll also need these." She reveals a plain white case with a handle and sets it on the table. Opening it with a click, she angles it so we can see what's inside.

Tea vials.

"There is one serving of *Beast's Blend* for each of you, thanks to Raving's expertise."

He huffs and says, "I'm a Game Master, not a Tea Master. I

can't guarantee the brew is perfect. The smart thing to do would be to wait for my sister."

Rabekah waves him off. "Don't mind him," she says. "Being a Game Master teaches you to consider the worst-case scenario."

Raving huffs again.

One by one we each remove a vial. I've never tried this blend, and I hope it doesn't turn me into a cat. While I adore Chess, Dinah ruined the animal for me. *Please, let my beast form be anything but feline.*

"Use it wisely."

We don't ask for further explanation. Charlotte trusts this woman. She trusts Raving. I trust Charlotte, despite how long it's taken me to do so.

"Thank you," I say.

Rabekah hugs each of us in turn, and the sober importance of our next move hits afresh. She swipes at her eyes, and her emotion is deep as she takes us in. "We will all be watching from the Wabe. You won't be able to contact me once you're past the barrier separating visible from invisible, but I'll tap into your WVs from an encrypted computer when you go back online. Let's just hope your devices don't glitch."

I suddenly wish we could make this a lengthier goodbye. That we could spend hours and days and weeks filling in every blank and eliminating every question mark. But we have to keep moving forwards on the board. We did come to finish, after all.

And all of Wonderland—even if they don't know it yet—is counting on us to reveal the truth.

"Good luck," Rabekah says to our quad. "I'll escort you to the bridge."

She exits the room followed by our small team. I snag Knave by his sleeve at the door and whisper, "I'll catch up. There's something I need to do first."

He frowns but nods.

I watch him and the others walk up the corridor, then I catch

Raving before he leaves the conference room. "Can I ask you an odd question?"

"There's no such thing, but sure." He still doesn't look pleased he has to stay at the Wabe, but at least he doesn't appear to hold any ill will towards me about the matter.

Quickly, I pull out the almanac and flip to the first page, revealing the inscription.

To my darling, Charlee. Best of luck in the Trials this year. I hope this book will help you find your way. With all my love, R.S.H.

The recognition in his eyes confirms what I already suspected. "Are these your initials? R.S.H.?"

After a moment, one corner of his mouth twitches. "My mother thought she was being clever. Naming me Raving Stark and my brother Stark Raving." He shakes his head. "It got downright confusing at times, if you ask me."

I close the book and return it to my bag. He's about to walk away, but before he can, I blurt, "Do you remember the year the Wonderland Trials began?"

He looks back at me, and his expression twists, as if he doesn't have an answer prepared. After a minute he says, "Twenty-five years ago."

That's what I was afraid he'd say. This can only mean he's been fooled by Scarlet's lies too.

"To clarify," he says, granting me an inkling of hope, "twenty-five years in the *real* Wonderland, which is unquestionably where this mess got started. Where the original Trials began."

"Charlotte mentioned something about that in her audio diary." I pat my rucksack. "What do you know about the original Trials?"

"To clarify again, everything you've endured thus far in this farce Scarlet calls the Heart Trial is really a series of eight Trials put into place by Wonderland itself." He gestures around. "What you experienced from the Spades and Diamonds and Clubs were child's play compared to this place. The human mind, even with the Wonder Gene, will only take you so far."

I can hardly wrap my own mind around the concept as it whirls like a spun teacup. "You said there are eight Trials? The same number as my mother's looking-glass memories?"

"You're just like the professor."

"How so?"

"Rabekah believes there's a connection, as well, and that Catherine chose eight memories to help you pass the final Trial—the Eighth Square. Some of the Trials can be skipped or skirted, but the eighth must be passed in order to find the way into Wonderland. As you are aware, no one has accomplished the task yet. That's where the Jabberwock is said to reside."

I don't tell him I've already had the unfortunate displeasure of encountering the dreadful creature. "How can you be certain Wonderland created these Trials?"

"Just as time passes differently in the real Wonderland, it slows on this side of the Gateway. A decade in the real Wonderland might be several in the Normal Reality. The same is true for these Trials."

"And in Scarlet's Wonderland?"

"Her version is like a virtual overlay. Plenty of fancy bells and whistles, but nothing of true substance. Time in her version is as it would be to a Normal. Hour for hour. Day for day."

"So . . . you remember the real Wonderland, then?" I wring my hands behind my back, unable to hold still.

Raving closes his eyes. "I remember how it felt. I know it was real, that I was there. I have memories of my family. Of Charlee. Things we did and games we played. But no." His eyes meet mine once more. "Wonderland and the Ivory King are so far removed from my memories, they might as well be children's stories."

I relate all too well. "One last question," I plead. "Promise."

He gives me a skeptical look but stays put.

"Where did you get the almanac?"

Raving answers slowly, "It's not so much where I got it. It's more where I found it. Or where *it* found *me*."

My curiosity is piqued as I hang on his every word.

"Wonderland didn't disappear all at once," Raving says. "It

happened piece by piece as more Wonders began to look to their own abilities rather than rely on where those abilities came from. The day before Charlotte went after your mother . . ." He pauses, and I can tell this is difficult for him. "The day before, I was in one of the only places that still contained something of what we'd lost—the Tulgey Wood. I was looking for the Gateway, hoping to find a way to keep Charlotte from leaving. I couldn't just abandon my siblings, not when we'd already lost our mother."

He takes a breath. "But I would do whatever it took to help my Charlee. The almanac with its red leather cover was just lying on the ground, open as if it had been dropped or discarded. It was almost like . . ." He breaks off.

I'm nearly on my toes, leaning in. Whatever he's about to say matters, and I don't want to miss it. "Like what?"

Raving's eyes are distant. They crinkle at the corners and it's the first time I've noticed how much older he really is, closer to Charlotte's true age. Finally he says, "Like it had been waiting for me to find it." He looks back at me. "I know it doesn't make sense, but what in Wonderland does these days?"

I'm about to wholeheartedly agree when—

"A!" Knave pokes his head around a corner a ways up the corridor. "Let's go!"

It feels we are just scraping the surface here, but I have to leave. "Thank you," I tell Raving.

"No problem."

He gives me a quick side hug before bidding farewell, and I get a whiff of something like the inside of a writing desk and newly sharpened pencils. He really is perfect for Charlotte.

With new dots connected that add endless possibilities to this rather complicated puzzle, I hurry to catch up to my team.

Now I understand why the bridge can only hold four people.

It's not a real bridge.

Where there was nothing connecting the platform Knave showed me to the inky black cloud in the distance before, a bridge made of glass now extends over the false sea.

Except, it isn't glass.

The first thing I notice when I step onto the hard surface is that it wavers under my weight. The effect reminds me of splashing in a puddle, though the substance isn't quite liquid. I'm thrown off balance and my teammates steady me on either side.

"Together?" Knave says.

"Together," I reply.

Much like we did during the Spade Trial, we grab onto one another's hands and run. With each step, the ground beneath our feet is a little less stable. I make the mistake of peeking over my shoulder and discover the bridge is collapsing behind us at a rapid pace.

I try to go faster. My heart pounds and my lungs catch fire. How does Knave do this with such ease? Since the ocean is a ruse, if we fall, where do we go? Into a ravine or forest? Onto jagged rocks or soft earth?

I have no intention of finding out.

When at last we've reached the black cloud, we pause and look back. The bridge is in ruins, no more genuine than the imitation waves swallowing it whole.

"Ready?" I ask.

"Ready," the others say in unison.

As one, we enter the heart of darkness.

I hold my breath and close my eyes as if I'm about to dive underwater. I don't register the moment we lose hold of each other's hands until after the fact. At first, nothing happens. I feel as if I'm drifting off to sleep, caught in that quiet space between consciousness and unconsciousness. My lids grow heavy and my breathing slows. It's lovely, actually. Warm and inviting. Wouldn't it be splendid to simply lie down, if only for a minute or two? I allow my body to relax, and at the same instant, I'm pulled under.

The sensation of entering a looking glass is familiar, and I don't fight it this time. I try to open my eyes, but the heaviness there remains, drawing me deeper into what could be a dream or nightmare. I'm floating, falling, waiting to emerge from the shadows.

A female voice, soft and cruel, says, "You can't do this, Catherine. You cannot just leave your child behind to chase a Wonderland that no longer wants us there. It's not worth it."

In an instant I'm standing face-to-face with an older Charlotte. Her hair hangs over one shoulder in a loose plait, and red silk pyjamas adorn her frame.

I don't need to seek out my reflection to know I'm playing the role of my mother again, seeing the past through her eyes.

I'm standing inside a Heart Palace suite, a packed-to-the-brim satchel lying on the bed beside me. The space is different from what I remember, though—more concrete. The sense that Buckingham Palace sits beneath Wonderland's veil is absent, leaving this suite to stand on its own. Unlike the gown from the previous party memory, I'm wearing a simple pair of black trousers and a hooded blue pullover.

"I know you think you're doing this for Alice," Charlotte goes on. "I know you believe I've given up hope and that's part of the reason Wonderland is abandoning us. But you can't go your own way. It isn't right, and worse, it isn't safe. This reality is crumbling. We have to leave here together, before Wonderland disappears and takes us with it. Your husband died to save you in that London fire last year. He wouldn't want Alice to grow up without a mother as well."

All this time, the reports in the Normal Reality said my mother died in a lab fire. Speechless, I stare at the woman who raised me. I wish with all my heart I could hear my mother's response to this, but in the memories I've entered so far, my mind has remained fully my own.

And then, as if granting my deepest desire, the whisper of my mother's voice enters my thoughts. It's an odd sensation, her perspective intertwining with my own. This has never happened, and I feel as if my will is being invaded. I work to calm my immediate tension, allowing her to direct my words.

"We had an agreement." My voice is different now too, worn but wise. "You promised not to speak of Ivan."

Ivan. My father's name was Ivan Pillar.

"I'm sorry." Charlotte moves closer. "I know it pains you to hear of him. But you still have Alice."

Charlotte's words jostle my emotions in a way that makes me feel out of control.

"I know you'll care for her." The words gag me as they pass between my lips. "One child's needs do not compare to the needs of an entire society. I must do this. For all Wonders, including Alice. You go. Take Alice and Knave with you. As for me, I'm staying. And if I'm lost to the Trials, I'm lost."

Best of luck in the Trials . . .

The almanac. It was Raving's send-off before Charlotte took me and Knave and went after my mother.

. . . this year . . .

Time passes differently on this side of the Gateway. A few days here might mean a year for Raving if he stayed on the outside.

. . . I hope this book will help you find your way.

My mother isn't the only one who got lost. Somewhere along the way, we lost Knave too.

The memory fades and so does the illusion. I'm sucked back and out and away, a trail of silver dust exploding before my vision. When the dust clears, I'm left with nothing but panic as I take in my new surroundings.

Did I mistakenly drink Dwindler's Draught, or are the flowers surrounding me as tall as trees?

Where are the others?

And why is a massive, serpent-like vine coiled centimetres from my face?

CHESS

Three knocks sound on the keep's dungeon tower door. I expect Madi to walk across the threshold and launch into some pep talk that will make me feel bad enough to traipse back downstairs and join my team. I'm fully prepared to offer a proverbial protest.

But it isn't Madi with all her bubbly positivity who appears at the opening of the cell where I sit alone sulking. It's Stark.

"Care for some company?" Stark doesn't bother waiting for a formal invitation. He slides down the wall to sit beside me, knees bowed and forearms resting on top, just like mine.

I watch him from the corner of my eye. His approach couldn't be more different from his sister's. While Madi says everything she thinks the moment she thinks it, Stark keeps to himself until the opportune moment.

The anticipation is killing me, and I finally break. Patience is not my strong suit. "Did you come all the way up here to convince me to rejoin everyone in the game stables? Because if you did, I'm not in the mood."

"No," Stark says, picking at a weed that's grown between

the cracks in the stone floor. "I came up here because misery loves company, and I haven't had a lot of that over the past miserable year."

Ouch. Guilt rears its ugly head, making me feel worse than I already do.

"I had a lot of time to think on that train." Stark digs at the dirt around the weed with his finger now. Still, it stands strong. "I'd go in and out of being alert, knowing who I was and what I was meant to be doing. I'd hear Madi's voice through my headphones, and I knew as long as she kept transmitting, our Realities were connected. I can't explain how it was possible for me to hear her. Whether it was a connection through the WV or the Trial allowing me that small bit of solace, either way, it happened."

His words strike me. We're the same age, but he's beyond our years in this conversation. "I think the train did something to you, mate," I say, forcing a chuckle that comes out all wrong. "That time loop made you sound like a grandfather."

Stark laughs a little at the comment but keeps his focus on the dirt. He digs deeper and deeper. "Like I said, I had a lot of time to think." He finally pulls the weed free with all its roots intact, holding the sad specimen up to the minimal light provided by the cell window. "Sometimes we become something other than what we imagine. Our lives turn out differently than we expected. To those on the outside looking in, we are nothing and no one. A nuisance. A weed."

I let the words sink in. I have the urge to keep giving him a hard time for sounding so ridiculously ancient, to say some sarcastic thing or another to lighten to mood. But, with Stark sitting so annoyingly grown up and mature beside me, my jesting only proves I'm out of my league here.

Twisting the weed this way and that, Stark continues. "The outcome doesn't have to be perfect. Take this weed. We're on the topmost level of a keep, and yet, somehow, a seed found its way into the cracks and soil within this cell. Eventually, life found a way to take root and grow towards the only light it could find. Its roots spread thin but strong."

I try not to be a dolt and roll my eyes at this philosophy lesson. "What are you getting at?"

Stark shoots me a glance. "The weed may have been forced to adapt to its limited environment, yet it still has the potential to expand and grow."

He may be onto something.

"It's never too late to increase your potential." Stark rises, keeping the sorry excuse for a plant pinched between his thumb and forefinger. "Sometimes you simply need an extra hand to help take you there." He heads for the stairwell, no doubt intending to deposit the weed outside where it can flourish.

His lesson is less than subtle. In the past I would have laughed it off. Then again, what if my past is the reason I feel the need to coat everything with comedy?

Stark disappears beyond the door, his footsteps growing distant in his descent.

Quick as a cat, I hop to my feet and jog after him. By the time I reach him, he's nearly at ground level. "Stark," I say in a rush, "I never blamed your mum." I fall into step beside him. "I blamed mine." Why is it so difficult to talk about this?

Maybe because I never have.

"What?" Stark sounds truly taken aback. "Why?"

I comb my fingers through my hair, which just falls back into my eyes.

"My dad was hardly around, always holed up in his study, staring at a chessboard. The pieces were his real family. And us?" I wave a hand. "We were an inconvenience. My parents had a spat the day your mum popped over for tea. My own mum was an emotional wreck and fled the scene."

"My mom went after her, to try and calm her down." Stark stops at the undercroft door that leads outside. When he turns to face me, I can't read his expression. But then he says, "I remember."

And it's my turn to be taken aback. "You do?"

"I was there as well."

As if a switch has been flipped, my mind comes to life and fills in the blanks of that dreadful day. Stark and I had been playing our favourite game of Mock Trials on the lawn, and we could hear my parents' shouts through the kitchen window. Stark had tried to distract me by making me list off statistics and facts from previous Trials.

"You're a true nerd when it comes to the Trials," Stark said, to which I bowed and replied, "It takes one to know one."

"My mum," I say now, "She just . . . left. She left us." It's the first time I've uttered the words out loud.

Placing a firm hand on my shoulder, my best mate and longest rival gives me a good jostle. "She would have come back," he assures me. "If she . . . If they hadn't . . ." He can't seem to find the words, so he starts over. "My mom would have brought her to her senses."

"And if she left anyway?"

"Then my parents would have adopted you, of course. You would have had to sleep on the floor though." His smile is all teeth. But there's a seriousness in his tone that tells me, despite his teasing, he's one hundred percent certain Kit and I wouldn't have been forgotten.

"You're too sentimental." I pocket my hands, unsure if this is an awkward hug-between-mates moment or not.

"And you're too jaded." He quirks one eyebrow, and I sense our old camaraderie might still have a chance.

We seem to come to an unspoken understanding then. I move past him and open the door wide, fully expecting to be bathed in sunlight.

Thunder bellows its greeting instead.

We exchange a worried glance and make a break for the stables.

Stark and I are drenched. In the minute it took to sprint from the keep to the game room, the sky decided that was the opportune time to burst into tears.

I am not amused.

"There you two are!" Madi scolds, ever playing the role of Team Mother. "Took you long enough." She glares at her brother, but it's immediately softened with a wink.

Madi seems ready to explode. And she does. "Jack has finished a solo game!"

It's then I see that, in the stall directly across from the one that holds Knightley's horse, a new steed has materialised. This one is chocolate brown with a black mane and reddish speckles all over. If Jack were a horse, he'd look like this one. At the thought, I examine Erin's mare with new eyes. A glance made me think the animal was pure midnight, but now I notice her tail is auburn like Erin's hair, and freckles dot her muzzle.

What if . . . ?

Turning in a full 360-degree rotation, I survey what's left of the game room. What I'm about to suggest is going to sound absurd, and yet . . . I consider my teammates, realisation building. "There's one game meant for—designed for—each of us. In other words, the reason Knightley could only get results from completing one solo game is because that game was coded for her." Buckley mentioned coding at the last checkpoint.

"What if the Trial has a mind of its own?" I pose. "And it knows exactly who will reach which checkpoint and move forwards? Stark couldn't leave the train until I found him. Erin's been stranded here, waiting for the right players to show up."

For *us* to show up.

A mixture of emotions passes over everyone's faces. Confusion, doubt, concern, hope.

Stark comes to my aid, finishing my thought. "Shire's points are valid. It would also explain the memory-loss issue." His gaze locks onto mine.

Why didn't I think of it? The challenge Stark faced on the train is no different from what happens when we pass back through the supposed Gateway and reenter the false version of Wonderland. No one remembers the Fourth Trial when they leave because the Trial doesn't *want* us to remember. If this is true, what else could the Trial be capable of?

The storm outside responds to my thoughts in tandem, growing more ferocious by the second.

As if warning us to leave this place as soon as possible.

And that's precisely what we're going to do. I count the remaining chessboards. Four left. Madi, Stark, Sophia, and I have yet to play a solo game. I turn to Jack, urgency in my tone. "How did your game end? What pieces took the king and queen?"

Our Team Heart Puzzle Master is all confidence, unfazed by my frantic questioning. His Jack position suits him well, the king of decoding and dissecting. He's also the most calm and collected of us all. It's similar to being a Game Master, I suppose, but on a more scrutinising scale. "My white knight took the red queen," he says. "Then my bishop went in for the kill."

My eyes dart to Knightley next.

She must know what I'm about to ask, because she gives a slow nod.

"Is that how you ended your first game, Erin?" Madi asks gently, using Knightley's real name for once. "With a white knight to the red queen and a bishop to the king?"

Erin approaches her horse and begins to stroke the beast's long muzzle. "It's been so long—years—but yes, that's how my first game ended. That day will remain forever stamped in my mind." The horse presses into her owner's palm in response, nuzzling against Erin's touch like a tame house pet. "I honestly can't remember a time before I had Song. She's been my best girl, my only company."

Rain pounds and pelts the barn's tin roof. Leaks drip water in various places, turning the dirt to mud, only serving to enhance the farm-fresh—or not so fresh—smell.

I wrinkle my noise to avoid sneezing and aim to focus. Erin has nothing else she can say, but I can see she understands we have to work together or none of us will make it out. The wind picks up, ranting and raving beyond the barn walls, shaking the wooden boards that barely hold this place in one piece. I steal a glance between the structure's slats, the keep in all its towering solitude sparking sudden recognition.

Tall and slender and pointed at the top. How did I fail to notice the design? The keep isn't a keep at all.

It's a chess piece, the bishop to be exact.

And the horses—knights—are somehow pieces too.

This is so simple. Too simple, really. Yet, if my theory is correct, we could move on and reach the next square by morning.

Taking my Team King position seriously for probably the first time since this year's Trials began, I direct the others to each one of the remaining boards in order of our positions. Erin played a Two, so Sophia—a Four—would be next to hers. Madi's a Nine so she's after Sophia. Jack already completed his, which just leaves the two Team Kings. A Diamond teaming up with a former-Spade-turned-Heart? I never thought I'd see it.

Stark and I march to the final two stalls, one on the left, and one on the right.

"You ready for this, Shire?"

"Ready as I'll ever be, Hatter."

"One hundred points says I'll finish my game first."

"I don't think this is about points anymore, mate."

"Is the great Chess Shire backing down from a challenge?"

He knows me too well. "Never. Make it two hundred points."

"You're on."

We part ways, each entering our respective stalls. I sit on the white side of the board, taking a deep breath before moving a centre pawn two spaces forwards. The game is brief, and since I only care about the moves I make for white, it's easy to leave the openings I need for the opposing side. It doesn't take long before my white knight takes the red queen, followed by my white bishop checkmating the red king.

The red king falls.

My chessboard quakes, then vanishes, leaving nothing but my white knight piece abandoned in the hay. I stoop to retrieve it. The piece is hot, burning my hand. I hiss through my teeth and drop the wretched thing. A visible blister is already forming over the creases of my palm. I don't have time to nurse my injury though. Something heavy either lands or falls on the barn roof. A tree? The castle tower? A giant bird?

I take a defensive position, tensing my muscles and hunching my shoulders to my ears.

Then the white knight explodes.

This is the second time I've been in this position today. I'm lying on my back on the soggy ground. A massive headache pounds from my temples to the base of my skull. When I blink my eyes open, the first thing I see is Jack's hand.

"Sorry, mate," he says. "I meant to warn you about that part."

I take his hand and he helps me to my feet. My eyes widen. The stall where I just finished my game is no longer empty.

A copper-brown horse with turquoise eyes stares back at me. His mane, just a shade darker than his body, bears a single pink streak. "Copper," I say without thinking, and he nods his long head in response. I grin and add, "Buckley says 'hi.'"

The moment of respite doesn't last though. Calm turns to chaos with my next breath. Did I expect anything different at this point?

The same horrible screech we heard rise from the wood when we entered this Trial sounds frighteningly close. In an instant I know what landed on the roof earlier. The sound of talons against tin vibrates every nerve ending in my body. I clench my teeth.

"Jabberwock," I curse under my breath. Then I raise my voice. "Everyone, mount your steeds! Now!"

"But I've never ridden a horse," Sophia protests, panic pinching her voice. Her stricken expression is a punch to my gut.

I wish Willow were here. She and Sophia don't fare well without one another, and I'll do everything in my power to reunite us all.

The minute the thought occurs, I realise it's true. I can't pinpoint the exact moment I stopped caring about my personal motives and began thinking about the good of the whole. A new energy surges through me, filling me with renewed purpose. With everything in me, I want my team to come out of this on the other side.

We will finish this Trial, together.

"Trust your instincts," Erin hollers, opening the first stall gate and mounting her own mare with an ease I'm sure even a trained knight couldn't match. Seems Knightley suits her after all. "These creatures are designed to carry you and you alone."

I wonder if other players have tried to steal her horse and failed, but that's a question for another day. I scan my stall for a stool or crate or something to give me a boost so I can mount my horse. Too bad everything vanished when the chessboard did. Then, as if he's been trained for this, Copper lowers himself to a kneeling position and waits for me to climb on.

Copper rises, and I steady myself, feeling the power of his muscles as they ripple under my thighs. My trembling fingers curl around his coarse mane. In another time and place, I'd take this nice and slow, ease into it, work my way up from a walk to a trot to a gallop. I don't say as much to Sophia, but I've never ridden a horse either. Now, though—with the Jabberwock about to break through the barn at any moment—is not the time to be timid.

It's as if Copper senses the urgency of the situation. He rears back on his hind legs, and I have to cling to him with all my strength. When his front hooves pound the ground, he takes off, bursting out of the stall as if his tail has caught fire.

"Follow us!" I can barely hear my own command over the Jabberwock's scathing scream. There's no time to repeat it as Copper charges forwards, through the barn doors, and out into the storm.

Leaning into his neck, I force myself not to look back. I've no idea where Copper's headed, but I trust he knows better than I do what comes next. If the Trial designed him, then the Trial can guide us where we need to be. Soon, the resonant rumble of several sets of hooves matches our thunderous pace. A massive shadow I'm certain doesn't belong to a cloud passes over us, and I dig my heels deeper into Copper's sides, willing him to move at an impossible speed.

We race across the muddied chessboard fields, my team at my heels and the Jabberwock screeching above. It stays with us, following but never attacking. Is it simply trying to invoke fear? We won't stop to find out. When at last we reach an L-shaped fork in the road, much like the one where Knightley found me and Stark, Copper doesn't pause, barrelling straight forwards along the narrow road.

"I see you've finally come around to taking my advice," Stark calls from his plum-purple steed, bolting past me.

"That's a horse of a different colour!"

"You owe me two hundred points!"

"Only if you can catch me first!"

Copper appears to relish the challenge because he speeds up. It isn't long before we're neck and neck with Stark and Plum. They pose a challenge, but we eventually pass them. Soon, the weather changes. Like night and day, the clouds clear and the sunset shines. I finally take the opportunity to look skyward. To my exhaled relief, the Jabberwock has vanished too. We gallop up and over a hill, then down an incline, towards a sandy shore and, beyond that, a glassy sea. The road levels out and narrows into a beaten path. In the distance, on the opposite side of the sea, I can just make out the crest of a rising moon above a new horizon.

We slow to a walk, and I pat Copper's side. "Nice work, mate."

Knightley sidles up beside us. "I've seen it from the keep's telescope, but I'd lost hope I would ever reach it."

"What is it?" I ask, attempting to make out the unfamiliar shapes and colours of the trees beyond the water.

"I've no idea," she says. "But it must be the next square."

It isn't until we're within a kilometre of the shoreline that the water shifts. The calm surface from moments before laps and rises into curling waves. Spooked, Copper backs up.

"Whoa, boy." I tug on his mane and pat his neck. He replies with a snort and a sigh.

"Are you seeing this, Shire?" Stark says when he pulls up, attempting to calm his own steed.

I nod, momentarily speechless. We look on in awe as the sea parts, creating a clear path to what lies on the opposite shore. I might even go so far as to call it a shortcut. A coincidence, or the Trial's way of directing our next move?

"Another wood?" Jack asks.

It's Sophia who answers. Her horse is bronze, its mane and tail black. A mixture of wonder and joy illuminates her next words. "It's not another wood," she breathes. "It's a garden."

CHESS

Anything that appears this harmless never ought to be trusted. We leave the parted sea behind, waves crashing down in our wake, and enter the Garden Wood. The floral scents surrounding us are so potent I can't help but sneeze. Again. First the barn and now this? What's next? If the Jabberwock doesn't kill us, this place might just do me in.

Our horses trot cautiously along the sandy pink path that cuts and winds between stems in every shade of green. They're as thick and tall as mature tree trunks, producing petals of various shapes and colours. The towering roses with their jagged thorns, warning us not to draw too near, I at least recognise. The odd white blossoms with petals like propellers and papery ribbons trailing off their ends? Now those are a mystery.

"Ghost orchids," Sophia explains, a reverence to her tone. "Extremely rare. When used in a tea blend, they're said to not only contain healing properties, but to make the drinker temporarily invisible and immune to injury as well. Ghost's Grog, some call it, though I've never personally encountered it."

And here I thought I was the master of illusion, when all along there was a tea to do the job. It doesn't seem fair. I don't say as much to Sophia, but I'll have to pester Madi to make me a brew when this is all over. A smile plays on my lips. Ace won't know what hit her.

"At least there's only one path," Jack comments. "We don't have to guess the way."

Ah, Jack, ever the optimist. "That's exactly what I'm afraid of," I say, clutching Copper's mane.

"Don't be such a worrywart." Madi's mare marches on ahead, confident steps kicking up sand. She's like her rider in every way from her lavender mane right down to her silver hooves. "We escaped the Jabberwock, didn't we? We helped Knightley move on from the keep. Surely you're not going to let a bunch of oversized flowers scare you, Shire. The Trial has brought us this far."

"The Trial has also made the way more difficult the closer we get to obtaining our goal," Stark reminds her. "It's testing us."

An unseen snapping sound makes me tug on Copper's mane as I jerk my head left. But I detect no movement in the flowering purple bushes blossoming beneath a tiger lily tree. I loosen my hold, and Copper continues forwards. He moves cautiously, as if he too was spooked by the noise.

"The pink-haired boy is right." To my surprise, it's Knightley who speaks up. She apparently hasn't taken the time to learn my name, thus I no longer feel bad calling her Knightley. And she's been so reserved, keeping her distance, sometimes I nearly forget she's here. "Something's not right," she adds. "It's too quiet."

I follow her gaze, searching the path ahead. The stems only grow thicker and closer together the farther we venture, and I'm starting to question if we're headed straight for a dead end.

Or a trap.

Another snapping sound followed by a rustle plays behind us. On instinct, I dismount Copper to investigate. Holding one fist in the air and finger to my lips, I weave between my teammates, sitting above me on their respective horses. The nervous glances they exchange tell me I'm not imagining things, and they, too, heard the disturbance.

When I reach the end of our line, all appears calm. We likely frightened a harmless critter. But then the rustling sound rises again. Or . . . I tilt my head, lifting an ear to listen closer . . . That's not a rustle. It's a hiss.

I whip around just in time to witness a long, leafy vine with yellow flowers curling around Sophia's waist, lifting her off her horse. Her expression changes from concern to terror in the amount of time it takes her to scream, *"Hibbertia Scandens!"*

"In English!" My hand darts to my hip as if I'll unsheathe some magical weapon that has appeared from thin air. Why didn't I think to rummage through the undercroft barracks before we left?

Maybe because we were trying to escape the Jabberwock, you idiot.

Fair point, Shire, fair point.

Sophia chokes out her words just before the vine closes around her throat. "Snake vines!" She grabs at them, clawing and gasping, no doubt hoping to use her Mastery to beg the blasted things to spare her life. Her eyes bulge, and her skin turns paler than the ghost orchid petals. Either this plant knows what it's up against and chose to attack Sophia first as a strategy, or it did so out of sheer dumb luck.

What do we do? We have no weapons, no defence. All the Trial has given us are the horses that brought us to this abhorrent excuse for a garden.

The horses!

I bolt past the others, straight for Copper. As if sensing my approach, he kneels, giving me a swift mount as he did before. Treating his mane as reins again, I coax him to turn, kicking him in the side, sending him into a full-on charge towards Sophia, who is fighting for her life midair.

"Run!" I order the others, hoping they can avoid the same fate.

They do no such thing. To my horror, each one of them has been snatched up by a snake vine too. I'm surrounded by teammates dangling, dying, the Fate lights on their WV bangles glitching and fading.

The WV. What happens if their Fate lights go out in this Trial? Stark's WV died on him during his extended train ride. I've chosen to remove mine for . . . personal reasons. Knightley's been in this Trial ten years, so I imagine whatever outdated version of the WV she had is long since out of commission.

But the others. Sophia, Madi, and Jack. They all still wear a bangle. Dread turns my stomach. Why do I get the sense that if their Fates vanish, they'll be booted back to square one? Is that what happened to me during last year's Trial? Did I lose my Fates and in turn abandon Kit? Is that how the quarter heads are controlling things from outside the Trial?

For now I need to get those bangles off before we lose half of our team. Using all the courage I can manage, I jump from my moving horse, aiming to grab onto Sophia and pull her from the vine's clutches. It's a moron's move, and I'm reminded of the unfortunate truth that the Wonder Gene does not make one superhuman. One look at Soph proves it. The very life is being squeezed out of our best chance at taming the flora, or at least reasoning with it. I have to free her first.

But I can't. I fall short, helpless. Copper and the other horses have galloped off somewhere, likely unnerved by the flowering snakes. And what am I good for? *Who* am I good for?

"Help!" I cry out to someone, anyone. The plea is pathetic, desperate, cracked down the centre and too weak to reach anywhere that matters.

Can the Trial see what this place is doing to us? Did it know the horses it provided would run when things grew bleak? I fall to my knees, half expecting a snake vine to take me next. And maybe it should. I've failed my team yet again.

It's then, when I've reached my breaking point, that the last thing I expect to see comes charging through the Garden Wood.

Do my eyes deceive me? It can't be real.

But it is. A dazzling white unicorn with a golden horn aimed like a spear.

I scramble to my feet, certain the unicorn will deliver the miracle we need and bring the snake vines down with a single slash of its horn. The mythical beast does no such thing. Now I'm backing away. Because the unicorn isn't after the enemy vines.

It's after me.

If snake vines weren't bad enough, evidently this place breeds killer unicorns as well.

There's no way I can outrun it. And I won't. Not when my teammates are fading with their Fates by the second. I'm at the ready. It's probably the most idiotic idea I've had yet. But if I can't outrun it, maybe I can join it.

As soon as it closes in, I turn and begin my sprint, running alongside the unicorn as it passes. I reach out, attempting a feat I've only seen in stories. It's a fool's errand and I'm left stumbling, nearly falling flat on my face. Did I really think I could mount a charging unicorn? I shake my head and wipe my hands on my mostly dry trousers. Well, that was entertaining.

When I look up, I'm fully prepared for the unicorn to round on me and charge again. Instead I find it rearing back on its hind legs, neighing wildly. It stomps down hard just as two arms of ivy reach out from beneath a bramble bush, their leaves snapping like tiny little jaws. But the menacing undergrowth is no match for the brilliant beast. It rears and stomps again, and I'd swear that's a growl radiating from its muzzle.

"Chess, watch out!"

Every muscle goes rigid. Madi never uses my first name. It's then I sense the heat close behind me, the feeling of a much larger and more powerful body just a handbreadth away. Slowly, I turn to face whatever monstrosity awaits.

I keep my gaze skyward, and the first thing I see is Madi, still struggling against the snake vines, but half free. It's no longer gagging her, and she bites and claws and squirms. Anything to keep herself alive. My situation, on the other hand, has escalated. Worse than the vines and the unicorn and maybe even the Jabberwock.

Who, after all, can kill a lion with his bare hands?

Several things happen in succession, too quick for me to count or observe them all. I brace myself, fully expecting to be mauled and dragged off to some nearby den where I'll no doubt become supper. But when has anything in the Trials met my expectations?

The lion doesn't bite. He smiles. If I didn't know any better, I'd think this beast is playing some sort of game, having a good laugh at watching me sweat where I stand. I glance between him and the unicorn.

"Well," I say to the lion, because what do I have left to lose? "Are you going to help my mates?"

The lion, of course, shakes his head. Why wouldn't he? I'm about to ask again, gesture frantically or something to try and explain what I mean to this animal. But I don't have to make myself look more ridiculous than I already feel because a bird that's a mix between a vulture and a chicken swoops down from nowhere with talons outstretched and beak snapping. It slices through the snake vines as if they're nothing more than bread and butter. One by one, my teammates are released.

The moment Sophia's on her feet again, she finds her voice. It's raspy, but with all the poise and presence of a queen, she commands the flowers to let us pass. "We mean you no harm! We beseech you to let us through."

The garden grows silent. The thick stems ahead bow and back away from the path, giving us a straight way forwards. Seemingly satisfied he's done absolutely nothing to help, the lion turns and retreats, strolling along as if no one almost died here. The strange bird flies off with a caw at the same moment the unicorn pauses beside me.

I face the glorious creature, bowing my head in thanks. It shakes the white mane from its eyes, revealing a spot of blood, which smears the space above its right brow. Then it lowers into a full kneel that almost looks like a curtsy.

Ace would think this creature very curious indeed. My heart aches. I wish she were here to see this. But as I reach out to stroke the unicorn's neck, I catch a glimpse of my reflection in her blue eyes. Ace always did see me differently than everyone else. More than that, she saw *through* me. It's as if this animal bears the same gift and somehow sees who I truly am too. The unicorn lingers only a moment longer before following the lion up the path.

With no promising options on the horizon, I gather my teammates, giving them a quick once-over to ensure they're all right for now.

Most everyone is stunned to silence. Except Stark. I suppose he's had enough silence for a lifetime. "Where to, Shire?"

Perhaps it's the way he says it. Or maybe it has something to do with the fact that he doesn't hesitate to trust me for guidance, even after I couldn't save them.

But I decide from here on out, I'll do everything in my power to be worthy of that trust.

"Where else, mate?" I hitch a thumb over my shoulder, then follow the lion and the unicorn wherever they may lead.

It's taking longer than I expected to reach the unknown destination. As we walk past jagged stems and ominous petals that look as if they might devour us at any moment, I keep an eye out for Copper and the other horses. Have they served their purpose, or will we see them again? Or did the Garden Wood attack them too?

At least we're not bothered by the snake vines again. It pays to have a Flower Master on our team.

I'm idly watching the lion and the unicorn ahead as Jack jogs to catch up to me. "How much farther, do you think?"

"Your guess is as good as mine," I admit.

He slows his pace, falling behind me again. The last thing we need is for our most optimistic teammate to turn into the precise opposite. If we don't refuel soon, there's no telling the toll this place will take.

I lift my gaze to the garden's canopy. Moonlight filters through the petals and my thoughts wander backwards as the lion and unicorn continue forwards. They remain a courtyard's length ahead, but I'm travelling back to London, creeping along the streets at night with Ace by my side.

"Alright, Ace?" I'd asked then.

"Alright," she'd replied.

The blush was clear on her cheeks, even beneath the shadows. And then I held her. Her scent was different from most girls. Not fruity or flowery or reminiscent of some sugary treat or another. Instead she smelled like the best part of a summer's eve, when sunset splashes the horizon in rosy pink and the glow-worms come out to play.

My thoughts shift to the present as the beastly pair rounds a bend, vanishing from view. Our groups slows, a collective question hanging in the air. Is this really the best idea? They may have helped us, but that doesn't make these creatures safe by any means. What if they only offered aid with the intention of leading our team to something more deadly? We could very well be walking to our doom, unarmed and unaware.

I take the lead, make my way around the corner, and halt at a small clearing. The lion and the unicorn have gone. I blink, looking this way and that.

"Where'd they go?" Madi asks.

And then . . . oh, then . . . My throat catches and my heart leaps.

It isn't until this precise moment that I realise it's been stopped for days. It can only ever truly beat when she's near, because it only beats for her.

Ace stands between a pair of daisy-tree stems, smiling. Dried leaves and weeds adorn her hair like a misshapen crown. There's a rip in the right sleeve of her blue blouse that looks like it was inspired by her eyes. Her glasses slip down her nose, and blood stains her right brow.

She's never looked more glorious than she does in this moment. Except . . .

The blood on her brow draws my attention, and now my heart stops. Ace is the Unicorn? My reaction to Beast's Blend turns me into a common nuisance of a house cat, and she gets to transform into a unicorn? It's entirely unfair and perfectly suitable at once.

A grin bursts over my face, and I trip over myself, rushing to reach her. She keeps still, letting me come to her, as if she's been waiting for me to find her from the moment we parted.

"Chess," is all she says when I'm close enough to inhale her sunset scent, engulfing her in my arms. My name on her lips is pure gold. Unlike our first kiss, we're out in the open, exposed, but I don't care who's watching. I slip one arm around her waist while I thread my fingers through her sunshine hair. I want her to feel my apology for not reaching her sooner and my regret for not telling her the truth in its entirety. But, more than anything, I want her to feel my utter joy at finding her. And I want her to know that I never intend to lose her again.

She rises on her toes, and I bow my head to meet her.

When I pull away, we're both breathless and beaming.

"Chess," she says again, keeping her palms resting on my chest. I close my fingers around hers, holding them over my heart, and she steps back. "I found him. Or . . . he found me, actually. He's alive."

A second passes before I register who she means. It's then I gaze past her into a set of eyes very much like my own. Ace withdraws her fingers from mine, stepping to one side, allowing me a clear path to the boy beyond.

Along with ecstatic relief, the dread that's been growing inside since the day I left him behind a year ago blooms like the flora surrounding us.

"Hello, big brother," Kit says, his stance carved from stone. "It's been a long time."

SQUARE EIGHT

THE QUEEN

"'Well, now that we have seen each other,' said the Unicorn, 'if you'll believe in me, I'll believe in you.'"

— Lewis Carroll,
Through the Looking-Glass and What Alice Found There

ALICE

When Charlotte was still my big sister and not my aunt and the rightful Queen of Wonderland, seeing her again after the Spade Trial undid me. I clung to her and wept. I forgot any malice I'd had towards her for hiding the truth because I was so thankful she was alive.

This moment is not like that one.

An awkward silence between Chess and Kit turns into an excruciating minute of nothing said. The only emotion conveyed between the Shire brothers is one of . . . what, exactly?

Madi breaks the stillness, thank goodness. She comes over and drapes an arm around my neck. "Well, now that we're all together, I suppose we should regroup and discuss how we plan to make it out of here and onto the next square. First up, though, introductions. Alice, this is Knightley."

A young woman dressed entirely in form-fitting black extends a hand. She has auburn hair and a gaze so piercing it startles me at first. "Erin," she says.

"Knightley here isn't too fond of nicknames," Madi explains

after I've made the acquaintance. "But I'm on a mission to convince her otherwise."

I lean into my best friend and sister at heart. "I've missed you."

Madi gives me a quick squeeze. Then she gets to work, bossy as ever, instructing the others like the Nine she is. She sets up a fire at the clearing's centre and fashions oversized petals into sleeping shelters. I catch Jack's smile when he meets my eyes and embrace Sophia before Madi steals her away. Though I've never met him, one boy is both strange and familiar.

"Stark Hatter?"

"The very same."

I offer my hand. "Lovely to meet the Team Diamond King I've heard so much about."

He shifts his load of firewood to one arm and shakes my hand. "The feeling is mutual. You don't remember me, do you?"

That guilt of forgetting strikes anew. Walking through my mother's memories has helped some, but I still haven't recovered my childhood in Wonderland. Maybe I never will.

"You seem different," Stark comments.

I adjust my glasses. "Is that a bad thing?"

"I guess it depends on your point of view," he merely says and walks away, only to be met with more of Madi's barking orders. At the angle he kneels beside the now-crackling fire, I can see his face. While most older brothers might find a bossy sister a nuisance, Stark only grins as he stacks.

Thinking of siblings turns me back to Chess, who is determinedly following Kit deeper into the expanse of the garden, no doubt refusing to lose sight of his brother again.

What did I miss? I glance at my cousin, who has avoided the entire encounter from the shadows of a lilac thistle. He starts whistling.

I mirror Chess's march and close the distance between myself and Knave. "You know, just because Beast's Blend transforms you into a lion—"

"Easy now, A," he says. "I have no control whatsoever over my

Gene's reaction to the tea. Willow became that strange-looking vulture. You turned into a creature I didn't think existed. If my Wonder-ness makes me a lion, who am I to argue?"

He's being far too casual about all of this. "You think whatever's going on between Chess and Kit is funny?"

"No, actually, I don't." His demeanour shifts from satisfied to serious. "I thought seeing Shire getting exactly what he deserved would be rewarding, but . . ."

"But what?"

Knave sighs. "But it just made me feel sorry for him."

I emulate my best version of Madi, planting both hands on my hips like a cross mother might. "And?"

"And," he says, "I suppose I ought to go after them to see if I can be of assistance."

Relief flows through me. This is the kind and compassionate cousin everyone else rarely sees. But old habits die hard. It's easy to guess Knave's defences are up. Our team doesn't know him like I do, and he doesn't seem ready to show that side, let his guard down. Maybe he just needs a chance to process the reunion too.

"No," I say, resigned. "Give them some space. Perhaps they'll work it out once the shock wears off."

"Perhaps," Knave says.

"Care to fill me in on things in the meantime?" I try, guessing the answer before he gives it.

"Shire's story isn't mine to tell. It's his. The Trial took most of our memories when we left last year, but what we do remember?" He leans against the thistle stem, closing his eyes. He doesn't go on.

I'm both surprised and more than a little proud of him. After the anger and resentment Knave showed Chess during the Spade Trial, I'd expect him to say whatever he could to make Chess appear the villain. But he doesn't. Maybe the noble and kingly lion does fit his personality after all. Or, at the very least, he has the potential to grow into that role.

Still, I can't help but ask. "What you do remember? Chess

taking the credit for the almost-win?" I suggest. "Or when you couldn't show your face in Spade Quarter?"

"It's more than that, A." He opens his eyes. "I don't care about praise and glory." He mumbles something under his breath.

"What *do* you care about?" My question sounds so jaded, but I want to know.

"You," he says, fixing his dark eyes on mine. "Kit. Madi. The team. Wonderland. Maybe even Shire." I note that he chooses to name Madi, rather than group her in with the team. Curiously interesting.

"But, once again"—his voice is somewhat bitter now—"I am covering for the Team King. And, once again, I'm bearing the brunt of his mistakes." He pivots away in the opposite direction of Chess and Kit, leaving me alone.

Perfect. I've managed to push away Chess and my cousin in the span of a few minutes, and I am completely confused. I trudge over to join Willow and Sophia by the fire. Stacked stones ring the wood pile, and embers flicker beneath the already-dying flames. I find and toss a fresh log onto the lot, watching the way the base logs shift to make room for the added weight.

As I gaze at the flowers, Sophia gives my shoulder a quick squeeze, and we both look on while Willow makes some concoction out of pollen and multicoloured stems. It doesn't look edible in this state, but Willow's already proven she has a knack for turning a mediocre meal into a masterpiece. She's never said what her Mastery is, but I'd bet all the golden petals left in my malfunctioning WV that it's got something to do with cooking.

I sit cross-legged, drawing in the sand with one finger. No matter how reunited we may look in the physical sense, we remain divided. This Trial has changed us—*is* changing us. Some of that change is for the better.

The rest I'm not so sure about.

CHESS

I knew there would be no rest for me after coming face-to-face with the ghost of my past.

This part of the Garden Wood is thick. Tiny spikes break off stems as thick as tree trunks, impaling my clothes and skin. I pick them off one by one, scratching the itches they leave behind.

"Kit, it's not the time to go wandering off where no one can find you. Not when more snake vines could be lurking about."

"Someone did find me, but it wasn't you. You're too late."

I try to respond the way our mother would have. She always did have a softer approach, though maybe too soft. My brother needs me to understand him, but he also needs me to guide him. So I try to do both with what I say next.

"You're right. I am too late. But I'm here now. I haven't stopped looking for you since the day I lost you."

"You didn't lose me; you left me."

"Right again."

"So, you admit it then? That's not like you." The skeptic in him braves eye contact. "What's the catch?"

"No catch," I say, hands up in surrender. "I can't make up for my cowardice back then. I wish I could say I remember it all and apologise for each and every shortcoming. Yet I can't give you that either. I can only vow to do better now."

"Prove it," he says before striding past me and back towards the camp.

"I will!" I holler after him between cupped hands. I can't help but smile.

Challenge accepted.

Once I reenter the clearing, my eyes are immediately drawn to Ace. I ought to go and sit beside her, explain myself so we can start with a clean slate and get everything out in the open. But Ace isn't Kit. It was one thing to confess something my brother already knew. It's entirely another to tell Ace about my deal with Dinah and the quarter heads.

So I keep my distance, choosing a spot opposite to where she warms her hands over the fire.

She straightens when she sees me and smiles in a way that makes me want to kiss her again. She tilts her head to one side, a gesture that clearly says, *Come sit with me.* But I need to clear my head, organise my thoughts, and figure out how to begin. I feign a yawn.

Ace nods as if she understands, and I offer a half-smile apology accompanied by a shrug. The hurt in her eyes at my distance is unmistakable, but it's nothing compared to the hurt I know she will feel when she discovers all I've done. I stretch out on the ground, my back to her, and close my eyes.

Sleep eludes me. Something rustles then snaps, drawing my eyes to reluctantly open. I spot Knave who leans against a nearby flower-stem trunk.

"Blast it, Knave," I say for his ears alone. "Why didn't you just tell her?"

"That would be too easy, Shire." He's enjoying my agony far too much.

I don't blame him, but I flick a pebble at him anyway.

It soars towards his smug face. Just before it hits him square between the eyes, he vanishes, and Kit stands in his place. He's younger by a year and far less jaded. Terror drowns out any sign of childhood joy he once wore.

"Chess!" he cries. "Help me! Please! Don't leave. Come back! Chess! You promised!"

I don't hear whatever else he says. Anything that remains is distorted by the sound of snapping jaws and Kit's screams.

I bolt upright, drenched and out of breath. No matter how many times I face the nightmare, what took place leading up to that moment is never clear. I tick off the next few seconds as I wait for my pulse to slow. Insects chirp to the tune of a midnight breeze while the fire crackles lowly.

"Rough night?" I cock my head to find the real Knave staring down at me. He's bathed in moonlight and has some sort of purple fruit in his hand that he's tossing up and down, up and down. He takes a bite and juice drips down his chin, which he wipes with the sleeve of his black jacket.

"Now's not a good time." I comb splayed fingers through my hair.

"It never will be." Knave looks like he might chuck the fruit at my face. Instead he offers me the unbitten side.

I take it. It's overripe, but the taste is worth the mush, a mix between banana and cherry. "Thanks."

He hunkers down across from me, poking a stick at the fire then adding fresh kindling. "You want to talk about it?" This is a surprise. He made it perfectly clear during the Spade Trial he's held a grudge against me for some time.

Still, the opening seems genuine. So I take it. "What do you remember from the Heart Trial last year?"

Knave doesn't respond right away. Then, he says, "Look, Kit's alive. We're moving forwards as a team. We can drop the past."

I'd really like an answer to my questions, but I eye him. "You've changed."

"Yeah, well, A has that effect on people."

A? It dawns on me, and the knife of jealousy cuts deep. Since when does Knave have a nickname for Ace?

Knave knocks a fist to my knee. "Relax. Alice is my cousin." My jaw drops. Knave must take pity on me because he immediately gives me the rundown of his family tree from Queen Cordelia to Catherine R. Pillar to Charlotte to Ace.

"That's . . . incredible." It strikes me I'm talking to the crown prince. "Uh, do I bow or . . . ?"

"Bow to me even one time and you'll regret it."

He then says something my ears don't quite catch.

"Come again?"

"I said, 'You've changed too.'"

"How do you figure that one?"

"Kit told me what you said to him."

Ah. And on that note, "I suppose I owe you an apology as well."

Knave lifts a hand to stop me. "Don't go all soft on me now, Shire. Not when we still have a Jabberwock to slay."

While I appreciate his attempt to lighten the mood and let me off the hook, it doesn't change what happened. "I still want to know what I can't remember."

"Why don't you ask Kit?"

"I want to hear it from your perspective first."

He stares at the fire, and the light makes his eyes look as if they're full of flames. The image triggers a similar one in my memories, and I sit still, waiting for him to give some clue as to what took place that day.

"I remember running," Knave begins. "There was this scorching heat we couldn't escape. I actually came out with some pretty nasty burns afterwards." He rolls up his right trouser leg to his knee, then twists so I can see the back of his calf where the shadow of a scar as wide as my fist has yet to completely fade. "I don't know what started the fire, or where it came from, but it was beyond what even those dragon-flamingoes in the Diamond Trial could have conjured."

Concealing his scar once more, he goes on. "Kit was with us one minute, and then he'd somehow fallen behind. I realised then that you, our Team Spade King, had been delayed too, though I couldn't figure out why. You were alone when you rejoined us, in a panic. I'd never seen you so scared out of your mind. Truth is, it scared me. I had to practically drag you out with us."

A sound that's suspiciously close to a hiss rises from a nearby bramble bush, and we both go stark still, our eyes focused on where the noise originated. Ten seconds, twenty, thirty. Nothing.

Finally, Knave says, "Maybe we'd better call it a night. Get some shuteye. I'll keep watch and wake you in a couple of hours."

His tale wasn't all told, but I've heard enough to get a sense of why Knave's been distant. In his mind, my fear caused me to abandon Kit. And without Knave, I might not have made it out of the Trial in one piece.

He stands, and I lie back down on the sandy ground. There's no need for a "goodnight" nor a "thanks" nor a proper "see you on the morrow." A new understanding settles between us. And if we live to tell the tale of this year's Trials, I know exactly what I'm going to say to every Wonder who has ever made a joke at Knave's expense. Any idiot who so much as thinks the words "Sir Knave will take us to our grave" will wish they'd never crossed paths with me.

Except Sir Knave the Brave isn't quite right for him either.

I smile to myself as I let my lids fall closed. I can't help it.

Prince Knave the Brave will eventually forgive me for his new nickname, and I'm sure he'll find a way to repay me and make things square.

In fact, I'm counting on it.

ALICE

I dream of mayhem and monsters.

They never appear, but their snarls and growls keep me tossing and turning. They claw at the dark walls of my nightmare, desperate to be seen.

The scene shifts and brightens to a dim glow, transporting me to the cottage where I encountered the Jabberwock. I open my mouth to belt my unbelief, but nothing comes out. I grasp at my throat, as if this will help me find my voice. The attempt is futile. A set of talons smashes through the cottage window, snatches me up, and yanks me through. Shards of broken glass bite and scratch. Then the beast relinquishes its hold, dropping me into a dark abyss.

And I'm falling. Down, down, down through the simulation filled with bubbled memory trinkets. I continue my descent until a Jabberwock talon reaches from the darkness and pops each and every bubble. The trinkets plummet and crash, shattering into unsalvageable pieces on the floor of the Wabe. I tense and shield my face before the inevitable landing, only to shoot straight through the floor and come out the other side on two feet.

Chess struts towards me along a path in the wood, a full toothy grin accenting his natural swagger. The light cutting through the branches and leaves above hits him at just the right angle, shrouding half his face in shadow. My heart soars at the sight of him. He's more than the boy who charmed me. He's my confidant and best friend. He knows me better than anyone, and I trust him without question or reservation.

But, just as he nears to draw me into the embrace I long for, the light shifts, revealing the opposite side of his demeanour. It's like looking at an alternate, mirrored version of him. Where one side of his expression emits joy, the other side expresses a deep-seated pain. I avert my gaze, and the instant I do, I sense the absence of his presence. When I glance up once more, the space he occupied is empty.

And so am I.

My silent, gasping scream jerks me awake. I'm drenched in sweat. Our fire has died down to ash and embers. The rest of my teammates still sleep soundly, using giant-sized petals for blankets and huge, rolled-up leaves for pillows. My WV bangle lies dormant and lifeless in my rucksack. I could put it on and try to check the time, but there's no need. By my best guess, it's the middle of the night. Of course, with how time works here, that might change from one square to the next.

My heart seeks out Chess first. He rests on his side, too far away, crooked arm propped beneath his head and legs outstretched. I rise to a sitting position and find I'm blanketed with a silky rose petal, though I don't recall tucking myself in for the night. Did Chess cover me?

I see Kit next. He's slouched against a bowed daisy stem, head lolling to one side and mouth hanging open. At least we're all in one place, though I selfishly wish one of the Shire brothers would wake and explain themselves.

Now fully alert, I shift and reach for my rucksack, withdrawing the almanac and flipping to the chess section. I've perused it a few times now, turning it upside down and in a circle, squinting at the notes scrawled in the margins, attempting to sift what's useful from what isn't. As I've observed previously, some of the notes are penned by another hand that doesn't belong to Charlotte. Now that I've confirmed Raving is R.S.H., I compare his inscription to the unfamiliar annotations. Though the former was written in haste, his failure to dot his i's makes his latter, more orderly handwriting a definite match.

I ponder the clues Charlotte left behind in the audio diary that's revealed so much about Dinah's schemes and what happened to Wonderland. Especially Charlotte's last clue: *The palace is afraid.* I'm almost certain that means *Scarlet* is afraid. But of what I still don't know. It must be something within these eight Trials, otherwise she would brave them herself. For isn't that why we've come? To face our fears and defeat the Jabberwock?

Then there was the underlined code in the "The Crocodile" poem from before I left Oxford and found *hearts are wild.* It's truer than ever as I think of everything we've faced here thus far. This place, this Trial, truly is a wild beast even Scarlet hasn't been able to tame.

As I flip through the pages now, I'm careful not to rip them. Before, I was looking for Charlotte's handwriting. Now I search for anything and everything that matches Raving's. But my burst of midnight energy has ebbed, and I'm suddenly struggling to keep my eyes open.

Taking off my glasses, I set them on top of the open book in my lap. My blurred gaze wanders to a blurred Knave, who appears to sit awake and ready on a boulder at the edge of our camp.

I think I see him nod, but it could just be the astigmatism playing tricks on me. I offer a wave then shake myself awake and turn back to the task at hand, settling my glasses back in place.

The firelight has dimmed to the point I have to strain my eyes to read. It's times like this I miss the convenience of my pocketscreen or WV. Tech has its uses, and an electronic torch would be nice right now. Hmm. Maybe I'm onto something. It will only be for a little while. What could it hurt? I dig through my rucksack and retrieve my WV bangle, turning it over in my palm. I clasp it onto my wrist and hold my breath. *One, two, three* . . . I exhale when it lights up and the view I've grown so accustomed to settles over my eyes. I let my wish for a proper reading light capture my thoughts, and almost immediately, the bangle illuminates. My three Fates beat heart red, but the rest of the bangle is like a miniature ring lamp. Perfect.

I don't know how long I stay that way. Hunched over the almanac's words, scrutinising every missing dot I can find that points to Raving. It isn't until the hazy grey glow of morning filters in through the petals above that I realise I've been up all night.

Sophia is the first to wake, followed by Willow. They fumble around for a few minutes before Willow traipses up a path, no doubt in search of something she can forage for breakfast. I catch Sophia's eye as she yawns and wave her over, standing to greet her.

"Soph, have you seen this poem before?" I pass her the almanac, pointing out a page with a rhyme entitled "The Mad Gardener's Song."

She gives it a once-over. "Looks like nonsense to me."

"That's what I thought, too, but take a peek at this stanza." I scroll down the page with one finger, stopping at the eighth grouping of lines.

> *"He thought he saw a Garden-Door*
> *That opened with a key:*
> *He looked again, and found it was*
> *A Double Rule of Three:*
> *'And all its mystery,' he said,*
> *'Is clear as day to me!'"*

"What do you make of it?" Sophia asks after studying the verse. "Since we arrived in this Trial, I thought the goal was to make it out." *Face our fears. Slay the Jabberwock. Find the king.* "But what if we're not seeking a way out of the Trial?" I glance at Chess. He stirs but doesn't wake. I wish I could talk to him. "I think we're looking for a door," I say to Sophia, recalling the two shortcuts I've already found and the key that let me through. "I think we're looking for a way in."

CHESS

"You were supposed to wake me so we could trade." My complaint to Knave is only half-hearted. I raise my arms and stretch. Despite my stiff back, a few hours' sleep did the trick.

"Don't mention it, mate." He claps me on the shoulder once before joining the rest of our group.

It's the first time he's referred to me as his mate in over a year. I don't want to embarrass myself and act like I care too much. Because I absolutely care too much. First Stark and now Knave? I simply have to get Kit on board with the everyone-forgives-Chess-for-being-a-foul-git trend, and we're on our way to becoming Team of the Year.

If only things were that simple.

For now, there's another trend to hop on and it's one I don't mind in the slightest. Everyone's gathering around Ace, looking over her shoulder to take a gander at something she's perusing with Sophia. I come around the side of them both to get a better look.

"What's so interesting?" I say, doing my best to sound playful. I offer her a half grin, hoping to smooth things over from last night.

She does not return the smile. In fact, she doesn't even look up from the book that's apparently more interesting than I am. Instead, she steps back and says, "This almanac has been a key component to understanding the Trials on several levels." She holds up the red leather book Charlotte gave her. "The rightful Queen of Wonderland gave this to me, and Madi's eldest brother, Raving, gave it to her. Now that we're all reunited, I think it's time I caught you up."

The explanation she dives into next is quite the trip down a rabbit hole. Queen Scarlet is an imposter. Charlotte is the true Queen of Hearts. Knave is the son of Queen Cordelia and the rightful heir to England's throne.

All eyes turn to Knave at that tidbit. Knave tells them the same thing he told me last night.

"Bow or curtsy or call me Your Majesty, and you'll immediately regret it as the most imbecile decision you've ever made."

A few teammates grin over exchanged glances, but no one says a word otherwise. It's clear they're a tad amazed, just as I was.

Ace carries on about Catherine R. Pillar next and the clues she planted for her daughter to find.

"They're looking glasses or reflections," she says, "bits of memories my mother left as a trail that leads to the truth. There are eight in all and apparently only I can view what's inside. It's similar to Wonder Vision, but these simulations—or illusions, if you prefer—are coded to respond to my specific DNA makeup."

"How many of these memories have you seen so far?" Madi asks.

"Six. Which means two remain."

It's Jack who poses the next question. "What happens when you find them all?"

I can tell Ace is trying to steady her expression. This is all a mystery to her, too, and I can see she feels less than qualified to handle it.

So I jump in. "They make a riddle." All eyes shift to me, and I immediately realise why. I shouldn't know this. "I mean, it makes sense, right?" I shrug, trying to play it off as a guess. "Every Trial has had a problem or riddle or clue to solve. Why would this be any different?"

My reasoning isn't the best, but Ace seems to buy it. "Exactly," she says slowly, keeping her eyes on mine for a lingering moment before addressing the group as a whole. "As I was saying . . ."

The longer she talks, the more I perspire where I stand. When she reaches the part about Dinah's plot to overthrow Charlotte and replace her with a new queen, my head is spinning and I'm blanking, missing most of what she says next. So it takes a second to pick up on the fact that she's addressing me.

"Chess, did you hear what I said?"

Her blue eyes pierce and probe. "Come again?"

"I asked," Ace repeats patiently, "if there was anything you wanted to add about Dinah. You've been the closest to her. I'm sure it's difficult to know she betrayed you too."

I swallow. "Yes." I clear my throat. "What I mean to say . . ." Just get it over with. You've made it this far. "Yes," I say lamely, "it's difficult to hear my grandmother is not who she claimed to be." I really do deserve whatever wrath or end befalls me after this.

Kit obviously thinks so too because his glare hardens with each cowardly word I utter. I catch him mouthing something to me.

Prove it.

Once again, I've failed to do what I vowed.

"Here's what I've concluded." Ace's declaration puts my thoughts and the task at hand back on track. "Though Raving and Charlotte both left notes behind, those commentaries can only take us so far. I spent so much time searching for hidden meanings and clues written in between the lines and margins of the almanac that I failed to see the most important aspect."

She's brought us all to the edges of our nonexistent seats. If games weren't her specialty, she'd make a fantastic storyteller.

"The original author of the book is who really deserves our attention. My theory is . . ."

Were drums present, they would roll for all her dramatic

pausing. Her serious style is one of the things I like most about her, of course.

"This book"—she holds it up again for effect—"was written by the Ivory King. He left it behind for the right person to find. I've been looking at the almanac in sections, but every poem, every game listed, every story, every historical fact inside this book is part of the bigger picture. It all connects, not in parts but as one complete tale. Or, as I like to think of it, a map. And each coordinate points true north, also known as the real Wonderland."

Adjusting her glasses and tucking a stray wisp of hair behind her ear, Ace waits for our reaction. I'm in awe of her, as usual, so when no one else speaks, I do. "Brilliant."

Her bashful grin charms me. Ace's mere presence makes me feel as if I could conquer anything—including, but not limited to, myself. Next time I can steal her away, I'll lay everything out and allow the cards to fall where they will. It's a risk I must take.

For her I'd risk Wonderland.

With all eyes fixed on our Team Queen, Ace takes her cue and begins to read. The poem is about a garden door. Where have I heard those words before?

"What does it mean?" Willow's query is directed at Sophia.

Though Soph is our resident expert on all things flora, her expression shows she's as stumped as most of us.

But not all of us.

Ace looks at me then. "To go out . . ." she begins.

"You must first go in," I complete for her. Of course. I knew I'd heard the poem. "The double rule of three is mathematical," I explain. "Something Catherine R. Pillar undoubtedly well understood."

"Great." Madi tosses her hands in the air. "A math lesson. Just what we needed."

"But," I inform her, "it's also a term used for an old card game." I nod to Ace. This is her area of expertise. She can take it from here.

"Not only does this poem share a page with the rules for

THE LOOKING-GLASS ILLUSION 223

Palace," Ace says, "but it seems the eighth stanza in particular is a clue in correlation to the eight smaller Trials within the larger one." She passes the journal around so we can each take a closer look.

When the book reaches me, I read the stanza twice, then review the rules of the game it's connected to. A glimmer of memory comes to mind of when Ace and I spent days holed up in an East End London house after the Diamond Trial, laughing and playing Palace and wishing life could simply stay that way forever.

Unfortunately, dabbling in complications tends to be my specialty.

"Palace is played in sets of three," Ace is explaining. "Play begins with three cards face down in front of you, three face up, and three in your hand."

"Wouldn't that be a triple rule of three?" Jack asks. "You know, nine cards?"

Ace flashes him a smile. "Great point. But you only *see* six of those cards—double three."

"But nine total," Madi persists. "There are nine of us . . ."

"Ten, actually." Knightley raises a hand. There's something in her expression that says she's used to being forgotten. "But who's counting?" Madi looks a little abashed.

"Don't forget about the draw pile. That counts as ten." The suggestion comes from Stark, who winks at Erin. Though he's barely eighteen, and she's several years older, I can instantly tell he sees age as only a number.

"Ten then." Knightley agrees.

Ace continues, "The six visible cards count as those who will move forwards. The three face-down cards plus the draw pile represent those who will stay behind."

"How are we supposed to choose which four?" Sophia asks.

"And how can we be sure this clue applies to this square?"

In the past, I would have heard Knave's question as a challenge, full of skepticism and doubt. But his concern is warranted. How *can* we be sure?

"We can't." Ace doesn't miss a beat. "But the poem is called 'The Mad Gardener's Song,' and this wood is like one tremendous mad garden. The snake vines that tried to kill us are proof enough, and I don't intend to wait around for whatever else this place has lurking about, ready to pounce or snap or bite. Splitting up is not ideal, but it can be a good strategy, which is something the game of chess relies on. If those of us who journey deeper into the wood don't come out, the others can move on and still have a chance at making it to the end. We were brought back together here once. I have faith it will happen again."

"So we play by the rules of the game set before us," I add. "Simple as that."

Kit shakes his head. "Normally I'm all for taking risks, but leaving something like this to chance seems irresponsible. We should think this through more and see if there's an alternative plan."

"I disagree," I say swiftly. "Ace hasn't steered us wrong before. I trust her. You should too," I reprimand before I can stop myself, then I hold up a hand and start over. "I agree with Ace that we have to split up, but Kit has a point as well." Hopefully this compromise will help make amends.

"Enough arguing," Knave declares, pushing off from the stem trunk on which he was leaning. "We can't keep standing around, waiting for a better solution." He drops his things to the ground. "So I'll be the first to decide. I'm the strongest, so it's only natural I should stay behind."

"Or it's only natural you move forwards," Ace counters.

"Be that as it may"—Knave's jaw is set—"I'm staying. One down. Three to go."

"I'll stay," Sophia says. "I can navigate the Garden Wood more easily than anyone else, so if there's another way out, I'll find it."

"Well, if you're staying, so am I," Willow says, her tone begrudging. "Now you have three. Only one left."

I can see the conflict in Ace's eyes. "Willow," she says carefully, "I need you with us. If anything should happen to me, it will be up to you to take my place."

Willow opens her mouth to protest, but Sophia touches her arm. "Alice is right."

Willow pauses, then nods as Sophia joins Knave.

"I'll be three," Erin says. "I'd like to stay and find my horse. She's the closest thing I have to family."

Which still leaves one. I look between Ace and Kit. I could keep quiet, let someone else stay behind so I can keep close to the two people I care about most. All eyes are on me, waiting to see what I will do. Waiting to see if I will make the right move.

The move of the king I'm supposed to be playing.

"I'll stay," Kit says. He eyes me in challenge, daring me to protest. No matter what I do, I'll look like I'm making a selfish decision.

We stare at each other a long time, then I nod and watch him take his place beside Knave, Sophia, and Knightley.

"The four of us will continue on the path," Sophia says. "Any idea where this garden door is?" She points to the almanac.

"I don't know if it's a door in the literal sense," Ace replies. "But I do know we need to explore the wood deeper rather than try to escape. I think our next clue will wait at the heart of this place, and hopefully we'll meet you at the next square before another day has passed. If the door leads to a shortcut, it may even put us slightly ahead. If that's the case, we'll wait for you, of course."

We bid our goodbyes, and I watch as Knave gives Ace a brief hug. If he hadn't explained how they're related, I might not be handling it so well. I'm actually sad to see him go, surprised when he approaches me next.

"Keep her safe." He extends a hand.

I shake it firmly. "I wouldn't have it any other way."

We part then, the crew of four heading towards the edge of the wood, along the sandy pink path, while our half-dozen remains in the clearing.

Ace, Stark, Willow, Madi, Jack, and me.

I cast one final glance in Kit's direction.

As if mirroring my final move in the Heart Trial last year, my brother does not look back.

ALICE

"It's settled then." I stow the almanac away and look at each of my remaining teammates in turn. None of us knows what to expect next, but we all agree we'll face it together. "With the previous shortcuts I've come across, maybe when we find this door it will let us skip to the Eighth Square. If not, the others will have to go on without us."

We abandon our temporary camp and trek through the Garden Wood, veering off the path and braving the wild tangles of vines and petals. I have the slightest bit of Beast's Blend left, though I'd prefer not to finish it. I still haven't asked Madi about the tea I used on Willow. Could she have more stashed in her utility belt?

Jack and Madi chat casually several paces behind me. I glance at my oldest friend and notice the way she blushes when Jack gives her a playful elbow to the side or brushes his arm against hers. They look content. Happy. As if they haven't a care in all of Wonderland and this is simply another Trial season.

I honestly wish that's all it was.

My thoughts drift to the moment before Knave and the others

left. He probably didn't think anyone saw the sharp look he sent
Jack's way. It lasted only a moment, dissipating quickly, replaced
with an expression of admiration for the girl with the wild
lavender locks.

It's funny, really. They're such opposites. Knave, the quiet and
brooding secret crown prince of England. Madi, the bubbly and
colourful podcaster with as many sides to her personality as there
are tea blends.

I do like Jack, but even Madi once said of Knave, *"Not your
classic type of handsome, but there's something about him . . ."*

There is something about Knave that makes you want to peel
back his layers. An unbidden tear pricks my eye. I hope I see my
cousin again.

I take a deep breath and shake off the nip of fear.

Now Chess takes up the rear of our human train. I still don't
understand what happened between him and Kit last night, and I
want to ask him about the revelations regarding Dinah.

As if sensing my wish, he suddenly appears beside me. "Hey,
Ace." His greeting is cautious. He keeps his hands in his trouser
pockets rather than intertwining his fingers with mine.

Apparently my insecurities are far from gone. I'm the Team
Queen, and instead of calculating strategies and thinking one step
ahead, I'm wondering why my—why *Chess*—won't hold my hand.
Ridiculous.

We have to move past this. "Hi," I reply. This new chasm
between us feels wide, and I'm not sure how to build the bridge.
"I'm sorry you had to separate from Kit again. I'm sure that must
have been difficult."

He nods at the ground.

"Do you want to talk about it?"

"Not particularly." His words come out slow and unsure, very
un-Chess-like.

I prod further. "Don't you want to know how I found him?
Don't you have any questions whatsoever?"

A twig snaps beneath his boot. He flips his head to get his

hair out of his eyes. "Go on then, Ace." He smiles but it falls short, though I know he's prowling around in there somewhere, like a cat lurking behind a locked door. "How *did* you find my brother?" I link my arm through his. "I thought you'd never ask." Keeping close as we walk, I tell him everything. About the crossroads, and Willow and Sophia versus the mome raths, and Kit, and the Wabe, and the E.G.G.

He listens intently, nodding along or offering an "mmm-hmm" here and there.

My arm falls to my side as we continue straight on. I do my best to keep my voice low, just between us. I want the real Chess Shire back. "What's wrong with you?"

His eyes meet mine. It's about time. "What do you mean?"

"Don't play dumb with me, Chess Shire. You know *exactectlee* what I mean." My words tumble out so quickly I revert to using a nonsense word from my childhood.

When he doesn't confess, I press on. "What I want to know is what *you* mean by the way you're behaving? Your brother is alive. We're together. We're closer than ever to finding the real Wonderland. What more could you possibly want?"

His eyes narrow, and I almost think I see a spark of the Chess I encountered back in London's Hyde Park. All he says is, "I didn't get much sleep last night." But his tone lets on to some of what's brewing behind those turquoise eyes. I know it's not mere exhaustion causing his internal storm.

I pose the question I've been dying to ask. "Did you know about Dinah?"

He slows his pace and doesn't respond right away. At least he doesn't outright deny it.

Finally he takes a measured breath. "Ace, I didn't lie to you that day, in the Diamond Trial timeout. I really didn't know Dinah reported Charlotte to the Normal authorities. I honestly didn't think the woman could be so conniving."

"What did you know?"

"I knew she was close with the quarter heads. That they

look to her for council. She's one of the oldest Wonders around, practically a legend, and the quarter heads—the Minister of Spades in particular—want something, though I'm not sure—"

A little gasp escapes me. I put a hand on his arm and stop walking. "Say that again."

"Which part?"

"The part about Dinah being one of the oldest Wonders around. A legend."

Something like understanding dawns in his expression. We lock eyes. He knows what I know, and we both know it, and how didn't we know it before? We've been standing on our heads, and now we're right side up.

"Care to fill us in, you two?" Stark and the others walk directly behind us now.

Chess and I look at one another and say exactly what the other has realised. "Dinah is the bride from the Ivory King's story," I whisper at the same time Chess nearly shouts, "The tale wasn't about Scarlet!"

The sun has finally made an official appearance, and the garden floor blooms into a canvas of watercolours as light filters through a variety of petals above. Pink and yellow and blue and violet. Chess reaches for my hand, and I grab tight to his. Together we turn to the stunned faces of our teammates.

This changes everything.

I'm frantic, flipping through the almanac's pages. It has to be in here. "Why isn't it in here?"

Chess gently draws the book out of my hands. "Let me look."

I need to pace but there's no room. If I go too far left, I'll be greeted by an ornery thorn bush, and if I move too far right, I'll run straight into a tangle of ivy. Although, thankfully, whatever Sophia said or did yesterday has led the wood to leave us alone since.

"Are you certain the story Dinah told you both is in there?" Willow's doubt drenches her tone.

"I thought it was." Removing my glasses, I wipe the lenses over and over. They're the cleanest they've been in a while when I put them back on. But no. There's a smudge. I'd better clean them again.

"Let me have a go." Madi takes the almanac next, scanning and searching with Jack peering over her shoulder.

Chess pulls me aside, allowing the others their respective turns with the book. He takes my glasses out of my jittery hands, then slips the frames onto the top of my head.

"I can't see that way," I protest.

He's blurred and out of focus, but I can see his hand coming towards my face. I almost swat him away, but he moves slowly. Then, with the greatest care, he touches a thumb and finger to my eyelids and gently nudges them closed.

"What do you see now?" He says the words low and soft enough so only I can hear.

"Still nothing," I reply, though I can already tell whatever trick he's pulled out of his invisible hat is working. My heartbeat has slowed, and my breaths come easier.

"Now," Chess says, placing his hands firmly on my shoulders. "Think about this for a moment. You know Dinah's story by heart. You shared it with our team in the Tulgey Wood before we abandoned the Club Trial."

He's right. But still . . . "I need to see it. What if I've forgotten something important?"

"If you've forgotten it"—Chess is so close I can feel his breath on my forehead—"then I'd say it's rather unimportant." He kisses the skin above my brow before sliding my glasses off my head and down over my nose where they belong.

I open my eyes.

My mouth forms an *O*.

Chess smirks in response. "See? You just needed to clear your head, and—"

"It isn't that." I step around him. How could we have missed it?

A door made of pure gold stands just steps away. Unlike the doors at the Foundling House and cottage, this entrance doesn't seem to be attached to anything. In fact, I see now why it was easy to miss. If I move a smidge to one side or the other, the door appears to vanish. It's clearly some sort of illusion, though not of the simulation variety. The gold is simply paper thin, but even then, it isn't exactly solid.

The closer I examine it, the sooner I decide it's not a door at all, but a gate. Cutout designs of climbing, blooming roses caused it to blend in with its surroundings. The light hits the gold just right, and it glimmers, nearly blinding anyone who might look at it for any length of time.

The others flock around me. "Cool trick," Jack says, admiring the gem-like apparition before us.

"Do you think this is the garden door from the poem?" Stark hands the almanac back to me. "The story you speak of isn't in there, and I've never heard of it." He quirks an eyebrow at Chess. "You said Dinah told you it was a children's story, Shire."

Chess nods.

"Your mom ever tell you a story like that?"

Pressing his lips, Chess gives a slow shake of his head.

"Mine didn't either," Stark says. "If it isn't a Wonder story and it isn't in that book, did Dinah make it up?"

"If it's about her, she must have," Madi muses.

It's the only explanation, but all thoughts of Dinah must be put on hold. Now we have nothing left to do but try the gate.

"Locked," I inform my team with disappointment. Did I expect anything to the contrary?

"Shall we try knocking?" Jack offers.

"Couldn't hurt." I rap my knuckles on a metal carving of a golden rose, one, two, three times. I'm prepared to pull out my locket watch and play the song that's worked on the previous two shortcuts, but this door is not the same, and I'm curious to see if this situation might unfold differently, so I wait.

After a pause, something sounds behind the door. Not footsteps moving like one might expect, though. Instead, there's a rustle and a hiss.

Chess hears it too. Before I know what's happening, he extends an arm in front of me and shoves me back. Stark and Jack do the same with Madi and Willow, acting like human shields.

"Quiet," a hushed and muffled voice says.

"You be quiet, Calla. I'm the one in charge here."

"Like thorns you are, Bud."

"I told you to stop calling me that," the other voice whines.

The gate opens a notch, and two small blossoms peek through. Chess lowers his arm, letting me by.

It's a strange sight to see flowers with mouths and eyes. Maybe we should have kept Sophia with us after all.

"Who are you?" The smaller of the two, a rosebud, asks.

"I'm Alice," I explain. "And this is my team, Chess—"

"No, no, no," the other flower, a calla lily, interrupts. "What Bud means is *what* are you? What genus?"

"I'm sorry? I'm afraid I don't understand."

"Are you flora or fauna?" Calla asks.

"We are neither," Madi says with full confidence in her tone. "We are *Genus humanus.*"

I try to keep from giggling. Surely she made that one up.

The flowers whisper to one another. That would explain the hissing we heard before. Then Calla nods. "Do you have a key?"

I move my hand towards my locket, but Willow's irritated question stops me.

"Why do we need a key? You can open the gate just fine."

"Oh, no!" Bud exclaims. "We can't. We've been specifically instructed only to let those with a key pass. So, do you have one?"

Slightly bemused, I withdraw the silver chain and reveal my locket watch. I open it, twist the knob on the side, and let the miniature music box play. "Will this do?" I ask, stifling an unexpected yawn. The tune is making me slightly sleepy.

"What's that?" Bud asks suspiciously.

Puzzled, I kneel and give him a closer look. "You've never

seen a watch before?" Strange. This worked at the other doors. Why would–?

"I don't know what petal you're trying to pull," Calla huffs, "but that is not a key." She starts to draw back and shut the gate. Part of me thinks we ought to ram our way through, overpowering the little blossoms. But the other part knows better. This shortcut quite possibly holds my mother's next clue. And where there is a clue, there is always something else lurking in the shadows, whether it be the Jabberwock's claws or confusing memories I'm meant to untangle.

Whatever it is, it will not be as harmless as a pair of kid flowers. We have to follow the rules.

New plan. "Can you tell us what the key looks like?" I venture.

The flowers exchange a glance. "You mean, like a clue?" Calla says.

"Yes," I say, smiling. "Just like a clue."

"The other *humanus* who came years ago mentioned a clue too," Bud tells us. "But we weren't planted yet."

"But we've heard stories about her," Calla says, sounding snobbish. "White petals and pollen like yours." She reaches out a leafy stem and pats my hair. "She had these strange things on her face too."

My heart soars. She's referring to my mother, I'm almost certain. Glasses and hair like mine and white petals–perhaps a lab coat? It has to be Catherine R. Pillar.

"Well, why not give us the clue she was given?" I try.

"Oh, no one gave her a clue," Bud clarifies. "She left one behind."

Another looking-glass memory? "Can I see it?" I ask quickly.

"Not without a key." Bud's voice is almost sing-song.

This is getting us nowhere.

"Is there any other way through?"

"Only flowers allowed," Calla states. "All other genera are simply too wild for our garden."

Flower. Wild.

Wildflower!

"I'm a Wildflower!" I blurt, jumping up and nearly trampling the gatekeepers in my excitement.

"You said you were a *Genus humanus.*" Calla looks accusingly at Madi.

"That's true," I agree. "But I'm also a Wildflower."

"Prove it," Bud challenges.

Chess shifts uncomfortably beside me.

I ignore him. "Can you read?"

"Of course we can read." Calla scoffs. "Do we look uneducated to you?"

I'm learning a lot of things about the flowers. Sophia and Blanche-Rabekah were right. I find my invitation to the Trials, a playing card bearing the Royal Seal of Wonderland, tucked between the pages of the almanac. I offer it to the pair of blossoms.

Please accept this cordial invitation to participate in this year's annual Wonderland Trials as a Wildflower player for Team Heart . . .

"Well, I'll be," Bud says in awe. "She is a Wildflower."

"I don't know if this counts." Calla eyes the invitation skeptically.

"Let's let Mother decide," Bud says.

Calla pauses. "Yes," she agrees, then smiles a little too sweetly. "What a fine idea. We'll let Mother decide." She opens the door and allows us to pass. One step closer to the next square and joining the others.

So why do I feel as if we're walking straight into a trap?

CHESS

I don't like this one bit.

As a child, I was known for my ability to sniff out foul play. Grandmother called it quick instincts.

"It's the reason we become cats when given Beast's Blend. We're clever. Fast on our feet and sharp in our minds."

Now, as we walk deeper into the inner garden past the gilded gate, my catlike instincts kick in. "Ace," I say aside to her. "This doesn't feel right."

"I agree," she says, squeezing my hand. "But we have to stop avoiding what doesn't feel right. We must face it head on. If we stand scared on the spot, how will we ever make it to the Eighth Square?"

She has a point, but I keep my eyes and ears alert. I don't buy the inviting façade of our surroundings for a minute.

The path has turned from pink to purple as we weave past an onslaught of blossoms. The rainbow of hues is blinding.

"Soph is going to be sorry she missed this," Willow observes.

"Or she'll be grateful," Stark comments, ever the blunt one.

I glance back to check on Madi and Jack. They've been so quiet since we separated from the others. Jack has an arm around Madi, and he seems to be comforting her.

What happened? I mouth to Jack when I catch his attention.

He juts his chin pointedly as if to say, *Not now.*

I face forwards again a little dismayed. If something's got Madi down and Jack stern, we're really being tested.

The path finally winds through archways wrapped in vines and ivy which, thankfully, appear harmless. Soon we find ourselves in a wide-open courtyard. Steps lead to an elaborate vase up ahead, as tiered planters, overflowing with every colour imaginable and unimaginable, rise to our left and right. At first it seems we're alone, but then Bud and Calla scurry on their tiny stems to the vase. No, not a vase. It's only then I comprehend what this place really is.

A throne room.

The details blossom before us. Chandeliers made of vines and thorns with yellow bulbs on their ends. The bulbs encase glowing fireflies. The tiers hold chattering flowers of every species. And at the base of the steps, which I now see is a dais, two flowers converse in soft tones. On the left, a white calla lily, and on the right, a red rose.

"Welcome to the living garden," the lily says regally. "I am Lily, the White Queen of the Northern Garden."

"And I am Rose," the one beside her says. "The Red Queen of the Southern Garden."

Ace curtsies, and I don't know whether to laugh or follow suit and bow.

"Your Majesties," Ace replies in return. "I am Alice, Queen of Team Heart and Wildflower from the Normal Reality."

A few flowers in the audience snicker. I've seen plenty of absurd sights in Wonderland. Impossible scenes created by the minds of extraordinary Wonders. But this is different, because this scene of talking flowers appears to simply be here. Not created by a Wonder's mind. It's as if these flowers are Wonders too. Another checkpoint? A riddle to solve or a game to play?

I look around. If this is a checkpoint, there's no going back now.

"Silence." Queen Rose hushes the garden with a single word.

Queen Lily nods, pleased, as if she were the one to do the silencing.

"Now then," Rose says, addressing Ace. "What is this business about you being a wildflower?" She looks down her petals at Bud and Calla, then glares at each of us in turn.

"Well, you see, it all started when—"

"I've heard enough," Queen Lily interrupts. "Have you seen her petals?" She whispers loud enough for everyone to hear. "Looks more like a common weed to me."

More snickering rises from the garden. I move to speak in Ace's defence, but she stops me with a single look.

"I say let the girl speak," a male voice says. A new rose appears. Or maybe he's been in the background all along. Either way, he's impossible to miss now for his rooted sturdiness and gracious strength.

"This doesn't concern you, Crim," Lily tells him.

"Shouldn't it?" the rose who is Crim replies. "I am, after all, the Garden King."

A hush falls over the garden, different from the one that occurred mere moments before. This hush is not one of fear, but of reverence and awe.

"Now then, if you'll forgive my daughters," the king apologises, "who are—may I remind them—princesses and *not* queens—I would like to welcome you to our garden court, Queen Alice." The king bows. When he rises, he makes eye contact with each of us, inclining his head to Ace.

It takes a moment to catch on, but then Madi bows. Ah, that's the ticket! The rest of us bow to Ace in turn.

"Oh, that's really not necessary," Ace protests, her cheeks flushed.

"I believe," the king says firmly, "you are mistaken. I have merely been given rule over this garden. I am its keeper, its protector. It's written directly into my code, you see."

Code. So this is a checkpoint.

"No Wonder has come this far in the eight squares for many years," Crim states. "Not since the woman who left something behind. Something she believed her very own daughter would turn up to find."

I sense Ace start beside me. It's not difficult to determine he's talking about Catherine and her daughter. But something strikes me about this strange encounter. Crim is too welcoming. Too . . . accommodating. If this is a checkpoint, there's a certain order to things. Like on the train or at the chessboard barn.

"That woman came looking for Wonderland too. She came seeking the Ivory King."

"Where is Wonderland?" Ace asks eagerly. "How do we find it?"

Crim laughs, petals shaking. "Haven't you guessed by now, young friend? It's here. You're standing in it."

We take a moment to let the notion sink in.

"But . . . " Ace falters. "But we haven't reached the Eighth Square."

I hear it in her voice and in her sudden shuddering breath. She's fighting back tears, trying not to let her emotions get the best of her.

"Oh, but you have, my dear," Crim says with a fragrant smile. "The gate was the shortcut. This is the Eighth Square. This is Wonderland. Or the entrance to it."

I reach out and take Ace's hand. For a brief moment, relief washes over me. But that relief is quickly replaced by reason. Ace holds fast to my grip, and I know she's realised it as well.

We're being lied to.

Whatever this checkpoint holds is far worse than we feared.

The Rose King eyes me as if he knows my thoughts, then he directs his attention back to Ace.

"Your mother sought to uncover the truth. And here is where she found it."

Ace doesn't contradict, nor does she stand up to this deceiver and demand we be allowed to pass. She's far too clever for that, of course.

"Well then." She lifts her chin. "If this is the entrance to the real Wonderland, by all means"—her words are steady as stone— "show us the way."

ALICE

Breathe. Just breathe.

My natural ability to keep a straight face kicks in. This is no different than playing a game of cards. I can't let this farce king know I have the advantage here. And I'd bet a hand full of aces this Red Rose King is somehow connected to Scarlet.

Which means he's connected to Dinah.

I take a step forwards. "Go on, Your Majesty. We're ready."

"Of course, of course," the Rose King says. "But first it would be better for you to freshen up. Please, make yourselves comfortable. You are Wonderland's most honoured guests." He bows.

I cast a side glance at Chess. He eyes me with the same look. When we're alone, without petals prying from double-edged stems, we'll fill the rest of the team in too.

"We are most obliged," I tell the king, offering a curtsy. "And we're more than willing to wait while we gladly accept your hospitality."

"Wonderful," Crim says. "My servants will attend to you and usher you to the garden beds."

Two buttercups rush from behind the vase throne. "This way," the smaller, more-crooked one says.

"Yes, indeed. Right this way," the second, straighter-stemmed flower echoes.

We follow them out of the throne room and through a side arch boasting lush ivy and vine. While the feeling of being outdoors is prominent, the further we walk, the more I'm certain this is the garden of my recurring dream. Was I seeing into the real Wonderland then? Or was it a memory trying to tell me something?

When we at last reach the end of the long floral corridor, we're led through another ivy arch and into a glorious greenhouse room, filled with four-poster trellis beds. The posts are fashioned from thick, twisted stems, and swathed across each bed from poster to poster, the loveliest purple flowers hang like drapes.

"This will be your room," the smaller buttercup informs us. "We will come for you before the king's banquet begins. You'll find everything you need in the wardrobes to prepare for this evening."

They take their leave, tittering all the way.

Once they're out of earshot, Madi plops down on one of the beds. "Does anyone else feel like we're being duped?"

I nod, pondering our next move. I may be Team Queen, but I have no experience with this particular predicament. "Chess," I say, "do you remember anything from last year? Anything at all that could help us?"

He shakes his head. "I only recall the moment right before the Trial ended. Everything else is a mystery."

He doesn't say more. I know he's keeping something from me, but somehow I trust Chess will tell me when he's ready.

I hope he will.

"So what then? Are we supposed to sit idly by until someone calls for us?" Willow's sour expression matches her tone.

"Contrariwise," I say. "We're going to go along with it."

"Which means . . . ?" Stark draws out the question.

"If whoever's behind this thinks they can fool us, well, we'll

just have to fool them. So naturally we're going with Sophia's
advice on this one."

"But Soph isn't here," Willow reminds me.

"Yes, she is." I put a hand to my heart then tap my temple as I
smile at each of them intentionally.

"We can learn a lot of things from the flowers," I remark
casually. "My mother must have thought so too."

Sparks light my teammate's eyes.

I head for the archway exit and they follow.

Time to find Catherine R. Pillar's next clue.

Oddly enough, I never did well in science class. My mother may
have been a renowned genome researcher, but that particular
gene she did not pass on to me. Still, I think other traits of
mine must be from her. Curiosity, for example. How else does a
researcher . . . well . . . research?

We pad quietly through the halls of the garden palace. Each
corridor is reminiscent of a rosebush, branching off here and
cutting us off there.

Jack surveys the area. "It's like a labyrinth."

"Except a labyrinth has an end," Madi replies.

"No," I say. "Not an end, a centre."

"Well," Jack comments. "The throne room is clearly the centre."

When we happen upon a circular room that branches off in
three different directions, I stop and face my team. "Should we
split up?"

"Is that wise?" Willow has truly suffered the most in these
partings. "To split up and then split up again?"

"Staying together isn't getting us anywhere," Chess counters.
"Think of what Ace told us about the mirrors. We're looking for
a reflection of some sort. A looking glass, an out-of-place puddle,
a dew drop."

"And what do we do if we find one?" Madi asks. "Alice is the only one who can go through."

Willow nods. "Madi has a point."

"We meet back here," Chess says. "Keep track of your turns. We'll pair off in twos. One person at a time walks up a corridor, and when you reach a corner, your partner will meet you. Then you walk to the next corner while your partner waits, and so on."

I'm thankful Chess seems to have a plan since mine was simply to wander around until someone found something. Not my most brilliant idea.

"Jack and Madi can take this hall." Chess gestures to the one nearest Madi. "Stark and Willow will walk the left one, and Ace and I will take the middle."

Willow looks less than amused. "It seems rather convenient to *couple* us off that way, Shire."

Her emphasized word does not go unnoticed, but now that I think of it, Chess and I are supposed to be leading and Stark's also a Team King. Two leaders together could mean two leaders lost together. Perhaps we ought to—

"Lay off, Willow." Chess's pointed retort startles me. "You don't know what you're talking about." He glares.

I blink. Doesn't she? "Perhaps Willow is right," I say, standing a centimetre taller. I could cry but I won't. What did he mean? We may not be a couple, but we're surely something more than teammates. I clear the lump in my throat. "Maybe we should rearrange our arrangements."

I give no further suggestions, swiftly grabbing Madi's hand to drag her down the centre corridor. Let Chess deal with divvying the others up.

"Alice," Madi says, tugging on my hand. "*Alice.*" She yanks her hand from my grasp and comes to a halt. "Alice!"

I whirl on her, directing my hurt and anger at the person who least deserves it. Hurt and anger at Charlotte for not being here. At Chess for making me care but confusing me when things grow too serious. At my mother for leaving in search of Wonderland rather than staying with me.

"What, Madi?" I fume. "What is so important right now that you'd risk alerting every flower guard as to our location?"

I expect her to want to talk about what just occurred. To try and comfort me or stand up for Chess or suggest we go. Instead she says, "Listen."

My mood isn't much for stopping and waiting, but I do as she says. The rush of blood slows. The pulse in my ears fades as the pounding in my chest reaches its natural rhythm. A distinct sound remains. One so small and weak and fragile, it's almost inaudible.

"Is that—" I break off.

"It is," Madi responds. "Someone is singing."

It's a sad tune, and I can't quite make out the lyrics. We move farther, our paces quickening, our strides syncing.

When at last we reach a curtain of red flowers on blue vines that has an odd resemblance to bleeding tears, we hesitate. Beyond the vines, a waterfall awaits. Whoever sings on the other side of this curtain is most likely the answer to our questions. Madi offers a solemn nod, and I return it by holding fast to her hand.

We step through the vines as one, swallowed by the familiar silver liquid of a looking glass beyond.

Another clue left behind by my mother. She's been here.

Now we're going to find out why.

CHESS

"This is absurd. Why must girls always jump to conclusions?" I storm down a spiral staircase, Stark at my heels. He doesn't answer, opting to either ignore me or silently endure my heated frustrations. He wasn't supposed to follow me at all. Two Team Kings getting themselves lost. Brilliant.

Our footsteps echo against stone. The stairs remind me of a garden path, lined with all sorts of flowers I can't name. At the bottom, the stone levels out into a rounded room, the curving wall interrupted by four, saucer-sized windows.

Stark peers out the closest opening.

"What do you see, mate?"

"Look for yourself," Stark says.

I step up to the window nearest his. No pane of glass obscures my view, but if I wanted to escape, the circular opening isn't nearly wide enough to fit more than my head.

Beyond the stone, I see this Trial. The bishop-shaped keep in the distance. The rolling chessboard fields and hills. I can even make out the time-loop train to nowhere, steam rising from its engine. As far as my eyes can see, a stormy sky, broken by cracks of lightning, brews trouble. But the weather flashing its warnings is the least of my concerns. It's what's swirling around those ominous clouds that has me shuddering where I stand.

"Are you seeing this?"

"I see it," Stark says.

"Did you have any idea?"

"Not a clue."

I turn and slide my back down the cold stone to sit with knees bent. One Jabberwock to defeat was plenty, even if we didn't know exactly what it was, but the number of beasts soaring through the air now? There must be dozens, each one more terrifying than the next.

"This is far worse than we feared," I say quietly.

Stark crouches beside me. "Our fear is the problem."

I face him. "All right, Hatter. Let's hear it. I know you've got a theory swirling around in that thick head of yours." I fling my hand towards the windows above.

"I don't know how it was for you, Shire, but in Team Diamond training we were taught one thing—the only thing anyone would tell us about the Heart Trial."

"The Jabberwock takes on the form of what you most fear," we chant together.

"I haven't seen anything like that play out since we've been here, have you?" Stark says. "I don't believe it—they—take on different forms based on fear. I think our fear is what creates them, breeds them. Essentially, we *are* them. Every Wonder is. It's why no one reaches the real Wonderland. Because we're afraid of what we might find. We're afraid of the truth, and it's more comfortable to keep living the lie."

His words make sense, and I'm kicking myself for not seeing it sooner.

"How did you come up with this?" I ask curiously.

He rocks back on his haunches. "I had a lot of time coming in and out of consciousness during my extended train ride to think. And," he adds, "I saw you."

A strange ache squeezes my sternum, as if preparing me for what he's about to say next.

"Much of it's a blur," Stark begins. "This place'll do that to you." He pauses a moment. It's in that brief space of time I know. However awful it was for Stark, it was just as bad for Kit.

"I saw everything from the train window," he says. "It had looped around to where we'd entered—the First Square. I couldn't disembark the checkpoint, but I could see clearly the Gateway. Do you know . . . did the other Diamonds make it out? Was I the only one to go missing?"

"Yes," I assure him. "Back home, you're a hero. At least that's what the scores showed. Most points earned by one player in a single Trial all season."

Stark laughs. It's good to see he's kept his sense of humour. "I would've loved to have known that. My WV just . . . died. It was working one minute, showing me my stats, my Fates, then the next it went dark." He rubs his wrist, where the bangle undoubtedly used to be. "I saw you, though. And Kit."

I still.

"You were together, running. A Jabberwock flew after you, screeching, breathing fire. I'd never seen anything like it. The beast was angry, and the more fear you both showed, the angrier it grew. You couldn't fight the Jabberwock, that much was clear. So you hid."

My throat is dry. Do I want to know what comes next?

"But the Jabberwock kept after you. It thrashed and snapped, clawing at the boulders surrounding the small cave where you'd taken refuge. Time seemed to slow and so did the train. What I saw next was the bravest thing I've ever witnessed."

He's going to mention Knave now. How I ran. Then froze. How Knave got me and the rest of Team Spade out alive.

"You ran," Stark says, confirming what I already know. What I've lived with for the past year.

I hang my head now, shame burning my face. Stark shakes me, forcing me to look up at him. "You're not hearing me, mate. That Jabberwock was not going to relent. You left Kit in hiding while you ran in the opposite direction, leading the beast away."

What? I stare at him for a long time. Then I close my eyes and force the fog away, recalling those last moments more clearly now, though they're still a bit muddled. Maybe they always will be. "Why didn't you say something before?"

"I thought you knew. I figured leaving Kit was eating at you, because you were questioning if you did the right thing. It's hard to explain, but it's agonizingly difficult to talk about my year lost on the train. I figured if you wanted to talk about it, you'd be the one to bring it up. But after witnessing all your uncertainty, I had to set the record straight."

Wow. "Thanks," I tell him sincerely. He's shown me more kindness than I could ever repay. But I guess that's the point, isn't it? Kindness isn't something that has to be repaid. I could get used to having Stark as my mate again. I hear Ace's voice in my head, repeating back something I once told her.

"And wouldn't it be a pity to lose something you've only just discovered?"

Yes, yes it would. I'm such a dolt. I've been believing that I destroy everything I touch. But, maybe I don't, not according to Stark and what he saw . . .

It dawns on me then. "The train goes in a loop. It passes through every square."

"Right." Stark nods slowly. "We've established that. But anyone on board would never be in their right mind long enough to get off."

He's made a fair point. But still. "There must be a way to disembark the train when it passes the Eighth Square."

Stark and I both rise as he answers. "I doubt it. Otherwise someone would have done it. What are you getting at?"

"Nothing is impossible," I state at the same moment a Jabberwock screeches in the background. Its call is reminiscent of talons scraping stone, grating my nerves. I ignore it. "We've already solved the train checkpoint's riddle, so we know exactly how to solve it again." My idea chugs along, gaining steam. It just might work.

"You still have one problem though. How do we *catch* the train?"

"That's a conundrum." I glance out the window. "But last things last and first things first, as I always say. And the train is last on our list right now. First, we find whatever it is Ace is looking for. Seeing the flying beasts outside might be bonus information, but I doubt it's what she had in mind." I pocket my hands and look directly at my best mate. "Hatter," I say.

"Yeah, Shire?"

"I'm sorry I've been such an idiot all these years."

He laughs. "I knew you'd come around eventually." He shoves my shoulder. "You've always been the slower sort."

I grin. "I won't argue with that."

"It's cold in here," Stark says as he takes the lead down the next stairwell.

I follow him but lose sight of his figure in the shadows. "Hey, Hatter?" I call. "Stark?"

He doesn't answer.

I jog down the steps two at a time to catch up. "Mate?"

Silence.

My pulse quickens. "We can play tricks later, but right now I think we—"

One more step around a bend and I'm falling, tumbling headfirst into liquid silver.

A looking glass, just as Ace described. Somehow, this one appears to allow me through as well.

I only hope the open invitation is worth whatever awaits on the other side.

ALICE

This is not like the other looking-glass clues. Something about this one stands apart.

Perhaps it's the fact I don't feel as if I've been transported anywhere at all. With the other memories, it seemed I had travelled to a different time and place. But this is still the garden palace. I glance down to find I am still very much myself as well. Madi's herself, too, though a little worse for the wear.

Madi bends forwards, gasping for air. "What happened?"

According to Rabekah, if this was something left by my mother, only I should be able to access it. So I'm not sure how to answer.

"It's similar to one of my mother's—Catherine's—memories." I don't tell her what it actually is since I don't yet know myself. "Don't worry. You get used to the sensation of drowning after a while. Follow me."

Madi nods, and after she inhales a huge breath, we proceed with caution through the silver fog. As the fog clears and the memory takes form, filling out in full colour, I watch as a young woman with a toddler on her hip and a young boy of maybe five or six clinging to her side shuffles quickly up a corridor. I recognise the trio immediately.

Charlotte. Knave. Me.

Alice grasps the rabbit lovey I found at the cottage in a fisted hand, its body dangling down Charlotte's back. The scene reminds me of one I encountered upon my entrance into what I first thought was Wonderland. When a distraught woman named Viola came rushing into Wonderland Abbey, a little boy hiding in the folds of her skirt as she lamented over her lost son, Dan. He'd been a player, lost to the Trials last year. He did return, and when he did, he seemed as if he'd gone out of his mind with memories muddled and eyes filled with terror. A snippet from the news story on the matter comes back to me now.

Boy claims he never left, only that he saw what's real.

That's the word Dan kept repeating whenever someone tried to interview him.

Real.

My mind switches back to this scene from much longer ago. Each detail is so tangible, it's as if the moment is happening in real time. This is the first I've experienced it completely as myself. I have the urge to reach out and touch Charlotte's arm, but as Madi and I follow her trail, I refrain, sensing she can neither see nor hear us.

"Is that . . . Charlotte?" Madi keeps her voice low, as if we've happened upon something sacred. "And you. That's you as a little girl." She sounds stunned.

I nod, an ache in my throat.

"And Knave?"

"Yes," I say, my voice catching. Is this just before he was left behind?

"Do you remember this?"

I shake my head, and we continue on in silence, our shallow breaths and guarded footsteps the only sounds. Charlotte rounds a corner, and we double our pace to catch up, only to stop short of nearly barging into her.

Or, at least, the memory of her.

Being this close to Charlotte, even if she isn't truly here, sends a pang through my heart. Why can't I remember any of this? Why didn't she tell me about it? Her excuse was *protection*, but was there something else, something she was trying to hide?

She raps on the red door before her three times.

Tap. Rap. Tap.

"Enter," a female voice drones from the other side.

My smaller self clings tightly to Charlotte's neck, burying her round face into my aunt's shoulder. Charlotte responds by hitching the child higher onto her hip and murmuring softly.

"There, there, love. You have nothing to fear."

But young Alice only holds tighter to the woman who was more of a mother to her than I knew.

The door opens, seemingly of its own volition, like a flower blossoming wide at the appearance of the sun. The entire room beyond the red door matches its entrance, red and crimson and scarlet and auburn and brick and rust coating everything from floor to ceiling to tapestry. Red picture frames encasing red paintings in every tone of red. Red tassels on red drapes. Even the grout between the red tiles is, in fact, red.

Charlotte and her charges contrast the setting. My aunt sports simple travel clothes in grey and black, and the youngster on her hip wears a cornflower nightgown to match her eyes. Knave is dressed in pyjamas, too, his wavy, dark hair mussed and in need of a trim. He yawns and stretches, reaching up to hold Charlotte's free hand.

"Why are we here, Aunty Sarlet?"

Is Knave trying to say Charlotte? His childlike pronunciation tears at my heart. It was so easy for Dinah to fool him. To fool everyone.

At first it doesn't appear anyone else is present in this room with bleeding walls. But then a throat clears, and the slightest shift in movement ahead sets everything into focus.

Dinah.

"You're really going through with this?" Charlotte stands tall. Her words don't waver.

Dinah makes a show of yawning before replying, "Did you have any doubt I would? I am a woman of my word, after all."

"You can have the crown," Charlotte informs her. "But I'm going after Catherine. And I'm taking my niece and nephew with me."

"You may take the *Normal*-born girl." Dinah speaks as if she has a foul taste in her mouth. "The boy, on the other hand . . ." She nods to Knave. "He remains with me."

Charlotte draws Knave closer to her side. He looks up at her, confusion contorting the features he hasn't grown into yet. "He's none of your concern," Charlotte says. "What could you possibly want with him?" But her voice quivers slightly on the last word. She knows exactly what Dinah wants with my cousin.

Dinah laughs darkly. "Do not play innocent with me, Charlotte. I practically raised you and your sisters. I can tell when you're lying."

Charlotte keeps her head high. "Cordelia entrusted Knave to *my* care."

Another dark laugh from the former governess. "Only because he was an embarrassment to her and put a wrench in her plans to control our kind. She couldn't stand that he was a Wonder, just as his father, Wonderland's king, had been."

Wonderland's king? Knave is not only the son of the Queen of England, but of the King of Wonderland as well?

Could Dinah be referring to the Ivory King? Chess and I just assumed the bride from the story was Scarlet. Was Cordelia the girl who cried so hard and so long, inspiring the legend behind the Pool of Tears?

The possibility sparks something my mother said in the recording from the Wabe's Archives. I hear it with new ears as it replays in my mind.

"Just as anyone can become Wonder, so anyone can unbecome *Wonder. We all have a choice what to believe."*

Queen Cordelia was once a Wonder. It makes sense. If she

unbecame one, that would explain her hatred, the reason for the Registry, the cordial to keep the Gene subdued, all of it.

Was her rejection of the king the beginning of Wonderland's end? When she stopped believing, maybe others did too. The story Dinah told us at the London café wasn't in the almanac. Maybe that's because whoever left the almanac for Raving to find removed it. But the mystery remains . . .

Who would have something to gain by changing history?

I glare at Dinah despite the fact she can't see me. Her own admission in the memory with Sevine made her intentions clear. It was Dinah who wanted to alter the story, Dinah who stood to gain from the falsehood and lies. All this time we've assumed the deception began with Dinah's schemes to replace Charlotte. That this was the original event which triggered the domino effect that eventually led to forming a lesser version of Wonderland.

So this is why the story wasn't in the almanac. Dinah didn't want anyone to make the connection between Cordelia and the Wonder King. But why?

Dinah rises now, crossing to a floor-length mirror. She tucks a stray lock of orange hair back into its perfect place. Then she adjusts the onyx broach at her collar. The one she's never without. What Dinah says next reveals the true version of this twisted tale for the first time.

"You know," she begins, watching Charlotte and the frightened children through her reflection, "Cordelia was always my favourite of you triplets. So easily swayed she was, a lump of clay not difficult to mould. When I introduced her to the Wonder King, everything was falling perfectly into place." Dinah sighs. "Through their match, I had everything I'd ever wanted. My own suite in Wonderland's palace. A high position in the king's house. I was practically Cordelia's second-in-command. Should something unfortunate happen to her and the king, it would have been my solemn duty to take charge, a sacrifice I was more than willing to make."

Sacrifice, indeed.

"When your sister left, it destroyed the king. My plans were falling perfectly into place. The poor man needed a companion, someone to comfort him as a mother would in his time of need. I encouraged him to go after her, fully expecting him to entrust the palace and Wonder people to me." She levels her piercing gaze at Charlotte. "But then you showed up with that child in your arms." Dinah casts a disgusted glance at Knave, and he responds, not in fear, but by sticking out his tongue. Dinah's eyes turn to cat slits.

My cousin is quite literally my favourite person in any reality at this moment.

Charlotte remains silent and Dinah continues. "Rather than transfer power to me, the king named you Queen of Hearts in his absence. And should he never return? Well, you would raise Knave as your own, and he would one day become King of Wonderland."

Madi grabs my hand. I can feel her pulse explode against mine.

"But, despite your efforts, dear Charlotte, you have failed. Wonderland is nearly lost. It was rejected and so it rejects us. Clearly, you are less than worthy of the throne. Wonderland chooses its king or queen. How does it feel that it didn't choose you?"

Charlotte bristles. "I never claimed to be worthy. I only desired to raise a boy who was." She holds to Knave's hand faster still. "One day, mark my words, Wonderland will choose him as king. And when it does you will be so far removed from truth, *governess*, you won't be able to see it even if it's right in front of your nose."

"We'll see about that," Dinah snaps. "For now, I'll be taking your mess into my hands. The fake haven you and Catherine call Wonderland, a place for Wonders to seek refuge until a worthy ruler sits on the throne, is now under my jurisdiction." Her words are all pretence, as poised and practiced as her pompous speech.

It's what she reveals next that truly locks everything into place. The tea vial she showed Sevine in my mother's memory rests in Dinah's flattened palm.

"What is that?" I know Charlotte best, so I can hear the fear in her question though her voice doesn't waver.

"A little something Lavender Hatter brewed up."

"Lavender? Help *you*? I don't believe it."

"You would be surprised what people are willing to do when the lives of those they love are at stake." Dinah casts a pointed glance first at little Alice, then at Knave. "Changeling Chai, it's called."

She offers no further prelude or dramatic pause. Instead she uncorks the vial and drinks its contents in one swallow. She tosses the container to the ground, and it shatters. It's a small sound and entirely underwhelming.

But the transformation taking place before us now is enough to overwhelm anyone.

Her catlike eyes are the first to shift, rounding out into a deep-brown gaze that is somehow innocent and lethal at once. Next her skin brightens and smooths, bidding farewell to decades of aging and exchanging them for a youthful yet mature glow.

One by one, Dinah's features alter until she is both unrecognisable and familiar. "Might I introduce you," Dinah says in a voice that rings of regality, "to Wonderland's new queen—Scarlet Heart."

Charlotte stumbles backwards, tucking a stunned Knave behind her. Little Alice refuses to look, keeping her face buried in her aunty's shoulder.

"You are free to go," Scarlet says, "but the boy stays with me."

Alice drops the rabbit and begins to wail. With that, the memory vanishes, leaving Madi and I staring straight ahead.

Scarlet didn't create the false version of Wonderland.

My mother and Charlotte did. Though they had the best intentions, they're partly to blame for the façade Wonders have come to believe.

My knees go weak, and I crumble, falling into Madi's arms, sobbing. We end up clinging to one another. This news has shaken her too.

"What happened to Knave?" Her voice breaks. "Did Dinah—*Scarlet*—take him from Charlotte?"

"I don't know," I say as we ease apart. "What about the king after he followed Cordelia? Do you think he could still be alive?"

"It's possible, isn't it?" Madi goes quiet and her expression falters.

I touch her shoulder. "Your mother's choice to protect you and your brothers was not your fault. Anyone would have done the same."

Madi only nods as the silver memory mist clears the entirety of the illusion, and our questions hang unanswered in the air. The red room vanishes around us, leaving us in the centre of a stone pavilion. A fountain bubbles nearby, and red roses climb each of the four pillars supporting the structure. The tinkle of a mirrored wind chime carries on a light breeze. Despite the immediate peace the atmosphere brings, a fierce foreboding follows.

We are not alone.

I sense her before I see her. The imposter queen emerges from around the side of a pillar, coming into view. She flashes a wicked sort of smile that is nothing like Charlotte's. Once you've seen the truth, you can't unsee it. And now that I know, it's obvious Scarlet and my aunt are nothing alike.

"Hello, Alice," the Queen of Hearts says. She glides towards us, her steps as lithe as a cat's. When she twists just so, I catch her reflection in the wind chime.

The face that scowls back at me does not belong to Scarlet. No matter what charade Dinah wishes to portray, her reflection reveals her true colours.

"Got you," I want to tell her, but I keep silent.

For now.

Then I see a new face in the tiny tinkling mirror. His expression is stricken, all blood drained from his face. He says one word, followed by another.

"Alice. Run."

CHESS

A house of cards always collapses. And a house of flowers? Well . . . what might one expect from a roof made of rose petals?

The ceiling caves in first, crumbling and crashing, shards of stems falling like daggers. Stark goes for Madi, and I dive for Ace. She's covering her head with both arms, ducking into herself, so small I could scoop her up in an instant.

And I do. With little effort I swing her off her feet and into my arms, and she stays there.

Sometimes it takes all the strength you can muster to allow another to carry your load.

I carry her as well as I'm able, glancing over one shoulder to check on Madi and Stark. He runs with Madi over one shoulder, bounding forwards in long strides that are quickly gaining on mine.

"Any ideas how to get out of here?" he calls.

"Not in the slightest," I holler.

"What about the others?" He's next to me now, panting.

"They've seen worse." My leg and arm muscles are burning. "Willow and Jack can handle themselves." Hopefully.

We barely escape the collapsing room as it caves in on itself, a heap of rubble and ruin within the threshold we just crossed.

This palace of flowers, the clue in the almanac, wasn't put into place by Wonderland. It wasn't a checkpoint or shortcut to the Eighth Square at all. It was a detour, an illusion of Dinah's. She fooled us again.

"I can walk now." Ace squirms to lower herself. "Please," she adds. "We'll go faster if I'm on foot."

"Same goes for me." Madi kicks, forcing her brother to put her upright as well.

Shouts resound from down the hall, but it's impossible to tell which direction they're coming from. The floors and walls and ceilings blend together in a blur of greenery. I'm in a daze in this garden palace maze. Which way is up? Left? Right?

Ace gains her bearings and takes my hand. "We stick together from here."

"Alice," I start, not sure how to begin.

She shakes her head. "Later. Please, Chess. Once we're safely to the Eighth Square."

"Ah. I have a theory about that," I remark.

Ace tilts her head. "I'm listening."

"We'll have to catch a train."

She merely nods.

Shouts grow closer, louder, as I urge my legs to propel me faster. A herd of guards rounds the corner at one end of the corridor. Our quartet bolts in the opposite direction. The maze of hedges that make up the palace walls grabs and claws as we pass. The entire garden is crumbling around us, like Wonderland crumbled without its king.

What if we can't catch the train? What if we don't make it out of this? I have to set things right. And I need to do it before my chance is gone.

"Not later," I say to Ace between gasps of breath as our feet slap against the stone. "Now."

Ace has picked up speed. For someone with such short legs,

she's surprisingly hard to keep up with. She's faster than I would anticipate, while at the same time exactly as fast as I'd expect. It's just like her to prove everyone wrong, to show that assumptions based on appearance are nothing more than blind guesses.

Stark and Madi pass us up when we reach the next corridor. It's narrow, and we run single file, creating distance between us.

"We have to talk." I pant and slow down.

"I know." Ace squeezes next to me and looks up. "What is it that's on your mind, Chess?"

You, I want to tell her. *Always you.* But rather than slip into my easy charm that wins most of the time, I opt to lose, to say the one thing I know may very well bring me the greatest loss I've yet to face.

But Stark is waving for us to catch up. "In here!" He eases through an open doorway, and the rest of us follow. I close the door quickly, clicking the lock into place for good measure.

The room before us is dark, and it's impossible to tell how deep or wide it stretches. It could be a suite or a broom closet for all we know.

"It smells like . . ." Madi begins.

"Fertilizer," Stark finishes.

There's another scent, too, just as potent.

"And blood," Ace notes sombrely. "It's like rusted metal and salted tears."

We're all smelling the same thing. I hate to think what this room is for.

"Hold on," Stark whispers. "I'll search for a light switch."

Ace's hand finds mine, and she pulls me down to sit in the deep shadows.

"Is it about Dinah?" Ace slides her rucksack off her back and lets it fall to the floor. "Because I need some time to process—"

"It's not about Dinah," I say. "Though she had all of us fooled, didn't she?"

"How could she be so selfish?"

Why is anyone selfish? I almost ask but refrain. I'm the last person who ought to be judging someone else's folly. Now that my moment of admission has arrived, nerves nip at my resolve. But I can't turn back now. "Last year, before the end of the Fourth Trial . . ."

I hesitate and she squeezes my hand. I bring her knuckles to my lips and press a light kiss upon them, hoping she understands just how much this moment means. And, more importantly, how much *she* means.

"My memories are scarce. I don't recall my reason for running. Stark says it was the Jabberwock." Or *a* Jabberwock, since apparently there is more than one. But the creatures we saw ruling the sky beyond the garden palace seemed too . . . cliché.

I don't fear the obvious. It's the subtle terrors, the beasts you don't expect that are truly the most frightening. Sometimes, those beasts are within, clawing away at you until they can be free.

"Chess?" Ace's gentle voice brings me back.

I clear my throat. "I left Kit to hide while I led the Jabberwock in the opposite direction. A wall of fire separated us, and I couldn't make it back to him. And, before I knew it, the Trial was over. Kit was trapped. And I couldn't tell a soul the first thing about what had occurred." My voice catches. "I do remember his pleas. 'Chess,' he'd called, among his various cries for help. 'Come back.'" I fall silent.

"Chess," Ace says softly, "it wasn't your fault."

"There's more." My eyes shut tight, and I steady myself. While I may not have abandoned Kit on purpose, my next move was completely my responsibility. *My* responsibility. "Ace, after that, I made a deal with the Minister of Spades and Dinah. If I helped them bring you back to Wonderland, if I got you to the Heart Trial, they guaranteed they would help me find Kit."

Her hand falls from mine. "That's why you joined Team Heart."

"Yes," I confess.

"And the Knight Society?" Her voice is dull and sharp at the same time.

"I didn't care who helped me as long as Kit was found. Dinah.

The minister. The Knight Society. Blanche wanted to bring you into the Trials for the Society's cause. Dinah and the minister had their reasons, though they wouldn't divulge their true intentions."

"Did you know Scarlet was Dinah all along?"

"No! Ace, no. I swear on my own life, I had no idea. I only wanted to find my brother."

"And it didn't matter if I got hurt."

"That's not true."

"True?" Her voice rises. "You want to talk to me about what's true?"

I hang my head, ashamed. I'm losing more than I was prepared to let go.

"You abandoned me. That night in Hyde Park."

"I did care," I tell her fervently. "I never wanted you to end up in the crossfire. That's why I returned for you."

"No," she corrects. "*I* found Wonderland. And you happened to be there. Circumstances pushed us together. You didn't choose—"

"Hold on," I say, defence building up inside. "You know I stayed and watched you. I made certain you discovered Wonderland, even if you couldn't see me."

"Yes, apparently you're always hiding. And very good at manipulating. You're—"

"A coward," I say for her because I can't bear to hear her speak the word.

"No." We are frozen in time an instant, then Ace sighs. Her anger from moments before fades. "I don't think you're a coward, Chess." To my shock, her hand finds mine again.

I desperately intertwine my fingers through hers, hoping against hope I can hold onto her, that we can hold on together.

"You're not a coward," she repeats. "You're Normal."

I'm taken aback. It's the last thing I expected her to say. "Pardon?"

She laughs, and it's the best sound in any Wonderland, real or otherwise. "Don't you see, Chess? You're Normal. And Wonder. I don't know how I didn't think of it before. Despite the fascinating things we're capable of, we all have the potential to do perfectly normal, human things. We lie and cheat and steal and swindle. I used to pick pockets, for goodness' sake." She tugs on my hand, and we balance one another to rise and stand.

"Kit will understand, Chess. And we've both made choices we regret. How can I hold such things against you, when here you are confessing the truth and striving to make amends? Maybe you *were* hiding, but you're not hiding anymore."

"Ace." I enfold her in my arms, and she nestles against my chest. "I thought for sure when you knew the truth, I'd lose you."

She tilts her head back. "You could never lose me. Maybe for a moment or a day. But lose me for good? My dear Chess Shire, I do believe that's impossible." She disengages from my embrace. "Now let's see what's taking Stark so long to find that switch."

My heart is lighter as we fumble around in the darkness. I run my hands along the walls, searching. How large is this room? The walls feel strange, like they're drenched in water. The sound of trickling fills my ears, and I notice how dewy and damp the air is. So humid it's making it difficult to breathe.

A light flicks on at last, and I let my eyes adjust. Where did Ace go? I'm relieved when I see her standing before a wall of water. When her face comes into view, she's smiling.

But there's something else about her too. My gaze falls to her lips. They're darker than normal, not their usual pink but bright crimson red.

She smiles a smile that doesn't belong to her.

I back away. "You're not you."

"Of course not," she says in a voice that doesn't belong to her either.

Her name tastes like poison, and I spew it out of my mouth. "Scarlet."

ALICE

We should never have entered that dark room. One moment, Chess was confessing everything, the next I was wishing I could talk to Charlotte about it all and falling through another reflection— another looking glass. I am on my own, which confirms one thing.

The memory the four of us witnessed together was an illusion crafted by Dinah. A real memory, yes, but not one planted by Catherine.

What I see before me now, however, must be another clue of my mother's, meant for me alone.

Newgate Reform Centre, London.

"Oy, you there," a voice says from my right.

I turn to find a burly-looking guard stalking towards me.

"Bill?" I can hardly believe my eyes as I take in the man who once guarded The Rabbit Hole door for a Clash of the Cards event. If this is a memory from years ago, how is Bill here now?

From the way he hesitates and furrows his brow, I can tell he recognises me, though he can't place why. Have I really changed so much in the weeks I've been gone? It's just as well. If he did remember me, I'd probably be in more trouble.

This isn't real. It's a memory of the past through my mother's eyes.

"Show yer papers," he demands. He's too close, and I can smell something foul on his breath.

I've never been asked for papers to prove I'm Normal before. Maybe it's because I have always looked too young, too unassuming. I catch a glimpse of my reflection in a Reform Centre window, and my eyes go wide. I'm exactly as I was with Chess. Not my mother, but me.

I'm in London? How can this be happening?

"I left them at home," I say quickly, fear creeping in. "I must have taken a wrong turn," I add. "Sorry. I'll be going now."

Bill grabs my arm, and there's no use protesting. He's three times my size. Still, I make it as difficult as I can for him to drag me up the steps and into the Reform Centre.

More guards stand before a thick glass door to the side of a desk that's secured by a pane of glass. It reaches from floor to ceiling, and a lone woman waits behind it. She looks up and her expression is unreadable. She sighs as we approach.

"It's nearly closing time, Bill," she says, clearly bored. Her voice crackles through the silver speaker in the glass. "I'd rather wait to process another stray until tomorrow."

"What do you s'pose oi do with her then?" Bill asks.

The woman shrugs. She glances at the clock, then stands, gathering a handbag and coat. "It's no longer my problem today. See you tomorrow." She pulls a shade down to cover the window, leaving Bill and me alone with the other guards.

He eyes me and takes in the others' glances. It's clear they don't want to stay late either.

"Go on, you two," Bill responds. "I'll deal with the girl. Just be sure ta lock up on yer way out."

"Yes, sir," one of the guards says. He seems familiar. I catch the name on his tag and then spy the other guard's tag as well.

Officer Deedum. Identical tags on the identical uniforms of

two men who appear to be identical twins. They were there the day Charlotte went missing. They broke into her flat along with Headmistress O'Hare. Back then I'd thought they worked for the Academy, but now it's clear their added presence was solely to collect a Rogue Wonder.

I gasp under my breath. If this is real, *I'm* a Rogue Wonder. Was this Dinah's intention all along? To send me here, have me processed and branded and forced to drink cordial that will suppress the Wonder Gene?

The room suddenly feels stifling. The click of the lock heightens my panic.

"This way." Bill shoves me through a security door that opens automatically when he nears. When it closes behind us, I sense that the door would not open the same way for me, most likely only recognising those with clearance.

Along a narrow hall he pulls me, then into a cell with four dingy, grey walls and no furniture.

"Wait 'ere," he instructs, as if I could go anywhere else. "You'll be processed in the mornin'."

"Wait!" I rush to speak before he closes the door. "How do you know I'm a Wonder? How do you know I'm not Normal?"

He grunts then flashes his teeth in a villainous smile. "'Cause," he says, "the cordial doesn't affect Normals the way it does you lot. With that terror in yer eyes, you've got Wonder written all over you." Bill slams and locks the door, leaving me alone with my thoughts. My fears. It's like a different kind of Jabberwock. One far worse than any Trial could conjure.

I close my eyes and try to find Wonderland again, but it isn't there.

Just like my mother, Wonderland has forsaken me too.

I didn't cry myself to sleep. I didn't dream. When I couldn't keep my eyes open any longer, I curled up into a ball on the hard floor, listening to the rattle of air through the vent in the ceiling. I eventually drifted off to its grim tune against my will.

I have no way of knowing if it's morning or midnight. My mouth is dry, and my tongue sticks to its roof. I try to swallow but this only agitates my parched throat more. I need water. And food. When's the last time I ate or drank?

As I force myself into a sitting position, voices echo from the hall outside my cell door. I sit straighter, smoothing my hair as if a proper appearance even matters. When the doorknob jiggles and the sound of a key turning a lock follows, I stand on weak legs. I couldn't fight a guard like Bill off, but that doesn't mean I have to sit and wait for him like a coward.

The door opens to reveal not Bill or another guard but a middle-aged woman. Her warm smile and kind blue eyes that match the streaks in her blonde hair is as familiar to me as her face on a fiver note.

"Hello, child," England's queen says.

I stand there, frozen. She shifts to one side of the threshold, giving me a clear path to escape if I had the strength. "No need to fear," she assures. "I shall not harm you."

I find my voice and blurt, "Then release me."

She shakes her head. "I am afraid I can fulfil no such request. But I can help you, Alice."

If I could retreat any further than the wall supporting my back, I would. "How do you know my name?"

"I know a lot of things about you, niece." Her voice is tender, but firm. "Charlotte has not ceased talking about you since the day she arrived. You had best come with me now. She has little time."

Suddenly I don't care that this woman has singlehandedly made it her mission to eliminate the Wonder Gene from existence. Charlotte arrived? She's here again? I'm bewildered and befuddled. How can this be?

I can't wrap my mind around it. But then, Queen Cordelia's last words make my world tilt as I register what they mean.

She has little time.

Charlotte is here.
And she is dying.

CHESS

Gone is the garden of live flowers, the palace, and the labyrinth. In their place stands an arched bridge, overlooking a deep chasm. Water rushes past rocks and boulders far below. The wall of water that was playing as Queen Scarlet's backdrop has revealed itself to be the thunderous waterfall it really is at the bridge's end.

It was all an illusion, a trap, right down to the very last rosebud.

Willow and Jack have rejoined us, though there's still no sign of Ace.

"I've been patient long enough," Queen Scarlet says, and I realise she's not actually present. This is a projection, a hologram, just like the one I encountered in the wood.

Stark stiffens beside me.

"Enough lies, Grandmother," I say.

"Grandmother?" Willow's question comes out as a high-pitched squeal that sounds nothing like her.

I steal a glance at her and Jack, who both appear to be processing the revelation. I'll have to fill them in later.

For now, I return my glower to the mock queen. "Show your true self or leave us to finish this Trial."

"That's precisely what I intend to have you do, Grandson."

I respond by spitting at her holographic feet.

"Now, now," she chides. "The Gateway closes at midnight tomorrow, and you're running out of time. We must proceed with the utmost decorum."

"Ha!" I scoff. "That's rich coming from you, Your Majesty."

"You have tried my patience long enough, Chesster. Where is the girl?"

I stare at her image. What game is she playing?

"I shall ask once more. What have you done with Alice?"

"I should ask you the same thing." Relief washes over me. If she doesn't have Ace, maybe we have a chance after all. Perhaps our Team Queen will pop into view at any moment to save us.

"What do you need Alice for?" Stark demands. "What do you need *any* of us for?" His anger is such that I have no doubt the false queen would be in serious danger were she, in fact, present.

"Let me break it down for you." Scarlet's voice is patronizing. "I promise I'll be brief." She paces the bridge's width from railing to railing.

I watch her closely, attempting to determine how she's sending the transmission. It can't be through my WV, long dead now and no longer connected to my mind.

"Now then," she states. "You've seen the memory, Chesster. You know what took place before Charlotte fled. Unfortunately, I made a grave error."

Maybe if we stall her long enough, the rest of our team can make it through to the end. Knave can take his place as Wonderland's rightful king. Then again, we'll be stronger as a whole. I glance nervously at the others. We need to find that train and catch it if we can.

"And what error is that?" Madi challenges.

I glance at her and note the single lit Fate pulsing on her WV bangle, still clasped tight to her wrist. And it's not just her. Jack wears one as well. So that's how my grandmother is transmitting. If I can catch Madi's and Jack's attention and get them to take off the bangles, we might cut this waste of time off at the source.

"It's simple, you dull girl," Dinah says derisively. "I chose the wrong child."

I can only assume she's referring to keeping Knave with her and allowing Charlotte to take Alice. I'm sure there's more to it, but history is the least of our concerns at present.

"Let's get to the point. You will—" Scarlet's transmission glitches for the briefest moment, and I take the opportunity to send a pointed look Madi's way, my glance travelling from her face to her wrist.

Understanding dawns. Madi tugs on Jack's sleeve and sends him the same silent message.

The transmission soon steadies, coming through quite clearly, but now Dinah is her old self again, no doubt in need of another dose of Changeling Chai.

"—then, and only then, will Alice see the truth. And when she sees it, she will crumble. And so will Wonderland."

We've missed some vital details thanks to the WVs and their constant unpredictability here, but I lose the will to care when Dinah pulls someone into the transmission with her.

The Minister of Spades appears by her side, and he's holding a knife to Kit's throat.

"You had best be on your way," Dinah says, "or you can say goodbye to your darling brother."

I don't think. I lunge for the hologram.

The transmission dissolves. Madi and Jack didn't even have to remove their bangles. Dinah promised she'd be brief. For once, she told the truth.

Stark pulls me back. "They aren't there, Shire."

I spin to face him, chest heaving. "What do we do?" I tug my hair. "We never should have separated from the others."

"I could have told you that," Willow mutters.

Madi shakes her head. "We didn't have a choice. We did what we thought we were supposed to do."

I'm wild, gripping the bridge's railing and staring straight down into the ravine. "Forget what we were supposed to do. She has Kit." My voice echoes across the chasm. "She has Kit!"

"It could have been an illusion." Jack speaks up. "Kit's smart. Even if Dinah holds the upper hand now, she won't have it for long."

They all wait in silence for me to make my next move. I've let fear take over my decisions before. Now I run our options through my mind. For whatever reason, Dinah wants us to finish this Trial. If that's the case, we ought to run in the opposite direction and refuse to give her what she so clearly desires. Jack is right. My brother is far from weak. He can handle our grandmother.

As tempting as leaving all of this in our wake sounds, though, something in me says we must see this through. We have to trust that the real Wonderland is out there and the Ivory King exists.

I turn away from the railing and face my team. "We can't run."

Slow smiles of approval find their way onto each Wonder's face. Even Willow appears on board. I inhale a long breath, giving myself time to formulate a plausible plan. I close my eyes in an attempt to clear my head. When I open them again, my gaze lands on something I didn't notice before, something Ace is never without.

Her rucksack. In all the commotion, she must have left it behind.

With catlike reflexes I slip my boot under one of the straps and flip the rucksack up into my open hand. I lift the flap and withdraw the worn almanac.

This Trial has challenged us at every turn. Yet somehow, someway, it's thrown us a lifeline at the moment we need it most. I can't chalk this up to coincidence. No, this is providence, and if Ace were here, I know she'd agree.

I turn to the section covering the game of chess. If this book helped Ace find her way, certainly it will aid us in navigating ours.

A quick scan through the chapter reveals nothing of importance. I search through strategies and tactics, openings and developments.

"Well?" Madi taps her foot, but the small sound is no match for the waterfall's roar behind us. "Don't leave us out of the story, Shire. What did you find?"

Story. "That's it." I flip a few pages back. My father taught me to see chess as a pure game of strategy, which only the best could best. But it's more than that. Each piece plays a part. "Here," I say, pointing to the title at the top of the page.

Chess—A Game for Queens or Legend of a Conquered King?

"What is that?" Stark cranes his neck to get a better view.

Madi comes to stand by my side. "It's a story Alice read when we entered the Heart Trial."

"Why would a story matter?" Willow asks.

The realisation solidifies, and I begin to see the bigger picture. "All this time we've been fighting our way through, hoping to slay the Jabberwock and find the elusive Ivory King, and we've done so trusting in our own merits and skills. But not one of our strategies has succeeded thus far. We rejected the idea of being Pawns in Scarlet's—*Dinah's*—game, and we strived to outwit her however we could. But this is not her Trial."

I give them a moment to see it too. One by one it dawns on them from Madi's wide eyes to Willow's slack jaw.

It's Stark who gives the answer. "The Trial protected me," he states. "I always looked at the train as a prison, when really it kept me safe from the Jabberwock. It even allowed me to hear Madi's voice during my time in solitude."

"The games of chess at the keep," Madi continues, expanding upon Stark's idea. "They kept Knightley from moving on. Maybe if she'd continued forwards on her own, she would have ended up hurt or lost or worse."

I close the book and slide it inside the rucksack. "This place definitely has its challenges," I agree, "and I don't presume to understand them all. But my brother is alive. As worried as I was about Kit for the year we were apart, there was an odd sort of relief in forgetting what happened."

Their thoughtful expressions show they're reflecting on each word. After I let everything sink in, I say what I know we're all thinking. "The Trial has not failed us yet, and neither has the king."

The sound I've been hoping to hear calls to us over the din then. It's long and loud and high, and I recognise it at once. I study the waterfall, peering past rather than at it. To either side of the rushing water, a slender path crawls along a recess in the ravine wall—a path paved with train tracks.

I shoulder Ace's bag and wave for my teammates to follow as I sprint for the end of the bridge. When I burst through the falls, I'm drenched, but there is more than one way to get dry. A good old-fashioned caucus race ought to do the trick, and from where I'm standing, all votes are against Dinah.

The train slows when it comes into view. Buckley leans from one car as the locomotive stops inside the waterfall tunnel, which houses a hidden platform.

"Hello, Hearts!" Buckley addresses us as if we're old chums. "Hop on."

We accept the invite, unsure what awaits us at the Eighth Square. But we are a part of this story, and we will see it through to its end.

The Trial, it seems, will make quite certain of that.

ALICE

Her Majesty leads me through the uninviting halls of the Reform Centre. It's exactly how a place like this ought to look. Harsh, fluorescent lights flicker in their cages. A vent near the floor pushes out tepid air. It's a short walk to the room where Charlotte's being held, which is lovely compared to the rest of this place. Pretty watercolour paintings hang on the walls, and a stack of old books sits on the nightstand. When I see Charlotte lying there, so frail in a four-poster bed, I rush to her side.

I take her limp hand tenderly in mine. "Charlotte." My words tumble out. "It was Dinah. Our stupid cat. It was Dinah all along—"

"I know," she says, patting my hand.

"How did you get here?" But I think I can fathom the answer. "I thought Dinah helped you escape."

"Dinah is clever." Charlotte's voice is so weak it hurts my heart. "She reported me to the authorities so they would bring me here to undergo a slow poisoning. She never had any intention of releasing me."

I knew this much, didn't I? The red *W* seared above Charlotte's collarbone when she joined me in Wonderland after the Spade Trial was proof enough. "The cordial just subdues the Gene," I tell her. "It isn't poison." But I glance over at Cordelia, whose expression bares all.

Guilty as charged.

"They've been testing the stuff on Wonders for years, trying to perfect the formula but failing miserably." Charlotte gives me a sad smile. "Some survive the treatments, but they're never quite the same. Others . . ."

Her voice trails but she needn't finish. I twist to face the queen, not caring in this moment if she makes me drink her stupid cordial. "You did this."

"Yes. And I think it is time for a change."

Her words aren't what I expect.

"When they informed me Charlotte was here"—Queen Cordelia comes to her sister's side and lays a hand on her arm—"I could scarcely believe it. Charlotte was supposed to be with my son in Wonderland. Yet here she was. She had already been given the cordial by the time I arrived, and there was nothing I could do except release her."

"*You* let her go?"

"I did." Something glistens in Cordelia's eyes. "She said she had something to do before she no longer had the chance."

No longer had the chance. I can't consider what that means. Not yet.

"And when you left for the Club Trial"—Charlotte's fingers tighten weakly around mine—"I returned."

Her note holds new meaning now. *I am always with you.*

The note wasn't a "see you soon." The note was Charlotte's goodbye.

My heart bursts into pieces, and I lay my head on the bed, but I don't allow myself to cry. Charlotte slips her hand out of mine and strokes my hair gently. She has always been my strength, but here, in her weakened state, it's time I was hers. I lift my head and make myself take in every detail down to her pallid, papery skin and the sunken half-moons under her eyes. She appears to have aged decades due to the poisoned cordial, plus a likely lack of Infinity Infusion. Even so, her brown eyes have kept their radiance.

I hold her gaze and swallow my emotions. "Why come back here?"

"To help me." Cordelia sits on the edge of the bed. "Charlotte was always the brightest of us three, despite what Catherine would say to any soul who dared listen."

Their exchanged smiles carry a sad sort of longing for all they've lost.

"It was Catherine's Wonder Gene research—or what was left of it, following the lab fire—which aided my team in developing the cordial. I never intended . . ." She breaks off, taking a moment to compose herself. "I know now it matters not what I intended, only what I have done. When I learned Charlotte had received multiple doses, the scales fell from my eyes, and I saw the damage I had caused. It was then I knew I had to make amends."

Charlotte coughs. "I've helped her draft a new initiative," she says between breaths. "And all it took was me dying to get her on board." She utters a little laugh, which lightens my heavy heart the slightest bit.

"Alice," Charlotte says to me, inserting strength into her voice. She's firm as she's always been, but beneath her serious tone, love abides. "You must go back. You must finish what you started."

"But how?" I want to do what she asks, to grant this final request— but I truly have no clue. "I don't even know how I ended up here. Is there an entrance nearby? Even then, how will I find the Gateway and catch up with my team?"

"Oh, dearest Alice," Charlotte says, "I think you know you never needed an entrance or a Gateway. You simply must close your eyes and believe."

We sit that way for what seems like hours. I share of my experiences in the Heart Trial and inquire about our past. Charlotte fills in the gaps between coughs and shallow breaths. She tells me of the birth certificate she had to forge to live in the Normal Reality and about her odd relationship regarding the Minister of Spades.

"He is obviously not my father," she explains, "but when I returned to the Trials this year—with Professor White's assistance, of course—I begged him to see reason. He was never completely on board with Dinah's plan to overthrow me, but he didn't see eye-to-eye with my views either. The minister is on the side of the minister—whatever that means in any given moment. I asked him to pose as my father in front of you, and he reluctantly agreed. In exchange, I gave my word that I had no plans to reclaim the throne, because I didn't. I wasn't ready for you to know who you were yet. I was still afraid of losing you."

The admission of her intricate lie stings a little less now than it would have previously. She shivers, and I tug the blanket closer to her chin. Cordelia brings her water and dabs her forehead with a damp cloth. It's a strange sort of sight to behold, the Queen of England acting as nursemaid to her bedridden sister.

I suppose servanthood is the mark of true royalty. My thoughts wander to Knave, and I smile. He'll make a perfect king one day.

"What happened to Knave?" I ask, changing the subject, hoping for happier memories.

No such memories exist. "I sought refuge with you both at the Foundling House." Charlotte frowns. "I had no idea it was part of Dinah's plan, nor that the property belonged to her."

New understanding straightens my posture. The woman who owned the Foundling House, the one who connected Charlotte to the position in Oxford from afar was . . . Dinah?

"One day, while we were still fairly new to living in London, I took you and your cousin on an outing to see Tower Bridge. I turned my back for one second . . ." Her voice catches before she continues. "That's all it took. Knave was gone."

I wasn't allowed to get lost. Charlotte's overprotectiveness, her constant need to keep a watchful eye, it all stemmed from not wanting to lose me too.

"There was no doubt in my mind Dinah kidnapped him," Charlotte says. "I could have gone after Knave. I should have." She sinks deeper into her flattened pillow. "I let fear control me, Alice, but you must not let it control you."

I nod, and her charge brings a new question to the forefront of my mind. "The palace is afraid," I reply. "Your message. Do you know what Dinah wants? What is she afraid of?"

Charlotte opens her mouth, but Cordelia speaks first. "My son would be fit to rule no matter his upbringing or circumstance. He takes after his father."

I sit in expectant silence. This is the rest of the story I've been waiting to hear.

"He gave up everything to be with me. He left Wonderland behind only to meet his own demise." She goes on to tell of the infamous lab fire, and how Knave's father tried to save Catherine and her husband, Ivan.

Hearing my father's name again tightens my throat.

"Cat was spared," Cordelia says, "but Ivan and Lewis did not survive."

Lewis. The name strikes an odd chord. It seems such a common name, certainly too common for Wonderland's king.

"If my mother didn't die in that fire, what really happened to her?"

Charlotte, whose eyes had closed briefly, rejoins the conversation. "I never saw her again after she left you behind in search of the real Wonderland." There's a soft sadness to her tone that is both reminiscent and distant. It tells me she grieved my mother a long time ago.

I expect more. I need more. But happy endings don't always come the way we need or expect.

"As far as what our former governess desires from all this," Cordelia cuts in, circling back to the original question, "that remains to be seen, child. The only way to know for certain is to return and face the end of the Trial."

Her statement ushers in the moment I've been dreading, the one I've tried to draw out as long as possible. Time may pass differently in the real Wonderland, and a day here might be only minutes there, but I can't stay Normal forever. Not when everyone is counting on me to solve my mother's riddle.

So I ask one final question before I part, hoping the sisters who knew Catherine best can help me find the answer I seek. "My mother left a riddle behind for me to solve." I look at each of them, but my eyes fix on Charlotte's. "I don't think I have all the clues quite yet, but if either of you could tell me anything that might—" I'm stopped midsentence when Charlotte and Cordelia exchange a knowing glance. "What is it?" I ask.

Charlotte closes her eyes and shakes her head, a smile curving at the corners of her mouth. Her cheeks almost look rosy, but the colour departs as quickly as it arrived. When she looks into my eyes again, I hold my breath.

"The answer, Alice, is you."

My brows scrunch. "Me? I don't understand."

"Catherine's riddle was one she could never solve," Charlotte explains. "Oh, sure, her theory of impossibility provided some explanation as to what she thought provided answers, but in the end you—your Wonder-ness—remained the greatest mystery of our lifetimes."

Born Normal, now Wonder.

Tears well, and I allow them to fall, free and unhindered. It takes all the strength I have to bid Charlotte—my sister, my aunt, and my mother, if I'm being truthful—goodbye for the last time. When I can't put it off any longer, I embrace her.

"Come now," Charlotte says. "Crying won't help."

"You know, for once, I don't really care." I cry-laugh.

She pats me on the back once more before weakly pushing me away. Cordelia stands by her bedside. Her blue eyes glisten and I know. Once I'm gone, Charlotte won't have a reason to stay. She will stop fighting. My favourite person in this reality or the next will let go.

"Tell Raving I—" She covers her mouth, choked up on her own words.

When she doesn't finish, I promise, "I'll tell him."

Charlotte nods her silent thanks.

This is it.

I want to stay.

I have to go.

"I love you, Alice."

"I love you, Charlotte."

She smiles.

My heart breaks.

Then I close my eyes, and I'm gone.

CHESS

Can't this never-ending train travel any faster?

We all sit anxious and knackered in the dining car, the six of us, including Buckley, crammed into a single booth. The others have had their fill of food and drink, and a mess of empty plates and glasses lies before us. I picked at my shepherd's pie, forcing a bite or two. I can't rightly eat when my stomach is in knots.

Jack didn't mind in the slightest, delighted to consume the helping I couldn't finish.

Our clothes have dried for the most part, though I had to sort Ace's rucksack things along an empty bench seat to air them out. The almanac survived, thanks to the leather cover, its pages only damp and crinkled along the edges. The rest of her items— an old deck of cards, the pocketscreen I gave her, her outdated soundbuds, a threadbare stuffed rabbit I've never seen, a hand mirror with fragmented glass—are a tad worse for wear.

I scoot out of the booth and pace up and down the aisle, unable to sit still a moment longer. "I don't understand," I tell Buckley.

I'm amazed to see that not a single soul occupies the dining car aside from us. "Where is everyone?"

"That's just the thing, my boy," Buckley replies jovially. "You two started a chain reaction when you solved my checkpoint riddle!" He wags a finger at me, then he nods towards Stark. "The other players began to wake and remember themselves. Several jumped just as you lads did, while some gathered in the caboose to wait it out until the Eighth Square."

So I was right. We can ride the train to the end.

"What happens when we reach the Eighth Square?" Willow asks.

Buckley strokes his goatee. "That depends."

Jack looks at him pointedly, speaking around his last mouthful of meat pie. "On what?"

"On you, most definitely, or indefinitely, as the case may be." He strokes his goatee once more before adding, "And the Jabberwocks, of course."

Madi, Willow, and Jack all express their own versions of shock. Jack spews mashed potatoes across the table, and Buckley wipes his cheek with a handkerchief.

"Sorry, old chap." A sheepish grin spreads across Jack's face.

Buckley eyes him but replies, "Quite all right, quite all right."

I cast a glance Stark's way, and he inclines his head. It's time to tell them what we saw.

The explanation I launch into is all jumbled words and frantic hand gestures. When I'm done, Madi repeats the same idea Stark relayed in the flower palace.

"We *are* the Jabberwocks."

They truly are related.

"So it would seem," Stark says.

"That's good though, right?" Jack sets his fork down with a clang. "If we created the beasts, then we can un-create them."

"Let's hope you lot are correct," Buckley pipes in. "Because the time has come."

At his words I follow the goat man's gaze beyond the window. More Jabberwocks than we've ever seen swoop and soar through a sky that appears to be darkening every second. Each of my teammates rises to gain a better view.

"This is your stop," Buckley says.

"But the train is still moving." Jack never fails to note the obvious.

"So it is, young chap, so it is."

Buckley makes no action to explain further, but there is no need. I shake his hand in silent thanks, gather Ace's rucksack and possessions, then let Stark take the lead as we follow him to the nearest exit. Once we're outside, a frigid wind whips and nips, throwing us off balance. Engine steam clouds the air, and we cling to the handrail, huddled in the small space, using one another for support.

"What are we doing?" Willow shouts at the same time a whistle blares.

I cover my ears and holler, "We jump. It's the only way."

There's no time to try and convince them. Instead I copy Ace's strategy from the Spade Trial, joining hands with my teammates. Once we're all linked, I prepare to take the leap that will be either our beginning or our end.

Our ride rounds the curve of a hill, and the Jabberwock hub comes into full view. If I wasn't witnessing the scene with my own eyes, I'd believe it a tale rather tall indeed. The beasts fly low and land in the centre of what appears to be ancient ruins. Just outside the ruins, the other half of our team, along with Knightley and Kit, wait with our horses at the ready.

My heart stops. And there, in the midst of it all, stands Alice.

Let the final Trial begin.

ALICE

The space between Realities is one I've yet to properly appreciate.

It's not so different from the silver liquid and temporary-drowning sensation I've experienced through the looking-glass memories. There's the feeling of being nowhere and everywhere at once. A nightmarish fear followed by a dream-like calm. I haven't been able to understand or explain how the most recent looking glass led me straight to Charlotte's door to say my goodbyes. But it's here, in this place where I am both Normal and Wonder, that I know without doubt or question . . .

My mother's memories showed me snippets of her reality, but she planted them with the hope that I'd find what was real in mine.

It's why the others could see the memory at the palace with Charlotte, Knave, and Dinah. The live garden illusion belonged to the former governess, but the memory was my own.

When I wished for Charlotte in the dark room with Chess by my side, a mere reflection or memory wouldn't do. Somehow, the Trial—dare I believe Wonderland?—allowed me to find the very person who would guide me back to where I needed to be.

I open my eyes and find Charlotte was right.

She's always been right.

I didn't need an entrance or a Trial's Gateway. I could see Wonderland all along.

It waited in my dreams, just beyond the door. It waited deep within my heart.

I'm standing in the midst of what appears to be an ancient castle's ruins. Colossal stones the colour of ivory lie fragmented and forgotten around me. Discarded weapons are strewn across the ground like bones in a graveyard. There's a long oak table that's been snapped in two. A floor-length looking glass in a gilded frame leans sideways against a cracked column, a red velvet chair that must have once been a throne beside it. Torn tapestries cover crumpled suits of armour. Battlement walls meant to guard from attack sit on the ground like fallen crowns.

Yet, despite its lowly state, one feature in the castle's architecture remains perfectly intact. An ivory tower rises before me, glistening and glorious. The turret at the top is adorned with crisscross arches, and at the heart of those arches stands a cross—a perfect replica of an imperial crown. The sight reminds me of the chapel next to London's Foundling House, where I entered Wonderland Abbey for the first time. But more than that, the cross and its crown and the tower beneath are the spitting image of a chess game's king.

Why didn't I see it? The Ivory King and Wonderland are one and the same.

It's part of what my mother was trying to show me. With every piece of her past she left behind for me to uncover, from Cordelia to Charlotte and every memory in between, Wonderland has always been here. While we've been searching, hoping, waiting, the truth has stood right before our eyes all along.

Boy claims he never left, only that he saw what's real.

Dan saw it. We all did.

And now I'll fight with everything in me to protect it and restore what was lost.

One by one, the Jabberwocks land like thunder inside the ruins. Each beast is unique in its own way. Some bare fangs and sweep long spiked tails through the decay, others have claws and horns protruding from their snouts. Some look like dragons and some more like griffins. Still others possess the head of a lion and the body of a bear.

The almanac's poem comes back to me with each thunderous landing. I know every word. The Jabberwocks are meant to invoke fear. They feed off it. They grow more ferocious with every beat of my racing heart. But the authors of the poem filled it with nonsense for a reason. And more than Charlotte's notes or Raving's scribbles, the original writers—the *Adventurers*—are who I turn to now. I'd been trying to piece the almanac together. Attempting to decipher this note or that. Now I recognise it's not just one author, but many who have contributed to it over the years, my mother and Charlotte included.

The almanac was penned by Wonders.

And, as one of them, I now see through the murk and mire to the poem's core purpose. On first glance, one might think it was written to make the reader afraid. But to come to that surface conclusion misses the mark as well.

Because the poem's purpose isn't to make the reader afraid.

It's to make the reader brave.

The ground trembles with each beast that joins the gathering, shifting the sand beneath my feet, sending a new crack through the already well-worn earth. I step over the cracks and crevices and climb on top of a pile of bricks to get a better view. The sky is ash, and the hills are shadows.

The Jabberwocks continue their descent.

Out of habit I move to open my rucksack, and my heart plummets. I left it behind at the garden palace. In the past I would have panicked. I've carried that canvas bag with the inked daisy chain with me for years. I even refused to accept a new one when Charlotte tried to convince me to switch to a boring old messenger bag. I would have no such nonsense, of course.

I've never fully appreciated nonsense. I've rolled my eyes and clicked my tongue. Huffed at Chess for his backwards riddles, wishing he would just say what he means for once. Now I know that impossible words with no meanings whatever can mean so much more.

For when the words do not matter, there is nothing to fear.

Rubble falls, and an echoing screech fills the sky as one Jabberwock calls to its brethren. If the sound wasn't so horrifying, it might mimic a song. I close my eyes and picture myself in the cottage filled with lost things. My mother's science experiment. The heart-shaped hand mirror. The rabbit lovey meant for me. Refusing to believe in the Jabberwock did the trick then. But that was one beast, one fear, compared to hundreds. Maybe even thousands. Here, just when I think the last Jabberwock has landed, two more circle the sky in its place.

I search those Jabberwock-filled skies, hoping help will appear. It's going to take more than me not believing in these beasts to defeat them. They are as real as I am. Only the sharpest vorpal sword can bring them down, or so the poem says. And like the authors of the almanac, I have something sharper than a sword.

I have faith. Against all odds, I found Wonderland and believed in its existence. But that wasn't enough. In the end, finding Wonderland wasn't based on anything I did. It wasn't my own abilities or talents or even a Mastery that brought me here.

It was Wonderland itself. And because Wonderland believed in me, I am not alone.

I close my eyes and tune out every sense. The pandemonium around me fades, and the air grows utterly still. And then something stirs it, something different from a Jabberwock.

That's when I open my eyes and see someone climbing up and over the rubble.

At first I think it might be Chess, but my hope falters when I find it's not. Instead, a young boy of maybe nine or ten with blond hair and a fierce look about him scales the stones. He's so young.

Too young. Something Madi once said during a podcast episode returns to me then.

"While it's rumoured players much younger were once permitted to compete, a tragic accident many years ago drove Trial officials to raise the age requirement to thirteen."

The boy is joined by a girl a few years older. They finish climbing together and race towards the brick pile where I stand.

"We heard the king is returning," the girl says, her eyes shining.

"You heard right," I tell them both. "But you must be prepared to fight. To defend." Like the chess pieces in the legend behind the game. Every piece is important, just as every Wonder matters to Wonderland.

More lost players appear, trickling in through collapsed archways and hurdling over fallen spires. Each one is a stranger, but we have the Trials in common. Trials designed to prepare us for this moment. Players from the Spades, the Diamonds, the Hearts, the Clubs.

Together we are strong.

Amazingly, the beasts are outnumbered two to one. For every single fearsome creature there are two more, three more, now four more Wonders.

Several Jabberwocks breathe rings of fire around the ruins. This obstacle is nothing compared to the flames rising inside, of course. Standing tall on my pile of bricks, I shout through cupped hands so everyone can hear.

"Wonders!" I yell. "My aunt Charlotte was once your true and loyal Queen of Hearts. But, like so many, she lost faith. She lost sight of what being Wonder truly means."

The beasts take notice as we band together. They creep closer, forming a wall of trepidation, blocking every exit. I watch the expression on each player's face. Their uncertainty is anything but foreign. If they lose hope, they lose Wonderland.

I won't let that happen.

I find my resolve. Then I turn the "Jabberwocky" poem etched into my mind upside down and on its head. I speak it out loud, not as I originally understood it, with its dark words and malicious meanings. I say it now with victory in my heart. These words are my weapons, just as I believe the authors intended them to be.

> "'Twas brillig, and the slithy toves
> Did gyre and gimble in the wabe:
> All mimsy were the borogoves,
> And the mome raths outgrabe."

I laugh at the last line, and a few Wonder players laugh along with me. The mome raths led us to the Wabe. They were feisty little things, but we grew stronger because of them. Sophia broke out of her shell and saw she was capable of standing on her own. Willow learned to accept help—to see that sometimes the strongest thing you can do is to let someone else's strength carry you.

I find renewed strength with each stanza and line.

> "Beware the Jabberwock, my son!
> The jaws that bite, the claws that catch!
> Beware the Jubjub bird, and shun
> The frumious Bandersnatch!"

"We've lost sight of the truth," I announce. "We've become careless in our care for Wonderland. We must always be on guard against the Jabberwocks. They've taken our home, but today we claim it as our own once more."

Whoops and hollers rise from the crowd. One beast begins to retreat, cowering with its tail between its legs. Another follows suit and then another. It's working. Without fear to feed on, the Jabberwocks cannot survive.

> "He took his vorpal sword in hand;
> Long time the manxome foe he sought—
> So rested he by the Tumtum tree
> And stood awhile in thought."

I think of the Tumtum tree fruit at the Wabe. Of the laughter and joy and respite I found there.

> "And, as in uffish thought he stood,
> The Jabberwock, with eyes of flame,
> Came whiffling through the tulgey wood,
> And burbled as it came!"

We came here through the Tulgey Wood. It separated us. But we found one another. My newest teammates roar louder than any Jabberwock ever could.

> "One, two! One, two! And through and through
> The vorpal blade went snicker-snack!
> He left it dead, and with its head
> He went galumphing back."

More beasts retreat. The Wonders fight with their voices. They say the words I know Wonderland wants to hear. Nonsense words that cause the beasts to cry out in agony.

Uffish!

Tulgey!

Frumious!

Burbled!

The Wonders are laughing, coming up with more nonsense words, reminding one another the Jabberwocks are only as strong as our fears allow them to be. I finish the last stanza before the first one repeats, and the final Jabberwock takes flight, moving up and out and away.

> "And hast thou slain the Jabberwock?
> Come to my arms, my beamish boy!
> O frabjous day! Callooh! Callay!"
> He chortled in his joy."

At those words, my own joy manifests. The clouds part, and a glorious sunrise paints the hills in vivid, full-fledged colour. It's not even breakfast yet, and I've already believed my fair share of impossible things, including, but not limited to the boy charging straight for us.

Chess comes galloping in on a copper-haired steed, leaping over the fire ring and through the arch that must have once housed a drawbridge, the remainder of our team in tow.

Knave.

Sophia.

Willow.

Madi.

Jack.

Kit and Erin and Stark join them too.

Sophia wields a snake vine like a whip. Knave approaches in full Beast's Blend form, lion's teeth bared and ready. The sight makes my heart full.

Chess dismounts his steed and sprints to greet me with open arms, my rucksack attached to his back. I scramble down my brick-pile platform. When we embrace, I know everything is going to be okay. "We're safe," I say when I draw back. "Wonderland is restored." But just when I think I can breathe and finally cry over Charlotte or collapse into Chess's arms, I look around, taking in the unaltered state of our setting. "Why hasn't anything changed? Why is this castle still in ruins?"

"I . . . don't know, Ace." Chess, rarely at a loss for words, appears just as confused as I am.

Everyone else present seems to sense it too. A lack of victory settles on our shoulders. I don't know what I expected. For the castle to magically rebuild? For music to swell or trumpets to resound, ushering in a new king's reign?

This isn't over. The morning remains bright, but the new Jabberwock soaring overhead casts a dark and ominous shadow. Another joins it. And another. Soon, four-winged creatures circle the skies. Unlike the previous beasts, these are more vibrant, more real than any foe we've faced thus far.

As the fire rings surrounding the ruins die down, the Jabberwock quartet circles closer, and closer still. I shade my eyes and squint through my glasses, straining and searching for something that might be promising as our next possible strategy.

Why do these beasts seem so familiar?

One by scaly one, they perch on the four cornerstones of the conquered castle. Their tails with pointed spikes flick this way and that, and their talons click and scrape against stone. I suddenly know where I've seen a dragon like this before.

Wonderland's coat of arms.

There was the lion and the horse I now know was a unicorn. But behind them, a dragon black as night lurked, just waiting to pounce. Four stones to represent the four suits were embedded into the coat. A red ruby for hearts, a dazzling diamond for Diamonds, a jade opal for Clubs, and a black onyx for Spades.

I gasp when it hits me. Black scales that shine like onyx. Catlike eyes. Orange markings on its horned tail. The largest Jabberwock of the quartet is Dinah. Does she have a tea for everything?

Is this nightmare ever going to end?

She sneers and sniffs. Then she makes her move, the play she'd been holding back. This is the hand she's held just out of sight since the beginning, waiting to reveal all until it would inflict the most damage.

Dinah takes flight.

Then she dives straight for us.

Every Wonder present looks on, stricken into silence. I can sense their fear returning, brewing beneath the surface as they watch this terrifying Jabberwock come in for the kill.

Taking Chess's hand, I stand firm. Knave roars, warning Dinah to stay back. She responds with a breath of fire to the ground far too close to where we stand. Chess steps in front of me, acting like a human shield. If we stick together, everything will be fine.

Everything is not fine.

It's as if Dinah has been waiting for this moment to pull out every stop. She soars then dives again, this time stretching out her claws and snatching me up in her talons. I wiggle and squirm, but she's too strong. She keeps low and drops me carelessly on the other end of the castle grounds, far away from Chess and the others. I tuck my head and roll right over a sharp rock. It tears the black trouser fabric and skin at my ankle. Wincing, I take a deep breath and rise to my feet.

Dinah returns to Chess and lands a metre from him, sweeping her tail along the ground, stopping Chess mid-run so he can't reach me. I cry out and pick up the same rock I rolled over. Then I limp-run towards them. When I'm close enough, I hurl the stone at Dinah.

"Leave him be!" I shout. "It's me you came for. Me, the Wonder anomaly born Normal!" I pick up rock upon rock, each throw echoing the truth beating in my heart.

I am not afraid.

I am not afraid.

I am not afraid.

The Jabberwock turns her attention from Chess to me, a leer curling her black lips. She prowls towards me like a hungry wildcat. I look past her to where my team is now in full battle mode. The other three Jabberwocks, who I assume are the quarter heads, fly in for the fight.

All around, the lost Wonders stand in place, refusing to run. They must see a lack of fear won't drive the Jabberwocks away, but it seems words won't stop whatever Dinah has planned either. If she knows I do not fear her, what is she—?

"*No!*" The choked-out scream can't be my own. It's too far away and too high to be mine.

Her catlike eyes on me, Dinah's tail becomes a deadly weapon. She raises it high then slices the air clean through before going in for the move she's been wanting to make all along.

Dinah takes Chess out of the game.

CHESS

I groan. I'm lying on my back, hard stone beneath me. It's quiet. I could curl up and take a cat nap. My eyes close. Am I dead?

Muffled noises strike my ears from all angles, but a closer, garbled voice stands out.

"Hmm?" I ask, my words slurred. "Come again?"

The voice comes through clearer now, finer tuned, until I can make out what's being said.

"Get up, Chess! Get *up!*"

My eyes open and my body goes rigid. Who's shaking me?

"Don't be a loafer. Get up!"

Kit.

I roll to a crouch then lurch to my feet. Ouch. I rub the back of my head. That smarts. Every muscle and bone aches something awful, but Kit stands before me, making me abandon all complaints. He's holding one arm to a gash in his side. My gaze shifts from him to the structure around us. We're inside the stairwell of the remaining tower.

"What happened?"

Kit sits on the bottom step, hissing a breath through his teeth. "The Jabberwock's tail hurled you a good fifteen metres or so. Knave took the lead and I dragged you in here."

I don't ask how my brother ended up bloody and bruised. He probably wouldn't tell me if I did. All I know is he's worse off than I am, which means he likely stepped in during the attack. I look out the small window in the arched door and spy the battle beyond.

The Jabberwocks remain unscathed despite everyone's efforts to thwart them. I know without a doubt the largest beast is a transformed Dinah, the woman who deigned to call herself our family.

This is why Dinah was so adamant from the start that I help with her investigation, keep an eye on Ace, and stay near her throughout every Trial.

"I chose the wrong child."

It was all leading to this moment. As Wonderland hangs in the balance, years of wreckage around us, Ace's belief remains the key. Dinah plans to break her.

To do that, she's going to kill us.

Dinah is going to kill me.

I join Kit on the stairwell's bottom step, thoughts reeling. We don't have much time.

"Got any brilliant ideas?" Kit winces with each small movement.

"You've always been the brighter Shire, brother."

"Obviously." He quirks an eyebrow.

"I was coming back for you," I blurt. If these are our last moments together, I need to set things straight.

"What?" Kit rises, using the curved wall for support.

"I was coming back for you," I repeat, standing as well. "I never intended to run during the Heart Trial last year. I was trying to distract the Jabberwock while you hid. I had every intention of coming back for you."

He's looking at me strangely. "Is that why you've seemed so odd around me? Don't you think I know my big brother well enough by now? The same big brother who stood in Dad's way when he was off his trolley so he would lash out at you instead of me? The same big brother who let me win every game we ever played? The same big brother who streaked his hair with that horrid pink in memory of Mum's favourite rose after Dad burned every photo, just so I wouldn't forget her?"

"She never did like red," I say absently, combing my fingers through my hair.

He folds his arms over his chest, clearly amused. "The same big brother who ran into the Jabberwock's path because I was so scared out of my mind I couldn't move?"

All this time, he knew? "You remember," I breathe.

"Of course I remember. You left the Trial, not me. I didn't end up on some time loop checkpoint train like Stark Hatter either. I remember everything."

"But, you told me to prove it, to prove I wouldn't leave again."

"We all have something we fear, don't we?" Kit gives his head a shake. "You've had it all wrong, Chess. If you would have just asked me, you would have known." He looks away for a moment, then a hesitant smile comes to his face. "I guess I was wrong too. I wasn't sure if you thought I was a coward." We stand looking at each other for a moment as the sounds outside intensify.

I find my words again. "A coward, you? Never." I clap him on the shoulder and grin.

Before I can say more, someone screams beyond the safety of the stone walls. There's a clash, a clang, a shout. The others aren't backing down, buying us time to come up with some way to end this. Ace's rucksack weighs heavier than it ought to on my back as I peer through a crack in the stone wall.

The battle rages on outside. The Jabberwocks will soon claim victory. Wonders have grabbed swords and spears and javelins. They throw rocks and shout, their voices hoarse. Fire rains from the beasts circling the sky. I scan the ruins, searching for some weapon or defence we could use to help.

My eye catches something glinting in the sunlight at the other end of the grounds. My fingers curl tightly around the straps of the rucksack. It just might work. I've had enough of Dinah's illusions. Maybe it's time we create one of our own.

"Come on." I grab my brother by the arm, and we head up the spiralling steps two at a time.

He matches my pace despite his injury. "What's the plan?"

I hitch Ace's rucksack higher and flash a full-toothed grin. "It's time to give that old cat a taste of her own tea."

ALICE

Dinah and the other Jabberwocks do not relent, no matter what we try to ward them off. The tremendous relief from seeing Kit drag Chess to safety gave me a surge of strength, but now my energy is depleting. If I had any Fates, they'd be long gone by now. Even the extra Fate the Trial provided to give me hope and the courage to move forwards couldn't save me. Fates and golden petals and Wonder Vision were never the answer anyway.

Knave looks worn too, his fur mangled and matted. Poor Jack is limping horribly and blood spreads across Madi's middle. Her expression is stricken as she downs what must be her last vial of tea. As soon as she does, she disappears, and I know it must be the same blend she gave me. The one I used to heal Willow that made her momentarily vanish in the wood.

This can't go on. Soon, Knave will turn back into his human self and Madi won't have any more tea up her sleeve. Sophia's snake vine has already died, and Stark's and Erin's horses can't keep galloping circles around the beasts. They'll tire out soon enough and then what?

I look to the Ivory King tower, hoping for an answer.

"Help us," I plea, throat parched and words weak.

That's when I catch two copper-haired heads pop into view through a window near the tower's top. I can't see Chess's turquoise gaze from here, but something tells me he's smiling. My heart leaps. What do those brothers have up their sleeves?

Whatever it is, I only hope they don't do something stupid.

"A!" Knave shouts.

I whip around to see my cousin is human once more. Blood and dirt mat the hair at his temples.

"Why isn't it working?" He grabs a rock and hurls it at the Jabberwock with a spade burned into its scales—the minister.

"I don't know!" I cry, lungs ready to burst. "These beasts seem different. Fear isn't feeding them, so what is?"

His answer drowns in the tumult. Dinah whirls, and I barely dodge her massive tail. I run in the opposite direction just as she emits another fiery breath. The heat is so close, too close. My clothing smells of smoke and my forehead is drenched in sweat. My injured ankle has gone numb, but I know when the adrenaline ceases its rush I'm in for a world of pain.

If we make it out of this.

We *will* make it out of this.

Rubble soars overhead, and I duck behind a boulder. Too many Wonders are screaming, fighting, maybe even dying. We were not prepared. I'd attempt to imagine a different outcome into reality, but my mind is spent. Besides, it's been clear from the start of this Trial the Gene works differently here.

I press my back against the boulder and adjust my glasses. One, two, three quick breaths before I'm turning, peering around the curve of stone to see where I might be of use. A boy with a sword bigger than he is swings the weapon at one Jabberwock, while a young woman races back and forth, trying to distract the beast. My eyes widen when what's ahead comes into focus. Chess and Kit sit together on steps that must have once led to a dais. How did they move from the tower to the opposite end of the ruins so quickly? It doesn't matter. The sight of them boosts my confidence. Exhaustion consumes every muscle, but if I can just reach them, maybe we can come up with a plan together to end this fight.

End. This. Fight.

I take in the ivory tower again. Its high arches and double-edged cross make it more fitting for a fortress than a castle. I'd pled for help and thought I'd received silence in return. The battle pressed on as we fought with everything in us. But what's in us still isn't enough.

What's in me still isn't enough.

A screech louder than any we've heard yet fills the air and quakes the ground. I cover my ears and step out from behind the boulder. It takes a few moments, but I stand still, watching, waiting.

One by one, all eyes land on me. The battle stills. Dust settles. The Jabberwocks quiet and Wonders cease their shouting. Swords and spears clatter to the ground as if in slow motion. Then, with my last shred of hope, I raise my hands high in surrender and fall to my knees. Hard earth and rubble dig into my torn trousers and broken skin. I pull out my locket watch, just as I have done so many times before, turn the tiny key, and let the music play.

It's a small sound, and I don't know if everyone present can hear. I don't even know the lyrics aside from the title. I only know this tiny tune has saved me from my nightmares more than once. It's opened locked doors. When nothing else worked, trusting in the simplicity of a golden afternoon's song did.

Once the melody has finished, I rise on shaky legs, lift my chin, and find the face of the boy who helped me believe in the impossible.

Our eyes meet for only a second before Chess and his brother are consumed by the Jabberwock's flames.

Death is not the end. This is.

My mouth opens in silent agony, releasing no sound. I fall to my knees again, unable to breathe. I want to look away, but I can't. Chess wouldn't look away if it were me.

The Jabberwocks vanish then, one by one, leaving mere humans in their stead. The Minister of Spades, Lord of Clubs, and Duchess of Diamonds wear mixed expressions of fear and relief, victory and defeat. They utter not a word. It appears they don't dare. For all their fanfare during the first three Trials, here they are, nothing but common cards.

Queen Scarlet struts to where I kneel, adjusting her ruby gown and fussing with her dark curls.

I'm shaking, and tears drip from my eyes, muddying the ground.

She clicks her tongue as she nears. "There, there. Why the long face?"

Hatred, raw and wrathful, surges, overshadowing every other emotion. The quarter heads appear to cower at her presence. I, however, do not. "You sent Charlotte to her death." The words start tense and low, then rise. "Now you've taken Chess from me." I can barely get the words out. To say them makes them real. But there's power in truth, and right now truth is all I have.

"Poor, pathetic, Alice," the queen says. "All alone. Did you truly believe a song would save you?" She may insist on continuing this ridiculous masquerade, but she's not fooling anyone. Scarlet strides around me, prowling. I can just see her in her old form now, flicking her tail this way and that, maddening as ever.

Who would have guessed it was the cat all along?

"How?" is all I ask.

"It was simple, really." She touches the onyx stone on her WV bangle with one finger. "A bit of Fear's Fancy did the trick."

"A tea turned you into Jabberwocks?"

"No, you daft girl." A sneer doesn't begin to describe the look on her proud face. "You did."

My fingers curl into fists. "I do not fear you."

"Silly child, I don't need you to fear me. Not now."

"Explain yourself."

"Very well." She sighs, apparently annoyed though she continues as if she's been waiting to divulge her secret all along. "Fear's Fancy is a code I've worked to perfect over the years, thanks to Catherine's Wonder Vision technology. It has allowed me to explore the hearts and minds of players. To see who they *really* are at their rotten cores. Your courage may have sent those other Jabberwocks fleeing, but it will do nothing to defeat me."

"We are not interested in the possibilities of defeat. They do not exist."

Charlotte's favourite Queen Victoria quote returns to me. Have I been looking at this all wrong? Focused on possibilities when it is the impossible that continues to reign?

"Many lost Wonders became Jabberwocks, while others hid and waited," Scarlet continues. "Still others returned to my Wonderland, their memories wiped. It was rather inconvenient, I must say, having to start from square one every year."

Of course. How did I fail to recognise it? If we let our fears consume us, we inevitably become them.

"We coded ourselves into this Trial and you did the rest, dear Alice. The closer you came to the Eighth Square, the more data we gathered. The more data we gathered, the more real our Jabberwock forms became, give or take a few minor setbacks with the WV technology." She touches the onyx stone again.

The code. It's in the stone. No wonder she wears that thing everywhere she goes. Do the other quarter heads possess it as well? I glance at the Minister of Spades, finding his tattooed hand. There, on his ring finger, sits a black, spade-shaped stone.

They all carry the Fear's Fancy code with them. But this Trial bears its own code as well. We've seen it in the obstacles we've overcome. In the varying shortcuts and checkpoints we've faced. My mother left behind a code in each looking glass, visible to me alone until the memories and experiences became my own.

"Have you solved your mother's riddle yet?" Dinah prods, circling me a third time.

"Yes." I force myself to stand. Chess wouldn't cower, and he wouldn't want me to either. I hear his voice in my head even now. *"There now, Ace. That wasn't so difficult, was it?"*

Dinah may think she's taken everything, but she can't steal what will always remain in my heart and mind. Every moment feels measured. I find my teammates and take in their current states.

They're injured and bloodied and bruised. Knave carries Madi to sit on a nearby boulder, though he looks like he can hardly stand himself. Willow, Stark, and Erin aid some of the other players who arrived to help, checking their wounds and wearing solemn expressions.

Sophia kneels beside Jack, who appears unable to move his legs.

I can't allow their sacrifices to be for naught. And I will not let the deaths of Kit, Chess, and Charlotte be in vain. If I am the answer to my mother's riddle, both Normal and Wonder, then I can grieve my losses and still find joy in the victories.

In Wonderland's victory.

"It's simple," I say to Scarlet, mimicking her tone. I stand at my full height now, though still a head shorter than the woman who pretends to be queen. I lift my chin.

"Tell me, then, and let's get this over with."

"No." Despite my tears, I look her straight in the eye. "I don't think I will. Not when it's quite clear you need what I possess." She thinks I trusted in a song—in myself—to save us. She couldn't see the surrender meant so much more. "Was this your plan all along, *Your Majesty?*" I spread my arms wide then let them fall to my sides. "To reach the end of the Trial, to solve the clues in hopes that doing so would finally make you a ruler worthy of Wonderland?"

"Oh, my dear girl, I do not wish to take the throne now. It's clear Wonderland doesn't want me. The last king certainly didn't trust me to run things, though I can't say Charlotte did much better."

I want to tell her not to dare speak Charlotte's name, but I won't give her the satisfaction of knowing the fury her irreverence causes.

"So what, then? If you do not wish to restore Wonderland and rule it?"

Dinah chuckles. She's far too pleased with her schemes, but maybe I can use this to my advantage.

"Isn't it obvious? I wish to destroy it. Just as the lab fire I started destroyed the king who once sat upon that throne."

The revelation should pierce me like a talon to my chest. Then again, after everything else this woman has done, adding arson and premeditated homicide to her list of crimes doesn't astound me. Besides, she's feeding my anger and she knows it. I want to hold onto it, to make her pay for her wretched deeds. Yet, just as fear isn't the answer, hatred isn't either. My grief is still too raw to process, but if I let it consume me now, Dinah wins.

I follow her gaze to where I last saw Chess and Kit. A scorched chair sits beside an equally damaged looking glass. I narrow my eyes. No sign of one body let alone two. My pulse canters. Could it be possible?

I face Dinah once more, courage building. "You might be able to destroy men, but you could never destroy Wonderland."

"And yet I have," she taunts. "If the real Wonderland still existed, this castle would have raised itself. It would have been restored."

Charlotte's words come back to me, her hidden meaning clearer than ever before.

The palace is afraid. All this time, Dinah has been afraid of what's real because she can't see it. She could never see it.

The first time I thought I'd found Wonderland, I spoke four words out loud. Now I say them with my heart, knowing without a doubt they'll be heard.

I believe in Wonderland.

To Dinah I say, "I have nothing to fear, because you have *everything* to fear. You may have won this battle, but Wonderland claims victory in the war."

She doesn't look surprised in the least to hear me say this. Instead she looks bored. "Is that all?"

"No. There's something else too."

"Get on with it, then."

I choose each word before I say it, claiming them as truth. "I forgive you." The release I feel at this final surrender is immediate. The words aren't for Dinah as much as they are for me. Though they don't erase the pain, they do pave the way for healing.

Her eyes widen then narrow into slits. Her expression shifts from victorious to uncertain for an instant before she says, "If the Normal-born girl turned Wonder can't restore Wonderland, then no one can. Which means Wonders must continue to rely on me and the quarter heads. Every citizen from the greatest to the least will need to start wearing a WV bangle. And unless they do, they'll never get as much as a glimpse of anything resembling Wonderland at all."

She thinks she's won. That by bringing me to my breaking point she's destroyed what I've become. She thinks I'm ever so Normal. Ordinary. Unworthy to stand where she does. And that's precisely the point, I suppose. None of us is worthy. Being Wonder isn't earned, it's a gift, so I can't help but smile as wide as Chess when I say, "That's rather curious." I look around at the faces of my teammates, and the other Wonders who stood by our side. "From where I'm standing, it seems Wonderland has been restored."

At the same moment I speak what I know to be true with all my heart, my surroundings alter. It's like knowing I've won a high-stakes card game, and I'm about to lay down my best hand.

The Ivory Castle's throne room is glorious. Tapestries that tell stories I can't wait to hear line the walls. Columns encircled with ivy and roses support marble arches. A carpeted dais rises ahead, a throne at its helm. Behind the throne, a gilded looking glass stands.

I walk past Dinah and take my time ascending the steps. My fingers brush the throne's golden arms.

"What are you doing?" For the first time, Dinah's voice wavers.

Rather than answer, I continue my quest, stopping to stand

before the pristine looking glass in its golden frame. I almost expect to see my mother staring back at me, and I suppose in a way I do. Two blue eyes behind crooked black-framed glasses, and tangled blonde hair that is neither gold nor white but somewhere in between. I see a bit of Charlotte there too. I smile wide, but not because of my reflection.

I turn slowly, fully believing he's there and not just a refraction of my Wonder imagination. Across the throne room, high above the crowd that has gathered close to watch the scene unfold, Kit waves a shattered hand mirror in the shape of a heart.

It's a sight to behold, but more than Kit's triumphant visage, it's Chess's wide grin that sends my heart soaring.

It appears the Shire brothers created their own illusion. How very clever indeed.

Chess places his arm around Kit's shoulder, then he lifts something else into the air. It's seemingly insignificant to any onlooker, but it gives me the final nudge he knew I'd need. A reminder of where I've come from.

The tattered rabbit lovey. The one I lost when Charlotte fled. She never held her circumstances against anyone, despite all that was taken from her. She was true royalty, but she chose to make herself low so I could eventually rise.

I mouth a silent *thank you* and return my attention to Scarlet, whose façade is beginning to fade. Her brown hair turns to orange and grey, and her onyx broach appears dull and ordinary. Her data and codes are no match for anomalies, it seems.

"Dinah." I curtsy as it's likely the last one she will ever receive. "So nice to see you again, even if it is a goodbye."

Knave joins me on the dais, where he belongs. He says nothing though his eyes are filled with awe.

Dinah's mask of certainty falters, replaced by dread. "No," she says, trembling and backing away. "You're lying."

"I'm afraid not." Knave sounds rather regal. "It would appear, just like my mother Cordelia, you have lost sight of what's right in front of you." Then he does something I don't expect. He moves to the side and says, "Now bow before your queen."

My heart stops. I shake my head, side-eyeing him. "Knave," I say through the corner of my mouth. "It's you. You're meant to be the new king."

"I think I'm better suited to take after my mother," Knave says. "England needs a change, and I might be just the lion for the job." He winks. "Besides, I'm pretty sure you saw the truth first."

"So?"

"So," a new voice says, "Wonderland chose you."

I whirl to find Chess waiting on the next step down. We stare at one another for a long moment, then I throw my arms around him, abandoning all decorum. "We did it, Chess."

He draws back and brushes the fringe from my eyes with his fingertips. "You did it, Ace."

"It wasn't me." I blink back my tears, bursting to say more. But we have plenty of time for explanations. My heart is full at the mere thought of the hours we'll no doubt spend talking about this—about the wonders of Wonderland.

Chess kneels, kissing my hand. My new charge weighs heavy, and soon everyone in the throne room takes a knee too.

Everyone except Dinah and the quarter heads. They're backing towards the exit, pressing against one another like shuffled cards. When they reach the tall oak doors at the back, they vanish entirely.

I can only assume they've returned to their false reality, unable to see this gift we've been given. Knave, no doubt, will deal with them soon enough, if and when they cross his path.

For now, I fight the urge to hide. I may be the new queen, entrusted with this immense responsibility, but I am still just one of many Wonders seeking the truth.

"I am Alice," I say.

"All hail Queen Alice," Knave bellows, and a chorus of echoes follows.

My heart beats wildly with every new voice that cries out.

When the refrain has quieted to a low hum, I clear my throat and start anew.

"I am Alice," I say again, "but Wonderland is King."

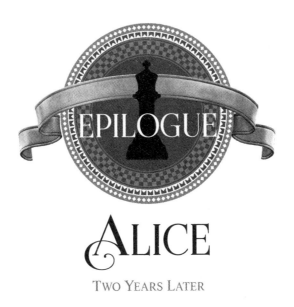

ALICE

TWO YEARS LATER

One thing is certain . . .

There once was a time when no room existed at the Normal table for a Wonder. Likewise, a version of Wonderland was closed off to those who didn't yet have eyes to see.

That time is coming to an end.

Anticipation brews and bubbles over as I stand inside a quaint Buckingham Palace parlour. Once known as the Queen's Audience Chamber, it now belongs to England's king. His painted portrait hangs over a hearth, his frozen-in-time expression making me swallow a giggle. He must have hated posing. I wonder how long he lasted before loosing his tie and mussing his slicked hair.

Nearing footsteps from the closest corridor remind me to stand straight, though I can't help but twiddle my fingers as I wait for him to appear.

When my cousin crosses the chamber's threshold wearing a crisp, dark blue suit and tie, I pinch the folds of my skirt and offer a curtsy. Nothing will irk him more, and I watch for his inevitable reaction.

"Your Majesty," I say, exaggerating my vowels and dipping far too low. I peek up at him under my lashes.

He rolls his eyes. Despite being a pair of years older and wiser, he's still the boy who ran with me through the corridors of the Wabe. Still my Knave.

"Would you stop that, A? I don't take myself seriously enough as it is." He adjusts and loosens his tie slightly, only supporting my theory about his impatience with portrait posing.

I stand and fold my hands in front of me, schooling my expression.

"You're making it worse!"

I can't help it. I laugh and cross the rug to meet him.

He extends his hands and holds fast to both of mine. "It's so good to see you."

"You too." I beam at him.

King Knave Civilius Heart gestures for me to sit in one of the damask armchairs before the hearth. A true gentleman, he remains standing until I've settled onto my seat, then he takes the one across from mine.

I smooth my skirt over my legs, still not quite accustomed to the bold colour choice. It was one thing to wear the Team Heart colours of red and black during the Trials, but the hues I choose to don mean more now. An ivory blouse with puffed lace sleeves to my wrists represents my kingdom—Wonderland. A heart-red skirt that shimmers in the sunlight to remind me of the rightful queen, who once reigned there.

Even now, the thought of Charlotte not joining us tonight brings an ache. The loss of seeing her face when Knave and I embark on the next chapter of this journey we've begun tugs. Though Charlotte, proper and poised as ever, would have attempted to conceal her emotions, deep down I know she'd be bursting at the seams with pride.

"Are you ready for tonight?" Knave asks, his tone warm and

genuine. He leans forwards, clasping—no, wringing—both hands between his knees.

"You aren't nervous, are you, cousin?" I tease, if only to mask my own pre-game jitters.

"Alice Heart, do you dare address the King of England so informally?"

We both decided to keep the Heart in our names, a symbol to unify our very different kingdoms. A reminder of where we came from. And of where we intend to go. "That's *Queen* Alice Heart to you," I quip.

He flashes a rare grin my way. "So it is."

The easy banter between us is nice. I've missed having him near, but we'll never accomplish what we've set out to do if it's fun and games all the time. This is the part of politics I despise. The formalities and policies and procedures in a confined room, discussing visions for the future. It's precisely why I've instated courtyard meetings with the new Wonderland quarter heads. Far less stuffy and rather an ingenious idea, if I do say so myself.

Madi agreed, of course, and as my new royal advisor, I hold her opinion in the highest regard.

As if reading my mind, Knave looks at me intently. I know what he wants to ask, but he's hesitant, still unsure if he ought to be so open about his feelings.

"Yes." I smile at him. "She'll be here tonight."

He shifts in his seat, satisfaction and a bit of nerves apparent on his face. It's yet another reminder he's still quite young, not yet twenty-one until later this year.

How in the Divided Kingdom did we get here? Two unlikely rulers about to change history? It's impossible. Then again, so is Wonderland.

"Well, then," Knave says, rising. "I guess we mustn't dawdle."

I stand and take his offered arm. "I suppose we mustn't."

Then my cousin, the king, leads me out into the corridor, hand in arm, where we eventually part to prepare for the evening ahead.

"Eet's positively glorious! Vait until you see! Really, zee Normal palace haz outdone themselves!"

A straight pin between her teeth, Rabekah fusses with the final details on my evening gown, her dialect slipping on occasion. England's new ambassador regarding all things Wonder Gene development may be a Brit, but she played the part of Blanche de Lapin for so long, sometimes she still manages to mix her consonants and vowels.

"Nearly there," Rabekah says, a final tug on the ribbon lacing my bodice. "And . . . perfection!"

I'm about to turn around to face the floor-length looking glass when Madi comes bursting through the suite door.

"Really, Madi Hatter, you need to learn to knock before you enter a queen's chambers!"

My dearest friend ignores Rabekah's reprimand and skips over. She's the picture of everything that is uniquely Wonderland with black-lace, high-heeled boots that tie with a ribbon at her knees, a matching tiered, high-low tutu that bounces when she walks, and a sequined silver bodice that drips glass beads. Her hair is a deep amethyst tonight, pulled up in an extravagant plait that begins at her forehead and trails past her hips. The finishing touch is her signature headband, a miniature top hat tilted to one side.

"Wow, Rabs, you really outdid yourself." Madi gives me a once-over followed by two thumbs up.

"I told you not to call me zat."

"Oh." Madi gives a wink only I can see. "I must have forgotten."

Rabekah rolls her eyes before excusing herself and heading for the door. Just before she takes her leave, she looks back at the two of us. "Don't you dare be late to the party." Her words are for us both, but her eyes are on Madi.

Madi waves Rabekah off as if such an accusation is nonsense. "Never would I ever," she says.

Rabekah shakes her head but goes just the same. I exhale. Or try to. My bodice is laced so tight, it's hard to move, let alone breathe. Madi jumps into action, undoing Rabekah's work and starting over on the ribbon. "Better?" she asks.

I take three deep breaths, testing them for good measure. One good breath deserves another, after all. "Much," I say. My voice shakes on the single word. Why am I so nervous? I practice my breaths again. Just when I think I've got the hang of them, the sharp sound of scissors snipping something close to my body sends me into a panic.

Craning my neck to look back at Madi, I gasp. "Oh, your head is going to roll, Madi Hatter!"

"What Rabs doesn't know won't hurt her. Besides, there was plenty of leftover ribbon after I loosened your torso prison." Madi reveals the length of satin black ribbon she cut from the one lacing up my gown.

I pull my loose curls off my shoulders and Madi helps me tie a bow on top of my head. When I let my hair fall loose and long again—longer than I've ever let it grow, I might add—Madi turns me around by my shoulders. Then she steps to one side, leaving me to face my reflection in the looking glass.

The first thought that comes to mind is that I look exactly how I expected. A title doesn't make one taller, and a gorgeous gown doesn't turn a girl into a woman. And yet . . .

Despite the truth I'm still very much me, I also notice the subtle changes that have taken place over the past two years. Changes like my hair that now falls to the middle of my back. It's a darker blonde now, the yellow from my childhood and younger teen years replaced by a deep gold. Though it will never be brown like Knave's or Charlotte's, I look more like our aunt than ever, and that sight alone makes me smile.

I feel I've aged years beyond eighteen. I focus on my eyes, but I don't just see their colour or the glasses frames surrounding them. My eyes speak of what I've seen and what I've experienced.

Centuries ago, a famous Wonder poet once said, "The eyes are the windows to the soul." He was right on one account, but he forgot another very important thing. Our eyes reveal more than what's inside us. They show what's outside us too. They reflect those who love us, believe in us, protect us. And it isn't until we close our eyes and trust that what we can't see still remains, that we finally can believe in the impossible.

I close my eyes now, taking these final few moments before Knave and I announce our plan to the world. As word continues to spread, more and more Normal-borns like me are becoming Wonder through pure and simple belief. It is our hope that every Normal might eventually witness what we've had a chance to see. And when that happens, fear of Wonders and Wonderland may finally be defeated for good.

There's still so much to be done, though. In the two years since Charlotte's passing, we've managed to eliminate the Registry, destroy every last trace of cordial, and, slowly but surely, warm Normals up to the idea of living in unity with the Wonders around them. No more hiding, no more haven. Just two kingdoms, separate but united. Different but working together.

The lion and the unicorn.

Here and there, a former Jabberwock will seek refuge at the Ivory Castle, lost and confused Wonders who finally surrender and let go of their fear and choose to trust in truth. Knave visits and offers counsel when he can, but he's been busier than ever. In his short time as king, he's reinstated the Houses of Lords and Commons, visiting Scotland and Northern Ireland, negotiating peace treaties that were broken long ago. Erin Knightley has travelled with him, working as a liaison with the Irish and helping him find common ground. I've hardly seen the king since his coronation last spring, but tonight he owes me more than peace and a party.

He owes me a dance.

"It's time," Madi says softly, drawing me back to the present.

I reach for her hand. But the fingers that find mine aren't her delicate ones. Instead they're firm and strong, intertwining with my own in a way I've come to know so well.

Opening my eyes, I find him in the looking-glass reflection. He stands slightly behind me and to one side, his full grin lighting the room and my heart in one instant. His magenta waistcoat plays in brilliant contrast to his cream-coloured tuxedo. Though any sign of pink in his hair has faded, his copper locks remain stubborn, continuously falling in his eyes.

When he brings my hand to his lips, flutters of bread-and-butterflies take flight, and I don't know whether to throw my arms around him or give him a playful slap to the shoulder for making me nervous all over again.

I opt for something in between as I lean back against him, relaxing into his embrace.

"Ace," he says, circling his arms around my waist. "You look positively stunning."

"Do you think I should have worn red? It's what Charlotte would have—"

Chess shakes his head against my cheek. I inhale his peppermint cocoa scent with delight.

"You are not Charlotte," he says. "And should you ever try to become anything other than exactly Alice, I may very well have to alert the authorities to your treasonous ways. I have mates in high places, you know." He winks and kisses my cheek, lingering there too briefly before pulling away too soon. He keeps hold of my hand and twirls me once before kissing it again.

"That's enough, you two," Madi interrupts.

My cheeks warm. For a moment, I'd forgotten she was here.

"And, in case you wanted my most fashionable opinion," she adds, "I've always thought blue was your best colour."

With a final glance at my cornflower gown with the black lace overlay and gold beads sewn on to look like stars, I glide towards the door, Madi on my right and Chess on my left. Looping one arm through Chess's and picking up my gown so I don't trip, I catch a glimpse of my Mary Jane shoes and black-and-white striped tights. Reminders of where I've come from taking me to where I am going.

The Heart Ball.

Rabekah wasn't exaggerating. Knave has pulled out all the stops and then some. Paper lanterns swing along zigzagged string lights overhead as we enter the palace courtyard. A man in a funny hat with bells bursting from its pointed ends flips in the air then takes a dramatic fall, causing a group of ladies to roar with laughter. There are stilt walkers and jugglers and even a girl who appears to eat fire off a stick, which is possibly the most curious thing I've witnessed this side of Wonderland.

The moment he sees us enter the party, King Knave approaches with open arms. His eyes light up, staying on Madi with every step he takes. He doesn't look nervous, which works out well, as I'm jumpy enough for the both of us.

"Welcome." He shakes Chess's extended hand first.

"I'd bow," Chess says, "but someone once warned me I'd regret it, Your Maj—"

Knave eyes him, and Chess grins.

"It's good to see you, mate."

"And you, Shire. How are things in Spade Quarter? Alice tells me you stepped into the role as Minister of Spades quite nicely."

"I don't like to brag, but things are better than ever. In fact, I've got some ideas I'd like to run by you, when you have a moment."

Knave looks around. "I have some time now. Walk with me."

Madi and I watch them go. I notice how her gaze lingers on the king. She bites her lower lip.

"You should ask him to dance." I nudge her with my gloved elbow.

Her eyes widen. "He's the King of England, Alice."

"And you're advisor to a queen. There's nothing wrong with a little public relations." She doesn't seem convinced, so I raise the stakes. "I *command* you to dance with him."

She flashes a twinkling smile. "Yes, Your Majesty." She dips a quick curtsy.

A waiter with a tray of something that smells divine passes by, and Madi hurries after him, no doubt ready to swindle the entire platter out of his hands. I wander deeper into the party, taking in sights I never thought I'd see.

Wonders and Normals laughing together. Dancing together. There's no fear or resentment to be found, and my heart is full. A few lords and ladies I recognise from my most recent visit in the spring nod their greetings as I pass. Now it's summer and the air hums with the excitement of fun and frivolity. It's been two years since the Trials officially met their end. Without them this season feels full of new possibilities.

A string quartet begins an upbeat tune near the courtyard's centre, where a hardwood floor has been laid for dancing. I see several of my favourite people. Jack B. Nimble—now the Minister of Clubs—has all the dance moves and more, the master of the wheelchair he wields. Rather than let his injury slow him down, it's made him stronger, more confident. He spins this way and that, leading Sophia around the floor.

Perhaps a little too confident.

Jack's chair runs over Sophia's toes. She laughs it off. Willow approaches the pair and wags a finger in his face, but he bows at his waist and extends a hand. Soon Jack is wheeling Willow around in a waltz, Sophia's toes forgotten.

But Sophia isn't forgotten. Kit, who is far too grown up in my opinion, nears and presents her with a flower. Truly frabjous.

I spy Stark and Raving next. They chat with a few gentlemen by the refreshment table, no doubt bringing in more investors for their project. Though I offered Raving the Spade Quarter head position first, he insisted Chess take it.

"Charlotte and I had other ideas in mind," he shared then. "If I have your support, I'd like to bring them to fruition."

How could I protest? The brothers now run a school right here in London. Impossible Academy has become a place unlike any other. Anyone can attend and study anything from Wonderland's history to Tea Mastery. If Stark and Raving had their way, they'd do away with Occupational Exams altogether and turn every student who walks through their doors into full-fledged believing Wonders.

"One step at a time," I told them. "You still have the WV at your disposal. Use it at your discretion to show them what they're missing."

"We're more old-fashioned," Stark had replied. "We made copies of the almanac and find that the students prefer to study and come to conclusions on their own. It's amazing what gems that book contains, if you know where to look."

Raving had nodded but remained quiet. Even now I sense the sorrow he bears for losing the girl he always loved. I hope, in time, he'll learn to love again. It's what Charlotte would have wanted.

By the time Chess makes his rounds and finds me again, I've settled on a garden bench beneath a rose vine arch.

"Is this seat taken?"

I scoot to one side, relishing his warmth when he joins me. We stay that way for a time, quiet together, through Knave and Madi's eighth dance. Until partygoers trickle out and on their way. Until the crescent moon is at its highest point, smiling down amidst all the twinkling stars that remind me of home. Of Wonderland.

Chess speaks first. "What's on your mind, Ace?"

I'm not sure how to answer. Too many thoughts battle for attention.

Chess must sense my unease. He always does.

He pulls me close and looks at me in a way that says more than his words ever could. His kiss on my lips is brief but steals my breath just the same. I keep thinking that part will fade with time, but if anything, my love for him has only grown stronger.

"Want to talk about it?" His thumb is soft on my cheek.

I know I can tell him anything. "There's still so much to do.

It feels like we'll never accomplish it all." And then I share every concern and worry, every hope and dream.

He listens intently, his gaze locked on mine. I can see the pain that still lingers there, in the dark spot at the corner of his right iris. It's the place where he holds his father, tucked away in the shadows. I don't begrudge him for avoiding the topic of his dad. It's hard for me to talk about Charlotte too. For now, I let it be. When the time is right, I know he'll tell me everything, just as I've done with him now.

After listening to all I have to say, he's thoughtful for a moment. "You're right. Things may never be perfect. You could spend years as Wonderland's queen and still never achieve everything you've set out to do. Some people will never accept the truth about Wonderland. Normals will refuse to believe, and Wonders will walk away when things grow too difficult."

"Is that supposed to make me feel better?"

He smiles. "No. But I don't think you need to feel better."

I tilt my head up at him. "And what do I need, Chess Shire?"

"I think you already know, Ace." He lowers his hand and tangles my fingers with his.

I sigh. And smile. He's right. I do know. Here I've been fretting over the ball tonight, tomorrow's meetings, even an upcoming visit to Oxford—what Chess likes to call his unbirthday present to me. My mind has been so occupied with all I have on my endless checklist that I've neglected the very thing I need.

"Are you coming with me?" I ask timidly.

"I wouldn't miss it," Chess says.

We stand together. I look deeply into his turquoise eyes before closing mine. Next I say the four words I know will take me the way I ought to go. No illusions. No tricks. No simulations. Everything else fades away, drawing me to the place that's been my true home all along.

"I believe in Wonderland," I tell him.

Turns out it wasn't so impossible after all.

AUTHOR'S NOTE

"Write a duology," I said. "It will be fun," I said.

If only I could go back and tell myself how it was really all going to go down.

It wasn't until I started writing this story that I realised the rabbit hole I'd gotten myself into by promising a sequel. After writing a trilogy, I thought a standalone would be hard. Then I discovered wrapping up a plot with one book was even more difficult. I assumed a duology would be a happy medium, so much easier than one or three books.

I was, of course, completely naive. The more time I spent writing this book, the more I caught myself having to delete plot threads I couldn't tie off by the end. I'd introduce a new character only to discover that wouldn't quite do. Too many new characters would equal a third Curious Realities book, and I knew there could only ever be two.

And then there was the ending to consider. I couldn't quite get it right. It felt rushed and poorly paced. I turned in this story after a round of edits only to be entirely dissatisfied with the ending still. My best friend (you all know who she is by now) promised me clarity would come. She's always right, but I still doubted. Maybe this would be the book I couldn't figure out. Maybe this would be the time the epiphany didn't arrive.

It's funny how the things we learn in real life as authors often shape the characters we create. Just as Alice had to trust in what she couldn't yet see, I too had to trust that my King would show me what He wanted this book to be—and how He wanted it to end.

Then, on the Sunday following Thanksgiving—after I had already turned an already late revised manuscript in to my poor editors—the answer came through a song. As Phil Wickham's "Battle Belongs" played during worship at church, it all became clear. The thirty-seventh chapter of this story wouldn't be what it is without the reminder that the most difficult battles are fought in surrender to the One the battles belong to. Sometimes it's the simplicity of a song that reminds us all we need to do is let go and believe.

Thank you for coming along on this journey to Wonderland with me. It's been truly real.

Sincerely,

Sara Ella

1 Corinthians 13:12

ACKNOWLEDGEMENTS

We made it. If you've stuck with me this far, thank you. With every book I write, I continue to be astounded by the loyalty and support my readers continue to pour out. It is to you I tip my hat. You're the real Wonders—thank you for believing in me.

No acknowledgements would be complete without saluting my amazing family—both found and related. My husband, Caiden, is my daily hero. My girls, N & M, are my cheerleaders. And my adventurous boy, J, is forever my inspiration for all things written from a male perspective.

Thanks to my mama in heaven who still inspires me all these years later, as well as to all the parents who still love me here on earth. Dad, Mama Jodi, Aunt Terri, Paul Dad, Jen Mom, Erika, and everyone else who loves on me like their own kid—you're the best!

Nadine Brandes—How many different ways can I thank you before I start to sound redundant? You know what you did and continue to do. No book could be finished without you reminding me of why I write to begin with. Thank you for being my bestie and partner in crime.

Ashley Townsend—Sister! You are the bubbly Madi Hatter incarnate. Thank you for introducing me to coffee with lemon. Yes, I included that in this book just for you. You're welcome.

Erin McFarland—Yes, I used your name, and yes, I think I shall start calling you Knightley, just because. That way I can say I put a famous author in my story before she became famous. ;) Thank you for your constant encouragement and friendship.

Steve Laube—Thank you for being an unshakable rock as both agent and publisher. I feel like I need to say more, but I don't have room. Then again, I think you know by now just how fantastic you are, even though you'd never admit it. So I'll say it for the world to hear (or at least the small world of those reading this book)—Steve Laube is a fantastic human who is kind and gracious and incredibly generous. Anyone who says differently is selling something.

Steve Smith, Lisa Smith, Charmagne Kaushal, and the entire team at Oasis Family Media—Thanks to each and every one of you for the roles you play behind the scenes. I am forever grateful for how you've come alongside this series and look forward to working on more books with you all!

Lisa Laube—You are, in a word, brilliant. You know it, I know it, Steve L. knows it (and he always reminds me of that fact). Thank you for taking my stories to the next level (and for making sure Chess sounded like himself). You are truly Frabjous.

Trissina—Thank you for letting me pester you daily (and often late at night). You are a rock star and marketing would be lame (and non-existent) without you.

Sarah Grimm—You are the most encouraging copy editor ever. Thank you for your attention to detail and your heart for this story.

Jamie Foley—You always handle my extended deadlines with grace upon grace. Thank you for being exactly who you are and for blessing me constantly.

Katie S. Williams—As I write this, you haven't even seen or

proofread this story yet, but I have so much confidence in you I know I'll owe you oodles of thanks! You are the best! (And now that I've reached this final proofreading pass, I am adding WOW! You knocked this one out of Wonderland with your attention to detail. I'd be lost without you!)

Megan Gerig—Mwahahaha! You thought you could get away with having Katie remove your name since you didn't proofread this one? Well, too bad! This is *my* book and I say whose name goes where! But seriously, you may not have proofread this time, but you did work on Wonderland from its beginning, along with providing encouragement and creating the most lovely candles for my world. Thank you!

To all my other family and friends who continue to support me and cheer me on—Brooke Larson, Shannon Dittemore, Staci Talbert, Janalyn Owens, Carolyn Schanta . . . who else? I am sure I forgot someone. If that's you, insert your name here. THANK YOU!

Panera Ladies—What would I do without you all? Liz Johnson, Lindsay Harrel, Ruth Douthitt, Breana Johnson, Sarah Poppovich, Tari Faris, Erin McFarland (again), Kim Wilkes, Jennifer Deibel, Rhia G. Adley, thank you! Our group grows every year! Thank you for encouraging me and being a place of escape where I can just be myself (and eat cookies)!

Rebekah Fletcher—Thank you for helping me when I needed it most and for watching my kids so I could meet my deadline. I'm so grateful to have a neighbor and friend like you. I may have changed the spelling of "Rabekah" to fit with the character in this book, but just know I was thinking of you when I chose her name.

Janelle Amundsen—This book is dedicated to you in part, but I just had to thank you here as well. Thank you for always encouraging me and for teaching me how to play chess. I only hope this story lives up to this complicated game you love. You're the best!

To My Audiobook Narrators—Thank you for narrating this story and for bringing Alice and Chess to life. At the writing of these acknowledgements, I have no idea who has been assigned to narrate this book yet. All I know is that the story will sound fantastic thanks to you!

Kirk DouPonce of DogEared Design—You did it again! Thanks for listening to my ideas at Realm Makers and for bringing them to life! The cover is beyond what I dreamed. You are a true artist and I hope you will design many more covers for my books to come.

Hanna Sandvig—I don't know how you take my messy mock ups and turn them into art, but you do. And you did it again with this book. Thank you using your talents to make my world come to life.

A huge thank you to Stephanie @theespressoedition for all of her support and enthusiasm over *The Wonderland Trials*, and for lending an early copy of the first book to her nephew Noah. He is the sole reason I remembered to brainstorm what animal Alice turns into when drinking Beast's Blend. Noah, if you're reading this, thank you for being curiouser and curiouser!

Thanks to my Wonder Team and their tireless efforts promoting Alice's story. You went above and beyond and for that I give you all the tea and jam.

Thanks to my readers, as always, for picking up another book. I hope this conclusion is everything you waited for and more.

I'd like to take a moment to thank Alice. She's been with me all these years. Waving from the teacups at Disneyland and eventually showing herself in the looking glass during my college years. Sometimes people still say I look like her. I laugh and brush it off, saying it was twenty years ago. So much has changed since then. But so much has stayed *exacteclee* the same as well. So hats off to Alice and Lewis Carroll for inspiring me over the years. You are the OG Wonders, as my teenager would say.

No story is complete without giving glory to the One to whom it all goes. Thank you, Jesus, for giving me that worship song in the moment I needed it, and for reminding me it is through You alone that my books carry any sort of meaningful theme. This story is Yours. Thank you for allowing me to be a part of it.

GLOSSARY

BRITISH TERMS/PHRASES

Advert–Advertisement or commercial

Alright–Slang greeting, often used as a way to say "hello"

Anorak–Slang term for someone who is overly enthusiastic about a subject others find boring

Bloke–Slang for boy, guy, fellow, etc.

Broadsheet–Newspaper

Brolly–Umbrella

Bugger off–Go away

Crisps–Equivalent to American chips

Fiver–Five-pound note (currency)

Frock–Dress

Git–Jerk

Handbag–Purse

Knackered–Tired

Lift–Elevator

Loafer–A lazy or idle person

Notes–Paper money/currency

Not my cup of tea–Not my preference

Off your trolley–Drunk

Plait–Braid

Pullover–Hooded sweatshirt or "hoodie"

Pulling one's leg–Joking

Serviette—Table napkin
Settee—Sofa
Slowcoach—Slowpoke
Tenner—Ten-pound note (currency)

BRITISH VS. AMERICAN SPELLINGS

Apologise/Apologize
Analyse/Analyze
Backwards/Backward
Barrelling/Barreling
Behaviour/Behavior
Centre/Center
Colour/Color
Cosy/Cozy
Defence/Defense
Demeanour/Demeanor
Favourite/Favorite
Fibre/Fiber
Flavour/Flavor
Fulfil/Fulfill
Grey/Gray
Labelled/Labeled
Lacklustre/Lackluster
Meagre/Meager
Metre/Meter
Mould/Mold
Neighbour/Neighbor
Pyjamas/Pajamas
Realise/Realize
Recognise/Recognize
Rumour/Rumor
Sombrely/Somberly
Spiralling/Spiraling
Towards/Toward
Travelling/Traveling

TERMS OF THE CURIOUS REALITIES

Brillig–Precisely four o'clock in the afternoon or the time to boil dinner

Borogove–An impish bird with long legs, red feathers, and a beak too large for its tiny head. Borogove feathers contain healing properties.

Burble–A murmuring noise

Callooh callay–An exclamation of joy or excitement

Cards–Friends/mates linked in Wonder Vision

Checkpoint–A part of the Heart Trial that is coded specifically to either let those who reach it move on or stay put

Fates–The four lives/chances each player has in the Trials, coinciding with four lit team symbols (Spades, Clubs, Hearts, Diamonds) on one's WV bangle.

Fiddlesticks–A term for nonsense

Frabjous–A combination of fabulous and joyous

Golden petals–Wonder Vision money/currency allotted to players

Lost–Those living in the Divided Kingdom with no papers, no job, no home, and no family

Mastery–A special skillset a Wonder player has and uses in the Trials

Mome raths–No one quite knows what a mome rath is. We do know that they live in the Tulgey Wood and bite if you step on them, but it's nearly impossible not to step on one since we don't know what they look like. How unfair is that?

Outgrabe–To emit a strange noise

Registered–A Wonder living in the Normal Reality who has been branded and chipped

Shortcut–A faster way to move from one square to the next in the Heart Trial

Slithy–A combination of "slimy" and "lithe"

Suits/Quarters/Houses–**Suits** are the four symbols representing the four quarters/houses of Wonderland. The **quarters** divide Wonderland's geography by suit, and the **houses** are made up of quarter heads, such as the Minister of Spades or Duchess of Diamonds, and their families.

Toves—Badger-like creatures

Tumtum Tree—A shrub-like tree bearing luscious orange fruit that is plum-like in texture. It was designed to put an end to hunger, and the flavours are a bit different for everyone.

Unregistered—Wonders living undercover in the Normal Reality

Vorpal—Sharp or deadly

Wildflower—A "wild card" Wonder raised in the Normal Reality who is invited to play in the Trials

Wonder-born—Raised to know, see, and believe in Wonderland from birth

Wonderground—The underground of the Normal Reality where Wonders hide and mingle with the Normals who don't mind their company

Wonder Gene—The anomaly in some DNA discovered by renowned genome researcher Catherine R. Pillar.

Wonder-less/Unders/Normals—All terms referring to those born without the Wonder Gene

Jabberwock(y)—The monster described by Lewis Carroll as having "jaws that bite and claws that catch." Though believed to be a dragon beast of some sort, it takes on many forms depending of what you fear most.

Wonder Vision (WV)—Invented by Catherine R. Pillar, this unique bit of Wonder tech worn as a bangle on the wrist was originally designed to enhance the Wonderland experience. It is used in the Trials as a way to gather and keep track of data on players/teams.

WONDERLAND TEA (AND COFFEE) BLENDS

Dwindler's Draught—A unique blend of lavender and black currant causing one to shrink.

Flourisher's Fate—Lemongrass, ginger, and honey made from sunflower pollen. Potent stuff. Serves as an antidote for most other blends.

Beast's Blend—A mixture of cinnamon, cloves, and bergamot. Turns Wonders into animals. Every Wonder reacts differently.

Café au Citron—An Irish coffee brew infused with lemon. Surprisingly refreshing.

Changeling Chai—Works together with the Wonder Gene to create a chemical reaction that alters one's appearance.

Focus Fix—Yerba mate and peppermint. Wakes the brain and sets all nerves to rest.

Ghost's Grog—Contains the petals of the extremely rare ghost orchid flower. It has healing properties and can also make its drinker temporarily invisible. Notes of citrus and chocolate.

Infinity Infusion—One drop a day keeps the aging away. Plant of origin remains unknown.

Rainbow Regimen—Rose petals and cardamom. Meant to cause a frabjous effect of colour-changing and joy.

Serenity's Slumber—Potent mixture of chamomile, valerian root, and passionflower. Causes a deep sleep.

Seren-i-Tea— Lavender Hatter's blend of lavender and chamomile, infused with honeysuckle and vanilla. A mild concoction causing one to relax, but should one get the recipe wrong, it won't cause any side effects.

Tranquil-i-Tea—Madi Hatter's own blend of lavender and chamomile. Just enough to calm the nerves.

TEAMS

Team Colours

- ♥ **Hearts**—red and black
- ♠ **Spades**—white and black
- ♣ **Clubs**—green and black
- ♦ **Diamonds**—silver and black

Team Positions

Ace—Most important player; as long as the Ace is still standing at the end of each Trial, the team gets an automatic one hundred points added to their score (Alice and Willow)

King or Queen–Team captain; usually the most experienced player who has competed in the Trials previously (Alice, Chess, and Stark)

Jack–Player with the highest IQ; skilled at solving riddles/puzzles/codes (Jack)

Ten–The most physically capable team member (Knave)

Nine–Support system player; can play any position aside from Ace; fills in when other teammates are down (Madi)

Four–Most creative team member; solves problems and thinks outside of the box (Sophia)

Two–Lowest position and often written off as unimportant, but the Two can also step in as an Ace if needed (Willow)

ABOUT THE AUTHOR

Once upon a time, **Sara Ella** dreamed she would marry a prince and live in a castle. Now she spends her days homeschooling her three Jedi in training, braving the Arizona summers, and reminding her superhero husband that it's almost Christmas (even if it's only January). When she's not writing, Sara might be found behind her camera lens or planning her next adventure in the great wide somewhere. Sara is the author of the Unblemished trilogy and *Coral*, a reimagining of *The Little Mermaid* that focuses on mental health. Her latest journey into the world of *The Wonderland Trials* feels like coming full circle after her time spent chasing a white rabbit around Walt Disney World. Sara loves fairy tales and Jesus, and she believes "Happily Ever After is Never Far Away." Connect with her online at SaraElla.com or find her on Instagram at @saraellawrites.